HOMELAND

★ ★ ★

ALSO BY THE AUTHOR

FICTION
The Palace of Fears

NON-FICTION
A War Against Truth
Smokescreen
The Demonic Comedy
Journey of the Magi
Empire of the Soul
River in the Desert

HOMELAND

★ ★ ★

PAUL WILLIAM ROBERTS

A NOVEL

KEY PORTER BOOKS

Library and Archives Canada Cataloguing in Publication

Roberts, Paul William
    Homeland / Paul William Roberts.

ISBN-13: 978-1-55263-818-7, ISBN-10: 1-55263-818-9

    I. Title.

PS8585.O299H64 2006   C813'.54   C2006-901808-1

The publisher gratefully acknowledges the support of the Canada Council for the Arts and the Ontario Arts Council for its publishing program. We acknowledge the support of the Government of Ontario through the Ontario Media Development Corporation's Ontario Book Initiative.

We acknowledge the financial support of the Government of Canada through the Book Publishing Industry Development Program (BPIDP) for our publishing activities.

Key Porter Books Limited
Six Adelaide Street East, Tenth Floor
Toronto, Ontario
Canada M5C 1H6

www.keyporter.com

Text design: Martin Gould
Electronic formatting: Jean Lightfoot Peters

Printed and bound in Canada

06 07 08 09 10 5 4 3 2 1

For Lewis H. Lapham
A great American

What goes by the name of love is banishment, with now and then a postcard from the homeland.

—Samuel Beckett, "First Love"

Perhaps the history of the errors of mankind, all things considered, is more valuable and interesting than that of their discoveries. Truth is uniform and narrow; it constantly exists, and does not seem to require so much an active energy, as a passive aptitude of the soul in order to encounter it. But error is endlessly diversified; it has no reality, but is the pure and simple creation of the mind that invents it. In this field the soul has room enough to expand herself, to display all her boundless faculties, and all her beautiful and interesting extravagancies and absurdities.

—Benjamin Franklin

Of all the teachings of history the clearest is this: that those who seek to realize ideal aims by force of law are always unscrupulous and always cruel.

—Lord Eustace Percy, *John Knox*

PREFACE

* * *

*Caelum non animum mutant qui trans mare currunt** (Horace)

IT IS A COLD BRIGHT DAY IN APRIL, and the terror alert stands at thirteen. We seem to be heading back into dual front war. Two separate Chinese factions have been caught aiding terrorists and the Mongolians are suspected of remilitarizing in violation of US–Global protocols, so security will be tight again until Central Command has the situation under control. The Department of Homeland Security believes a sleeper cell has been activated. There is a possibility that some kind of nuclear device is going to be detonated at the heart of a major city.

War. The wars are endless, and the details become less and less relevant. Images on the news show bodies being carried through swirling smoke, people yelling, military vehicles pulling up, faces distorted by shock or spattered with blood. Television takes care of the details, as it always has. We even execute our enemies on prime time these days. *UB Judge* is the most popular show in the brief but noisy history of the medium, or so they tell me, and *InstaKarma's* not far behind. I would have thought no one wanted to watch people get killed. I hadn't factored in terrorists, though. They have evidently lost their right to be treated as human beings.

---

* They change the sky, not their soul, who run across the sea.

I sit looking out at the untidy countryside. The fields resemble dirty hair someone has slept on. The bare trees are scary marionettes. But the great cities have seen better days too. Their towering fortresses of culture have disintegrated into fermented memories of a bygone glory. Most of the great East Coast capitals never recovered from a deluge that came with the arctic meltdown, although human ingenuity knows no limits. Like the multitrillion-dollar transformation of the former New York City into Big Aqua, the world's first underwater city theme park, one of whose main attractions is a simulation of the attack on and collapse of the World Trade Towers. All under the sea.

Washington has long been sealed off, its slums cleared out, and only those on official business ever visit the capital. The President and Vice President, along with the Secretaries of State and Defense, are no longer identified for reasons of national security, and elections occur only to vote for the party, not an actual candidate. Indeed, no one knows where the President lives now. Or what he looks like. Or his name.

I have been a guilty bystander for too long.

We have been lying to ourselves for too long.

I wanted to correct the problem in some kind of irrevocable way before I carried this egregious flaw of character with me into a hundredth year of life. I am now begrudgingly convinced, having had more than enough evidence, that some deep aspect of our being retains the scarring of our errors until we find a means of undoing what was done or replacing it with a thing done right. Although many regard me solely as a politician, I have chiefly been a writer for my entire career, yet what follows is the first real writing I have ever wanted anyone to see. It is also the first document I have ever written about myself, and the first one in which my sole intention was to be clear and truthful and honest, although I have never made a practice of obfuscation. But it is a bolus. It is an old man's mind.

You are doubtless perusing this text in a typescript form, and I am sure that most will know the reason it will always be thus, but in case someone does not, as well as for the safety of all concerned, it now behooves me to caution the reader that the very act of reading beyond this first page will constitute very serious violations of so many pages of our fatuous and self-important legislation regarding treasonable activities, espionage, national security, and official secrets, that it is scarcely worth the trouble to cite them nor the trouble to list the mandatory minimum sentences a judge will be obliged to hand down to the guilty. Suffice it to say, none of you would be free women or free men again, even if you lived to be twice my age.

I now have nothing but contempt and scorn for the nation to which I gave my best years in diligent and faithful service. Contempt not for its people so much as for its institutions, which failed it most disastrously when they were most needed, and revealed themselves to have been sabotaged with flaws since their inception by and for the corrupt and unscrupulous, who are always with us. Such institutions and their legislation deserve to be betrayed, unveiled, torn down and crushed back into dust. It is my sincerest hope that what follows will impel you to do this yourselves, in whatever capacity you are able and to the utmost of your abilities, for as long as you live. I can think of no task more appropriate nor any more noble, when a choice is as limited as yours is to freedom or slavery.

The culprits are all dead now. I am the only one left alive, and your scorn cannot hope to match the level of self-loathing I have achieved on my own in lieu of any punishment fitting for such a crime. My only wish is that I do not live quite for ever, because my days stretch out like decades with this thing I have to face in the mirror of my conscience every moment I'm awake, and then in dreams more cruel and heartless than the torture pits of a Grand Inquisitor. Oh, yes, I know where I am all right. I know. But I want you to know where you are too.

I do not want you to like me, nor am I asking you to forgive me, for no one can forgive what I have done and what I am. The calling of that dateless night is now in every heartbeat, and I know that what I am will survive even there and beyond that too in a loneliness too terrible for imaginings. I want you to despise me, to despise what I have done and what I am, for your own future depends on it. I do not want you to like me, but I do want you to learn what happened so you can correct it. Some day.

Beyond this, I am a waste of your time. I wasted mine too; thus and forever time is all I will have to waste. In what follows, therefore, are only the relevant points in my progress through circles of fire down to where they burn in darkness, giving off no light.

These are my confessions.

David Derklin Leverett
Caledon, ON, USNA
April 2, 2050

CHAPTER ONE

★ ★ ★

Omnium rerum principia parva sunt[*] (Cicero)

I WAS BORN INTO A LIFE OF SINGULAR privilege and wealth, though not one lacking in responsibility. James Leverett was our patriarch, or as far back in search of one as I can get, and he ran a dry goods store in Dumfriesshire until 1796, when he left for Massachusetts under a dark cloud of some sort. Since my great-grandfather, Lewis Derklin Leverett, all the men in my family have been involved in public service, either in the federal government or on a local level. His father, Daniel Augustus Leverett, had amassed a great fortune in the railroads—the Leverett Line still runs out of Hartford—so great a fortune, indeed, that he knew his descendants were in danger of losing the work ethic he always swore by as the mainstay of life. The Leverett Trust was thus arranged so that beneficiaries would receive its support only as long as they were in public office. If they remained in office for fifty years, the Trust was authorized to hand them a single payment of $20 million or its equivalent in inflated currency. My father received nearly $120 million. I would go on to be handed a check for nearly twice that.

Throughout my fifty years of public service, I received every month a check for precisely three times the amount of my

---

[*] Everything has a small beginning.

government salary, besides the right to live rent free in any of six different homes. Those who surmise that I have no understanding of the way an ordinary person lives are right. Great-great-grandpa Daniel may have ensured hard-working descendants but he also guaranteed they'd be insulated against the heat and cold afflicting their fellow man, and thus he created a line of dedicated but very solitary men, who were invariably attracted to gregarious yet serious women.

My mother was Alice Barnham, the biologist, who, along with five colleagues, received a Nobel Prize for something I don't pretend to understand but that paved the way for the correction of many genetic diseases.

My first clear memory is of being told I would be moving to England. I was nearly five years old. I pictured England as a wild and savage country where we would live a life close to nature, hunting, trapping, fishing and building teepee-like structures. I wondered what we would wear.

My father, Warren Lewis Leverett, had been appointed by President Truman to the post of ambassador to the Court of St. James in London, which, as liaison to our most important ally, representing US interests across the whole quadrant of Western Europe, was Washington's top diplomatic position, its plum. Put the wrong man in that position, as has happened occasionally, and things can get fouled up very quickly. The Leverett Trust contained a special provision to purchase property for any descendant who received an ambassadorial position, which explains how I came to grow up at Kingrove, a 40-acre estate on the banks of the Thames near Windsor, with a sunny spacious Regency mansion that looked out over the swift iron waters and had been designed by John Nash himself. My father went on to be so successful at this job that his tenure was extended through three administrations—at least once probably at the request of the British government, which also took the rare step of offering him a knighthood that all concerned knew he would politely decline. Trusted implicitly by three presidents, and brilliantly gifted at diplomacy, he was respected and popular too, perhaps because in an era when the American abroad had become a vulgar stereotype of overweight, underschooled crassness, few ever realized, faced with the tall narrow frame, the patrician head, and the self-deprecating courteousness of his manner, that my father was an American in the first place.

I grew up feeling not just more English than American, but more English than many of the English. The first five years there were a heaven I would happily inhabit forever. My mother had reduced her career to one day a week, Friday, when she drove the half-hour it took, through Henley, to Oxford, where she delivered one lecture and supervised the doctoral research of a rather frightening Scots girl at St. Anne's. The main purpose of her day, however, was to lunch with her colleagues at a thatch-roofed pub in Binsey, keeping up with developments in research and gossip. This must have been a happy, carefree time for her too. She often took her "boy" along, dumping me in the lap of the frightening Scots girl while she lectured.

I was home-schooled until I was ten, mainly by a series of tutors who came to the house four days a week at 9 AM sharp, but also by my mother for whom the natural world contained an eternal course of study. From April to November, we roamed the woods and fields of Surrey and Berkshire observing every step in the glorious progress of nature's ineffable pageant, from the first snowdrop emerging warily from its February mulch on a forest floor to the last umber leaf clutched by the crooked arm of some ancient oak as it tried to fend off the legions of impending winter. To everything we noticed there was always attached a story or lesson. The sight of a wild daffodil contained a little yarn about Wordsworth that concluded with his famous poem, as well as an account of how bees made honey. The terrifying sight of a large bouncing frog had a disquisition on metamorphosis in it, as well as a fairy tale and then an account of how warts grew and were cured. It also handed me a homework project that entailed nursing a jar of frogs' spawn until its tadpoles began to turn into tiny black frogs, at which point I was supposed to return them to their pond. I can still see all those frogs in their little prison, slowly dying. In the winter, Mother read to me beside the wrought-iron hearth's tiny magical planet of glowing coals and crackling wood, setting fire to my imagination with such marvels as *The Wind in the Willows* and *Treasure Island*, which she always managed to make sound as if they occurred at the end of our garden or in the nearby village.

My dear, dear mother, the great cycle of seasons, the palpable mysteries, the magical nature of the countryside, the old footpaths, the circles of ancient stones at whose function we can merely surmise, the tea and crumpets, fireworks and a bonfire on November 5, the tingling mystery of Father Christmas, the snapping and crackling of goblin drummers in the grate— I imagined that life would be like this forever, just the same even around the impossible bend in time whence no man may look. The thought was a comfort and a joy. But it all came crashing down a month before my eleventh birthday, when I was told my mother would soon begin full-time work and I would be going away to school. *Going away to school*...At ten, I had no clear understanding of what "away" meant, and wasn't even certain if this "away" was a punishment or a reward. Such arrangements were normal then, but I still wonder who could have thought it a good idea to give a child everything for the first few years only to snatch it all back again.

I was enrolled at the venerable boys' school, Eton College, where I blossomed forth from child to man. It had been operating since the year 1440, founded by King Henry VI, and apart from a very strong and clear idea of what it was about, it had many arcane and sometimes silly traditions that went largely unchallenged because their roots receded into the earth and vanished from sight at such a depth they seemed as much a part of the school's structure as the yellowing, pitted stones or the wrought-iron street lamps.

Initially, it was a place I endured solely because I was allowed to return home from it every Friday evening and have the precious weekends to myself. On that first day, nearly ninety years ago when I was due to attend kitted out in the antiquated uniform of tail coat and vest I refused to leave the safety of my bathroom. I'd locked myself in. Kingrove had these huge old oak doors that had been fitted with modern deadbolts, so I knew nothing was going to budge me from my hidey-hole. My parents were forced to negotiate with this terrorist, and even my father—who became something of a legend in hostage negotiation—obviously didn't feel they had much in the way of bargaining chips. Within minutes, they promised I could come home at the weekend if I would open the door. Both of them believed in a word being a bond—something considered an almost tragic failing these days—so their promise of weekend returns simply *had* to be delivered.

Along with private traditions and a uniform so far away from the edge of fashion it had recycled twice and was again somewhat fashionable by the time my mid-teens loped around, Eton also had a vocabulary of its own with words and phrases from an antique English but with meanings quite unique. For example, I was never late for class once during my five years at Eton—I was late for "div," and my division master noted it, as indeed did I in the school office's "Tardy Book." I was similarly noted for being a "Slack Bob" in my first "half" or term, avoiding anything that smacked of physical exercise, particularly any activity involving an inflatable leather sphere or water, which added rowing and cricket to my list of hateful things. A year later, I couldn't even be made to remember I'd hated boats and what they floated in, sculling through the dawn mists daily in preparation for Fourth of June and its Procession of Boats—a passion that made me now a "Wet Bob."

Anywhere else I'd have been a junior student during these first years, or at least *some* kind of student; here I was an "Oppidan." Tradition dictated that Oppidans were better off boarding full time, and indeed those denied the privilege once they'd reached the upper school frequently resented being pulled from the fun of Etonian weekends—or so I recall us being told on that traumatic first day. Allowing new Oppidans to miss this vital period of socializing and handicrafts proved to be a concession Eton rarely made, though, and it was agreed upon for me that morning only after much agitated talking, and also because I lived so absurdly near the school, in Datchet, that I could walk to div without setting foot on a paved road or path. From my first window in my first classroom in fact I could have seen, had I looked for bearings and markers, the steep gray lead sheeting of our roof, just behind the shaking skein of limp green leaves that curtained off the view beyond Dutchman's Field.

I can still remember vividly sitting in the lower master's study with my father as he lied through his teeth about the extensive weekend military courses and martial arts lessons that were a Leverett family tradition dating back to the fourteenth century. He had not warned me in advance—had not solicited my agreement or compliance with this lie—and I recall the amused glint in his eye as he looked over at me while he was recounting fictional military careers that adorned our ancestors with imaginary laurels. Then and there I learned that lying was all right in a matter of honor.

"I, myself," said the lower master—which meant deputy headmaster—"am an army man. Queen's Own Rifles, yes indeed, sir. Spent five years as tutor for the Wali of Swat's children, I did. Enjoyed them *immensely*..."

He made English sound like a foreign language to me.

"Ah," said my father.

"Yes, sir," said the headmaster. "*Immensely*! Magnificent country! Enjoyed it *immensely*. That is how we arranged the enjoyment in those days...By the way, do you happen to know the Maharaja of Kut?"

"Is it a limerick?" said my father.

"No, sir," said the headmaster, "it is an Indian princely state..."

"Then I do not, alas," said my father.

"The Rajkumar will be joining your son's division, yes indeed. Poor chap's got a bit of a gammy leg..."

"Yes?" My father did not appear to understand the headmaster, which made two of us, and that presumably accounts for the clarity of my remembrance too.

"I thought you *might* know him," said the headmaster.

"I thought the princely titles had been abolished by Nehru?" said my father.

"Yes, I believe that was so," said the headmaster, staring at my father as if he were just another four-foot Slack Bob. "And being *so*, it ought to make us question why it is not *more* so, rather than *so-so*..."

The long silence that followed made this exchange stick in my mind like Excalibar. I did not understand why what had been said could have caused any offence. I wasn't even sure if offence had been caused, but I knew the increasingly tense atmosphere indicated *something*. It took me many years to grasp what was going on.

My father was a great tester of men, a great believer that there were tests to which men could be put in order to assess their *value*. The assessment was vital in deciding what tasks to allot them. As his sole heir, I now realize, I was often if obliquely tested myself, and the experience of it has profoundly affected my life.

"Let's test your memory," my father is saying. He holds up a book. "We shall both memorize lines and then perform some scenes. Howzat sound? Do you want to be the *king*, or Hamlet?"

I had never even *heard* of the play—and he knew this, just as he knew he'd made the king's part sound huge, guaranteeing I'd pick the part of Hamlet. At the time, of course, I felt I was being treated equitably.

One sweltering Sunday in late July I found a five-pound note on the gravel path leading up to the kitchen door. I asked my father if he'd lost five pounds, and I vividly recall the genuineness of his reply, the baffled expression, the faint air of annoyance at being distracted from something important.

"Not I," he said, turning back to the file he was reading.

It became a sort of quest, the return of the five pounds to its owner. I was eight or nine at the time. I asked my mother, her housekeeper, the gardener, the maids, the embassy chauffeur, the stable boy, and Mr. Pellet, the handyman, who always wore bicycle clips on his pants. No one had lost any money. So I fashioned a sign. At first it read HAVE YOU LOST FIVE POUNDS? I can vividly remember suddenly thinking this sign was no good because it made it too easy for dishonest people to come and claim the money. How would I be able to know the rightful owner? I thus changed it to DID YOU LOSE MONEY AT KINGROVE HOUSE? TELL ME WHEN AND WHERE AND HOW MUCH AND YOU WILL BE REUNITED WITH YOUR MONEY. It is the first thing I remember writing.

Some thirty minutes after I'd placed this sign by the driveway leading up to the wrought-iron gates of Kingrove's private road my father appeared holding it. I was scared of him at that moment, thinking I'd done something wrong.

"I claim the money," he said.

"But you *said* you didn't lose any," I said.

"Testing your honesty, David. It was a test, old chap, and I am *proud* of the result...."

He picked me up in his big strong arms and held me over his head, beaming.

I suspect that when I failed one of these tests he simply did not let me know I'd been tested. I was happy to pass them, of course, and thus never had the opportunity to consider how very wrong my father was in his thinking.

Back in those days, people still imagined they had to bring up boys to be Aeneas or Ulysses, as if our lives would be epic struggles, interminable journeys, impossible feats of brilliance or daring. They were not to know that the computer, motor car, telephone and automatic submachine gun would change everything.

I loathed the physicality of Eton most, I suppose, when I was least equipped to deal with it, most ineffectual in those games that were played out on the legendary fields, where no war of the future would ever be won. I was a smallish child, elfin and frail, and after my lost paradise I cannot blame me for withdrawing from the world somewhat for a spell—if indeed that's what I did. I disliked the other boys, collegers and Oppidans alike; I hated the div, the dry Bob cricket—I loathed it all, the rugby, tennis, gym, running and rope climbing, beagling, shooting, archery, badminton, basketball, canoeing, clay pigeon, croquet, cross-country, eventing, fencing, fives, golf, gymnastics, judo, karate, lacrosse, mountaineering, polo, rackets, sailing, sevens, squash, swimming, table tennis, volleyball, water polo, windsurfing, and the bloody Wall Game. But all this hate was really due to not knowing how to dislike the school itself effectively, not knowing how anything worked, what anything meant—not knowing much at all about Life. It is a feeling I now have about Death.

Ironically, however, this was where the school truly excelled. It taught us about Life and how best to live it. The day I learned I could row a boat made an extraordinary impact on me. I felt as if someone had taken me up to the summit of a mountain, showed me how to unfurl my wings then hurled me out into a warm twilight of convective currents where I soared, sank, glided, swooped, and did absolutely everything else possible—except land.

In photographs one can still discern what an awe-inspiring trauma it must have been for me suddenly to grow up and out of my four-foot elf's chrysalis and into six feet one inch of long-limbed, muscular young man, a frame intended for grace under pressure, intended for *achievement*.

Eton did not believe in creating loners to toil in solitary splendor over their obsessions. It believed in turning out individuals who were capable of appreciating eccentricity or uniqueness in others, but for whom personally achievement existed in the team created to achieve it. This is really just a variant of the adoration of the human mind, though, and as such it always strikes me as merely a vain way to be humble. When my mother and her colleagues won their Nobel Prize, the acceptance speech in Stockholm was so self-effacing and humble that it made me proud of the steadiness and determination I knew was behind the façade. Humility is never appreciated for its own sake.

Obsession or a great interest in something are not the same as love, and I came to love the subject of History profoundly, since through it all the other subjects opened up to me, offering their secret worlds for exploration. It was scholarly success that I first observed as a most potent medicine for the ills of this world. Perception is what counts here, and I perceived that scholarly success transformed my body from its scrawny beginnings into a chap who could yell,

"Howzat!"

Cricket. The smack of leather on willow replaced the hum of bees as the sound of my summers. How I have missed that sound. I ceased looking back, and my life became something serious, earnest, diligent and long. But it never returned me to Eden.

CHAPTER TWO

★ ★ ★

*Omnes aequo animo parent ubi digni imperant** (Syrus)

AFTER ETON, LIKE MANY OF MY CLASSMATES, I went up to Oxford, reading Greats at Lincoln, a small college on Turl Street, backing onto Radcliffe Square and James Gibbs' magnificent Camera. My father and grandfather had been undergraduates there. The Leverett Trust gave the college a sizeable sum each year specifically designated for "restoration costs and bursaries to be offered only to needier students." I could tell some of the dons thought I'd bought my way in, and that the headmaster seemed relieved to find in me an adequately intelligent freshman—because throwing me out would have been difficult.

My tutor was J.N. Maxwell, the great classicist, annotator of Plato, biographer of Solon. I learnt more about the art of contemporary politics from him than I did from anyone else I have ever known or read. Still, after eighty years, I hear his voice when I read Plato, and when I avoid the dictates of conscience too. I am deeply grateful to have studied under him and deeply ashamed I wasted his time.

We studied the language, history, politics and philosophy of the people whose foundation became Western culture. It is the only complete civilization that can be studied in its entirety, or

---

*All men cheerfully obey where worthy men rule.

so we believed. Perhaps a measure of the relevance such a course was thought to possess by the three-quarters mark of the twentieth century is that it was officially dropped from the university's syllabus the year after my matriculation.

I spent two months of every summer thereafter helping with Maxwell's archaeological dig near the Artemis Temple at Ephesus, and indeed was there when he first brushed the mud from the Platonic inscriptions that so briefly captured the world's imagination. I remember how his big dark eyes burned beneath their dense white brows as he sat trying to decipher the letters. He was not a man usually given to excesses of emotion.

"Good grief!" he said, repeatedly, and I could hear for the first time faint strains of a Welsh accent in his voice. "Good grief!" I thought at the time his discovery would change the world utterly, such was the force and infectiousness of his enthusiasm, but of course it barely altered one small area of classical history. Maxwell's ambitions were no doubt modest, though his accomplishments were many. I realize I was the one who wanted to change the world. I should have aimed at changing one small area of ancient history, though, because I was not capable of more. Perhaps I would not have been able to do even that properly, yet I know I would have found the work toward it more fulfilling than what I went on to do with my life.

Like most who had the good fortune to study there, I wanted to stay on at Oxford and do my doctoral work under Maxwell, but a tyrant named tradition dictated I now had to return to the land of my birth and get a PhD from Harvard. After Oxford, Harvard loomed up like a banishment in the wasteland. I felt I was being wrenched away from everything I held dear, everything I'd worked for, the only kind of life worth living. I still recall the outrage, the righteous indignation that puffed me up like a televangelist. For a week there I was the Reverend

Rectitude himself, staking a mighty claim on the moral high ground. This was the only serious argument I ever had with my father, who, for the first and last time in my life, lost his temper so completely that a glass was shattered, a chair overturned, a door slammed. When he lost his mind to alcohol decades later, I fondly wished it had only claimed his temper.

"Goddammit!" he roared. "*I* didn't *want* to do it either—that's what a tradition is all about. *This* is what *we* do!"

"It's *my* life," I yelled back. "If I want to devote it to scholarship, I will!"

"You will *not*!" said my father, many decibels louder. "You have a *duty*. You don't think all *this*—" He gestured around him at the room and its treasures like Satan showing all the kingdoms of the world. "—comes without a price attached to it, do you? You will do your duty. You will *not* defy me!"

I didn't, of course. We went a few more rounds, had a couple more games in which I held my own until I couldn't, returned all his blistering serves until I didn't. I slammed a few doors shut, a few receivers down, and I may have scorched a bit of earth but I never burned any bridges.

My mother set fire to one, though. She was all for me staying at Oxford, and she said so. It caused an immense rift between her and my father. Their arguments drifted up to my room in the night like a poisonous cloud, making nothing seem solid any more.

In the end, I wrote my doctoral dissertation at Harvard on "Athenian Elites: the relationship between money and class in Plato's thinking" under the watchful eye of Samuel Gelb, who was by then also a Connecticut senator.

I may as well have been born at Harvard, for the David Leverett who grew up in England must have died there. I scarcely knew him, and wish I'd known him better.

* * *

I had expected to hate everything about America because I'd been forced back there, but I did not hate it. I loved it, soon shedding the stuffiness I'd absorbed from England, while keeping a little of the accent that was so mysteriously popular in the renegade colonies.

While still in my first year at Harvard, I had received in the mail an envelope I'd been expecting for some time. Inside it was an invitation on curiously crested notepaper to join one of the secret societies you heard so much about. This one was called simply A-3, and in fact one did not hear anything about it. The stationery reeked of wealth, class and tradition, acknowledging nothing of the twentieth century in its embossed copperplate script and ivory vellum. Its heraldic crest was this:

And there was a motto: *Beati possidentes**. I was probably the first person in a long time who knew (or cared) it was from Euripides.

As it was known I would, and not without some curiosity, I wrote back to a V.S. Parks who identified himself as treasurer, saying I was flattered but knew nothing of the society's purpose, thus was not sure if I'd want to accept the invitation. This was the traditional response.

A few days later I received another invitation from Parks, this time to join him for dinner. There was a telephone number

---

*The blessed who possess

that proved to be the Fogg Museum, yet when I asked for Parks, the man who answered said:

"Will you be able to meet Mr. Parks here at 6.30 this evening for dinner?"

I said I would, although my evening was far from free.

You will understand how hard it is for me to tell the truth from the lies when I say that the reason I had to attend Harvard was to join the A-3. The ritual of ignorance was important for my diary entry, perhaps, but I do not know why I persist in the deception here. A double life is not difficult to live if you have never known any other kind of existence. Perhaps this is why the rich are different: they all lead double lives.

I had just begun turning a creaky carousel of the Fogg Museum's postcards when a voice behind me said:

"Leverett."

It was not a question; the voice had a rich decisive timbre that left one in no doubt about this. I turned to find myself looking at a small deformed man in his mid-twenties, whose torso leaned over on the left side so precipitously that he seemed to be attempting to reach his ankle with his hand.

"Parks?"

The woeful little man thrust a crooked arm up at me.

"Donner," he said. "C.P.—but call me Chris."

I shook a little crumpled hand gently, fearing it might break.

"Have we met?" I asked him.

"Mr. Parks sent me to escort you over to the clubhouse," he said.

He led me out and we walked up Quincy, then turned down Broadway. Donner did not exactly lope like Quasimodo, but his gait was an ambulatory nightmare all the same. I tried slowing the pace, thinking this might help him, but he hobbled ahead at the same pace, occasionally twisting his neck around painfully to check I was still there. I did, of course, appreciate that any true treasure must be guarded by a dwarf.

In this fashion we'd walked about ten minutes when a black Lincoln drew up beside us. Its rear window slid down and a gaunt, pale but rather charming face leaned out.

"Dave Leverett!" said the face, cheerily. "Hop in."

I thought I would recognize this person, but I did not. No one had ever called me "Dave" before. Not ever. Donner opened the car's rear door.

"I'm Val Parks," the man inside added. "Thank you so much, Chris."

I climbed into a spacious rear seat, thinking Donner would get in behind me. I was surprised to find him closing the door and waving as we pulled out into Broadway's traffic. As I waved back, Donner's expression changed dramatically from cheerful affability to cold stern authority, and he pointed an accusing finger at me saying something I couldn't decipher. It was odd. The change in expression was almost inhuman. I sat back on the soft leather, puzzled and disturbed. A liveried chauffeur of advanced years sat beyond the glass panel isolating our passenger area. Parks spoke to him with an intercom.

"To Jay's, please, Sam."

"Donner's not coming?" I asked. "Poor little fellow."

"To the Hindu," said Parks, "the concept of karma does not mean you are being punished for your sins in a previous life, it means you have paid for them. It's over and done with. There's a difference, do you see what I mean?"

"Not really..."

He was immaculately dressed in a bespoke pinstripe suit, with highly polished black wingtips and an azure blue tab-collared shirt with gold tie bar. It was his necktie that stood out most, though. A club tie of some kind, it was highly unusual, with lavender diagonals over a Sienna red ground dotted with tiny crests. He caught me staring at it.

"I hope you like it, my friend, because nothing would give

me more pleasure than to have you wearing one yourself before the week is out."

Tiny as it was, I recognized the necktie's crest as the one on my invitation.

We drove west, following the Charles River's meander loop, pulling up outside a nondescript building near the Arsenal. During the trip, Parks and I discussed the war in Vietnam in terms of its winnability, rather than the desirability of pulling out, which was of course the view being expressed increasingly by the general public.

We entered the rather shabby building, which was startlingly opulent on the inside and appeared to be offices of some sort, although I saw very little of the rest of it. I was shown down a corridor and then through a set of double doors leading to a small dining room. An oval table had been set with freshly polished silver and fine Staffordshire bone china. There were just two chairs at opposite ends, where Parks and I were seated by a gloomy butler. As an exceptionally fine meal of trout and lamb was served, we embarked on a long and detailed conversation chiefly concerning the Soviet Union. Both of us were well informed on the subject, yet Parks had the edge on me. I noted down as accurately as possible in my diary his last comment since it impressed me greatly:

"We have here a political force committed fanatically to the belief that with the US there can be no permanent *modus vivendi*, that it is desirable and necessary that the internal harmony of our society be disrupted, our traditional way of life be destroyed, the international authority of our state be broken, if Soviet power is to be secure. This political force has complete power of disposition over energies of one of the world's greatest peoples and resources of the world's richest national territory, and is borne along by deep and powerful currents of Russian nationalism. In addition, it has an elaborate and far-flung apparatus for the exertion of its influence in other countries, an apparatus of amazing flexibility and versatility, managed by people whose experience and skill in underground methods are presumably without any parallel in history. Finally, it is seemingly inaccessible to considerations of reality in its basic reactions. For it, the vast fund of objective fact about human society is not, as with us, the measure against which one's outlook is constantly being tested and re-formed, but a grab bag from which individual items are selected arbitrarily and tendentiously to bolster an outlook that is already preconceived. This is admittedly not a pleasant picture. The problem of how to cope with this force is undoubtedly the greatest task our diplomacy has ever faced and probably the greatest it will ever have to face. It should be the point of departure from which our political general staff's work at the present juncture should proceed. It should be approached with the same thoroughness and care as the solution of any major strategic problem in a war, and, if necessary, with no smaller outlay in planning effort. Of course, I cannot attempt to suggest all the answers that may exist here. But I would like to put on record my conviction that this problem is within our power to solve—and without recourse to any general military conflict."

The combination of his knowledge and his desire for peaceful solutions to international problems was immensely attractive to me. I felt instantly that I had a lot in common with V.S. Parks. We moved with our coffee and port to a pair of leather wingback armchairs situated conveniently nearby. It occurred to me that I'd not yet asked a single question about the A-3 Society, so I attempted to correct that.

"Do?" said Parks, laughing raucously. "What do we *do*? *This* is what we *do*, old boy."

I must have looked perplexed.

"We dine well and we yak about international affairs. What did you imagine? Ladies of the night and opium pipes?"

"I'm not sure what I imagined," I confessed. "I did not expect—and if you knew me better you'd know I am not a flatterer—such brilliantly conducive conversation…You are remarkably well informed, Parks. Are you postgrad here still, or—"

He cut me off.

"No, no. I work in Washington now. Got my scroll some time back." He smiled, looking at me with a sudden intensity I found unnerving. "I used to be the A-3 president, but I agreed to stay on as treasurer because I simply couldn't imagine life without the club." Then he leaned toward me with a conspiratorial air. "And naturally I am a very useful contact for anyone seeking to work in government…very favorably disposed to A-3 alumni…"

He poured another glass of vintage Fonseca.

"How do I go about applying for membership?" I inquired, as I had known I would. "I have no doubts whatsoever about it. You have certainly persuaded me."

He reached for something in his inside pockets, suddenly throwing a small package wrapped in black tissue paper at me. It was a necktie like his.

"Oh, you're in all right, Leverett. I merely have to see what the brothers thought."

"Brothers?" I asked.

He leaned back and reached for a book in the shelves to his left. Instead of coming right out in his hand, the book leaned at a 45-degree angle on a hinge. Panels on three of the room's four walls slid aside, and some dozen men walked out and circled my chair, applauding raucously and holding up score cards. My conversation was being rated or ranked: I saw nines and tens, nothing else.

I was most amused. Indeed, it was more what I had expected from a secret society. With this laddish finale of good cheer, a relief from the series of strange disjointed events preceding it, I was welcomed into A-3, which provided much stimulating and intelligent conversation over the coming years, and the most thorough and intimate grounding in *realpolitik* to be found anywhere on earth. It also introduced me to three of my closest friends: Dean Torrance, Lester Sturvis Melton, and Melvin Cassel.

Friendships that endure a lifetime are worth something, to be sure. I deeply enjoyed being young with those three men. Dean Torrance, sandy-haired eternal boy, the most gregarious human being I can imagine. As one might expect, his father was the same—he even knew my father—and his grandfather before him was so famed for his friendliness that there are still Vermonters who use the expression "a real Torrance of affability." You could not walk down a street or sit in a restaurant with Dean Torrance for more than ten minutes without coming across someone he knew. It wasn't surprising, he was so likeable, too, always smiling, never depressed—which was just as well since tragedies followed him like a pack of pariah dogs. Les Melton was stuck with the nickname "Apollo" after Torrance and I overheard a girlfriend of his tell him he had the features of a Greek god. He did too: high cheekbones, noble Patrician nose coming in a line from the fore-head, long delicate yet powerful limbs, sculpted by swimming. He had an air of authority even when relaxed. His grandfather, the newspaper tycoon, had married Jessica Sturvis, whose brief career in Hollywood is still of great interest to some, bringing the Melton gene pool this overabundance of good looks, which the harsher critics claim is what won Lester's father, John S. Melton, the governorship of Rhode Island. The only feature that did not fit Les was his voice, a crackly high-pitched, almost girlish sound that confounded telephone callers and made strangers wonder where it came from. He had the kind of voice you associate with female thespians after a long summer season. When he died from throat cancer fifty years later, I was not surprised to learn the source of his fatal weakness.

With these two charismatic personalities, Melvin Cassel stood out by contrast. A melancholy, moody red-haired anglophile Jew, his glass was always half empty, and he was guaranteed to find the worrying point in any piece of good news. I think we chose each other very carefully as friends, looking back on it. Melvin served to remind us of the perils entailed in excessive negativity, and we served to remind him of the folly in unwarranted optimism. Every time one of us met with grief, Melvin was there to point an accusing finger at the shameless positivism that now caused only pain. On occasion, he even said, "I told you so." But he was very funny, and could be exceedingly acute in his analysis of world affairs. His grandfather had come over from Ukraine and worked very hard. So hard, indeed, that his father, Irving Cassel, could afford to be a noted literary editor and notorious curmudgeon. This, however, is probably what gave Melvin his critical edge and put the biting irony in his humor. I was sorry to see him lose them both in the bitterness of old age.

Strangely enough, I never saw Parks again at the club, nor Donner, the little handicapped man. Soon after my induction, I learned Parks had received an overseas posting that was "classified," which meant CIA, and was now rumored to be in Berlin. As one does when close friends come by the legion and a year seems a long time, I forgot about him.

You might well ask why a club devoted to nothing more covert than conversation about current affairs needed the designation of "secret society" along with all its trappings. The reason was not something we ever discussed, but we were all conscious of it in selecting new members, all of whom had one thing in common: conservatism. I know this word has now lost most of its original meaning, so I need to point out that, when I was at Harvard, it still meant a political ideology centered on faith in the status quo. There were as many conservative Democrats as there were Republicans. But it was not a popular position to take politically in an era when the status quo had seemingly revealed itself as flawed. Those in the A-3 were not oblivious to the catastrophic decision making behind such disasters as Vietnam or Watergate, but we did not feel they warranted the kind of response they were getting from a public unknowingly manipulated by ultra-leftist organizations intent on fomenting revolution. We thought of ourselves as realists, pragmatists cut from the same cloth as the Founding Fathers. We did not believe America had any great mission in the world—the pernicious doctrine of exceptionalism crept in later. We were aware that Fortune had favored us in the wake of WW II, but felt the duty of our government was to sustain and improve upon these conditions for the benefit of the people as a whole.

I leave the above paragraph intact in order to show the reader how deeply ingrained habits of mind become. For, while nothing in it is untrue, there is one striking omission. Besides conservatism, A-3 members had something else in common: we were all sons of privilege, wealth and power. Our faith in the status quo thus also entailed vested interest. If things remained as they were, we stood to inherit the earth—and most of us had been told so since we were children. We saw nothing wrong with it, and indeed there *was* nothing wrong with it. We did not believe we had an automatic right to power, merely the right to stake a claim.

In selecting its members, the A-3 was in effect forming a future ruling class—not a make-believe one either but the thing itself. It wasn't the presidents who had been members that imbued A-3 with the aura of power—although there had been three in the early days—it was the administrations. There had scarcely been a governing body that did not contain at least one A in a key position, and many were dominated by them.

And you could not apply to join, you were *invited*. Thus few were ever disallowed, since an invitation implied acceptance. Some had their membership revoked, however. We were not petty about this, but our values were unshakeable, or so we flattered ourselves. We did not care if someone smoked a little pot in the privacy of his home or if he discreetly purchased the occasional sexual favor—be it hetero or homo. However, the *flaunting* of any vice would bring you a single warning. If the indiscretion recurred, you were out.

There were some moral lapses that did not warrant a warning, however. During my term as A-3 president, for example, I revoked the membership of a state governor's son upon learning he had cheated in a card game. The son of an incumbent president was thrown out for promoting stock in a company in which his brother sold a majority holding the day it peaked, which was the day before it crashed. Another fellow was terminated for having a drunken and very public fight with his mother. The consequences of having A-3 membership revoked sounded direr than they really were: "A man's name shall be removed from all records of the Society, and henceforth and forever no member of the Society shall have any manner of business with him except for public civility. This being adamantine, irreversible and the observance of it strictly enforced, on pain of a member's own expulsion." The first clause was, of course, merciful: it meant that only the current membership would be aware of a man's expulsion, thus only they would be forbidden from doing business with him. We were all nonetheless aware, given the club's venerable history, that expulsion from it would make a life in business or politics not impossible, but very very hard. And that was the intention.

The handful that persisted in opposing club rules found out just how powerful we were, but over two hundred years there were remarkably few of them, and they were easily dispensed with. Cherniak Colbert: bankrupt, suicide. Maynard Grainger Pusey: sentenced to life imprisonment in an asylum for the criminally insane. Garner Leonard Teva: stripped of US citizenship, died in Cuba. Luther Gabel Harriman: disappeared in hot-air balloon over Kansas. Nathan Ghali Johnson: bankrupt, suicide. Daniel Lynch Beveridge: Trappist monk. S.O. Bellman: self-exile in Germany. Lyndon Pearce: bankrupt, suicide. Matthew Harrop Linsdale: disappeared. Lorien Lucibello Kane: remained in the position of chief financial advisor to the emir of Ubai, where he was unofficial finance minister, and, in marrying the Emir's only child, eventually became heir to the throne. Rudolfo Battalion: drowned at sea when his yacht sprang a large hole in its hull. D. Gallard Rossiter: bankrupt, suicide. Elijah Fistoonth: emigrated to Hungary. Enamorata T'ezee-B'i: last seen in Trieste applying for merchant banking credentials. And lastly, ***** ********.

The last name is not known. I list them all; indeed I have remembered them all, because in a better world they would be honored as heroes. They stood their ground, denouncing a foul conspiracy until their money, will, or minds gave out.

Had you asked the young men that we were if they felt themselves wise enough to stand in judgment and hold the keys of life and death, wise enough to mete out a punishment that was uniquely awesome in its breadth and finality, I have no doubt they would have affirmed it, nodding sagely, confident in matters where in reality no confidence is to be found. I have always found confidence such an inappropriate response to life's holocaust. If you survived the blitz of malevolence and greed with your body and mind intact, you survived it merely in order to die. The best outcome is a death that comes because you're too old and worn out to live, as opposed to the one that comes because you were in someone's way or posed another kind of threat to their need for too much. After all this, you *die*. What is there to be confident about here? I shudder when men use that word. Only the insane would find anything in this world that inspired confidence. I'm confident only of this verity.

CHAPTER THREE

★ ★ ★

Vitiis nemo sine nascitur[*] (Horace)

THE FOUR OF US NEXT FOUND ourselves transplanted from Cambridge to Washington, with Torrance at the Pentagon, Melton, Cassel and myself at the State Department. We rented a big old house in Georgetown together, and from it sallied forth each day side by side to conquer the known world, along with its womenfolk. We have all been young, so the reader will forgive me if I do not dwell on the sweetness of these years. Everything we did was of momentous importance and everyone we met was crucial, thus I remember little of it now. All I presumably did during those early years was familiarize myself with a world that members of the previous generation knew all too well but were preparing to leave.

We threw ourselves a lavish dinner party once we'd settled in. There were no other guests since it was supposed to be in celebration of us—that we had arrived.

"I'd like to propose a toast," said Dean Torrance. "To the hope of America and the glittering prizes."

"May we leave the place better than we found it," I said, raising my flute of champagne.

"I'll drink to that," said Les Melton.

* No one is born without faults.

"May we remember what pompous assholes we were," Melvin Cassel said, knocking back his glass.

"Boo, Mel," said Dean. "We're launching our ship here, don't curse her."

"Being realistic," Mel told him. "Are we really so different?"

"We're sure going to try to be," said Les.

"I don't know about the rest of you," Mel said, "but I'm beginning to feel the weight of this bureaucracy we've got sitting on us..."

"Not tonight, Mel," I told him. "Just wish us fair winds and plain sailing, eh?"

"No sharks?" said Mel.

"Just whales," I said.

"To Captain Ahab, then," said Dean, raising his glass again.

"Here be monsters all right," said Mel. "I can drink to that." And he did.

Most of the people I worked alongside had been at the State Department through several administrations. This in itself should have troubled citizens more than it ever did. The bureaucracy doesn't change with the government, but that does not bother the public, because they do not understand the relationship between permanent bureaucracy and elected government. Ideally, a government would draft policy and merely command its bureaucracy to follow accordingly. In practice, however, government policy is based on the advice of people like me, who represent a permanent government behind the façade of the elected one. If you examine the records, you will see that the Big Issues, such as our foreign policy, were barely affected by whether Democrats or Republicans held the White House—such was the force of our advice. The day we accepted this fact, instead of questioning its Constitutional legality, was the day we lost our political innocence. But we all rationalized it by telling ourselves that it was better to have experts on this job than to hand it over to novices every four years. This avoided the real issue, of course, which was that of who sets the course.

We did not start out this way, and I do not believe we entered into it deliberately. It happened slowly, and then all of a sudden it just was. There was nothing anyone could really do about it. A hard-nosed president could even appear to get his way. Heads would seem to roll. But no one ever thought it worth their while to explain to the taxpayers, the citizens, the people, the public in this public thing that was a republic, a *res publica*, that although undersecretary of defense sounded like a minor position, it was not. Defense secretaries came and went, presidents came and went, but the undersecretaries and the assistant secretaries, the deputy secretaries and the associates, they endured, cherishing above all else their serene anonymity. It was like Disneyland. Mickey Mouse and Donald Duck may seem to be the most important people there, but they're not even real.

Having just emerged from Watergate's crisis of faith in government, naturally enough, the Washington of Jimmy Carter that I arrived in was exceedingly humble and low-key. President Nixon had brought shame upon the town, which was now shriving itself with the peanut farmer from Georgia. That was the storyline of the season.

At the State Department, I found a mentor in Franklin Barker, a great bearded bear of a man who lectured on political science at Georgetown and was also, as undersecretary of political affairs, my boss. He had fled the Nazis in Hungary with his parents as a child, and something about the experience made him cherish his privacy. He never discussed these early years. But as everyone there knew, Barker's "private life" consisted of affairs with some of his female students, for which purpose he rented the top half of a duplex near the Georgetown campus, in addition to the house in West Virginia where his wife and eight children lived, the "cottage" on Martha's Vineyard, and the Manhattan apartment a block away from the park. Barker simply needed more of everything than other people, and I don't think anyone resented him having it. He was three hundred pounds of gleaming black bristle and *joie de vivre*, and he made you feel good because he felt good. Barker was also one of the new guards brought in by then-president Jimmy Carter and Secretary of State Cyrus Vance. He deeply distrusted those who had worked under Nixon. Because I accepted him for who he was, and did not pry into his complicated affairs, we became close, and he undertook to teach me all he knew about the ways of the world we were in.

It was, ultimately, an odd relationship, however, one of those unequal friendships that seem antagonistic but really aren't, that seem cruel but are merely playful. He was a prankster. Barker did not go by the rules, and I appreciated this greatly in the stuffy atmosphere that reigned in the institution. He also tried to dispose of the rumors that abounded, both on Capitol Hill generally and in our office.

For example, I'd been told that those, like me, who were considered bright and headed for high position, could expect to find themselves under surveillance, and Barker confirmed it, calling it a compliment. A training unit of CIA researchers was assigned to the task, he told me, and trainees are usually more zealous than seasoned pros.

"So you'd just better be squeaky clean in everything," Barker peered over his huge black horn-rims, "...as I'm *sure* you are."

A little later on that same day he told me the CIA liked a "man of independent means in government, because it makes him harder to corrupt." He went on to add that it would almost certainly mean too that their investigation would focus on my financial affairs and personal life. I should probably have wondered what they knew about A-3, but I did not. The society numbered many CIA heads and high-placed officials among its alumni. It was never in any danger of being investigated—not that it had anything to hide.

One conversation from the period stands out and warrants inclusion here verbatim because my notes on it have a preternatural intensity, an hallucinatory hyper-reality that must have been related to the malicious flu I'd come down with at the time, or the excessive amount of Benylin I'd consumed to soothe the dog-like cough that kept me barking all night long.[*]

"Oh, he really believes and all that," said Franklin Barker, returning from a weekend up at Camp David with Carter and Vance. "Vance ordered me to attend church with them both on Sunday—although his purpose was getting Carter to work the rest of the day."

We were in Barker's cluttered office, with its piles of books to review, books to read, books to teach with, all of them festooned with tattered tails of paper torn from magazines and newspapers to mark something significant. The place resembled a cavern full of grassy stalagmites. I had come to collect him for our lunch date.

"Kind of worrying," I agreed.

Vance was a decent upright man, a fine legal mind, and totally opposed to the use of force in our foreign policy. This made him ill equipped to deal with liars and the unscrupulous.

"There's more worrying things than a true believer in the White House," Barker said, leaning over toward me, his voice growing barely audible. "I was looking into it, out of sheer

---

[*] A note on language. I am attempting here to flee the worst excesses of the jargon we all used to avoid admitting to ourselves what was really going on in America's relationships with other nations, but back then we were timid. I suppose we still cared what the world thought of us, and what the public thought, so we developed a language to conceal the reality of actions that were difficult to justify in plain terms. My life became so entangled by this web of euphemism, oxymoron, and straightforward lies that I have to confess it is hard now to sort the truth from all the evasions.

curiosity, but it's disturbing to see where the people behind Nixon ran to for shelter."

"Why's that?" We were in a restaurant by now and the noise was incredible. I had my ear virtually on his mouth.

"You been around as long as me, you notice things," Barker said.

"Like what?"

"Law firms, corporations, trusts, that sort of thing. The same names keep coming up..."

"And?"

"I mean," he continued, "that you can narrow it down to a few dozen people but you can't be sure it isn't just one guy. Too many of the big shareholders are private corporations that don't have to reveal details of ownership. And, whoever it is, they're doing exactly what I'd do if I wanted to hijack this country."

"Hijack it?"

Barker had been sifting through his pockets all this time, looking for something. The effort had made him break out in a sweat. Now he turned to face me and the beads of perspiration on his brow suddenly made him appear untrustworthy. I was reminded of the sweat on Nixon's upper lip as he lied about Watergate.

"If you wanted to take over this country from within, a bloodless coup d'état, how would you do it?" he asked me.

"Make state governor in Florida or Ohio then run for the party nomination?"

"Nah," he said, waving my thought away like a moth with his paw. "You don't want to *appear* to run the country. You want to actually run it. Get me? You want the power, not the glory. How would you go about *that?*"

"You'd need hundreds of millions," I told him.

"You got it. So now what?"

I thought about this for a while, and then said, "I'd have my people in here and at the Pentagon, as close to the interface between industry and government as possible. I'd bring them in by the horde at the lowest level too."

"Exactly," Barker said, exhaling mightily.

I pressed him for details, but he wouldn't give them. I felt somewhat confused by the exchange and wondered if I'd been supposed to glean more from it.

"I bet Hank's in on it," Barker muttered to himself.

"Hank" was Henry Kissinger, who'd left Harvard just before I arrived, and then done the same in Washington. As Nixon's national security advisor then secretary of state, he was widely viewed as the *eminence grise* responsible for many of the darker incidents in recent foreign policy, particularly the covert operations that had installed or propped up brutal dictators in South America and elsewhere.

"Hank's a great front man," Barker told me. "Just look at the companies on whose boards he sits—a Who's Who of taxpayer fleecing."

"You really think someone is trying to buy control of America?" I tried to sound incredulous, but I was not sure what kind of response Barker was looking for in me.

"Sssh," said Barker, looking around, "let's not tell the press just yet, hmm? No, I don't think someone is trying to buy control. I think someone already owns control, and now they're trying to consolidate it by moving on the bureaucracy. That way there's no unpleasant surprise waiting after every election, is there?"

He was trying to wheedle it out of me, the bastard, the old bear of a bastard. Barker was a master of body language, and he was trying to get my body to talk.

"That's quite an allegation, Frank," I told him. "You're going to have to do better at persuading me."

"For fuck's sake," he said, wrinkling up his big face as if in agony. "Let's talk like grown-ups, hmm? Can we do that? I suggest you go ask your father who runs any country. Or say, 'Daddy, is it true that those who own the country also run it?'"

"You don't need to patronize me, Barker."

"I hope I don't. Look at your family, with fingers in the pie going back generations."

The metaphor didn't work for me. Our fingers were always clean and manicured. We paid people to get their hands dirty on our behalf. He did not understand—for how could he?—the difference between money and wealth. We didn't need his pies, or anyone else's pies; we had plenty of our own pies. He was the one who, with all his smarts, would be led astray with a pie when he could have had shares in the bakery.

"Oh, please," I said, growing impatient with him now. "You know damn well why we're in public service."

"No, not really. Suppose you tell me." He looked me straight in the eye. "And please don't give me the bullshit about public service."

How could he be so right yet also so wrong? His vision was all about striving, seeking, grasping at. He had no idea how men behaved when they already had everything they could possibly want and now merely sought to maintain that position. It wouldn't have surprised me to find he believed the meek would inherit the earth too, which of course, I imagined myself telling him, they will if they need to. But not its mineral rights.

"That's the truth, and you know it. There's no hidden agenda. My great-gr—"

He cut me off: "Your great ancestor nothing! He was just making sure you all kept your hand in the game, knowing that sooner or later one of you would be capable of a bit more. And that's where you come in, isn't it?"

"I really resent this."

"Shut up, David," he said, beckoning over a waitress. "What I'm saying is that you are here—Oh, we'd like some dessert, Miss, um, Sheryl, that's such a pretty name..."

"Thank you, sir," said Sheryl. "What kind of dessert can I bring you?"

"In an ideal world it would just be you, sweetheart..."

Barker was well known in his day, a highly visible *eminence*, a resident genius, and Washington was as full of young women seeking an entrée to politics as Los Angeles was of young women trying to break into movies—even if it only meant marrying the writer. I'd also observed that the great bear attracted women not in spite of his bearish bulk but because of it. His presence was unthreatening, cuddly. He was the writer.

"Would you like me to show you how best to serve such a dish?" Barker was saying.

The waitress, Sheryl, glanced nervously at me, then said, "Sure."

Sexuality, or rather the power it exerted over men, has always terrified me. I've seen it topple so many of the mighty. And my father poisoned its well for me, in ways not necessary to mention. So it wielded no power over me, and I'm glad of it. My parts functioned well enough, but it was merely a function. Nothing else. I have always disliked intensely any losing of control, and I disliked being touched for most of my life, until I was too old to be touched by anyone.

"Call me when your shift's over," Barker said, scribbling on the back of a business card and giving it to her. "I'll schedule in some tuition, OK?"

"The only thing you can't resist is temptation, isn't it?" I said when Sheryl had gone off to fill our order.

The bear's hackles were up. Barker looked at me like a weary old bedroom pirate. I wondered if he were locked in that cycle of repeating what gave him pleasure until it no longer pleasured him at all—as too many of us are. Was he pretending it gave him pleasure now? Was it merely the echo or memory of pleasure? Or was it still OK? I could never tell. Even if I had asked him, the answer would have been like explaining color to a blind man.

He looked at me strangely, as if expecting to find something that was not there. "We can't all be men of ice," he said, "laudable as it may be. Or is it just a physiological thing?"

"Are you asking me if I'm impotent or if I'm queer?" I said.

"Neither. I'm just giving you the view from here, which, to continue with my thought, is that you are not here to betray the interests of the Leverett fortune."

It was always back to those differences he could not hope to understand, differences that drive a wedge between men, differences that make a persuasive argument for outlawing inheritance. Leave a house, some furniture and paintings, fine. But that's enough. Why shackle the future to this wheel of fire? Why gamble that the truth and beauty will follow the wealth and power forever? Even if they do, they will no longer be true or beautiful. If money was really the root of all evil, the churches and synagogues and temples wouldn't be so thirsty for it, would they? Power is that root. Men will clutch onto it when all that's left of them is a grasping claw of gnarled fingers. Money is not power. A vast fortune is power.

"I'm here because the trust is set up that way."

I began to wonder whether this conversation was about me or about the country. Barker was one of those people who shows you how unaffected by class and wealth they are—how at ease with the new egalitarianism they've grown—by ceaselessly discussing the subject. His humble origins, as Barkuv or Barkuf in a Budapesht gazing back on the halcyon days of Franz-Josef so intently it didn't see either Hitler or Stalin coming, a mitteleuropa of oversweetened tea and chocolate coffee, with architecture, furniture and music so ornate its gullet wobbled with every attempt to swallow the foliage, and a tinker's son doomed merely to look on and yearn, not ever to be included in the gluttony and culture, no matter how despised....He was as comfortable with all that as he'd been with their flight on the mud flaps of Russian tanks, the tiny suitcase, the threadbare jerkin, the junior fisherman's cap, the memories of his heritage, and occidental Vienna now muddled up with oriental Budapesht. The right mix of attitude and sheer hard work stood all the huddled masses well once they were brave and free. If we gave you the impression it was one big happy huddled mass—no European vices, like hierarchy, God forbid oligarchy—it was just because that's the way we liked to view it ourselves. It's the national myth.

"Oh, come on," he said, waving a paw at someone behind me, "you surely don't believe great-great-grand pappy Leverett wanted merely to see his descendants toil on behalf of the nation, do you?"

"He did."

"No, no, no. He didn't. He just didn't know how else to guarantee you'd keep yourselves in the game."

"So you're saying I've been hoodwinked?"

"David, David," said Barker, "it isn't some great conspiracy. All of you have variations on it. Why did so many Kennedys go into politics? Rockefellers? Hmm? It merely makes sense to assure the wealth doesn't get marginalized."

"If accusing me of repping the oligarchy in government is what you wanted to say," I told him, "then you've been admirably clear."

"Sure sign you've hit the target when someone gets rattled," said Barker.

"I'm not rattled."

"Yeah," he looked at me with narrowed eyes. "Yeah, you're rattled. But I think you're missing the point."

"Which is what exactly?"

"I think of us as a team," he said. "And as a team I am suggesting we need to take sides or we'll be fucked in the coming war."

He went on to assure me that the political situation in Washington was polarizing, and that the two sides would wipe out anyone on the sidelines. In his mind, the sides consisted of vested interests that wished to see an isolationist America, and vested interests that believed we ought to seek control over the entire planet. This latter view Barker termed the "Roman model," meaning that ancient Rome had been the last great power to rule the entire world.

"What's your inclination?" he asked me.

"Not much of a choice, is it?"

"You're right, it isn't," he admitted. "Because only an idiot would take the losing side, and the Roman model will win out. FSD: full-spectrum domination. Fuck social democracies."

"Why's that?"

"More money involved in world domination than there is in isolationist utopia."

Follow the money. An American mantra. The trouble with the money is its weakness for critical mass. It always goes where the other money is. And birds of a feather end up baked in pies.

CHAPTER FOUR

★ ★ ★

*Libenter hominess id quod volunt credunt** (Julius Caesar)

IN POLITICS, THERE IS SUPPOSED TO BE vision, a governing ideology, a goal. In Washington, however, we put all this aside when we allowed into government vested interests. President Eisenhower saw it coming, and he warned the nation in his farewell speech about the dangers of a "military-industrial complex," by which was specifically meant the nexus of concerns feeding into and out of the Pentagon, the relationship between generals and the whole war industry, from Lockheed Martin's missiles, through Bechtel's underground cities, to Halliburton's ready-to-eat meals, and of course their lobbies, which turned our nation's political leaders into cash whores. From the modest practical vision of our Founding Fathers, who saw no great mission for our nation in the world, we went to a situational position without a philosophy behind it. At the end of WW II we were the only great power left unscathed by the carnage. We could have used this advantage for peace. Instead we started another war, which consumed the minds and the money that could have made America the earthly paradise.

Our job at the political affairs bureau of the State Department was to reassess daily our position with regard to

*Men will gladly believe that which they wish for.

[49]

international events and draft interim policy accordingly. As a result, over the closing years of the twentieth century, we were led by the nose when we weren't trying to shape events, and it is hard to say which consequence resulted in the most egregious actions on our part.

We danced around Central and South America, toppling regimes here, backing right-wing guerrillas there, with impunity. It was our backyard, and the world recognized that, so no one told us what to do in it. In the East, we had controlled Japan since the end of WW II, and used it as a check on the Chinese. I never viewed China as a threat. The Chinese have 5,000 years of continuous history behind them, so we know they have never been imperialists. When China was weak, its boundaries shrank. When it was strong, it regained those boundaries. The Chi'in state is the oldest political union on earth. When we respected that, we demonstrated our understanding of China. When we forgot it or ignored it, we lost their respect. The Taiwan Strait was the single most contentious issue in the politics of my time—it is thus to be expected that no one heard much about it.

The Middle East was where we came unglued, however. Barker kept directing my attention toward Iran, so when it blew up in our face I wasn't as surprised as most were. He had given me an intelligence report prepared for President Eisenhower back in 1955 that stated unequivocally some raw facts. There was, the report said, a pronounced hostility toward the US on the Arab street. America was perceived by the ordinary Arab as hypocritical, proclaiming democracy in public, while in private supporting brutal dictatorships across the region with complete disregard for the political will of the masses. The report went on to say that it was difficult to counter this perception largely because it was accurate. Furthermore, it concluded, we were doing the right thing in supporting status quo regimes, because they were the ones that could best protect our interests in the area. Any number of times, Barker told me our interests in the area boiled down to one interest: oil. We had seen first-hand the entire Nazi German war machine break down when its supply line to Middle East oil was cut. We were not going to allow ourselves to fall into that situation by letting the Russians get control of the oil, so we backed the very regimes Russia was targeting as ripe for revolution.

Of all the Arab regimes, Saudi Arabia was the most problematical, since it had the most money and could buy all the help it needed, but the process we used was similar to that we used on poorer nations. We built them cities and kept the princes in power, and in exchange they invested all their money in the US. They couldn't turn against us without losing their money, which we now controlled.

Iran was the first country we ever handled with the full range of options available to us, and events had dictated its necessity. In the fifties the Iranians had a democratically elected government headed by a very progressive prime minister, Mohammed Mossadeq. In those days, the big oil companies basically owned the Middle East fields, paying a royalty to the nations involved. When, in 1953, Mossadeq announced he would nationalize the Persian oil fields, alarm bells rang in Washington. Iran was on Russia's doorstep, so we were always concerned about it.

Initially, our concern had been to keep Russia's pipeline to Gulf oil open, however. In 1941, the British and the Soviet Russians had invaded Iran and removed its shah from power because he was about to become a Nazi German ally, a member of the original "axis of evil." They installed his son, Mohammed Reza Pahlavi, as shah, because he was more susceptible to Western influence—but it was a parliamentary monarchy. Mossadeq was thus an elected leader, which was a problem for us. The situation was solved by the 1941 precedent. This time, in 1955, the CIA teamed up with Britain's MI6, to conduct another coup d'état, overthrowing the Mossadeq regime and installing the Shah as dictator, with a nominal one-party parliament. It failed, and the Shah had to flee to Italy, but a second coup brought him back. We'd had 100,000 "advisors" in the country to help him rule.

There is no doubt that we killed off the first indigenous flowering of Iranian democracy. This, along with our unconditional support for Israel, was the kind of thing that made us hated in the region.

True to our word, we kept the Shah in power for as long as we could, and he made sure the Iranian Tudeh Communist party remained underground, building up the SAVAK secret police into a formidable force of terror and persecution. "Guardian of the Persian Gulf," that's what the Shah called himself. But events there got out of hand very fast.

★　★　★

I was sitting with Barker on the rooftop patio of Tony's Black Forest Inn, a tacky Bavarian theme restaurant—predictably, a Barker favorite—overlooking the Potomac. We usually lunched there on Fridays, when it was warm enough to sit outside. This was November, but it had been unseasonably warm, so Tony kept the patio open. I remember the burning red of the leaves, which were only just starting to fall, although in the Midwest it was freezing. I wanted there to be snow for them to fall on, and I pictured it, watching the foliage turn into florid faces of people I did not know. The faces looked surprised, but not unduly so, as they sank into the crystal whiteness and were buried.

"You've gotta know what *they're* thinking," he said. "You've gotta know what their take on history is like. I keep telling these clowns at the agency that they've gotta be able to think the way their opponent thinks in order to outwit him. But do they listen?"

I learned a lot about international affairs from Barker, but nothing about cliché and decorum.

"Yes?" I said.

"Nobody listens. Nobody."

"A prophet in his own land?"

"Something like that. Talking about a profit in land, how's your dad doing?"

My father was having little success negotiating through a back-channel with the Iranians, as I told Barker.

"That old-world stuff isn't working any more. I think the age of the gentleman diplomat is passed. You're gonna have to toughen up yourself if you want to survive, kid."

"Seems to me it's more a question of having something tangible to negotiate for, no? What do you understand about negotiating over ideals anyway?"

Barker was just about to fire something back at me when Alberto, the maitre d', came out to say there was an urgent phone call for the professor.

"I told you!" said Barker, returning after five minutes. "They've taken over our embassy in Teheran. Now we got more than ideals to negotiate over, I'd say."

The Iranian Revolution was a disaster for us already without this. The Shah had been forced to flee. We had him holed up on an island in Panama, courtesy of General Torrijos, who had a thing for the empress. But we'd allowed him to enter the US for cancer treatments, and although he'd registered under the name "Noriega," word got out. Ayatollah Khomeini, the cleric who had surprised the world by declaring Iran an Islamic republic, wanted the Shah back in Persia and on trial. It was a reasonable enough request, and we probably should have complied with it, but he'd been a good ally, and we still had plans to put him back on the Peacock Throne. There had been total chaos in Iran for over a year now, and Barker had been warning the secretary that our embassy would be a target. As we hurried back to the bureau, he told me why the problem was bigger than I realized. Evidently, the Teheran embassy was more like our base in the region. We used it to listen in to Soviet Russia, and the CIA used it to run covert ops all over the Middle East. There was a lot of sensitive material in the files there, details about how we'd been trying to undermine the new regime in particular, along with actual plates for printing US hundred-dollar bills.

"Why on earth would those be there?"

"The agency gets through a lot of cash. They prefer to print it."

"Doesn't that make it counterfeit?"

"Yep."

"I don't get it..."

"Whoever they pay off with it can't bank it *here* because the numbers are wrong. But you can't tell the notes from the real thing, so you can spend the stuff *anywhere*."

Now the Iranians would be able to flood the world with fake US currency indistinguishable from the real thing. I thought there was something very wrong with this the moment I heard about it, yet the exigencies of *realpolitik* are such that I was able to justify it as something for the greater good. It always bothered me that so much of the business we kept secret would have been hard to justify to the American public, and I think a lot of people involved with it felt the same way. But you get caught up in politics, skilled in the business of presenting things a certain way—lying, in fact.

The embassy takeover turned into a hostage episode, of course, the longest one in our history, 444 days. Even my father's skills proved useless. When it was over, Barker was out of a job and America had begun to chart the course that took her so far from liberty and democracy she would never return there, never again know a safe haven.

There was a lot of pressure on us during those 444 days, but it wasn't the benign pressure that produces good work. Barker had me assigned to the unit working on diplomatic efforts to free the hostages, so I had many meetings to brief the president. Despite the aura of sanctity and humbug with which we surrounded our presidents in those days, when you sat down in a room with Jimmy Carter, or any of the others I got to meet, you were with an overtired, overworked mortal. Look at pictures of those men before and after their presidencies: the difference is striking. It wore out the toughest. Now, though, the position may well be permanently vacant... or permanently filled. But I don't want to get ahead of myself here.

Many presidents had dined in our house when I was a child. But they were my father's presidents and they came ostensibly for money. This one was my president and he came for something else. I liked the feeling of being wanted for one's knowledge, and of having earned the right to dispense it. It struck me that this was what my great-great grandfather had wanted his heirs to experience: the rewards that money cannot buy. Like virtue, they are their own reward.

When you met with the president everyone in our little world knew it. Secretaries treated you differently; you caught your peers talking about you. In my case, it also drew V.S. Parks, my sponsor at the Harvard A-3 club, from cover.

It was the day our embassy in Tripoli had been attacked by a few thousand Libyans expressing their sympathy with the Iranian Islamic Revolution. I'd been woken early by Barker with the news, and was having Sunday breakfast with Melvin at Denny's. He was now working in Intelligence and Research, so we always had a lot to discuss at our weekly breakfast. I was then attempting to get the Pope to write personally to Khomeini on behalf of the hostages, but I had become ensnared in Vatican bureaucracy.

"In my tribe, you don't expect much help from the Vatican," Melvin was saying. "Besides, Carter's a Baptist. Why don't you send in Billy?"

Billy Carter, the president's brother, was a walking cliché, a Southern good ol' boy straight from central casting, full of booze and platitudes, with an unerring instinct for maximum embarrassment. Some Arabs had lured him into a deal that his own dog could have advised against, and now he was promoting the self-explanatory Billy Beer, a can of which was always in his paw. I believe Billy existed solely for the further delight of people like Melvin, who simply could not stop marveling at the low comedy provided by this Rake's Egress of a man who even looked like his brother remade as a moron and recast as malice in blunderland. You couldn't make this sort of stuff up.

"Billy's a sad story this week," I said. I'd been impressed by the president's handling of the family shame. *Billy's my brother*, he'd said, *and I love him.* "We should all leave him alone, and think there but for the grace of G—"

"You're not getting religious on me, are you?" Melvin looked over at me suspiciously. "I bet you have yourselves a little gospel hour over there in the oval orifice, don't you?"

"We're getting Jimmy his own gospel hour, pewside chat plus four-part harmony, every Sunday evening to go up against McNeil–Lehrer."

"What's the fuckin' Pope going to do for you anyway? Absolve the sin of stupidity?"

"We saw it more as a clerkly appeal, one multinational CEO to another. You know, throw in a bit monotheistic solidarity."

Melvin scowled. "Solidarnosc in Qom, that's a laugh. Let's see the fuckin' Arabs build a dinghy, let alone a ship."

"They're not Arabs, Mel. The Iranians don't like to be confused with Arabs. They're Aryans, in fact."

"I'm sure they are," he said. "If they don't want to be confused with Arabs they should stop acting as if it's AD 1350, take off the tablecloths, send the mobs home, stop screaming and start talking. They act like yard apes, they gonna be treated like shit. Simple as that."

"You should definitely run on that platform, Mel. Cassel for Uberlieutenant. No to Yard Apes. It has a ring to it..."

"Better than seeking sympathy because they had shitty childhoods."

"I expected more than a knee-jerk from you," I said.

"I know some Lebanese Christians," said Mel. "Grew up in Cairo. They said every night they sat down to dinner this subject comes up. And you know what? You burn out discussing it. You get into who are the Palestinians and why won't the Arabs help them...You get into Israel's right to exist...It's right to defend itself...You get into how many Palestinians left and how many want to come back...You get into facts and figures and statistics....You get into ethics and morals....But at the end of the dinner you're left with....what? The Israelis aren't going anywhere...and nor are the Palestinians. It's insoluble. If Balfour and those fucking anti-Semites who dreamt it up, and Weitzman and those fanatics who pushed it through had had any idea of the problem they were creating, they'd never have gone ahead. *Never.*"

That was when I heard the voice behind me say:

"One hears you're doing very well for yourself in Washington, Dave."

I turned to find Parks. He had aged dramatically, a skein of tiny wrinkles covering his face, and was dressed more casually than I'd imagined him capable of, in jeans and a sweater. It was a Sunday so I put it down to that, but I didn't recognize him at first.

I asked him to join us, and I could see Melvin scowl. He didn't like interruptions, and he made Parks conscious of interrupting, so he didn't stay long. All I knew was that he'd come back to Washington after a lengthy stay abroad. We arranged to meet for dinner the following day.

"So who's the faggot?" said Melvin, when Parks had gone.

I told him, mildly surprised he hadn't run into Parks at Harvard.

"CIA doesn't just wander over and say hi," Mel said. "You're not thinking that was a coincidence, I hope?"

"Why would they be interested in me?"

"You tell me. You're kinda cute looking, even if you are losing your hair."

"What's it like to be suspicious of everyone and everything?" I asked him, pointedly.

"It's okay."

"You never take anything at face value, do you?"

"When most things have two faces, why would I?"

"Be nice to feel that our friendship had earned me your trust."

"It's in the genes, I guess," said Mel, sighing. "This way at least I don't get let down."

"I feel I'm constantly being tested—it's wearing, Mel."

"It's me," he said. "It's who I am. It may even be why you love me."

"A stiff-necked contrary bastard."

"That's what they all say." He went on to relate a story about Senator Dellsworth that ended up in an arrest for public lewdness.

I wondered briefly if Parks had just happened to be in Denny's. Coincidences did not bother me so much then as they do now. I grew to be far more like Mel in that respect than I would ever have dreamed I'd become. In my business, you got to suspect everything, though, because you never got a second chance at being right. I looked forward to the dinner with Parks, yet I also had a sense of foreboding about it that was not really rational.

Monday was yet another harrowing day. It was becoming obvious to me that Carter was focusing on his re-election campaign and not on the situation at hand, and that there was a considerable amount of vanity tied up with it—a recipe for disaster if ever there was one. At least I managed to get a positive response from the Vatican. The Pope would apparently be happy to assist us. Just as I was about to leave to meet Parks, a draft of the papal letter came through. It was very formal, one pontiff to another, but it did get right to the point. I wondered how Khomeini would respond to it.

We met at The Monocle on D. St.—his decision, not mine. The place was a little too casual for my liking. He was twenty minutes late, which I found disconcerting, sitting there alone with a newspaper and Tio Pepe Fino, feeling increasingly apprehensive about the wave of hatred for us spreading through the Muslim world. When he finally did arrive, I was happy to see he was his old elegant self again. In fact, I am convinced he wore exactly the same blue pin-striped suit he'd worn when I first met him. No sooner had we finished giving our orders than he started into what struck me as a prepared speech.

"Let's not beat around the bush," he said, laughing somewhat nervously. "You know I didn't just happen to be in Denny's. I wanted to find a way to run into you that wasn't so... official. And I don't trust the telephones here anymore. The fact is, Leverett, that I'm working in New York with a group of—shall we call them *concerned citizens*?—yes, concerned citizens. And they don't like what's going on with this administration."

"Really?"

This precipitous lurch into business took me by surprise. I was astonished he would breach protocol in such a way, imposing on a fleeting acquaintanceship to discuss what were potentially matters of national security. But, as I was finding more and more, the Washington protocol that I learned from listening to my father was a thing of the past, and I'd have to unlearn a lot of it or get swept out with the cobwebs myself.

"Let me finish." Parks took a sip of martini. He seemed more flustered than he ought to be, than the kind of person I thought he was—but, of course, I didn't really know him. "These concerned citizens are also very powerful, wealthy citizens, who feel the country has lost its direction. We're embarrassed by this pussy-footing around with Teheran."

He went on to criticize the position we'd taken and state that we ought to have invaded and put the Shah back in power. Much as I wanted to disagree with him, I had to stop him right there.

"It's inappropriate for me to be discussing any of this with you," I said. "You know how it is."

"Of course I do." He swatted an imaginary fly. "But this is me, your old A-3 pal, and we can discuss anything, can't we? The way we used to."

I realized he didn't remember we had only met the once. He was under the impression I'd joined A-3 earlier than I had.

"Can't do it," I said. "This is national security. I have signed secrecy contracts. I'd be in violation of them."

"Yes, yes, but I'm one of you. I'm on the *inside...*"

"Doesn't sound like it," I said, surprised he would push this. "You said you were working with a group of concerned citizens."

"But I'm still with the agency, of course."

I knew he was lying. I can usually tell if people are lying.

"DC," he added. Deep cover. "Which is why you won't find me listed. Point is, I'm cleared for classified info."

"Then you'll have to make a formal request." I was firm. "I can't do it any other way."

The dinner was rather awkward after my refusal to discuss current business. Rather than brush against national security again, we chose the more neutral topic of China. But Parks was clearly not so well informed on the subject as he'd been on the Soviet Union, and he waffled horribly, then abruptly returned to what I thought was going to be another attempt to have me breaching official secrecy. It was not, however.

"Frankly, Leverett," he said, "Liberalism failed, didn't it? All it achieved was the freedom for individuals to focus on themselves and their own selfish interests, hedonism, relativism, nihilism."

"Well, I think that's—"

He silenced me with his hand.

"That's all relativism can achieve. You start questioning everything, then pretty soon nothing is true, everything is permitted. People lose direction, purpose. The average Joe needs something to believe in. Necessary illusions, Plato's 'Noble Lie.' You and I don't have to believe in it, but don't you feel it's wrong for us to deny Joe that which will give his life meaning, a goal?"

I was about to object to this but again I was silenced.

"Uh-uh," he said. "A-3 rules." He waved his Montblanc fountain pen at me.

One of the A-3 conversation rules—honored more in the breach than in the observance—was that as long as a fellow held his pen no one could interrupt him.

"Quite so," Parks continued. "If we carry on the way we're going, religion will be gone soon, and religion is Joe's most apparent vehicle of necessary illusion. A nation of individuals isn't a nation. Remember Socrates: something has to benefit both the city and the people for it to be considered good. We're among those to whom the future looks for everything it can be, yet we will render it a terrible disservice if we send along this crumbling foundation of nihilism, of relativism. It is still possible to turn things around, and . . . well, we're trying to do that, trying to bring back to America the good fight, the war against evil. Because that's what history has been, isn't it? Good versus evil. And we're the good guys here, the white hats."

"I'm sorry Parks, but I can't sit here listening to twaddle," I said, emphatically. "History is all gray, and you know it."

I wondered where on earth he'd come across these simplistic moralistic ideas. He waved the pen at me again, so I patiently sat it out. I should have left there and then, but I bit on the hook, and though I fought back, I was slowly reeled in.

"Of course it is," he said. "*We* know that. But *they* don't— the great unwashed, the *oiks*. They need the world to be more like *Gunsmoke*, where the evil are always identifiable and the good always gun them down. You know what the sensibility is out there ... in the suburbs, on the prairies, up in the Rockies, or down in the deserts. It's real basic, David, *real basic*. And it always will be. In any society you can imagine, man will still be man, with his hatreds and jealousies and spite. Some kind of coercive force will always be needed by the guardians to keep these tendencies in check. Always. There *is* no utopia, my friend. It's a dream. It was the liberal dream, and it's blown up in our faces. At home and abroad. Look at the ghettos, the riots, the spread of drugs and immorality. Look at the Iranians—no respect for us or our people. The Soviets too, they sign our treaties then behind our backs they increase their weapons research, they develop non-acoustic radar—our nuclear subs are obsolete—and they put their missiles so deep under the Urals that we don't know where they are."

"That's not true," I said. "I've looked at the CIA data. Russia is falling apart at the seams. Their missile system has completely broken down. They can't afford anything. They are bankrupt already, but they won't admit it."

"No, my friend," Parks said, pointing an index finger at me. "That's where you are dead wrong. *Dead* wrong. I was on Team B—"

Team B had been an independent unit set up by Gerald Ford's young defense secretary, Donald Rumsfeld, and his chief of staff, Dick Cheney, to investigate the CIA's data on Russia. Its findings were controversial and largely viewed as nonsense by the current administration. I was only vaguely familiar with them, and all I knew was that they flew in the face of the CIA contention that the Soviet Union was cracking apart. Not that we allowed the public to know this until the Berlin Wall came down.

"Team B seems to be discredited these days," I pointed out.

"I saw the data. I *know*, and, as you know, I'm not exactly ignorant when it comes to Russia. For Christ's sake, there's even a military manual called *The Art of Conquest*...Conquest! Does that sound like they've given up? I know the mindset. They *will* conquer America if we go on the way we are."

"You have me there," I admitted. "I defer to you on the subject of Russia. Why on earth is there this general perception that Team B's findings are baloney?"

"Kissinger," Parks said, hissing the name, "wants history to remember him as the founder of a new world of détente, of globalism. Very much against our findings, and very powerful." His face soured. "You know what globalism would be if we let it happen? The biggest goddamn tyranny the world has ever known, that's what. Can you imagine it? The power struggles, the ruthlessness, the sheer bureaucratic *bulk* of it...We're political animals, human beings, we're always going to look to government of some kind for guidance, and the nightmare of a global government doesn't even bear thinking about, does it? So we're left with the struggles between Eurasia, Europa, Pacifica, whatever....and America. There's only one way to make sure we aren't overrun, and you know it. We have to make sure that we are always the most powerful military force there is. Because if we aren't, we're finished."

I was lost for words. It was a dismal Hobbesian prospect, and it depressed me to view the future of the world through such a dark glass.

"Realistic view...That's the way it is, and you know it. Listen," he said, "there's someone I want you to meet, fellow named Luposki. He was the driving force behind Team B, but I think you'll appreciate each other. He's also very bright—*very* bright. Left Harvard just before your time and went to Chicago, studied under Strauss."

Maxwell, my Oxford tutor, loathed the very name Leo Strauss, referring to him, if he had to, as "the Jewish Nazi," or "Heidegger's heir." All I knew about him was that Maxwell had nothing but scorn for his readings of Plato and Thucydides, and that because he had claimed the argument for the pre-eminence of democracy is not an apodeictic principle—that is, it's not self-evident or beyond contradiction—he was an enemy of democracy. I did not know enough to start an argument on the subject, so I let it go by.

"Ah," I said. "Strauss, yes, yes of course. I'd be intrigued to meet this friend of yours."

We set up a loose drink and meal date for three days hence, and before long I was walking down Constitution Avenue alone. Parks' arguments against liberalism had the force of a certain logic behind them, and the evening had left me feeling deracinated. Some of my most deeply held convictions had been shaken badly. I kept thinking the arguments through. Could freedom and excellence coexist? Where would a struggle between rationalism and traditionalism end? Did liberalism contain the seeds of its own demise? And so on.

I needed to walk, and that night I must have walked six miles. When I got home, Dean Torrance and Les Melton were chatting in the kitchen.

"Good God," said Dean. "You look like shit."

"Nice of you to notice. I've been thinking—"

"Better cut that out, David," said Les. "Not good for you."

"What was that phrase Marx uses in the *Manifesto?* 'All that is solid melts into air. . . .' That's what I feel like," I said.

"Take an Alka-Seltzer," Dean suggested. "Probably flatulence."

I made myself some tea and started relating the story of my evening with Parks. Then we started throwing the ideas around. When Melvin got home, just before one, we were like a session of the first-year A-3 again, and that, after all, was what had brought us together in the first place. Mel joined in, and there we were at dawn still going at it. It wasn't about agreement or disagreement—the rules of A-3 forbad proselytizing—it was about the ideas as ideas, and the general consensus was that, as far as new ideas went, these weren't bad.

Around 5 AM, we were arguing over Plato, and on the spur of the moment I decided to telephone Maxwell in Oxford. As always, it was a joy to hear his rich, deep voice, a joy that was now accompanied by pangs of regret for the life I might have had. We updated one another on our lives, and then I mentioned the apparent growth of a Straussian movement, hearing mutterings of contempt in the receiver as I did.

"Enough with the chit-chat," said Dean. "What's his take on all of this?"

I told Maxwell I was putting him on speaker phone but I know he didn't have a clue what such a thing was.

"What's wrong with Strauss's take on Plato?" asked Les.

"He reads al-Farabi's commentary," said Maxwell, assuming Les was me, disdain leaking from his words. "He's not really reading Plato at all."

"But what's actually wrong about it?" Les said.

"Strauss sees the need to turn to classical political philosophy as a whole to be integral to recovering an understanding of nature. Nature, in a pre-modern sense, emerges when the governing opinions of the city come to be questioned and the need arises to come to know the relation of those opinions to an abiding reality, nature.

"Strauss's return to the ancients is premised upon the need for a contemporary recovery of a phenomenological or pre-philosophic awareness. That awareness is the necessary beginning point of philosophy if it is to recover a rationalism that is non-technological. In the rise from opinion to knowledge, the philosopher does not emerge as a subjectivity disengaged from nature. Indeed, precisely because the ideas are not metaphysical, causal realities but rather permanent problems, the philosopher can seek only for a knowing he can never attain or master. The method of the philosopher, which is embodied for Strauss in the life of Socrates, is to ask the '*What is...?*' questions about human and non-human things. In the dialectic of enquiry the natures or essences of these things emerge—not as metaphysical causes, but as phenomenological realities. Out of the questioning of philosophy, nature emerges as heterogeneity of various natures; the whole consists of different parts. However, the nature of these natures or parts is itself fundamentally problematic. The philosopher can never grasp the whole in all of its parts; nature can never be a pure object of thought. The Socratic philosopher is defined by knowledge of ignorance. In short, the philosopher never converts phenomenology into metaphysics."

"Right then," said Dean. "I'm glad that's clear."

"That's fairly devastating as a critique, I'd say," said Mel.

It struck me as a purely philosophical quibble, interesting in itself but not a devastating condemnation. I should have thought more carefully about its implications, though. Instead, I asked Maxwell what he thought Strauss contained for a contemporary American politician.

"Lord," he said, "one hates to think..."

I could hear him unwrapping one of the candies he always ate during his lectures. He sighed a few times, reminding me he was now in his eighties, and then continued:

"For Strauss, the enquiry that looks to human ends, to the question of the good, is an activity destructive of the good of the city. Strauss takes up the Nietzschean view that what holds together forms of human life (cities or cultures) is a certain horizon or opinion that gives significance and moral direction to people's lives.

"In Strauss's terms, the city is, and must be, closed. Here lies the ambivalence in Strauss's concept of nature. The city, the natural community of humans, is sustained by the engagement of its citizens. This engagement is premised upon a belief that the laws of the city are legitimate. For cities that have come to question their foundation and tradition, this legitimacy is premised on notions of justice and right, ultimately grounded in nature. But, for Strauss, no actual city can be just or be in accord with nature. Every city must be conventional, structured by determinate opinions, and thus not open to 'the whole.' Each city must have decided among the various alternatives and in order to retain the engagement of its citizens must by force and persuasion (even to the point of a noble lie), instill the engagement of its citizenry.

"There is an irresolvable conflict between the philosopher, the highest type of man who would live in openness to nature as a whole, and the city, which by nature must be closed to nature as a whole. The conflict between the philosopher and the city is at the heart of Strauss's position, and at the heart of his reading of Plato. For Strauss, the Platonic dialogues are not metaphysical but a 'psychological' and 'sociological' phenomenology of the relation between the philosopher and the city.

"It's all so damn wrongheaded! This all comes out of the Marburg School of Ernst Cassirer et al. Strauss is notable for the extremes of his perversity. He leans toward the outright philosophical fascism of Nietzsche, Heidegger, Jaspers, Adorno, Hannah Arendt, and the Schmitt school of law in Germany. Appalling stuff!"

"He's saying your new ideas are just Adolf Hitler's old ideas," said Dean.

I switched the phone off speaker, thanking Maxwell and making some vain promises about coming to see him soon. I wish I'd kept those promises. This was the last time I ever spoke to him. Seventy years later and I still miss that man's presence in this world. Words like 'reason,' 'rational,' 'erudite,' and 'decent' always wear his face.

"Just because Hitler liked Wagner doesn't mean we should ban Wagner, does it?" asked Les.

"I'd say yes to that," said Mel. "Although it is true that some of the early Zionists were fascists—Jabotinsky, for example."

"Well, let's be careful we haven't fallen into a rift between philosophical schools here," said Dean.

"You wouldn't be able to hide an eyelash in one of those, let alone fall into it," said Les.

"God knows," said Melvin, after hours of this, "if anyone's got an original thought out there, I could use it right now. Because right now I have to go to work with a bunch of very old and stale ideas."

I must admit that the exceptional beauty of that golden dawn made it seem indeed like a new morning. As Melvin left for work he threw in the newspapers from the step. They looked like burning bricks of light before they hit the floor and the front door closed out the busy sun. I expected momentous front-page news to match my mood, and I recall being surprised to find all that had happened the day my mind turned around on its inner self was that the auction house Christie's had sold a thimble for a record $18,400, and eleven people had died in the crush of fans mobbing The Who at Cincinnati's Riverfront Coliseum. In a month of earth-shaking news, December 3 had been devoid of anything more significant.

I ought to have believed more in omens, for I have seen enough of them to know everything in heaven and on earth conspires at the birth of great events.

CHAPTER FIVE

★ ★ ★

*Qequam memento rebus in arduis servare mentum** (Horace)

I KNEW MY FATHER'S NEGOTIATIONS with the Iranians were going nowhere because my mother advised me not to bring the subject up with him.

"I am so sick of politics and the poison they bring home," she said, "that I don't care if I never hear a word about the Middle East for the rest of my life."

I had hoped she would answer the phone because my father had been testy the last few times we'd spoken, and it also seemed ages since I had really talked to her because we spoke all the time yet said nothing.

"How's your work going?" I asked.

I heard her intake air then hiss it out through her teeth.

"What's that supposed to mean?" I said.

"Since when has anyone been interested in my work?" she said.

"We've always been interested," I protested. "We just don't understand it..."

"*We?*" she said. "Why is it that the men in my life both use *we* instead of *I*? It is a sickening monarchical affectation."

"I think you're making too—"

---

* When the path of life is steep, remember to keep your mind even.

"Well, I don't care what you think!" she yelled, and she hung up the telephone.

I have always taken great exception to having someone hang up on me. It strikes me as unpardonably rude, a symbolic act that says communication is no longer possible. There is no equivalent in a real conversation. I regard it as abuse of the medium. And my mother knew this about me.

★ ★ ★

We did not have to wait long for Ayatollah Khomeini's reply to the Pope. The Vatican sent us a copy not long after they'd received it, presumably as a sign of their annoyance. Where the Pope's letter had been gravely dignified, impersonal and formal, Khomeini's response to it was very personal, seething with righteous indignation. I doubted if the Holy Father had ever received anything like it before; it instilled in me a curious respect bordering on admiration for the leader of Iran's revolution, particularly knowing, as I did, the truth of its accusations.

The letter dismissed the papacy as a tool of American imperialism, telling the Pope he normally wasn't so concerned about individual human lives. *Where were you*, it asked angrily, *when the Shah was cutting off the hands and feet of my people?* It went on to state the rectitude of Iran's position, promising that the Shah would receive a fair trial if he was returned to Iran, and even inviting His Holiness to attend the trial personally. It was a blistering reply, and one I found unanswerable. I have no doubt that we would have sent the Shah back to answer to his people had we not been so complicit in his crimes, and had the Iranian demands not been so stringent. For they demanded not just the return of the Shah to Iran for trial, but also the return of the Shah's wealth to the Iranian people, as well as an admission of guilt by the United States for its past actions in Iran, plus an apology, and a promise from the United States not to interfere in Iran's affairs in the future. We couldn't comply.

As I sat contemplating the hopelessness of our situation with Iran, Barker asked me to attend on his behalf a meeting with Zbigniew Brzezinski, who was Carter's national security advisor and who propounded a tougher line toward Iran than we'd been following at the State Department. The press had been trumpeting hostilities between our two departments, but the reality was far less extreme than that, even if it did result in the replacement of Cyrus Vance by Warren Christopher. We suspected that Brzezinski had engaged in back-channel negotiations with foreign ambassadors, but then the State Department was overly turf-conscious, so we tended to over-look the specific circumstances of any incursion into our realm. Vance was a gentleman lawyer; he simply did not know how to negotiate with crooks and liars. Christopher was hardly Wyatt Earp, but he was somewhat tougher.

When I arrived for the meeting, I was somewhat taken aback to find no one else there. Brzezinski, who looked like a rather surprised and wizened old eagle, came walking briskly into the room precisely on time.

"No," he said, noticing me looking around, "it's just you and me."

There was the faintest trace of an accent in his voice.

"Yes, sir."

"Call me Zbig," he said, very friendly in his manner. "Everyone else does. I'll keep this brief. I've been told that you're a man of exceptional ability in foreign affairs. I know your father, so it does not surprise me."

His face belied this statement, with its permanent look of sur-prise, and I had to stifle an impulse to laugh. He clearly thought I was about to profess modesty, however, so he raised his hand.

"This is no place for modesty," he said. "I mean Washington." He smiled benignly. "With Professor Barker's permission, which I already have, I would like to offer you a rather unique position, which is that of conduit between my office and your own. I am prepared to put you on full salary here, in addition to what you earn there. In effect, you'd have two jobs. As you know, there are differences of opinion between our two stations, and it is my concern that they do not get in the way of the job we have to do. Well?"

"I'm honored, sir... Zbig." The name sounded ridiculous on my tongue. "Of course I accept."

"Good. Very good," he said, opening a file and taking from it a sheet of paper. "I have here a proposal for the rescue of the Iranian hostages." His penetrating stare went right through me, with an almost tangible force. "Before I let you read it—and you cannot take it from this room—I want to fill you in about the larger picture. Negotiations are proceeding at this very minute between the two Husseins, the king in Jordan and the president of Iraq, for a coup in Teheran. Nominally, it will involve Iranian officers loyal to Bahktiar, the ex-PM, who's currently in France. But the main muscle will be from Iraq. All the Arabs have a vested interest in it. They don't want this fundamentalism spreading into their countries, so we all understand each other.

"Also—and this information must remain between us—the Soviets are going to invade Afghanistan very soon. They have plenty of reasons to do it, but I think the most pressing is the need to make sure Iran doesn't export its Islamic revolution into Azerbaijan and the other Muslim republics in Soviet Central Asia.

"As I think you understand, politics aren't black and white. I'm in a better position than most to understand the Soviet mindset, and I do understand it. I also have very good contacts behind the Iron Curtain, so my understanding isn't speculation either. They have their eyes on Pakistan and India—they desperately need a warm-water port—and they would like to dominate the Gulf and its oil. This is not, in my opinion, anything that warrants détente. The secretary disagrees with me,

I'm well aware of *that*." He laughed, instantly growing serious again. "I'm not asking you to be disloyal—of course I'm not. I'm told you are a political realist, as am I. Perhaps between us we can attempt to smooth out the secretary's ruffled feathers...for the greater good of all concerned. Yes?"

"I am wholly in agreement, sir."

I was still reeling from the thought of a Soviet invasion of Afghanistan, trying to follow the falling dominoes.

"Excellent. Now take a look through this." He passed me the sheet of paper, which was single-space typing, heavily annotated, bearing the heading Operation Rice Bowl.

The operation was designed as a complex two-night mission. The first stage of the mission involved establishing a small staging site inside Iran itself, near Tabas in the Yazd Province of Iran. The site, known as Desert One, was to be used as a temporary airstrip for C-130 Hercules transport planes and RH-53 Sea Stallion minesweeper helicopters that would undertake the actual rescue operation. After refueling, the ground troops would board the helicopters and fly to Desert Two near Teheran. After locating and extracting the hostages from Teheran, the rescued would be transported by helicopter to Manzariyeh Air Base outside Teheran, in order to evacuate them out of the country under the protection of fighter aircraft. Some of the units to be involved in this operation were listed:

- USS *Nimitz* (CVN-68) & MarDet (Marine Detachment); and Battle Group
- USS *Coral Sea* (CV-43) & MarDet; and Battle Group
- 1st Special Forces Operational Detachment-Delta (Delta Force)
- 75th Ranger Regiment (US Army Rangers)
- US Army Special Forces (Green Berets)
- USS *Okinawa* (LPH-3), 31st Marine Amphibious Unit, Battalion Landing Team 3/3, and HMM 165

- USAF 1st Special Operations Wing, 8th and 16th Special Operations Squadrons (AC-130/MC-130), USAF RED HORSE and numerous support organizations

"Can it work?" I asked him. "It reads like a movie."

"To be honest," he said, "I don't know. But we have to do something, don't we? Otherwise we look weak, and that is not going to do us any good at all. Remember, we are also working on the coup."

I heard the faintest trace of desperation in his voice, and it made me nervous.

"What makes you so certain the Soviets will invade Afghanistan?" I asked.

He was so still I thought he'd momentarily transcended this earthly coil. Then he sighed and said, "Yes, now you're one of us, as it were, and I am going to trust you, all right?"

I nodded.

"Okay. This does not leave this office, are we understood?"

Again I nodded.

"Since July we have been provoking Moscow by backing Afghan warlords opposed to the pro-Soviet regime in Kabul, with its friendship treaty. They will have to invade or else lose their negotiating edge there, and with it their paths to both the oil and the warm water. Also, we are encouraging certain Muslim guerrillas to prepare for what they call *jihad*, a kind of holy war against the unbelievers. The *Sunnis* at least are with us."

"You don't think the Iranians will spread their revolution?"

"They're not Arabs, and they're Shia. There's never been a Shia government in any Arab country—unless you count the sect running Syria, but they're secular. The only possibility would be Iraq, but it's totally controlled by a Sunni elite that's also ideologically secular. Besides, if the Husseins' coup comes off, relations between Iran and Iraq will be soured for a generation at least."

"It strikes me," I said, impressed with his knowledge of the subject, "that a Soviet invasion of Afghanistan is not something we'd wholly object to—at least in terms of containing Iranian influence in Central Asia."

"Yes!" Brzezinski said, suddenly animated. "The invasion has a lot to be said for it, not least of which is that it drags the USSR into its own Vietnam quagmire—and I tell you now: it will be the end of the Russian empire. It's already cracking apart down the fault lines of ethnicity, and this will stretch their budget beyond its breaking point."

"You don't place any credence in the Team B findings?"

"Team B?" he said. "Team B was overly concerned with keeping the Cold War going for reasons that are not particularly altruistic. Vested interests have no place in the politics of this country. Or perhaps I should say they *ought* to have no place."

"What about the non-sonar radar and the missiles in the Urals?"

"Listen," Brzezinski said, folding his hands as if in prayer, "I'm all for keeping up the pressure on Moscow, don't get me wrong. But this isn't the way. Do you know how they concluded the Russians must have developed non-sonar radar?"

"Not specifically, no."

"We haven't picked up their radar signals, so rather than conclude they're simply not concerned about ocean traffic, these...these *people* decide they must be using something we cannot detect. There is no *proof* for it, no suggestion of how a non-acoustic radar would work. It's amateurish. Based on the data we have, the Russians have to focus on their principle areas of interest. It's not a maritime nation—no warm-water ports—so their interests have never been naval.

"As for the Ural missiles, again it's speculation. We can't prove or disprove it—and I suspect that the Team B people know that. Their report merely provides grist for any mill receptive to it. This one isn't. Our mill requires a far more focused effort to squeeze the Politburo's treasury." He demonstrated this squeezing with his hand. "Squeeze it until it's empty."

"I think that's correct, sir," I said. "A correct approach."

"Good. I'm glad about that."

He'd lived in the Soviet Union as a child, as well as in Poland and Nazi Germany, so he was better equipped than most US politicians to understand the mindset of this enemy. I felt he knew what he was talking about far better than Carter, Vance or Christopher did, and, somewhat imprudently, I said so.

"Well," he sighed, "the president is learning. And he's an able student. That's all I can say."

We exchanged more thoughts on Russia, then he looked at me quizzically, saying:

"Oxford, eh? That must have been wonderful."

"Best time I've ever had, sir."

"Then Harvard?"

"Yes."

"They wouldn't give me tenure." He scowled. "I had to go to Columbia."

"Harvard's loss, sir."

"Exactly the way I see it." He looked at his watch. "I have enjoyed this, David. What do you know about the Policy Planning Council?"

"The usual information."

"Look into it." He walked me to the door with an arm around my shoulders. "Look into it. I think you may find yourself a very conducive home there."

I was somewhat elated walking back to my section from the meeting. There were few clear indications of one's progress in the department, and I had not realized how much I must have craved one until now. I found Barker in his office.

"You might have tipped me off," I said.

"You don't enjoy surprises?"

"Thank you, Frank. I appreciate it."

"*Deserve.* You deserve it. It may save you during the coming cataclysm."

"You don't think there'll be a second term?"

"Listen," Barker said, "anything can happen. This is Washington. But the way things are going, Carter's pal Jesus is gonna have trouble winning him this next election. I won't survive—I've been too prominent to last. But you can if you make some prudent alliances before it's too late."

We discussed various academic avenues I ought to explore, then I asked him about the Straussians. I'd held off until now because I suspected I'd get a torrent of negativity in response and wanted to nurture my newly hatched ideas so they'd be strong enough to handle it.

He looked at his watch, then sat silently for a good minute. "Well, we got time," he eventually said. "You want my lecture on it?"

"Why not?"

"Okay." He lit a cigar, leaning back in his expansive mode. "The real significance of Strauss for mainstream conservatives is that he provides the deepest available philosophical analysis of what is wrong with liberalism. Technocratic, legalistic, and empirical criticism of liberalism is all very well, but it is not enough. He believes that contemporary liberalism is the logical outcome of the philosophical principles of modernity, taken to their extremes. In some sense, modernity itself is the problem, you see?

"Strauss believed that liberalism, as practiced in the advanced nations of the West in the twentieth century, contains within it an intrinsic tendency toward relativism, which leads to nihilism. He experienced this crisis firsthand, growing up in Germany's Weimar Republic of the 1920s, where the liberal state was so ultra-tolerant that it tolerated the Communists and Nazis who eventually destroyed it and tolerated the moral disorder that turned ordinary Germans against it. But he was a Jew; he fled Germany in 1938. We see this problem repeated today in multiculturalism, and in the tolerance of political ideologies whose foremost aim is the destruction of the Western society that makes that tolerance possible, and in an America so frightened of offending anyone that it refuses to carry out the basic duty of any normal state to guard its own borders. The parallels are undeniable.

"Strauss believed that America is founded on an uneasy mixture of classical—by which I mean Greco-Roman—Biblical, and modern political philosophy. Conservatives have not failed to note that a significant part of the mischief of liberalism consists in abandoning the biblical element. The story's been told many times and is well represented in Washington. Where Strauss comes in is that he is the outstanding critic of the abandonment of the classical element. His key contribution to fighting the crisis of modernity was to restore the intellectual legitimacy of classical political philosophy, especially Plato and Aristotle.

"Now, Strauss's first move, which came as a stunning shock to a 1950s academic world sunk in scientism and desirous of making 'political science' substitute for political philosophy, was to reactivate the legitimacy of ancient philosophy as real political critique. I can't overstate how unlikely this seemed at the time, it being then a casual article of faith that ancient philosophy had no more to say about modern political problems than ancient physics about modern engineering. But he succeeded.

"When leftists today feel obliged to denounce Great Books curricula, it's because they know, consciously or unconsciously, that classical thought is very much alive and is a real threat to them. The holy grail of Straussian scholarship has been to understand the ancient philosophers *not from a modern point of view* but from *their own* point of view. The implication, see, is that then we become free to adopt the ancient point of view toward modern political affairs, freeing us from the narrowness of the modern perspective and enabling us to step back from the distortions and corruptions of modernity. You follow?"

I nodded, not that he required any feedback. He merely wanted to puff his cigar before carrying on.

"Strauss contends that the modern view of politics is artificial and that the ancient one is direct and honest about the experience of political things. He wasn't ignorant of the reasons modern political philosophy had come about. He saw it as a grand compromise made when the demands of virtue made by ancient political philosophy seemed too high to be attainable. Modern political philosophy provides no rational basis for higher human achievement, but it provides a very solid basis for the moderate human achievement of stability and prosperity. He famously described modernity as built on, quote, 'low but solid ground.'"

Barker took another contented pull on his cigar.

"The key Straussian concept is the Straussian text—not his own writing, although it *could* be—it's generally a piece of philosophical writing that is deliberately written so that the average reader will understand it as saying one ('exoteric') thing but the special few for whom it is intended will grasp its real ('esoteric') meaning. The reason for this is cute: philosophy is dangerous. Philosophy calls into question the conventional morality upon which civil order in society depends; it also reveals ugly truths that weaken men's attachment to their societies. Ideally, it then offers an alternative based on reason, but understanding the reasoning is difficult and many people who read it will understand only the 'calling into question' part and not the other part that reconstructs ethics. Worse, it is unclear whether philosophy really can construct a rational basis for ethics. Therefore philosophy has a tendency to promote nihilism in mediocre minds, and they must be prevented from being exposed to it. The civil authorities are frequently aware of this, and therefore they persecute and seek to silence philosophers.

"Strauss openly states—and it pisses off liberal professors who teach him as a martyr to the First Amendment—the prosecution of Socrates was not entirely without point. This stuff about the dangers of philosophy is what I like. It gives Straussian thought a seriousness lacking in much contemporary philosophy; it's also a sign of the conviction that philosophy, contrary to the mythology of our 'practical' age, matters.

"Strauss not only believed that the great thinkers of the past wrote Straussian texts, you see, he heartily approved of it. It is a kind of class system of the intellect, which mirrors class systems like rulers and ruled, owners and workers, creators and audiences, which exist in politics, economics, and culture. He views the founding corruption of modern political philosophy, which hundreds of years later bears poisonous fruit in the form of liberal nihilism, to be an attempt to abolish this distinction. It's a kind of Bolshevism of the mind."

Barker smirked at the aptness of his analogy, puffing furiously to keep the cigar burning.

"Now, some dispute whether Straussian texts exist. But the great medieval Jewish Aristotelian Moses Maimonides admitted writing this way. And I can say only that I have found the concept fruitful in my own readings in philosophy.

"According to Strauss, Machiavelli is the key turning point that leads to modern political philosophy, and Machiavelli's sin was to speak esoteric truths openly. He told all within hearing that there is no certain God who punishes wrongdoing; the essence of Machiavellianism is that *you can get away with things*. Because of this, he turned his back on the Christian virtue that the belief in a retributive God had upheld. Pre-Machiavellian philosophy, be it Greco-Roman or Christian, taught that the good political order must be based upon human virtues. Machiavelli believed that sufficient virtue was not attainable and therefore taught that the good political order must be based on men *as they are*, that is, based upon their mediocrity and vices. This is not just realism, or mere cynicism, though. It amounts to a deliberate choice as to how society should be organized and a decided de-emphasis on personal virtue. It leads to the new discipline of political science, which is concerned with coldly describing men as they actually are, warts and all. And it leads ultimately to Kant's statement that, *We could devise a constitution for a race of devils, if only they were intelligent.* Okay?"

I nodded. He puffed.

"The ancient view is that this will get you nowhere, because only men with civic virtue will obey a constitution. The modern view leads naturally to value-free social science and social policies that seek to solve social problems through technocratic manipulation that refrains from"—he scored quote marks in the air—"*imposing value judgments on the objects of its concern.* The key hidden step in the Machiavellian view, a bold intellectual move that is made logically rigorous and then politically palatable by Hobbes and Locke, is to define man as outside nature. Strauss sees this as the key to modernity. Man exists in opposition to nature, conquering it to serve his comfort. Nature does not define what is good for man; man does. This view is the basis for the modern penchant to make freedom and comfort (read 'prosperity') the central concerns of political philosophy, whereas the ancients made virtue the center.

"Once man is outside nature, he has no natural teleology or purpose, and therefore no natural virtues. Since he has no natural purpose, anything that might give him one, like God, is suspect, and thus modernity tends toward atheism. Similarly, man's duties, as opposed to his rights, drop away, as does his natural sociability. The philosophical price of freedom is thus purposelessness, which ultimately gives rise to the alienation, anomie and nihilism of modern life.

"Now," Barker continued, "The interesting question is why Strauss chose to spill the beans about Straussian texts if they are supposed to remain a secret. The answer is that he felt he had to, given the severity of our crisis. Admittedly, the concept of the Straussian text is one that's susceptible to intellectual mischief in the form of wild claims about the esoteric meaning of texts, not to mention rather off-putting for anyone who doesn't like know-it-all elites.

"Before getting too huffy about this elitist view of the good society, we need to remind ourselves that it's strikingly similar to the view cultivated for centuries by the Catholic and Orthodox churches and by Orthodox Judaism, not to mention other religions: you *know*, there's a small number of men who know the detailed truth; the masses are told what they need to know and no more. Right? Free inquiry outside the bounds of revelation is dangerous. And yet Strauss practiced free inquiry and taught anyone who could afford the tuition at U-Chicago how to do so. Clearly he's not just an elitist trying to return to the past that he claims existed; besides, he hints this is impossible anyway.

"So what was his positive teaching about the good?" he said, leaning back. "In a nutshell, Strauss would lead us back to the Aristotelian conception of man as naturally political. Politics implies natural goods that are prior to human thinking about them. If man is political by nature, the goods of politics also exist by nature. The goods of politics are the ways man must behave to make political community work. If there are natural goods, there is a natural hierarchy of goods, and therefore a natural hierarchy of men, as different men pursue different goods. Right?

"Civic equality may be salutary for the functioning of society, but men are not truly equal in value. All these things and more follow. Following Strauss's arguments, it is not hard to realize that much of what conservatives find attractive in society is ultimately premised on philosophy that is pre-modern and to some extent anti-modern. We realize that our America is a modern society but not only a modern society. This alone, in my opinion, is worth the price of the Straussian ticket."

"That it?" I asked.

"Hold on, hold on." He puffed on his cigar again. "It goes without saying that one naturally wonders whether Strauss's own writings are Straussian texts. That is, what did Strauss really believe? Now, basically, there are two schools of thought on this question, which turn on whether or not one thinks that Strauss really believed he had found an answer to nihilism. Does the restoration of classical political philosophy really re-establish convincing values? Are Aristotle's virtues really virtues? Is Plato's critique of democracy true? Did Strauss find the answer? Did he think he did? Or was he just spinning a new myth for intellectuals to keep them from spreading relativism and nihilism? There are vigorous Straussian camps for both views. See?"

"Okay," I said.

He hadn't finished, though.

"Strauss believed that the great competitor of philosophy is revealed religion. He believed that reason and revelation cannot refute each other. He believed that religion was the great necessity for ordinary men. For him, religion is in essence revealed law, and he took his Judaism to be its paradigm. Strauss had an ambivalent attitude toward Christianity, though. On the one hand, Christianity is the only practicable religion for America. On the other hand, Christianity has troubling strands within it, like Aquinas's claim that reason and revelation are compatible, which for Strauss is the precise opposite of the most important truth. We all know that Christianity is a synthesis of Greek philosophy with biblical theism, okay? Yet Strauss rejects the idea that such a synthesis is possible. For him, religion is at bottom simply dogmatic and unapologetic about it. It is not quite *credo quia absurdum est*, but it's a very bright line in the sand. Nietzsche was right: man needs lies. Or maybe some men don't.... Strauss was an atheist, which is what troubles me most about him."

Barker noticed my puzzled expression (I knew he wasn't religious), and clarified himself.

"I mean as a philosopher," he said. "He never produces a proof that there is no God. More seriously, there's his apparent certainty that Judeo-Christian religion is false, not just uncertain. Of course, he combines this with a vigorous defense of that same religion, which is part of what makes him attractive to conservatives, but there's something unnecessary and rather dangerous about being an atheist rather than an agnostic, no? Agnosticism would fit in with the rest of his teachings just fine, and without either begging the question of how Strauss has proved the non-existence of God or tempting his followers with the impunity that atheism confers. Far better for the conservative intellectual who doesn't believe in God to be not quite sure on the point and to live his life so as to stay out of too much trouble with the Almighty—*if* he turns out to exist.

"In my view, this is the ultimate basis for the self-restraint and humility before existence that conservative thinkers must cultivate. True agnosticism, which is not a version either of lazy atheism or lazy theism, is a rare and difficult intellectual balancing act, requiring great intellectual poise and a skill for reasoning in terms of balanced probabilities and multiple simultaneous values. This Strauss doesn't teach. See?"

I nodded yet again. Barker surprised me endlessly with his intellect. More than most people I've ever known, he was genuinely capable of being objective. I'd initially taken him for a raging liberal, but he was not exactly that. Libertine, yes, but even that wasn't what it seemed to be. The lecture wasn't over yet, however.

"It's been leveled at Strauss that he was in a profound sense anti-American," Barker continued. "This is so because he is the profoundest modern critic of the modern natural-right teaching on which our society is based, but, as I said, this is an incomplete view of our foundation, and he criticizes modern natural right only because he thinks it destroys itself and becomes untenable. He says, quote, 'just because we are friends of liberal democracy does not entitle us to be flatterers of liberal democracy.'

"In his public statement on contemporary politics he was a conventional conservative patriot who backed the US against Nazi Germany in WW II, and the Soviets now. He was anti-Communist at a time when most Western intellectuals were dangerously equivocal, if not outright sympathetic. What is undeniable is that he did see the United States as the most advanced case of liberalism and therefore the most susceptible to the nihilism that his life was dedicated to fighting. But he also saw the US as partly founded on the classical and Biblical political wisdom that offered an answer. There is no doubt that he saw America as the world's only hope. One of the lessons we can draw from him is that the essence of liberal modernity is so problematic that America cannot afford for its essence to be liberal modernity, whether that liberalism takes a Lockean, classical (in the sense of nineteenth century) or postmodern form. Right?"

He puffed, and stared with gleaming eyes, forming his next sentence.

"Strauss describes the purpose or *project* of modernity as, quote, 'the universal society, a society consisting of free and equal nations, each consisting of free and equal men and women, with all these nations to be fully developed as regards their power of production, thanks to science.' See? It is interesting that this conception makes clear that globalism is not the inevitable culmination of modernity, as its proponents believe, but a perversion that would first make nations unfree and then abolish them outright. Strauss was a trenchant anti-globalist avant la lettre. He writes that '*no human being and no group of human beings can rule the whole of the human race justly.'* His most serious reservation about the Cold War was its lurking premise that the undesirability of Soviet world rule implied the desirability of American world rule. Okay? He believed that world citizenship is impossible, as citizenship, like friendship, implies a certain exclusivity, and universal love is a fraud. (If it exists, it is the province only of God.) Good men are patriots or lovers of their *patria*, their fatherland, which must by definition be specific. Let's face it, the United Nations has failed in its fundamental mission: to prevent war. No?"

"Unfortunately," I agreed.

"So what are Strauss's drawbacks?" Barker said. "Well, his followers are accused of being cultish, which they are to an extent, though not in my experience offensively so, and this is irrelevant to the truth of his ideas. When I was at U-Chicago, there was a circle clustered around Allan Bloom. He used to say that he liked his students to come to him 'virgins,' not having read philosophy before, so he could shape their entire outlooks. Straussians talk in a kind of code to one another."

"A code?" I said.

"Yeah. When somebody refers to someone as a 'gentleman,' for example, it means they are a morally admirable person but not capable of philosophy. They network in academia and in Washington and find one another jobs. A lot of their academic money comes from the John Olin Foundation. This is the worst I can tell you about them; I don't find it particularly damning, but some do.

"Listen, you can criticize Strauss with the simple question: are you really arguing that the classical view of man is true? If so, are you also defending classical physics and metaphysics, which the classical thinkers thought were essential to their teachings? If not, and the classical teaching is just a useful corrective for modernity, not a truth in its own right, then what is the good regime? What is your ideal?

"Unsurprisingly, Strauss is elusive on these points. He certainly argued in the direction of defending the classical view of man, but there is nowhere where he declares, QED: here I have proved it. To some extent, this is just honesty on his part. You see, the Straussian project really awaits others to complete it."

We stared at one another.

"That endeth the sermon," he said. "Questions?"

"Why do I get the feeling I still don't know what *you* think about Strauss?"

"'Cos my feelings got no place in an objective view," he said, affecting a Southern drawl. "If you want my feelings, you shoulda *asked* for them."

"Well, what's the worst accusation leveled at him?"

Barker laughed, rubbing his hands together.

"The worst?" he said. "Okay, but in my opinion it's unwarranted. He came to the US in the thirties on a Rockefeller grant arranged by Carl Schmitt..."

"I don't know Schmitt. Who is he?"

"*Was*. Schmitt was the legal brains behind the crafting of Adolf Hitler's administration. So Strauss is accused of being a Nazi. I think it's entirely unjustifiable, but you can see the elements in his thinking that give rise to it, no?"

"Forgive me, Frank," I said, "but you are beginning to sound like a believer."

He laughed uproariously, provoking a fit of coughing that made him stub out the cigar.

"Sorry, sorry," he said. "I'm not a follower *by nature*, you see? I find a lot of what he says very persuasive but I find a lot of Marx very persuasive too, and you know I'm not a Marxist. My misgivings about Strauss are that he provides a philosophy easy to abuse. If the movement spreads, most people will not be able to understand the full depth of his teachings. They'll take what they need and leave the rest. That's what I see some of the conservatives doing. They like the stuff about the end of liberalism, but they don't understand the classical philosophy. And that's dangerous. It would lead to totalitarianism. I mean, he's right about the stupidity of the masses, but I don't see any plan to educate them better, do you? It forecloses on the future in that respect. And American society doesn't resemble ancient Greece, so I have problems with applying the Greek principles the way he can do. But listen, it brings *philosophy* back into the game. It's political *philosophy* again, not just political *science*. And I'm all for that."

We walked back to the bureau, exchanging thoughts on the subject, but I knew in my gut that I'd crossed the line. I would get Strauss's books and study them, but I had already decided he was my man. Barker was right. Everyone needs a philosopher.

CHAPTER SIX

* * *

Lupus in fabula[*] (Terence)

I DO NOT REMEMBER WHEN I FIRST noticed the term "neoconservative" in print, but it was certainly bandied around in conversation a lot during this time, and I tended to view it as a pejorative. Traditional liberals, on the whole, were not taking seriously the Straussian charge that liberalism had failed, and those, like me, who did, failed to discuss the issues. If anything, I felt I was dabbling with a neoliberal movement, not a neoconservative one. The convergence of conservative goals with those of the Israel lobby was not yet defined sufficiently for me to see it clearly, too. In retrospect, I don't think I would have been less enthusiastic about Strauss if I had seen the nexus of interests forming around his ideas, because most of those interests were still ones I associated with classic liberalism. Jewish intellectuals were, however, undergoing a sea change in their traditional views and with their traditional relationships. Yet few of them were underlining the principles of this about-face, which led away from the labor movement and civil rights, that was clear enough, but what it led toward was not. Cynics may say that the change resulted from social upward mobility among Jews generally, who no longer had to fight a proxy war

[*] The wolf in the tale.

on behalf of black rights to assert their own. But I think it went deeper than this.

★ ★ ★

Caleb Luposki was then US deputy assistant secretary of defense for Regional Programs for the US Defense Department, working under Harold Brown, Carter's defense secretary. I met him at Parks' apartment in the Watergate building, where we had a drink before going over to the 600 for dinner. He was a small man, about ten years my senior, with large ears and a somewhat patrician nose that always made him seem bigger in photographs. His father, Isaac, lectured on physics at Cornell, and had come over from Poland in the twenties, sparing his family the Nazi Holocaust. Luposki's background had led me to expect a brasher, more intellectually arrogant man, but his manner, while authoritative, was deeply charming. I liked him almost instantly. Like me, I noticed, he drank plain tonic water, and nursed a single glass of wine throughout dinner. After exchanging pleasantries, we asked about each other's work. His was a great deal more interesting than mine. He was currently putting together what he called the Limited Contingency Study, which examined possible areas of threat to the US in the Third World.

"We're so used to thinking in terms of outright war with the Russians," said Parks, by way of explanation, "that we forget to think strategically, the way *they're* thinking. That's what Cale's been doing."

"I posited a Soviet move to grab the Persian Gulf fields," said Luposki, tremendous concentration in his eyes. "The consequences would be dire. It would instantly remove NATO and Japan from the field before any war started."

"Right, it probably would," I said. "Smart observation."

Cut off from oil, the armies of both would be helpless.

"Wait," Luposki told me, raising a forefinger. "We went on to look at the regional powers capable of such a move on their own, but presumably with Soviet approval. And Iraq emerges as a major—*the* major military power in the region. Potentially, Iraq will be big trouble for us." He counted off points on his fingers. "One, it has a radical-Arab stance. Two, anti-Western attitudes predominate in the country. Three, it's dependent on Soviet arms sales. And four, it has shown a willingness to foment trouble in other local nations. Iraq is one country that we should be watching very closely, because it is the only Arab state that could fight a proxy war for the Soviets, paving their way to the oil and a warm-water port. The important thing about contingency study is it allows you to work in terms of consequences."

"I'm not sure I follow," I said. "How can we deal with something that *might* happen? I mean, if a study like this got out, wouldn't it sour relations between us and Iraq? Wouldn't it provoke the situation rather than defend against it?"

"The way we deal with things has to change," Luposki said, smiling, more to himself than anyone else. "In the quest to spread democracy, our policy has to include a doctrine of preemption—if our intelligence sources identify a potential threat, we need to be able to deal with it *before* it occurs."

"Pre-emptive war?" The idea disturbed me.

"If necessary, yeah," he said. "It would ultimately save lives...and money."

"But how can we really distinguish between the legitimate defense of a country and its hostile intentions?"

"We have to develop the ability." He looked at Parks questioningly.

"I told him about the Team B," Parks said.

"So you know," Luposki continued, "what we found out about the Russians simply by looking through the same data that everyone else found reassuring?"

"What I keep hearing are doubts about the validity of your methods. For example," I went on, "what's the evidence for this non-sonar radar they're supposed to have?"

"We know they're not using acoustic radar," Luposki said, reaching with both hands as if to test for rain. "They must be using something—*ergo* they have clearly developed a new system."

I started to laugh, but it was clear he meant this seriously. Maybe Brzezinski had been wrong?

"I understand your objections," he said, "but the reality is this: anyone who understands the Soviet mindset knows they haven't given up the idea of waging war on us. We're their Satan. Democracy's their evil. So, as I see it, anything we can do to keep the state of vigilance at its peak is legitimate." I realized he was attempting to persuade me, not just explaining himself. "So we may be wrong in specifics, but it doesn't matter as long as we're right in general. If we're on our toes, they won't be tempted to test us. Thus we have to aim for full-spectrum domination."

This was Pentagon-speak for total control of the world's land, air and seas, as well as its media.

"I won't ask what you think of détente," I said, and we all chuckled.

I had been studying the United Nations Charter because of the Iranian crisis, and it now occurred to me that this doctrine of pre-emption would put us in violation of it. The charter was ratified by the US, which made it a treaty binding as domestic law. What Luposki was suggesting seemed to be in violation of Article 2, which stated, "All Members shall settle their international disputes by peaceful means in such a manner that international peace and security, and justice, are not endangered." I mentioned this.

"The UN has become a farce and a burden," said Luposki. "We're going to have to offer an alternative to it some day.

Besides, Article 1 of the Charter states: 'To maintain international peace and security, and to that end: to take effective collective measures for the prevention and removal of threats to the peace.'"

"Collective measures," I said. "Surely that use of the term 'collective measures' invalidates your proposal?"

"Listen," Luposki replied, "the UN isn't a world government—much as it would like to be one. The US is a sovereign nation, and we have a Constitution that specifies the war powers of both the president and the Congress, and *that* is the supreme law of this nation—not any UN measures."

"Ah, but doesn't the Constitution also specify that 'all Treaties made, or which shall be made, under the Authority of the United States, shall be the supreme Law of the Land?'"

"Well," said Luposki, smiling—he clearly enjoyed this kind of argument, "Article 2 itself says: 'The Organization is based on the principle of the sovereign equality of all its Members.'"

I admired the way he had his defense of his ideas so tightly organized that he could fend off attacks from any direction, and I told him so, told him the Devil's Advocate was a much-maligned position.

"Then you're good too—particularly since you couldn't have been prepared for this. I admire that."

He reached over to offer an awkward handshake, which I found odd, since he had not shaken hands when we'd first met earlier on. I have always maintained the British aversion to hand shaking. As I took his small, soft, moist palm in mine, I felt the pressure of his thumb on my middle knuckles. It was quite clearly a secret handshake of some sort, and I wished I was able to return it. The boy in me was fascinated. Instead of no reaction, I tapped his knuckles twice with my thumb. To this day, I believe it was, inadvertently, the correct response. A faint smile flickered around his mouth and eyes. What was it he wanted to convey that could not be done openly in front of Parks?

"Parks tells me you studied with Strauss?" I wanted to change the subject, in case it once more veered toward what I was not allowed to discuss.

"Well, yeah," Luposki examined the backs of his hands, "I took a couple of fantastic courses with him at Chicago. But he was winding things down then—although, even in old age his mind was fairly dynamic." He paused for several seconds, re-arranging objects on the tablecloth. "I'm more of a pragmatist, though. I owe more to Wohlstetter than to Strauss, but the two aren't contradictory in any real way."

Albert Wohlstetter was an historian and intelligence expert who taught at various campuses, including Chicago, and also worked as a consultant on policy for the Rand Corporation. He challenged the concept of Mutually Assured Destruction that formed the basis of nuclear policy at the time. It meant that if each side had sufficient nuclear arsenals to guarantee one another's obliteration in an atomic war, then no leader—certainly no US president—would engage in one because it would amount to an order for reciprocal suicide. He opposed the nuclear treaties between Russia and America too, on the grounds that they stifled technical creativity in the field of weaponry, which was the American Way. He advocated the development of tactical nukes and argued for more precision in conventional weapons. In this, he could be regarded as the father of modern warfare. Philosophically, Wohlstetter was a student of Quine and the analytical school, which I could see was more conducive to Luposki.

I could tell Luposki did not like discussing weapons and warfare. The corners of his mouth turned down, and he emitted little sighs as he discussed the merits of the tactical nukes, laser-guided bombs and 'smart' weapons that Wohlstetter rec-ommended to replace the mutually assured madness of the hydrogen bomb. It was his influence, via Luposki and Donald Rumsfeld, that had persuaded the Navy to keep the Cruise missile as a conventional weapon and bargaining chip in the SALT treaty negotiations.

"Where Strauss was a theoretician," Luposki said, "Wohlstetter is a realist. He looks at things the way they *are*, yet he still has a foundation of philosophy beneath his feet."

We bantered back and forth in this manner, with Parks occasionally clarifying a point on Luposki's behalf. Luposki proceeded to criticize the Carter administration's policies from a Cold War point of view, emphasizing several times that he himself was a Democrat and always would be, but that there were times when a man had to fight for what he believed to be true no matter whose feathers he ruffled in the process. It was the passion behind his arguments that wore me down. He struck me as an entirely sincere man willing to risk his career in order to do what he believed was right for his country.

I was also conscious that the two of them were presenting a case, not having a conversation, and I wondered why they needed me to approve it.

"What if you're wrong?" I asked, at some point.

"Yeah, *that's* a Straussian issue," he said. "You see, logically I can't be wrong. The worst that happens is we're stronger militarily. But remove the threat of Russia and you remove the governing mythology that society requires for its sense of purpose. There always has to be a war against evil, otherwise the masses are cut adrift. Their lives would deteriorate into petty concerns and hedonistic pursuits. I'm not being totalitarian here—God forbid!—I'm just being realistic. Styles of government affect character. As leaders, we have a responsibility to look at the larger issues, at what kind of future we are planting with the seeds we sow today. You can see the tendency in Americans for selfish isolationism, and also for seeking a war with evil within if the outer one fails. If we don't provide a mythological framework, an identifiable bogey-man, then they will turn on themselves. A liberal outlook doesn't mean you condone liberalism taken to any extent, does it? If you see a man sitting on the wrong side of the tree branch while sawing it, what do you do? You tell him, don't you? And if he doesn't listen or won't believe you, what do you do? Well, you let him fall, don't you? But if the branch is hanging over your house, what do you do? If necessary, you're going to climb that tree and drag him down yourself, aren't you? Because there's more at stake than his own life.

"In politics there's always more at stake, which is why there needs to be a governing philosophy. In a nutshell, that's what Strauss provides, but it's verifiable. It's reason not faith. He views religion as nothing more than revealed law, and *that's* what it is, *all of it*. A modern society also needs a tangible war against evil, though, and whether it's genuine or not doesn't matter. Because the organizing principle is what counts. The higher good. When Russia finally falls—and it must—we will need to find another evil to fight. Or we'll create one. Because without it society will crumble. If one *knows* this, it becomes one's duty to guard the fundamental principles as well as the physical reality of the state. If those principles were being replaced by others, it would not be so bad. But they're not.

"There is no opposing point of view here. Those who disagree merely posit a vague progress toward the liberal utopia, without any assurance that it exists, or that it *can* exist. That's not a philosophy, and that's what makes it an irresponsible position. Even if you create the perfect society, what do you do with those people who don't think it's perfect? Some people just want to sleep all day; others want to steal or fight. People are people; human nature is what it is. You and I are not going to change it. So we have to work with it as it is and apply principles that restore the order most of us require."

"If Russia fell," I said, "and, somehow, we became masters of the world. What then?"

Luposki smiled, saying, "It's a problem I'd *like* to work with. But we'd have to create a different kind of evil to fight. Perhaps something vaguer, more shadowy...Terrorist groups, maybe... or a plague...ecological catastrophe. Or all of them. As long as there's fear of an evil, the government will remain strong. And, of course, the nation with the greatest fear will have the strongest government. Don't you think the Soviets know it was a mistake to abandon religion? If we only took *that* lesson from them we'd be better off. The fabric of Russian society is rotten. It's corrupt from top to bottom. Remove the myth, the punishing god, and you leave people free to rape, kill, steal, cheat each other....merely because there's no reason not to. You think it would be any different here?"

"No," I said. "You're probably correct in your assumptions, but you have to admit they are somewhat dismaying."

I told them I had been giving the philosophical aspects a lot of thought, and that it was the very absence of an opposing philosophical view that made Straussian ideas so palatable. Liberalism had not delivered on its promises.

"Now what?" I asked, assuming this was what they wanted me to ask.

It seemed to take them by surprise, however. Parks protested they were not trying to win any debate, merely airing views.

"I wish I knew what the right course was," said Luposki. "But I don't. All I know is that I need to save my political neck, so I've taken a teaching post at Johns Hopkins. I want distance from this administration."

Parks threw up his hands defensively, saying, "It doesn't affect me. I can hang in. But you might want to think about your own neck, Dave."

Finally, as politely as possible, I told him no one called me "Dave," and, surprisingly, he was profusely apologetic. It embarrassed me, so I played the issue down, saying I felt an obligation to stay on at the State Department.

"I know it's not for me to say this," said Luposki, "but why don't you think about a lateral move into the policy planning council?"

"You're the second person to say that."

"Obviously, you're getting good advice." Luposki smiled. "If anything comes up in Baltimore, do you want me to let you know?"

"At the university, you mean?"

"Yeah. I have good connections, and I'd happily recommend you. Just say the word."

"Well," I said, "let me say it now. Yes. I've been thinking I ought to diversify a bit. And I miss the campus environment. Do me good to get back to academia. Maybe one day a week."

"I'll see what I can do," said Luposki. "This was a great evening, inspiring. We must do it again."

And we certainly did. Many times. But they didn't rush things. This was a seduction in the grand manner. By the time I gave in utterly to their importuning, I was barely aware I was being fucked—and I use the word advisedly.

CHAPTER SEVEN

★ ★ ★

*Nil homini certum est** (Ovid)

AROUND THIS TIME I BEGAN SUFFERING from migraine headaches that were so severe I would sometimes lose my eyesight and sometimes even thought I might lose my mind. The pain made it impossible to think, and I would lay down in a ball on the carpet and cry because there was no other way to express what I was going through. My doctor prescribed morphine, but its narcotic haze depressed me so much that I preferred to endure the pulsing black ball of torment in my brain than wallow in a listless indolence where I felt nothing, thought nothing, did nothing, and was nothing, but didn't care.

The affliction did, however, enable me to see another side of Luposki. As soon as Parks told him I was confined to the house and in a miserable state, he took to dropping by on his way to work and again when he'd finished for the day. He knew what I was going through because he'd had migraines himself as a student. Thus he never tried to engage me in conversation unless I made the first move. But it was his extraordinary thoughtfulness that affected me most. He would bring small items of food, and various beverages, all of which he had vetted by a physician, since he knew certain things could trigger

---

* Nothing is certain for man.

migraines in an allergic reaction. He introduced me to the
exotic world of herbal teas, bringing all manner of different
blends and flavors over for me to try, knowing that, since my
doctors had prescribed a diet free of caffeine, among many
other delights, the one thing I sorely missed was my tea. One
day he arrived with a tape-recorder and two boxes of audio cassettes, one full of blank tapes, in case I wanted to dictate
something, and the other full of what he called Misc Tapes.
There were talks and speeches given over the preceding weeks
in and around Washington, mostly of a highly technical nature
and relating to US policy; then there were recordings of radio
shows, mostly documentaries, on all manner of subjects, from
semantics to seismology; and there were CIA briefing tapes, used
to give agents ordered to a foreign country on short notice some
background information on the place, which often included a
sleep-learning language course, where one side of the tape was
designed to be played while you slept, repeating phrases that
would embed themselves in the mind, inculcating flawless pro-
nounciation and an inexplicable craving for Italian food. Lastly,
there were cassettes of classical music, each with a handwritten
label. The choice of music was especially touching: all gentle
string pieces, lullabies, sonatas, pastoral tone poems, selected
for their soothing qualities rather than their musical virtuosity.
The thought of this eminent, busy, brilliant man taking the
time to make such a selection of music and label each cassette
moved me to tears. Among the recorded cassettes I also found
an oddity labeled: Migraine and Severe Headache: Review of
Alternative Therapies. Side A dealt with, Hypnosis & Trad
Oriental Treatments. Side B was devoted to: T.H. Campion on
Ergotomine & Autofeedback Therapies.

This, naturally, was the first tape I played.

"Thank you so much for the migraine tape," I told Luposki,
one gray November evening, as a thin sleety rain fell and
Georgetown looked half-formed in a low billowing mist. "I

would have dismissed the alternative treatments as hokum, but I found that Campion fellow very persuasive."

"I hoped you might," said Luposki. "He fixed my migraines for good—or at least to date."

"So you were hypnotized?"

"Yeah. It isn't what people imagine it to be, though. More subtle."

"I think I'll get my physician to send me to his clinic. I've got to deal with this problem once and for all."

"A word of advice," said Luposki. "Don't ask your GP. They can't condone the alternative treatments without the AMA coming down on them. Just see him on your own. You want me to set up an appointment?"

"It worked for you?"

"It worked where nothing else did."

Luposki was kind enough to accompany me to the Campion Institute for Research in Orthobiology and Traditional Medicine in Langley, Virginia. I told him I'd be fine alone, but he insisted on coming. It was undoubtedly this side of his complex personality that helped me forgive the deeds of the other sides for far longer than reason dictated I ought to have done.

The thought of him sitting outside in the waiting room reading *The New York Times* while I lay on T.H. Campion's couch made it easier to relax into the state Campion was urging on me. The fact of friendship made the world itself seem secure and benign.

Hypnosis was not what I'd expected. I think I fell asleep. But one thing I do remember is Campion telling me to imagine a place where I felt utterly calm and relaxed. I found myself sitting at the oars of a boat in the Thames, hearing the slow dark water lapping at my side and the distant shouts of other boys. The couch was a chaise longue with arms on both sides of it, and I could feel the arms as oars, suddenly aware of emerging into another reality. It seemed to me that I was a Roman galley slave with sore arms, blistered hands and a wrecked back. Yet it was a tranquil thought, for some reason, a comforting reality where everything was straightforward and there were no gray issues. I was almost tempted to tell Luposki that it felt like the memory of another life, but I suspected he wouldn't be receptive to something that far away from conventional wisdom.

Driving back to Washington with him that afternoon is a memory I still find delightful. It seems like a perfect day, but for no tangible reason. The sky teemed with high embattled clouds, and the air was crisp, with a light that made the horizons clear on all sides. It created a sense of being in a world of known dimensions, whose problems were soluable given enough time, and where life would be conducted in a rewarding and orderly manner. I imagine it was the after-effects of the hypnosis, which, as it turned out, fixed my migraines for life. I have Luposki to thank for it too, and I can't take that away from him—even if I have taken all else away.

★ ★ ★

I spent that Christmas with my parents in West Virginia. An icy gulf had opened between them by now, and they filled it with people. There were so many guests staying at the house or dropping in that I felt like just another one—and indeed was treated like one by staff unaware of my actual status. I wanted to find out if my father was aware of how impersonal his home life had become, but I overheard him talking to someone—clearly a woman—on the phone, and realized he'd arranged himself another life. He drank far more than he ever had before too, and it did suit him. My mother talked only about her work, which was presumably *her* other life. So there we were, all strangers, with a communal past we never mentioned for fear of the consequences. The Leveretts viewed emotions the way other families view contagious disease; if you had one, you went somewhere alone and came back when it was gone.

Only once did I manage to have a conversation with my father on our own, and we talked about Iran. He'd been among those attempting to negotiate with the Islamists for the embassy hostages, and was frustrated by the lack of success he'd had.

"You can't talk to zealots," he kept saying. "They don't negotiate. They merely restate their demands. These people know nothing about politics. The whole country is being run by amateurs—it's frightening to contemplate."

This had been Cyrus Vance's impression too. Both of them were from a kinder, more gentlemanly world.

I told my father a rescue attempt was in the works, assuming he would know about it anyway. He always knew everything. But he didn't know about this.

"Oh, God!" he sighed. "What a bloody mistake that is!"

As if in Pavlovian response to the word "bloody," he mixed himself another huge Bloody Mary.

"Why?"

"It can't work, that's why!"

He cited facts, like the hostages being held in different places all over Teheran, and I had immediate misgivings about what was now Operation Eagle Claw.

"As far as I know," I said, "the Pentagon is operating on the idea that all the hostages are in one place. Why don't they know this?"

My father couldn't recall where he had obtained his information, pointing out that he wasn't responsible for what the Pentagon believed or didn't believe. I had not realized until then what an antiquated view of the world he had. He acted as if there were rules in politics, as if the Iranians could be called to account for breaking these rules. For the first time, I realized that we no longer lived in the same world, and that the State Department now operated as if there were no rules, hence I did too.

I tried broaching the subject of my newly acquired philosophy, but my father was from the old school of pragmatism.

Everything was a trade-off in his mind. You could get what you wanted only by identifying something your enemy wanted and trading the two off. It didn't work with an enemy that wanted only what you were not prepared to give, and it would not work with an enemy that wanted nothing tangible at all.

"Politics are a science," he said. "The Nazis had a philosophy, and look where it got them! My advice to you is stay clear of philosophies and keep your ear to the ground."

"That's not working with the Iranians, though, is it?"

He was confident something would work with them, however. It was just a question of finding what it was and then going to the bargaining table.

"We'll find it," he said, the creak of age appearing in his voice. "Don't you worry."

Neither of us was surprised when, on Boxing Day, we learned that the Soviet Union had invaded Afghanistan.

"Brzezinski told me too," my father admitted. "He's the only clever thing about that administration and he's hemmed in on all sides.... It's a pity."

Nearly everyone in the house had to rush off back to Washington the moment the news came in. The phone never ceased ringing.

"I wish I could stay," I told my mother, "but you know how it is."

"Oh, I do," she said. "I know."

"We don't talk any more," I said. "I wish we talked."

"We've talked." She sounded startled to hear otherwise.

"Not really. But I do love you very much. I want you to know that."

"Of course you do, darling."

"I mean it, mother."

"Of course you mean it," she said, her smile fixed and perfect, as it would be for all departing guests.

I felt dreadfully alone driving back. The radio blabbered on about the iniquitous Soviets and the poor Afghans. I wondered why it couldn't know what I knew about the invasion. But I have always been aware that I don't know how the common man lives, so I have always been ready to ascribe such musings to my ignorance. Most people work and watch television and sleep. That is their life. I never stopped to think about whether or not they had really chosen that life for themselves, though, or simply had it thrust upon them. No one has ever wanted to give the masses control over their own destinies, so we do not really know what they would choose to replace the condition of servitude in which we—the rulers—have placed them throughout all of history.

General Arbuthnot invited me to observe Operation Eagle Claw in the Pentagon's War Room. Technology has always impressed me, and I was amazed by the sophistication of what I saw around me, satellite images of the helicopters landing at Desert One, constant communication with the commanding officers, and so on. The boy in me found it all exciting, and that's all the operation was to those of us so closely involved with it yet so far removed from it there in mission control: a boys' game with very fancy toys.

It was while the helicopters were refueling in the Iranian desert that things started to go wrong. It began with an unexpected sandstorm. The storm was low level, yet it complicated things. As the first MH-53 helicopter took off, all hell broke loose. The War Room became a frenzy of activity, and the general explaining things to us visitors was no longer around, so it was a while before we knew precisely what was going on, although it was obvious something disastrous had occurred. The MH-53 had drifted into a C-130 transport plane, because its navigational equipment had failed and the poor visibility made it impossible to see. The helicopter had exploded, and both planes were now on fire. It soon became clear that at least eight servicemen were dead. The operation was swiftly aborted, and in an atmosphere of gloom we were hurried from the building. Only later did I learn that five intact MH-53s had been left behind, containing plans of the mission that identified CIA agents working within Iran. It was a diabolical mess.

At several meetings, I had raised my father's point about the hostages being held in different locations, but it was felt to be invalid since enough people could be rescued from the one location to make the mission a success.

"In voters' eyes, of course," Franklin Barker pointed out. "That's all Carter's thinking about now."

When I told him what had happened in the War Room he wasn't surprised.

"Then it's over," he said. "He'll never be re-elected. We've got to think about ourselves now, and you're lucky I'm screwed whichever way I turn, because it gave me time to think about you."

He had already cleared me for a position in the policy planning council, where I'd be safe from the ax that was bound to fall when Carter did. Whatever he was doing for himself was not clear, but I assumed it was something since he was not around much at all over the coming weeks. Although I missed his rambunctious presence, it was too chaotic a time to dwell much on sentimental attachments.

* * *

When powerful men know the source of their power is being cut off, they react like cornered beasts. The final months of the Carter administration were exactly like being on a sinking ship that had only enough lifeboats and vests to save a few. The stampede for salvation was highly indecorous, to say the least, and I was surprised by the number of people who betrayed their positions of trust by leaking information to the press or the Republicans. But then I have never been in the situation where I needed a job so badly that personal survival superseded everything else, so I ought not to judge those who were.

Of our little family in Georgetown, Les Melton was the most affected. He was by then working on the Carter campaign, and he knew he had to run for cover before the election had been decided, so I suggested he talk to Parks.

"That was a good idea you had," Les said, the morning after their meeting.

"He's well connected," I said. "I'm sure he'll find something for you."

"*Find*? He already had it waiting for me."

It was true I'd told Parks that Les needed something to put distance between himself and the imminent disaster, but I didn't expect him to do anything about it immediately. He'd found Les a partnership with a New York law firm, however, and I should have found this more suspicious than I did at the time. Yet Les was overjoyed. His degree was in law, yet he lacked the kind of raw ambition required to plot one's career strategically, and all his life he looked to others to supply it, which in retrospect is probably one of the things that endeared him to me.

Melvin, who reveled in the misfortunes of others, could barely conceal his glee at the panic he saw all around him. Through his father, he'd arranged for himself a regular column with the *Washington Post*, which within a year would be nationally syndicated, thus keeping him out of hands-on politics for the rest of his life, although of course he was never out of politics for a minute.

Dean Torrance was the least bothered. He'd recently learned his sister was dying of cancer, so he decided he'd return to Vermont and be there for her until the end. Then he'd think about his own future. Being Dean, of course, he ran for Congress while nursing his sister, and cynics say it was her death that secured him the sympathy vote that got him elected.

Melvin and I toyed with sharing another house, but we both knew we'd passed that stage of life—and, besides, neither of us fancied becoming Washington's Odd Couple. I moved into the apartment my father now rarely used, and Melvin moved in with the woman he eventually married, Ennis Parker-Loomis, the television personality.

"She's very smart and she's not Jewish." These were the only reasons he ever gave me for their relationship, where there was never much in the way of love, if indeed anything approaching it.

Rumors abounded during this time, and one of them concerned Franklin Barker. He'd been out of town several times, and it was said that he'd been having secret meetings with the Iranians in Paris.

By now, Parks and I met regularly, sometimes with Luposki, sometimes alone, and, because it didn't seem to matter any more, I had ceased citing national security in our discussions. We openly talked about everything, including matters that were supposedly secret. It was Parks who confirmed the rumors about Barker.

"He's supposed to be negotiating the hostages' release," he said. "Which he is, but with a twist...."

I must admit I was shocked when Parks told me that Barker was offering the Iranians a deal on behalf of the future government, not this one. Carter's people had concluded the only thing that would win them this election was a prior release of the hostages, and Barker had been sent to negotiate it, authorized to offer them the freeing up of Iranian assets abroad, an end to the trade embargo, and, within reason, anything else it might require. What he in fact was offering them was a totally different kind of deal. If the Iranians would hold off releasing the hostages until Ronald Reagan was elected president, Barker was telling them, the US would supply them with weapons.

Initially, Carter wanted to try a second rescue operation, this time using a specially modified airplane able to land in a soccer stadium. The operation had been abandoned after the craft exploded during a test run at Elgin Air Force base's Duke Field, Florida. The Husseins' coup did not come off either, and by now, with our encouragement, Saddam Hussein had declared war on Iran. The Iraqi army was massive and far better organized than its counterpart in Iran, so initially it looked as if Iraq would win. That was what made Barker's offer of sophisticated weaponry so attractive to Teheran.

"I hope we're doing the right thing," I told Parks. "There'll be hell to pay if this ever gets out, *you* know that. What makes you think it can even be kept secret?"

"We're exploring a couple of routes, but the Iranians are being told there's no problem, and we've arranged a token shipment through a broker overseas to show our good faith. Besides, it's good politics to make sure Iraq doesn't win this war. We don't trust them. Saddam Hussein is far closer to Moscow than he is to us, and we're going try to change that, but we still don't want him to win. We don't really want anyone to win, you see?"

"That won't be easy to pull off."

I tried to recall a war that neither side had won, but could not.

"The two World Wars," said Parks. "In real terms, no one won them."

"I thought we won the last one?"

"And we'll win the next one, the same way, without a single bomb falling on our continent. We're untouchable here—but the only side we should ever take is our own. We want the spoils, not the war."

We both laughed at this. Only later did it occur to me that we were laughing at the death of a hundred million and the misery of countless more. I cannot put it down to gallows humor. To this day, I cannot forgive it.

CHAPTER EIGHT

★ ★ ★

*Aspirat primo Fortuna labori** (Virgil)

THERE WAS A TENDENCY IN WASHINGTON to see things in terms of Before and After Nixon, ascribing all that was bad to the vagueness and barbarism of what seemed to me like another age, far from the light and wisdom of our new era. In reality, though, and certainly in the light of what was to come, Nixon was not such a bad president. Vietnam had been the blunder. As foreign policy, it was sheer folly, and as domestic policy, in the way we treated those who protested it, it opened up a rift in society wider than the Civil War. There were those who said, however, that enough was enough. The period of healing under Carter had done us no good abroad, said these people. America was perceived as weak. How else could you explain the Iranian hostage crisis? How else could you explain the Soviet invasion of Afghanistan? Knowing what I know now, I tend to ascribe all of it to a foreign policy that was belligerent, headstrong and tumescent with a hubris that came in the wake of WW II, which we may have helped the allies win but in no way won ourselves to the extent that we enjoyed the victor's spoils.

But Ronald Reagan was the first president of the United States of whom I was ashamed. He was a nice man, a kind man,

---

* Fortune smiles upon our first effort.

true, but he was also an uneducated fool, a blithering idiot when it came to grasping complex issues.

I was not working at the Policy Planning Council long before it was announced that we had a new boss. Richard V. Allen, who had Brzezinski's old job as national security advisor, appointed Caleb Luposki as director of policy planning. I'd dined with him the night before the announcement, so it came as no surprise. Both he and Parks were ecstatic. *Our time has come*, they said. When an opportunity arose, I floated Melvin's question, adding some spin of my own.

"Is Reagan the right man?" I asked. "He doesn't seem to be cut from the same cloth as other presidents."

"He's an imbecile," said Luposki. "Is that what you mean?"

"I wouldn't go that far."

"Go further," he told me. "I do. That's what makes him so perfect for the job."

"He's an actor," Parks added, somewhat redundantly.

"A very bad actor," I pointed out.

"It's a very bad part," said Luposki, "and doesn't require Marlon Brando."

"So if he's the actor," I said, "who's the director?"

"We are," Luposki said, giving me his glittering intent stare.

I should have dug a little further but it seemed churlish to do so at the time. Did he mean the public, or he and Parks? Or he and I? Or all three of us? Or was it some other 'we' to which he referred? By the time I discovered the answer to this, it was too late to do me any good.

Luposki went on to regale us with the story behind his appointment. His old boss, Fred Ickle, who was now undersecretary of defense for policy, had slotted him into the policy planning directorate, but Richard Allen nixed him.

"He assumed I was just another Carter democrat," Luposki said, "so I was a goner. John Lehman had to intercede, or I'd still be in Baltimore."

Lehman was a banker who'd once been Navy secretary and still wielded a lot of influence in Washington. He later served on the 9/11 Commission. Luposki wielded such contacts with a glee I did not quite understand. Was it merely that he had them? Or was it that he had them despite himself? No matter how deeply inside he was, he always acted as if he were an outsider.

"By the way," Luposki said, as I was leaving, "you will stay on at the PPC, won't you?"

"That would be up to you now," I said.

"Excellent. You'll be the only one." He asked if I were free for breakfast the following day, inviting me to join him. "I want you to meet your new colleagues," he said. "This is one Policy Planning Council the citizens of America are going to know by name. I promise you that."

The next morning, I had breakfast with Luposki, Lewis Libby, Francis Fukuyama, Dennis Ross, Alan Keyes, Zalmay Khalilzad, Stephen Sestanovich and James Roche, the men who, with me and a few others, would now be responsible for defining the Reagan administration's long-term foreign goals. It was an exhilarating meeting, ideas flashing back and forth around the table like heat lightning. I had no idea that Luposki would be such a skilled general—I'd imagined he might be a little shy—yet he conducted this meeting as if he'd been doing it all his life. His quiet charm was merely amplified, but he also had the necessary sense of power and was able to encourage or silence someone with a glance. I looked forward to working with him. We all did. Like me, everyone there seemed to have a personal connection to him—they'd been his students, classmates, coworkers, something—which created an intimacy not usually achieved by such groups without months or years of working together. Because I was the only one who had been on the PPC before Luposki headed it, I alone noticed the enormous difference in purpose and morale that swept over the place. It had been at best a notch above lugubrious and unimaginative, now it was all sparkling

quicksilver. The old ponderousness was replaced with bold innovation. It was a joy and a privilege to work there. We all arrived
just after dawn and, more often than not, were still there at midnight, reluctant to leave in case we missed out on decisions that
would reshape the future of the world.

My misgivings were born, I tend to think, the day of Reagan's
inauguration. Not when "the greasy Bog-Irish valet browned his
nose a deeper shade of peat," as Melvin Cassel described the
swearing-in, but two hours later when the hostages in Teheran
were released.

He did it, I thought, *the blackguardly bear did it*. It was a cheap
and pathetically obvious deception. The thought occurs to me
now that our hostages might have been held several months
longer than they would have been were they not earmarked to
be a dumb-show of foreign tribute along the triumphal way as
we crowned ourselves another puppet king. The public must
wish to remain blind and deaf, indeed they must strive to maintain this state against the torrents of reason and common sense
that batter against their frail walls and heave at their shallow
foundations.

The release of the hostages set the tone for Reagan's whole
presidency, an eight-year party during which the rich got so
much richer that the poor got fat just feeding on their crumbs.
To quash the rumors of secret negotiations to delay the
release—which had certainly got to Jimmy Carter—Reagan's
people decided it might be prudent to let Carter fly to Germany
to officially welcome the hostages, since he was the one who, in
the public's eyes, had suffered most during their captivity.
Besides, a ticker-tape welcome home was being planned in New
York for a little later on, and that would be the memorable
event, the Reagan-style event.

My ultimate boss was now the new secretary of state,
Alexander Haig, and I soon began to notice Luposki and he did
not get along that well. I mentioned it to Parks, who claimed

not to have heard anything on the subject. A few days later, when we were alone I broached the subject with Luposki. He shrugged, looking pensive for a while. Then he agreed that Haig didn't seem to like him, yet he had no idea why.

"Maybe he doesn't like Jews," he added, laughing. "Or mathematicians."

It was Melvin who told me Haig had spent some time as Henry Kissinger's assistant and probably still believed in détente. Mel had become increasingly interested in Luposki, and I had to be careful what I said now that he was a journalist.

"So there's conflict at the State Department is there?" he said. We were walking in Constitution Gardens after a brief lunch, and although I hadn't told him Haig and Luposki didn't get on with each other, he sensed it. "Haig shouldn't have that job anyway. He's too inflexible, and he's always tense. Makes people uneasy. Do you see much of him?"

I hadn't seen him at all, but I told Mel he seemed okay to me, and that my work at the PPC kept me out of any pressing affairs of state.

"But Luposki's in on everything isn't he?" Mel said. "I heard he was incredibly well connected, right up to the top."

I'd noticed this too. Luposki always had someone he could call if things weren't going his way, and the people he called all had one thing in common: none held a government position. Most were connected with banking or the oil business, and they were always very, very wealthy. They were also people I did not know personally, which at that level of big business was rare enough to be notable.

"No more than average," I said. "He's bright, he's personable, why shouldn't he have good connections?"

"It takes more than that to have those people behind you."

Mel had a deadline to meet, so we parted company and I walked on alone. The air was a high-contrast blue, focused, bone dry, cloudless. The sun's ball was low, a pale-lemon yellow with a sharp circumference, as if etched into the azure sky. It was only February but it felt like May. I must have been lost in thought, because the next thing I knew I was up at 16th and Church and hearing a very familiar voice.

Browsing through a tray of books on the sidewalk in front of Stanley's Bookstore was Franklin Barker, his arm around a willowy hippie girl with profuse and curly red hair. They were laughing raucously.

"Home is the soldier from across the sea," I said.

Without even looking up, Barker said, "Home is where I hang my head."

We hugged and told each other it had been ages. Then he introduced me to the girl, saying she was, "my brightest student."

"I'm sure she is," I said.

"What's that supposed to mean?" the girl said, looking very offended.

I quickly did myself some spin-doctoring, saying that Barker never liked to waste time on mediocre students so one ran into him only with the cream of his crop.

"I'm sorry, this is David Leverett."

"*You're* Leverett?" she said, greatly surprised. "Franklin always talks about you. Cyrus Vance's Diabolical Duo, right?"

I gave Barker a knowing look. "If he says so."

"Oh, I do say so," said Barker. "Let's all go get coffee...or something stronger."

"I gotta class," she told us, anxiously. "I can't. But I insist we do it soon. Make sure he invites me next time you get together." She planted a sloppy kiss right on my lips. It so took me by surprise that I didn't know how to react at all, so I just stood there smiling as she skipped away.

"She's nuts," said Franklin, "but she's also an incredible lay."

"I assumed that part."

We found a coffee shop near Dupont Circle, and when the waiter had finally brought our order I looked Barker straight in the eyes and asked him if it was true, if he really had negotiated to delay the hostage release until Reagan's inauguration.

"What do you think?" he said.

He had. The knowledge made me feel I stood on an eggshell above a bottomless pit, its void tangible, a maw breathing me down. My legs actually trembled, knowing there was nowhere to tread.

"I don't know what to say," I said.

It was the truth. Everything I thought I knew about him seemed to evaporate like gasoline leaving nothing but a stain on the road. I felt the man I sat with now was an imposter, someone who had cheated me out of genuine affection and respect when all he really merited was scorn.

"Why would you do something so immoral?" I finally asked.

"Immoral? Give me a break," Barker said. "This is Washington, it's about politics, which is a grown-ups' game, hardball, winner takes all. Where does morality come into it? Besides, it was done to make sure Carter didn't win, not so Reagan looked good."

"No," I said. "No sophistry this time, Frank. You kept those people imprisoned there for months because it would stop Carter winning or make Ronald Reagan look good? Jesus Christ, man! What were you thinking?"

"I—" Barker stopped himself. "I don't know what you're talking about," he said eventually.

I simply stared at him. I knew that for him to concede defeat so easily he must already feel fairly bad about what he'd done, so I backed down.

"I did it for me," he finally said. "It's been eating at my liver, though, the fact that I did it for me, not for Reagan. It was all I could see to save myself from exile there. Yeah, it was shitty.

And I didn't have the right to play with lives like that. But if I had the chance to go back in time, would I do it again? Yep, I would. Dog eat dog, pal."

"We're not dogs."

"That's right," said Barker, "I forgot. You're not one of us. You people simply throw down the scraps for us to fight over, don't you?"

He knew these feeble attempts at a defense held no water. I wasn't going to say anything else on the matter. I wanted to, but I was aware we were not on an even playing field. The great bear even looked physically smaller.

"If you're worried I might blab," I said, "there's no need. You have my word on that. You know I think rats warrant the death penalty. Besides, it's hardly going to do our government any good, is it, and if nothing else you know where my first loyalties lie."

Barker visibly relaxed, saying I was one of the few people whose word still meant something. He began telling me the details of the Iran-Contra deal, where profits from the sale of military equipment to Iran went to fund and arm the Nicaraguan Contra guerrillas, who were trying to overthrow their own democratically elected government and were also being used as proxies on various other tasks in the area by our own covert ops people. As Kissinger observed, covert ops is not missionary work, but even by these standards what Barker was telling me seemed to be pushing it. If it ever did get out, he'd be in deep trouble.

"If it were just me," he said, "maybe I'd worry a bit more. But if this got out it would bring down the government, from the very top."

"The president knew?"

"Yes.... insomuch as he knows anything. The real culprit is Bush."

George Herbert Walker Bush was then vice president. Before

that, however, he'd been CIA chief, and his contacts in the agency were some of the prime movers behind Iran-Contra.

"We've got a lot of nerve telling other nations how to behave," I said.

The thought stayed with me, and some time later I turned it into a policy paper, which I think still has merit, and at least shows how some of us were thinking as the storm clouds gathered and the skies struggled to hold onto the last glimmer of daylight.

POLICY PAPER 347

The conduct of diplomacy is the responsibility of governments. For purely practical reasons, this is unavoidable and inalterable. This responsibility is not diminished by the fact that government, in formulating foreign policy, may choose to be influenced by private opinion. What we are talking about, therefore, when we attempt to relate moral considerations to foreign policy, is the behavior of governments, not of individuals or entire peoples.

Let us recognize, then, that the functions, commitments and moral obligations of governments are not the same as those of the individual. Government is an agent, not a principal. Its primary obligation is to the interests of the national society it represents, not to the moral impulses that individual elements of that society may experience. No more than the attorney vis-à-vis the client, nor the doctor vis-à-vis the patient, can government attempt to insert itself into the consciences of those whose interests it represents.

The interests of the national society for which government has to concern itself are basically those of its military security, the integrity of its political life and the well-being of its people. These needs have no moral quality. They arise from the very existence of the national state in question and from the status of national sovereignty it enjoys. They are the unavoidable necessities of a national existence and therefore not subject to classification as either "good" or "bad." They may be questioned from a detached philosophic point of view.

But the government of the sovereign state cannot make such judgments. When it accepts the responsibilities of governing, implicit in that acceptance is the assumption that it is right that the state should be sovereign, that the integrity of its political life should be assured, that its people should enjoy the blessings of military security, material prosperity and a reasonable opportunity for, as the Declaration of Independence put it, the pursuit of happiness. For these assumptions the government needs no moral justification, nor need it accept any moral reproach for acting on the basis of them.

This assertion assumes, however, that the concept of national security taken as the basis for governmental concern is one reasonably, not extravagantly, conceived. In an age of nuclear striking power, national security can never be more than relative; and to the extent that it can be assured at all, it must find its sanction in the intentions of rival powers as well as in their capabilities. A concept of national security that ignores this reality and, above all, one that fails to concede the same legitimacy to the security needs of others that it claims for its own, lays itself open to the same moral reproach from which, in normal circumstances, it would be immune.

Whoever looks thoughtfully at the present situation of the United States in particular will have to agree that to assure these blessings to the American people is a task of such dimensions that the government attempting to meet it successfully will have very little, if any, energy and attention left to devote to other undertakings, including those suggested by the moral impulses of these or those of its citizens.

Finally, let us note that there are no internationally accepted standards of morality to which the US government could appeal if it wished to act in the name of moral principles.

It is true that there are certain words and phrases sufficiently high-sounding the world over so that most governments, when asked to declare themselves for or against, will cheerfully subscribe to them, considering that such is their vagueness that the mere act of subscribing to them carries with it no danger of having one's freedom of action significantly impaired. To this category of pronouncements belong such documents as the Kellogg-Briand Pact, the Atlantic Charter, the Yalta Declaration on Liberated Europe, and the prologues of innumerable other international agreements.

Ever since Secretary of State John Hay staged a political coup in 1899 by summoning the supposedly wicked European powers to sign up to the lofty principles of his Open Door notes (principles that neither they nor we had any awkward intention of observing), American statesmen have had a fondness for hurling just such semantic challenges at their foreign counterparts, thereby placing themselves in a graceful posture before domestic American opinion and reaping whatever political fruits are to be derived from the somewhat grudging and embarrassed responses these challenges evoke.

To say these things, I know, is to invite the question: how about the Helsinki accords of 1975? These, of course, were numerous and varied. There is no disposition here to question the value of many of them as refinements of the norms of international intercourse. But there were some, particularly those related to human rights, which it is hard to relegate to any category other than that of the high-minded but innocuous professions just referred to. These accords were declaratory in nature, not contractual. The very general terms in which they were drawn up, involving the use of words and phrases that had different meanings for different people, deprived them of the character of specific obligations to which signatory governments could usefully be held. The Western statesmen who pressed for Soviet adherence to these pronouncements must have been aware that some of them could not be implemented on the Soviet side, within the meanings we would normally attach to their workings, without fundamental changes in the Soviet system of power—changes we had no reason to expect would, or could, be introduced by the men then in power. Whether it is morally commendable to induce others to sign up to declarations, however high-minded in resonance, which one knows will not and cannot be implemented, is a reasonable question. The Western negotiators, in any case, had no reason to plead naïveté as their excuse for doing so.

When we talk about the application of moral standards to foreign policy, therefore, we are not talking about compliance with some clear and generally accepted international code of behavior. If the policies and actions of the US government are to be made to conform to moral standards, those standards will have to be America's own, founded on traditional American principles of justice and propriety. When others fail to conform to those principles, and when their failure to conform has an adverse effect on American interests, as distinct from political tastes, we have every right to complain and, if necessary, to take retaliatory action. What we cannot do is to assume that our moral standards are theirs as well, and to appeal to those standards as the source of our grievances.

II

Let us now consider some categories of action that the US government is frequently asked to take, and sometimes does take, in the name of moral principle.

These actions fall into two broad general categories: those that relate to the behavior of other governments that we find morally unacceptable, and those that relate to the behavior of our own government. Let us take them in that order.

There have been many instances, particularly in recent years, when the US government has taken umbrage at the behavior of other governments on grounds that at least implied moral criteria for judgment, and in some of these instances the verbal protests have been reinforced by more tangible means of pressure.

These various interventions have marched, so to speak, under a number of banners: democracy, human rights, majority rule, fidelity to treaties, fidelity to the UN Charter, and so on. Their targets have sometimes been the external policies and actions of the offending states, more often the internal practices. The interventions have served, in the eyes of their American inspirers, as demonstrations of not only the moral deficiencies of others but also the positive morality of ourselves; for it was seen as our moral duty to detect these lapses on the part of others, to denounce them before the world, and to assure—as far as we could with measures short of military action—that they were corrected.

Those who have inspired or initiated efforts of this nature would certainly have claimed to be acting in the name of moral principle, and in many instances they would no doubt have been sincere in doing so. But whether the results of this inspiration, like those of so many other good intentions, would justify this claim is questionable from a number of standpoints.

Let us take first those of our interventions that relate to internal practices of the offending governments. Let us reflect for a moment on how these interventions appear in the eyes of the governments in question and of many outsiders.

The situations that arouse our discontent are ones existing, as a rule, far from our own shores. Few of us can profess to be perfect judges of their rights and their wrongs. These are, for the governments in question, matters of internal affairs. It is customary for governments to resent interference by outside powers in affairs of this nature, and if our diplomatic history is any indication, we ourselves are not above resenting and resisting it when we find ourselves its object.

Interventions of this nature can be formally defensible only if the practices against which they are directed are seriously injurious to our interests, rather than just our sensibilities. There will, of course, be those readers who will argue that the encouragement and promotion of democracy elsewhere is always in the interests of the security, political integrity and prosperity of the United States. If this can be demonstrated in a given instance, well and good. But it is not invariably the case. Democracy is a loose term. Many varieties of folly and injustice contrive to masquerade under this designation. The mere fact that a country acquires the trappings of self-government does not automatically mean that the interests of the United States are thereby furthered. There are forms of plebiscitary "democracy" that may well prove less favorable to American interests than a wise and benevolent authoritarianism. There can be tyrannies of a majority as well as tyrannies of a minority, with the one hardly less odious than the other. Hitler came into power (albeit under highly unusual circumstances) with an electoral mandate, and there is scarcely a dictatorship of this age that would not claim the legitimacy of mass support.

There are parts of the world where the main requirement of American security is not an unnatural imitation of the American model but sheer stability, and this last is not always assured by a government of what appears to be popular acclaim. In approaching this question, Americans must overcome their tendency toward generalization and learn to examine each case on its own merits. The best measure of these merits is not the attractiveness of certain general semantic symbols but the effect of the given situation on the tangible and demonstrable interests of the United States.

Furthermore, while we are quick to allege that this or that practice in a foreign country is bad and deserves correction, seldom if ever do we seem to occupy ourselves seriously or realistically with the conceivable alternatives. It seems seldom to occur to us that even if a given situation is bad, the alternatives to it might be worse—even though history provides plenty of examples of just this phenomenon. In the eyes of many Americans it is enough for us to indicate the changes that ought, as we see it, to be made. We assume, of course, that the consequences will be benign and happy ones. But this is not always assured. It is, in any case, not we who are going to have to live with those consequences: it is the offending government and its people. We are demanding, in effect, a species of veto power over those of their practices that we dislike, while denying responsibility for whatever may flow from the acceptance of our demands.

Finally, we might note that our government, in raising such demands, is frequently responding not to its own moral impulses or to any wide general movements of American opinion but rather to pressures generated by politically influential minority elements among us that have some special interest—ethnic, racial, religious, ideological or several of these together—in the foreign situation in question. Sometimes it is the sympathies of these minorities that are most prominently aroused, sometimes their antipathies. But in view of this diversity of motive, the US government, in responding to such pressures and making itself their spokesman, seldom acts consistently. Practices or policies that arouse our official displeasure in one country are cheerfully condoned or ignored in another. What is bad in the behavior of our opponents is good, or at least acceptable, in the case of our friends. What is unobjectionable to us at one period of our history is seen as offensive in another.

This is unfortunate, for a lack of consistency implies a lack of principle in the eyes of much of the world; whereas morality, if not principled, is not really morality. Foreigners, observing these anomalies, may be forgiven for suspecting that what passes as the product of moral inspiration in the rhetoric of our government is more likely to be a fair reflection of the mosaic of residual ethnic loyalties and passions that make themselves felt in the rough and tumble of our political life.

Similar things could be said when it is not the internal practices of the offending government but its actions on the international scene that are at issue. There is, here, the same reluctance to occupy one's self with the conceivable alternatives to the procedures one complains about or with the consequences likely to flow from the acceptance of one's demands. And there is frequently the same lack of consistency in the reaction. The Soviet action in Afghanistan, for example, is condemned, resented and responded to by sanctions. One recalls little of such reaction in the case of the somewhat similar, and apparently no less drastic, action taken by China in Tibet some years ago. The question inevitably arises: is it principle that determines our reaction? Or are there other motives?

Where measures taken by foreign governments affect adversely American interests rather than just American moral sensibilities, protests and retaliation are obviously in order; but then they should be carried forward frankly for what they are, and not allowed to masquerade under the mantle of moral principle.

There will be a tendency, I know, on the part of some readers to see in these observations an apology for the various situations, both domestic and international, against which we have protested and acted in the past. They are not meant to have any such connotations. These words are being written—for whatever this is worth—by one who regards the action in Afghanistan as a grievous and reprehensible mistake of Soviet policy, a mistake that could and should certainly have been avoided. Certain of the procedures of the South African police have been no less odious to me than to many others.

What is being said here does not relate to the reactions of individual Americans, of private organizations in this country, or of the media, to the situations in question. All these may think and say what they like. It relates to the reactions of the US government, as a government among governments, and to the motivation cited for those reactions.

Democracy, as Americans understand it, is not necessarily the future of all mankind, nor is it the duty of the US government to assure that it becomes that. Despite frequent assertions to the contrary, not everyone in this world is responsible, after all, for the actions of everyone else, everywhere. Without the power to compel change, there is no responsibility for its absence. In the case of governments it is important for purely practical reasons that the lines of responsibility be kept straight, and that there be, in particular, a clear association of the power to act with the consequences of action or inaction.

III

If, then, the criticism and reproof of perceived moral lapses in the conduct of others are at best a dubious way of expressing our moral commitment, how about our own policies and actions? Here, at least, the connection between power and responsibility—between the sowing and the reaping—is integral. Can it be true that here, too, there is no room for the application of moral principle and that all must be left to the workings of expediency, national egoism and cynicism?

The answer, of course, is no, but the possibilities that exist are only too often ones that run against the grain of powerful tendencies and reflexes in our political establishment.

In a less than perfect world, where the ideal so obviously lies beyond human reach, it is natural that the avoidance of the worst should often be a more practical undertaking than the achievement of the best, and that some of the strongest imperatives of moral conduct should be ones of a negative rather than a positive nature. The strictures of the Ten Commandments are perhaps the best illustration of this state of affairs. This being the case, it is not surprising that some of the most significant possibilities for the observance of moral considerations in American foreign policy relate to the avoidance of actions that have a negative moral significance, rather than to those from which positive results are to be expected.

Many of these possibilities lie in the intuitive qualities of diplomacy—such things as the methodology, manners, style, restraint and elevation of diplomatic discourse—and they can be illustrated only on the basis of a multitude of minor practical examples, for which this article is not the place. There are, however, two negative considerations that deserve mention here.

The first of these relates to the avoidance of what might be called the histrionics of moralism at the expense of its substance. By that is meant the projection of attitudes, poses and rhetoric that cause us to appear noble and altruistic in the mirror of our own vanity but lack substance when related to the realities of international life. It is a sad feature of the human predicament, in personal as in public life, that whenever one has the agreeable sensation of being impressively moral, one probably is not. What one does without self-consciousness or self-admiration, as a matter of duty or common decency, is apt to be closer to the real thing.

The second of these negative considerations pertains to something commonly called secret operations—a branch of governmental activity closely connected with, but not to be confused with, secret intelligence.

Earlier in this century the great secular despotisms headed by Hitler and Stalin introduced into the pattern of their interaction with other governments' clandestine methods of operation that can be described only as ones of unbridled cynicism, audacity and brutality. These were expressed by not only a total lack of scruple on their own part but also a boundless contempt for the countries against which these efforts were directed (and, one feels, a certain contempt for themselves as well). This was in essence not new, of course; the relations among the nation-states of earlier centuries abounded in examples of clandestine iniquities of every conceivable variety. But these were usually moderated in practice by a greater underlying sense of humanity and a greater respect for at least the outward decencies of national power. Seldom was their intent so cynically destructive, and never was their scale remotely so great, as some of the efforts we have witnessed in this century.

In recent years these undertakings have been supplemented, in their effects on the Western public, by a wholly different phenomenon arising in a wholly different quarter: namely, the unrestrained personal terrorism that has been employed by certain governments or political movements on the fringes of Europe as well as by radical-criminal elements within Western society itself. These phenomena have represented, at different times, serious challenges to the security of nearly all Western countries. It is not surprising, therefore, that among the reactions evoked has been a demand that fire should be fought with fire, that the countries threatened by efforts of this nature should respond with similar efforts.

No one will deny that resistance to these attacks requires secret intelligence of a superior quality and a severe ruthlessness of punishment wherever they fall afoul of the judicial systems of the countries against which they are directed. It is not intended here to comment in any way on the means by which they might or should be opposed by countries other than the United States. Nor is it intended to suggest that any of these activities that carry into this country should not be met by anything less than the full rigor of the law. On the contrary, one could wish the laws were even more rigorous in this respect. But when it comes to governmental operations—

or disguised operations—beyond our borders, we Americans have a problem.

In the years immediately following the ww ii the practices of the Stalin regime in this respect were so far reaching, and presented so great an apparent danger to a Western Europe still weakened by the vicissitudes of war, that our government felt itself justified in setting up facilities for clandestine defensive operations of its own; all available evidence suggests that it has since conducted a number of activities under this heading. As one of those who, at the time, favored the decision to set up such facilities, I regret today, in light of the experience of the intervening years, that the decision was taken. Operations of this nature are not in character for this country. They do not accord with its traditions or with its established procedures of government. The effort to conduct them involves dilemmas and situations of moral ambiguity in which the American statesman is deprived of principled guidance and loses a sense of what is fitting and what is not. Excessive secrecy, duplicity and clandestine skulduggery are simply not our dish—not only because we are incapable of keeping a secret anyway (our commercial media of communication see to that) but also more importantly, because such operations conflict with our own traditional standards and compromise our diplomacy in other areas.

One must not be dogmatic about such matters, of course. Foreign policy is too intricate a topic to suffer any total taboos. There may be rare moments when a secret operation appears indispensable. A striking example of this was the action of the United States in apprehending the kidnappers of the *Achille Lauro*. But such operations should not be allowed to become a regular and routine feature of the governmental process, cast in the concrete of unquestioned habit and institutionalized bureaucracy. It is there that the dangers lie.

One may say that to deny ourselves this species of capability is to accept a serious limitation on our ability to contend with forces now directed against us. Perhaps; but if so, it is a limitation with which we shall have to live. The success of our diplomacy has always depended, and will continue to depend, on its inherent honesty and openness of purpose and on the forthrightness with which it is carried out. Deprive us of that and we are deprived of our strongest armor and our most effective weapon. If this is a limitation, it is one that reflects no discredit on us. We may accept it in good conscience, for in national as in personal affairs the acceptance of one's limitations is surely one of the first marks of a true morality.

IV

So much, then, for the negative imperatives. When we turn to the positive ones there are, again, two that stand out.

The first is closely connected with what has just been observed about the acceptance of one's limitations. It relates to the duty of bringing one's commitments and undertakings into a reasonable relationship with one's real possibilities for acting upon the international environment. This is not by any means just a question of military strength, and particularly not of the purely destructive and ultimately self-destructive sort of strength to be found in the nuclear weapon. It is not entirely, or even mainly, a question of foreign policy. It is a duty that requires the shaping of one's society in such a manner that one has maximum control over one's own resources and maximum ability to employ them effectively when they are needed for the advancement of the national interest and the interests of world peace.

A country that has a budgetary deficit and an adverse trade balance both so fantastically high that it is rapidly changing from a major creditor to a major debtor on the world's exchanges, a country whose own enormous internal indebtedness has been permitted to double in less than six years, a country that has permitted its military expenditures to grow so badly out of relationship to the other needs of its economy and so extensively out of reach of political control that the annual spending of hundreds of billions of dollars on "defense" has developed into a national addiction—a country that, in short, has allowed its financial and material affairs to drift into such disorder, is so obviously living beyond its means, and confesses itself unable to live otherwise—is simply not in a position to make the most effective use of its own resources on the international scene, because they are so largely out of its control.

This situation must be understood in relationship to the exorbitant dreams and aspirations of world influence, if not world hegemony—the feeling that we must have the solution to everyone's problems and a finger in every pie—that continue to figure in the assumptions underlying so many American reactions in matters of foreign policy. It must also be understood that in world affairs, as in personal life, example exerts a greater power than precept. A first step along the path of morality would be the frank recognition of the immense gap between what we dream of doing and what we really have to offer, and a resolve, conceived in all humility, to take ourselves under control and to establish a better relationship between our undertakings and our real capabilities.

The second major positive imperative is one that also involves the husbanding and effective use of resources, but it is essentially one of purpose and policy.

Except perhaps in some sectors of American government and opinion, there are few thoughtful people who would not agree that our world is at present faced with two unprecedented and supreme dangers. One is the danger not just of nuclear war but of any major war at all among great industrial powers—an exercise that modern technology has now made suicidal all around. The other is the devastating effect of modern industrialization and overpopulation on the world's natural environment. The one threatens the destruction of civilization through the recklessness and selfishness of its military rivalries, the other through the massive abuse of its natural habitat. Both are relatively new problems, for the solution of which past experience affords little guidance. Both are urgent. The problems of political misgovernment, to which so much of our thinking about moral values has recently related, is as old as the human species itself. It is a problem that will not be solved in our time, and need not be. But the environmental and nuclear crises will brook no delay.

The need for giving priority to the averting of these two overriding dangers has a purely rational basis—a basis in national interest—quite aside from morality. For short of a nuclear war, the worst that our Soviet rivals could do to us, even in our wildest worst-case imaginings, would be a far smaller tragedy than that which would assuredly confront us (and if not us, then our children) if we failed to face up to these two apocalyptic dangers in good time. But is there not also a moral component to this necessity?

Of all the multitudinous celestial bodies of which we have knowledge, our own earth seems to be the only one even remotely so richly endowed with the resources that make possible human life—not only make it possible but also surround it with so much natural beauty and healthfulness and magnificence. And to the degree that man has distanced himself from the other animals in such things as self-knowledge, historical awareness and the capacity for creating great beauty (along, alas, with great ugliness), we have to recognize a further mystery, similar to that of the unique endowment of the planet— a mystery that seems to surpass the possibilities of the purely accidental. Is there not, whatever the nature of one's particular God, an element of sacrilege involved in the placing of all this at stake just for the sake of the comforts, the fears and the national rivalries of a single generation? Is there not a moral obligation to recognize in this very uniqueness of the habitat and nature of man the greatest of our moral responsibilities, and to make of ourselves, in our national personification, its guardians and protectors rather than its destroyers?

This, it may be objected, is a religious question, not a moral-political one. But the objection invites the further question as to whether there is any such thing as morality that does not rest, consciously or otherwise, on some foundation of religious faith, for the renunciation of self-interest, which is what all morality implies, can never be rationalized by purely secular and materialistic considerations.

V

The above are only a few random reflections on the great question to which this paper is addressed. But they would seem to suggest, in their entirety, the outlines of an American foreign policy to which moral standards could be more suitably and naturally applied than to that policy which we are conducting today. This would be a policy founded on recognition of the national interest, reasonably conceived, as the legitimate motivation for a large portion of the nation's behavior, and prepared to pursue that interest without either moral pretension or apology.

It would be a policy that would seek the possibilities for service to morality primarily in our own behavior, not in our judgment of others. It would restrict our undertakings to the limits established by our own traditions and resources. It would see virtue in our minding our own business wherever there is not some overwhelming reason for minding the business of others. Priority would be given, here, not to the reforming of others but to the averting of the two apocalyptic catastrophes that now hover over the horizons of mankind.

But at the heart of this policy would lie the effort to distinguish at all times between the true substance and the mere
appearance of moral behavior. In an age when a number of
influences, including the limitations of the electronic media,
the widespread substitution of pictorial representation for verbal communication, and the ubiquitous devices of "public
relations" and electoral politics, all tend to exalt the image over
the essential reality to which that image is taken to relate—
in such an age there is a real danger that we may lose alto-
gether our ability to distinguish between the real and the
unreal, and, in doing so, lose both the credibility of true moral
behavior and the great force such behavior is, admittedly, capable of exerting. To do this would be foolish, unnecessary and
self-defeating. There may have been times when the United
States could afford such frivolity. This present age, unfortunately, is not one of them.

Writing such papers was, I think, in retrospect, my only outlet
for thoughts that would otherwise have had to scramble for
attention in conversations unwilling or unable to accommodate the kind of space they required. In my position, a
newspaper column or magazine articles were out of the question, and I received few invitations to speak that would have
warranted a disquisition of this nature. They are really more
like journal entries, which is certainly how I view their presence here.

The cut-and-thrust of *realpolitik* at this time was also such
that one had to be extremely cautious about presenting oneself
as "off-message." It was invariably viewed either as a grab for
power or as evidence that one was changing horses in mid-
stream—never a salutary thing to do in itself, let alone one to
be *perceived* as contemplating. With Reagan came the advent of

big PR as a staple of government, too. It had always been there, but never on this scale—which was largely a consequence of the fact that the public bought into the hype on an unprecedented scale. The public's perception was that this new government could do no wrong. In reality, the rich prospered on a scale they hadn't experienced in decades. And thus the markets soared, making wannabes in the upper middle class as rich or even richer than they wanted to be. Success breeds success, but it also spawns the illusion of success, and this "Me Decade" created an entire subculture of those whose success depended on creating an illusion of success for others, especially in the more dubious areas of financial enterprise whose sole product is money, and particularly in the trading of spurious bonds. You can always gauge how flimsy the general knowledge of economics is by the inability of those riding high to recognize their sudden wealth must inevitably be the consequence of equally sudden poverty in other areas of the community. But "Reaganomics," as they were laughably termed, were widely regarded with the awe reserved for sacred mysteries, with which, indeed, they had much in common. As for our foreign policy, it had reverted to the bullying bluster of the old pre-Nixonian dark age, with the Cold War promoted as if Soviet Russia was a mighty equal in military power, and an "Evil Empire" that it was our destiny to fight. We knew the reality was very different from this, and yet we kept the truth from the public, taking their hard-earned tax dollars and handing them over to a favored few in the sectors of big industry that clung like vampires onto the Pentagon's broad neck, sucking out the blood that could have otherwise been channeled into the nation's real life. The only people in America to whom Communism was an evil were the five percent who, like me, owned ninety-five percent of the wealth.

It was when Luposki was fired that I realized the full extent of his power. Someone—presumably Secretary of State Haig—had leaked the firing to the press, so we read about it in *The New York Times* the day it happened. "Mr. Luposki is being replaced," the article said, "because Mr. Haig finds him too theoretical. . . ."

Luposki was clearing out his office when I arrived. He seemed unflustered.

"It's not what it seems to be," he said. "I can't say more than that now. We've done a good job here, and the work will not be wasted. I want to concentrate on longer-term goals anyway." He smiled his knowing smile. "Don't think that Haig has won," he said. "The Kissinger doctrine is never coming back. It's history."

Several weeks later Alexander Haig was replaced as secretary of state by George Shultz, one of the most powerful men in America. He had been president and director of the Bechtel Corporation—the largest civil engineering company in the world—before taking up this government position. Before that he'd been Nixon's treasury secretary and was responsible for taking the US dollar off the gold standard. My father knew him, since my great-grandfather had been in business with Warren Bechtel, founder of the Bechtel Group, which was still a private family-owned concern, but they were no longer friends. My father severely disapproved of the decision to go off the gold standard, calling it the "highway to hell," and he was prone to call Shultz a "toady." Bechtel he would frequently refer to as "one of the fattest pigs at the trough." He claimed they received too many big and lucrative government commissions—dams, highways, mega-projects—because they wielded too much influence in Washington. I mentioned all this to Parks and Luposki at what proved to be our last supper for some time.

"I don't understand why there's such resentment over a company being successful," said Parks. "Bechtel is just the American Dream come true, after all, isn't it?"

"I can't answer for my father," I said. "I don't know enough to say whether it's true or not. I'm just telling you what he says."

"The Bechtels are as all-American as you can get," Luposki said. "They regularly donate hundreds of millions to this country, which they've literally helped build. I for one don't mind if they get something back."

"Like what?" I asked. "What do they get back?"

"The ability to participate in decision making, for example," Luposki said.

"Without being elected to government positions?" I wasn't sure if he meant this.

"Their financial commitment to this country overrides everything," Luposki said. "They are a part of America."

"You mean they own a part of it?"

"Yes, but it goes deeper than that. Their concerns are America's concerns. They have a vested interest in the country."

"No doubt you choose those words carefully?" I said.

"I do it only in this company," he said. "As a measure of my trust in you both."

"I second what you said," Parks told him, looking at me quizzically. "Wholeheartedly."

I knew I was supposed to cave in, admit that financial power ought to translate into political power, and I was too much of a diplomat not to do so, but I had severe reservations about what was being said. However, my apparent agreement was greeted with a little too much enthusiasm.

"Excellent," said Parks, pouring himself more wine. "I know some people who will be relieved to hear that."

Before I could express any alarm at this, Luposki said, "Don't frighten the kid," telling me, "He meant people we can take into our confidence. This country is no place for pragmatic common sense to mix with politics. It's just good to know we all see eye to eye. I'd never doubted you shared our views, David. After all, you have as big a slice of the pie as any Bechtel does—am I wrong?"

Rather than argue, I thought I would try delving into motivation, so I asked Luposki why he felt so strongly about supporting the oligarchy.

"I share their views," he said. "And now I shape their views. I believe in the system we have as the best possible—under the circumstances—and one of this system's features is that there will always be people like the Bechtels, and they will always demand their right to influence government. So, far better to join them and help influence things the right way."

"Their concerns are not making more money," said Parks. "They have more than enough of that. They want a say in the future, that's all. And they deserve it, since they have been a critical part of getting us here."

"Yeah," said Luposki. "They have a right to share in creating the social, financial and political climate of tomorrow because it will affect them more than it will most people in the country."

"What if they wanted to go in a direction of which you disapprove?" I asked.

"That's the whole point," said Luposki. "It is our job to make sure they're properly advised, given all the data, so our interests always converge."

"Exactly right," Parks said. "And it's in our interest to keep them financially competitive by making sure they get the big contracts they're after, because they're the devil we know. If too many cowboys rise to the top of the heap, we'll lose primacy. We advise the ones we know, so we're tied into their fortunes. It may seem fairer to let everybody at the trough, but it isn't practical, is it?"

"What if they pursue a course against your advice?" I asked.

"We'd have failed in our task," Luposki said. "Simple as that. And when one fails, it's time to resign." He folded his palms together, tapping a knuckle with his forefinger before concluding, "The fact that we are there says everything, though, doesn't it? Our advice is valued because we are who we are, not because we reflect their desires. If what we advise goes contrary to what they feel are their interests, they will still weigh it very carefully. The arrangement couldn't be more ideal. And I don't believe it undermines the essence of democracy at all."

"Nor do I," agreed Parks.

"I don't either," I told them. "But I know many who'd disagree."

"And so do I," Luposki said. "But they disagree because their interests are not being served in the same way, which kind of invalidates the objection."

"And the Trotskyites and socialists object for the same invalid reasons," Parks said, "don't they?"

This was when Luposki announced he was being promoted by Shultz to assistant secretary for East Asian and Pacific Affairs. He would be leaving for Indonesia the next day. Parks then announced he was relocating to San Francisco, "to do some consulting."

"Can we trust you to mind the shop?" said Luposki.

I asked him if he knew who was taking over the policy planning directorate and he smiled, saying, "I think you'll agree it was a good choice, won't he?"

"I would say so," Parks said. I wondered why Parks knew who it was.

"No doubt Shultz will fill you in," Luposki said. "It's improper for me to say more, but it's someone you'll be able to work with and relate to. Don't you think, Val?"

"Absolutely," Parks said. "In fact, you're the one person he won't be able to surprise and dazzle."

"So long as he's more logician than magician, we should get along fine then," I said.

Only a fool would have come away from this wondering who the new policy planning director would be. But I went to my meeting with George Shultz prepared to seem surprised when he offered the policy planning directorate to me. A cold, somewhat overbearing man with a disconcerting fleshiness to his face that made him seem sybaritic, Shultz was widely regarded as someone far more powerful than any position he had currently held. As treasury secretary under Nixon, he had been instrumental in taking the dollar off the gold standard, a move regarded by my father as "criminal" because it made the value of the dollar a fictional sum that came to be loosely based on the price of oil, which was why the greatest industrial powers hedged inflation by holding vast reserves of US currency or governement bonds.

"I have nothing but respect for your father," was how Shultz handled this potential source of embarrassment, "if not for all his views—especially those on subjects about which he is heinously ill informed."

I accepted the directorate with genuine gratitude, trusting that I would always make sure to be well informed before tackling contentious issues with Secretary Shultz.

"I have no doubt you will," he said, expansively. "No doubt whatsoever. And do not feel you have to make your mark in this position." He became suddenly very still, unblinking eyes locked on mine in a stare that was supposed to convey sheer will, and did. "I think I can safely assure you there will be many other opportunities for you to do that."

I knew what he was really telling me was that he wanted the PPC under my direction to stick closely to the course Luposki had charted for it. I saw little problem with assuring him that this was my own goal too, that Luposki and I had few differences of opinion in this area at all—and precious few in any other.

"So I've been told," said Shultz, "but I am deeply reassured to hear it from your lips."

CHAPTER NINE

★ ★ ★

*Pars maior lacrimas ridet et intus habet** (Martial)

MY INITIAL FEELINGS ABOUT REAGAN never changed, although I had many meetings with him and liked him as a person. It was impossible not to, but this still did not mean I thought he was the right choice for president. I did come to see, however, that Shultz and others had the same feelings I did, but they weren't disturbed by them. In fact, by many comments he made over the course of our relationship, which was not close but did necessitate an unexpected frequency of contact, I realized Shultz felt it was an ideal situation to have a president who was totally reliant on his advisers. The next best thing was a president whose views you could trust, who would take the advice he was given, who had no agenda of his own and did not believe in consulting the public over every issue.

I soon began to feel the pressure to invoke the Team B data in mapping out policy vis à vis the Soviets that projected Cold War strategy far into the future. It made me distinctly uncomfortable, especially in the light of more recent CIA reports that showed in enormous detail the disintegrating social fabric of the USSR, its tattered economy, and most significantly the pathetic state of its military capabilities since the onset of its

---

* You smile at your tears but have them in your heart.

own Vietnam quagmire in Afghanistan. Even the vaunted intercontinental ballistic missiles were barely a threat any more. Poor maintenance, substandard manufacture, and various other aspects of what happens when nineteenth century realities have to cope with twentieth century high-tech exigencies all combined to make it clear to me that we had grossly exaggerated Soviet achievements in the nuclear area in order to advance our own far, far beyond the requirements of mere deterrence.

It worried me that we had deceived the American people into funding a weapons program they did not need, by any stretch of the imagination, and, if the facts were put to them honestly, might not want. The tab was mounting into the hundreds of billions by now too. This was the kind of money that could have laid the foundations of free education and health care, both of which, as every poll on the subjects ever taken showed plainly, were the two things most American citizens most wanted for their country. I began to wonder what sense it even made from our perspective. Since we knew the USSR was no longer a threat, why were we developing weapons systems geared to intercontinental nuclear war when it was clear even then that the kind of wars we would most likely find ourselves waging would be small, contained geographically, and fought with conventional arms? I had no argument with those who wanted our policies kept secret when revealing them would have genuinely harmed our security and their success. But where I felt the secrecy was to conceal deliberate deception, and to promote unnecessary fears that helped sustain public acquiescence to government goals that were no longer tenable, I began to feel a sense of growing alienation from this administration's objectives and a profound apprehension about what lay behind the inherent duplicitousness so many of them entailed.

It became churlish to criticize Reagan on any level though, because the apparent successes of his presidency were too great to cast doubt on. The greatest event of the era was a good example. When the Soviet Union finally collapsed in utter disarray and debt, it was made to seem like a triumph on our part. The pulling down of the Berlin Wall symbolized this final defeat of communism, and Reagan was made to appear the victor of the entire Cold War. We all knew the Soviets were floundering on the brink over a decade earlier. It may have been the result of our continued pressure, militarily and economically, but we knew it was inevitable long before Reagan came along.

It was with Russia that I began to question Luposki's judgments. The Team B findings had continued to exert influence over US attitudes toward the Soviets, whether they were factual or not. And as a result we continued to be hostile long after we should have started extending a helping hand. It was a great opportunity and we passed it over. From my point of view in policy planning, we could have brought the Russians into our circle of allies by extending economic aid, but we chose to let them descend into chaos instead because...why? We still didn't trust them, perhaps? Or we wanted their descent into hell? Whatever the reasons, the result was that instead of fostering a democracy over there we created another totalitarian regime. Deprived of its empire, Russia was still as volatile as it had been, and perhaps more so because it felt threatened. I thought Luposki was just plain wrong in his approach.

He had continued to push for the overthrow of Saddam Hussein in Iraq too, but with little success. This was now largely because Shultz did not agree with it. Indeed, Luposki's old accomplice in Team B, Donald Rumsfeld, was sent to Baghdad as Reagan's special envoy purely for the purpose of smoothing Saddam's ruffled feathers. He had not been happy to find out we were arming the Iranians as well as himself in their war, so Rumsfeld went to offer him some good deals on military equipment and to reassure him of the esteem in which we held him. We were getting reports of Saddam's increasing brutality in dealing with the Kurds and other Iraqi minorities emboldened by the conflict with Iran, and Reagan's people had to work hard dissuading a few senators from passing a motion to publicly censure him on the grounds that he was more asset than liability.

Both the Kuwaitis and the Saudis told us they preferred Saddam in charge rather than the chaos and uncertainty his removal from power in Baghdad would leave. Shultz had long had close ties to Bechtel, which had built an entire city in Saudi Arabia, so he was presumably hardly indifferent to the House of Saud's princes and their wishes. We generally tended to defer to their views on local issues—as long as they did not affect Israel—which meant we revealed to Muslims a distinct Sunni bias. In those days such distinctions were lost on almost everyone though.

The Vice President was now George Herbert Walker Bush, who had previously been CIA Director. He hadn't been Reagan's choice, I'd learned, but had been foisted on him as the most sensible running mate because of his clout with the Republican Party—he had chaired the National Committee under Nixon—and the perception that he was a skilled international diplomat, having been US Ambassador to the United Nations, and chief of the US Liaison Office in the People's Republic of China (a position equivalent to ambassador, since thirty years after its advent we still did not officially recognize the place existed). This perception was somewhat belied by the embarrassing blunders that occurred during Bush's tenure at both postings, but at least there were photographs of him with world leaders. There were far too many photographs of Reagan for anyone's comfort, since none was particularly presidential and, rather than world leaders, all too many of them showed him hugging a chimpanzee or promoting Camel cigarettes.

Personally, I thought Bush fit right into the circus atmosphere of this administration, but I gradually came to see there was another aspect to the man that was not so amusing. His inherent weakness of personality had made him a pawn to some of the more shadowy figures behind both Shultz and Luposki, whose principle interests were money and power, both of which were manifested in business interests limited to oil and weapons. Bush also concerned himself with certain issues to a point where some said he was the first vice president ever to hold what the British called portfolios—in this case on terrorism and narcotics—but if two activities thrived more spectacularly than these during his period of "portfolio" management, neither I nor the media were aware of them.

What I most despised about George the First, however, was the unapologetic absence of conviction that seemed to coat all his political views and positions like aerosol glitter on tissue paper. While running against Reagan for the Republican nomination, he stood staunchly in favor of abortion and heaped scorn on the supply side–influenced massive tax cuts his opponent proposed, terming the policies "voodoo economics" and Reagan's position in general "too conservative." As Reagan's running mate, of course, Bush gave equally impassioned speeches decrying abortion and expounding on the genius of Reaganomics, presenting an image so ultra-conservative it squeaked when he moved. If the most important quality in a political leader is to say and do whatever it takes to win elections regardless of any issues or principles involved, then George H.W. Bush had everything a voter could dream of and he richly deserved his success in obtaining the highest offices in the land.

Bush was just one among many around Reagan to have very sound financial reasons not unconnected with petroleum that let it be known to mere mortals like myself in policy planning that, as a general rule, what was good for Saudi Arabia in the politics of the region was the course we wished to chart anyway.

When it came to Israel, I'm afraid I came to depend a little too much on Melvin Cassel's advice. Mel had become quite good about not reporting our conversations without asking me first—

probably because he realized I was better to preserve as a source than blow away with one sensational exposé—and I'd come to trust him more than prudence dictated I should have done.

His knee-jerk pro-Israel responses to issues were still by no means the norm they became, but, as I realized only later, they occurred with increasing frequency whenever a relevant issue arose. I still remembered the Mel who when we were at Harvard had even on occasion taken up the banner of the Palestinian cause. Indeed, he once debated a prominent Zionist on the subject, not only silencing the catcalls and hecklers with the sheer force and moral potency of his rhetoric, but winning the debate outright too in favor of Palestine's rights as the innocent party in a matter of grave injustice.

Although students can be forgiven most excesses, I somehow knew I didn't have to forgive him that one, because at least part of him believed sincerely in what he had said that evening, and always would.

This was why I tended to take his equally potent diatribes supporting the Israeli position with a pinch of gunpowder if not salt: I felt the reality of Mel's position lay firmly between the two extremes. It was a while before it crossed my mind that he no longer ever had a good word to say about Palestinians any more. Nor Arabs, nor Druse, nor any ethnicity or group that posed, through word or deed or suspicion, a threat of any nature to the State of Israel.

When I finally challenged him on it, he said, "And why not?"

"You've never even been there," I said, pointing out that I was more involved with Israeli charitable organizations than he was.

"I don't have your guilt to expunge," was his reply to this.

"At least you didn't accuse me of that second most heinous of crimes against the Jews," I said.

"Marrying one?"

"Close," I said. "But Philo-Semitism covers more territory, I think."

He rolled his eyes and made a gargling noise, saying, "Yes, a plague of poxes on that! Anti-Semites we can handle, we know where we are with *them*. But the *Philo*-Semite, ugh! What do they want? What's their problem? And when can we pass a fuckin' law against 'em? Holy Mother of a Gentile God, *you're* not becoming one of *those*, are you?"

"How can I tell? I am on the Israel Bonds drive committee, though."

"How many bonds did you buy?"

"Few thousand."

"Whew!" he said, mopping feigned perspiration from his brow. "It takes at least a million before you're up for a Righteous Gentile Award—admittedly a good plaque to have on your office wall when you start drafting that massive military aid to Arafat policy."

"If I didn't know you—" I began but he cut me off:

"—you definitely wouldn't want to!"

It was that moment I chose to ask him to be best man at my wedding.

I'd taken to spending summers at the family place on Martha's Vineyard, and on August 5, 1984, while shopping at Alley's General Store in West Tisbury, I'd run into an old friend of my father's, Theo Casgall, who was with his daughter Abigail. I hadn't seen either of them in many years. Theo had not changed at all, so I easily recognized him, but Abbie had been transformed from a sulking tomboy into a very beautiful young woman, and I had to be introduced before I realized who she was. Theo clearly noticed my interest and contrived to leave the two of us alone. The result was a dinner invitation, then many other invitations. We announced our engagement on Labor Day.

We were married the following spring. As we both knew would happen, our hopes for a small quiet wedding were quickly waived by two fathers bent on making it a society event.

The attraction of a small wedding is you can just invite close friends. But with a wedding like mine, you have to invite almost everyone you've ever known, which, between our two families, meant half of Washington. The guest list grew by the day. And the day itself became more and more an ordeal Abbie and I just wanted to get through intact. When I learned that the president and first lady would be coming I knew there was no hope left for a pleasant day. I was a little angry too, so I called my father to ask why a man neither of us respected as president would be invited in the first place. "You'd better ask your future father-in-law," he told me. "Casgall invited him, not me." So Abbie called her father to ask the same question. The answer was that it would have been rude not to invite him when his entire administration had been given invitations. Evidently Bush, the vice president, had insisted Reagan come. "What does Bush have to do with it?" I complained. I should have seen what was really going on, but I did not.

Theo Casgall was one of the richest men in America, although you would never have guessed it from meeting him. Soft-spoken, with delicate features and a neatly trimmed white beard, he was a small unassuming man whose family fortune had been made in the nineteenth century grain markets and now comprised a global empire involved in every aspect of the food business from cultivation to retail. The company was still privately owned, although no Casgall had run it personally for decades. The family hired people to do that sort of thing, but this did not mean they had no interest in its running. They were notoriously intrusive, and CEOs rarely stayed on the job for more than three years because of it. "People got to eat," was all Theo ever said about his business, but it clearly occupied much of his time all the same. The rest was devoted to philanthropic work, a good deal of it overseas in the countries where the company operated. He shunned publicity, so the public never knew the full extent of his generosity and concern for the less fortunate. Where many men I knew donated to charities for the tax deductions or even for the profile in *Fortune* magazine, Theo Casgall genuinely gave money away. Nor did he rely on charities to dispense his gifts; he oversaw the disbursements himself, building schools, hospitals, clinics, low-cost housing, roads, even airports in places where they were desperately needed. He disliked talking about himself, so I gradually gleaned this information from Abbie. When I expressed interest in helping with some of these projects one evening, he told me to pack a bag for hot weather and meet him at dawn.

His Lear jet flew us in three stages that took two days to a remote area of northern Zaire, where I was stunned to find him greeted by hordes of children as "Papa." We were at a housing project, a vast site that included schools, a hospital, and many industrial structures, and when word got out that he was there, people flocked from all over the place to greet him. He had ten kids hanging to each hand, and women gave him flowers or brought food, while men bowed in the tribal manner. He would introduce me as his son-in-law, and the people would look at me with wonder in their eyes, saying, "Mister Casgall good man, very good man. You welcome here, son of Casgall, always you have home here." And the kids, with their huge soft eyes and keyboard smiles, would hold my hands as well as his, saying, "Papa two, papa two."

When the rains came suddenly, cataracts pouring through the holes in heaven, to thunder down on the shuddering tin-roofed lean-tos in a shantytown that had sprung up near Casgall's site, we were rushed into the shelter of a tiny house with bare ocher mud-brick walls, and served a meal of sourdough bread and a curry of okra and gourd on banana leaves. I was amazed to see Theo eat it with his fingers, not the slightest hesitation in his movements, as he spoke with the elders in Swahili. The rains beat down, at times roaring like enormous beasts, cascading down walls, rushing along gutters and gulleys in a deafening static hiss, the white noise of nature. And there we were, surrounded by gleaming blue-black flesh, uncompromising bone-white smiles, great sparkling eyes leaking genuine affection. The children kept going back and forth, offering more leaf platters, bamboo cups of warm buffalo milk, smiling, asking if we liked their food, and laughing shyly when we said it was delicious. "Good for papa, this, good..." They rubbed their tummies.

Theo insisted everyone eat with him, and I could see the honor this entailed, and the old men looking disapprovingly at the women who shuffled closer, and the old women pinching children's arms to move them aside, but the whole thing conducted with grace and dignity, and, improbably, there was more than enough food for all. Then walking out into the steaming jungle as it came back to life with clicks and clucks and squawks and buzzes, and the steady drip-drip-drip from one great leaf to another, and the sun appearing in the skeins of mist like a headless ghost with an Afro. My linen suit clung to me like pond slime, rivulets of sweat streaming down my face, tickling my sides.

"Papa now raining," said the kids. "Look, papa, you raining!"

No malice at all, just genuine affection. And the man whom no one touched back home treated like the black stone of Mecca, an object of reverence, a source of blessing, a thousand hands stroking, dabbing, sweeping, pressing, gripping him. Old men circled in front and fell on their knees, to be hauled up by Theo, saying, "La-la, no. This is not necessary for me."

Casgall was building a small city here, even if he did call it "some public housing," and it was clearly no easy task. He examined a hundred structures, called over architects, site managers, foremen, bricklayers to point out a fault or question a decision or praise a finished building. He seemed to know about every trade and skill, every tool and fabric, and his words were listened to intently, his praise inhaled like oxygen, and his criticism received in sullen shame. In one place, the plans had been followed in reverse, creating a major problem where the structure was supposed to join up with an exterior wall, yet Theo explained patiently what had happened to the workers, and what they could do to correct it. He never seemed angry, and he was lavish with his praise.

People who were clearly dreading this visit ended up as joyful as the children, whose city this would one day be. The more I saw, the more immense I realized this undertaking was. We ended the tour in a school's library, where crates of books we had just flown in were still being unpacked. The children who had followed us all day obediently went to sit behind little desks from which they pulled out textbooks and at a sign from the woman who'd been introduced as principal they began to take turns reading. Each child read a paragraph, and almost all of them read faultlessly:

"There are three species of government: republican, monarchical, and despotic. In order to discover their nature, it is sufficient to recollect the common notion, which supposes three definitions, or rather three facts: that a republican government is that in which the body, or only a part of the people, is possessed of the supreme power; monarchy, that in which a single person governs by fixed and established laws; a despotic government, that in which a single person directs everything by his own will and caprice."

I realized they were reading from Montesquieu's *Spirit of the Laws*. I was moved to tears, and can say without hesitation that this was and is among the most memorable moments in my life.

"The laws of education are the first impressions we receive; and as they prepare us for civil life, every private family ought to be governed by the plan of that great household which comprehends them all. If the people in general have a principle, their constituent parts, that is, the several families, will have one also. The laws of education will be therefore different in each species of government: in monarchies they will have honor for their object; in republics, virtue; in despotic governments, fear."

The children sat quietly and attentively when they finished reading their paragraphs. It was extraordinary to see such discipline. The readings lasted over ninety minutes, and every one of the percipient French baron's insights about government seemed to be written in magnesium flares, but it was the last few paragraphs that were fired into my mind like burning coals, and still exist as glowing embers in the heart's bare grate:

"As education in monarchies tends to raise and ennoble the mind, in despotic governments its only aim is to debase it. Here it must necessarily be servile; even in power such an education will be an advantage, because every tyrant is at the same time a slave. Excessive obedience supposes ignorance in the person that obeys: the same it supposes in him that commands, for he has no occasion to deliberate, to doubt, to reason; he has only to will. In despotic states, each house is a separate government. As education, therefore, consists chiefly in social converse, it must be here very much limited; all it does is to strike the heart with fear, and to imprint on the understanding a very simple notion of a few principles of religion. Learning here proves dangerous, emulation fatal; and as to virtue, Aristotle cannot think that there is any one virtue belonging to slaves; if so, education in despotic countries is confined within a very narrow compass.

"It is in a republican government that the whole power of education is required. The fear of despotic governments naturally arises of itself amidst threats and punishments; the honor of monarchies is favored by the passions, and favors them in its turn; but virtue is a self-renunciation, which is ever arduous and painful. This virtue may be defined as the love of the laws and of our country. As such love requires a constant preference of public to private interest, it is the source of all private virtues; for they are nothing more than this very preference itself. This love is peculiar to democracies. In these alone the government is entrusted to private citizens. Now a government is like everything else: to preserve it we must love it."

The entire class recited the last sentence in chorus and from memory:

"It is not the young people that degenerate; they are not spoiled till those who are older are already sunk into corruption."

As Theo and I walked from the school, I asked him what these children could possibly understand from reading Montesquieu.

"What did you understand from reading him?" he asked me.

I smiled, thinking it a joke, but he was serious.

"You think they are less intelligent than you?" he said.

"No, but they are a little young."

"Poor diet," he said. "The youngest there is sixteen."

I had taken them all for no older than twelve or thirteen, with the youngest around eight or nine.

"People got to eat," he said, smiling at his joke. "And they've got to learn as much as they can while they can. I'm not going to have them reading *Dick and Jane* only so some bastard dictator can come along and close the schools to everyone except his own tribe. While they're learning they might as well learn something useful, yes?"

"You're a thorough man, aren't you?"

"And one of those kids might be that bastard dictator, so at least he will have something nagging at his conscience as he plants the killing fields."

He also believed that memorizing texts was as good an education as any. It flexed the mind, and the text remained with you for life, so the more useful it was the better.

"We're destroying our own educational system," he said quietly. "Look at the crap they do at school now, the lack of discipline, the hare-brained curriculum. We ought to pay more attention to Montesquieu ourselves. By his definition, we need to worry about our form of government too, because our education bears the hallmark of despotic government."

I thought about it, and saw it could be viewed that way, but it didn't have to be. Theo asked if I disagreed. I told him I could see how he interpreted it that way, but I saw it differently.

"You've got your father's diplomatic genes," he said.

We were once again surrounded by bright-eyed smiling people, now bidding us farewell. There were little gifts wrapped in leaves, which Theo gratefully accepted from one and handed to another. The children began singing some kind of traditional farewell song, and Theo gathered the tribal elders together, taking them onto the runway strip where a packing case had just been unloaded from the Lear. The old men gathered around the case as Theo levered off its top with a crow bar. Reaching in, he pulled out rifles wrapped in burlap, handing one to each man, and then giving them small boxes of bullets. He unwrapped a gun—they were semi-automatics of some kind—and demonstrated how it was loaded, slamming the cylinder shut and spinning round to fire three quick shots in succession at a faded notice reading KEEP OUT some hundred yards away. The old men whooped with delight and began loading their guns. Theo clearly told them no, no practicing, no messing around. Guns were dangerous. The men nodded and bowed, walking away with their weapons.

"Guns," I said lamely, trying to insert a questioning tone into the word.

"They've got to be able to defend themselves. You think others aren't envious of all this?" He gestured over at the enormous construction site.

"So you're making their lives more complicated?" I asked.

"Civilization is a complex business," he said. "They're going to have to learn how to deal with it sooner or later."

"By killing the 'others'?"

"They won't kill anyone unless their own lives are threatened."

"What makes you so sure of that?"

"I know the tribe. It's their way. They have always lived peaceably. That's why I chose to build here."

"A thorough man." I said again.

"If you wanted to do something useful here, as you claimed you did," he said, "you could build something similar for the Bekbe."

"The Bekbe?"

"That's the neighboring tribe. They aren't so peaceable, though. They eat the livers of their enemies—so I suppose you could say they're cannibals."

"I suppose so."

After seeing what this work entailed, the sheer scope of knowledge it required, I was no longer sure I could do it, and I said so.

"You learn as you go," Theo said. "Trial and error. But your heart has to be in it."

"I know my limitations," I confessed. "I couldn't do what you've done here. I'd happily support someone who could, though. I simply don't have the time to devote to it even if I could do it. Surely I can help in other ways?"

"You know something, David," he said, as we buckled our seat belts, "I've always thought I would pity the man who tried to take away my daughter—you know what fathers are like about their daughters. But I can't tell you how happy I am to have you as a son-in-law."

"Thank you."

"Let me finish. Anyone else would have felt obliged to match me here, building a city for the Bekbe and inevitably screwing it up. But you don't want to challenge me. You don't need to perhaps. Now why is that? Don't you respect me?"

I was startled. I had no idea he was thinking this. I protested that we were in Africa because I *did* respect him, what he did.

"You don't have to," he said. "You've got my daughter now anyway."

"You can't be serious," I said, looking at him in amazement.

"A politician in the family," he said, giggling in an oddly inappropriate manner. "Who would have ever thought it?"

The whole exchange, on top of such an unusual day, left me feeling anxious and discombobulated. I decided to take a couple of Valium and try to sleep. I had a dream-wracked fitful series of slumbers, and every time I awoke I saw Theo still sitting in his chair staring vacantly with glassy eyes, the same irrelevant grin on his lips. I would not take any more such trips with him—that I promised myself.

The first secret I kept from Abbie was the full account of my day in Africa. I wondered if she even realized her father was capable of such weirdness, but concluded she must be, since you cannot spend twenty-five years living with someone and not be aware of their extremes. But if she was like other people, she'd be ashamed of her father's rogue facet, the piece that did not fit. So I chose not to put her through such a scene. We had enough on our plates as it was.

And there were days when the tying of our knot, or its preparations, took a distant back seat to the swift unraveling of the tangled web that members of the media had already started referring to as Iran-Contra, although not yet in their mediums of choice. For this and much other helpful information about impending political doom Mel had become almost more useful to my career than I know I previously had been, and would be again, to his. Largely because the whole business appalled me so profoundly, I had already spilled him enough Iran-Contra beans to build an obelisk of shame easily tall enough for him to clamber up into the clouds and slay his fill of giant reputations. I was mildly puzzled that he had not taken even partial advantage of this inside track yet, but put it down to his reluctance to endanger me until another viable source came along to blame it on. I could not have been more wrong, but I don't think I would even have believed the real explanation then if he'd told me himself.

Because the president was attending, the Casgall–Leverett wedding party's guest list had to be checked with the Secret Service for undesirables.

"If they find some," said Abbie, "it'll be a little late because they're already running the country."

We were both, I think, tolerantly amused as well as exasperated, exhausted and frustrated by the whole jamboree by now, which seemed so far out of our hands it may have well been the wedding of total strangers. We had rendezvoused at a McDonald's in a twee olde-tyme mall near Falls Church because the place happened to be equidistant from where each of us found ourselves that morning around 6.30 AM. Beyond agreeing that the coffee seemed supernaturally hot—far hotter than boiling, somehow—we had nothing to say to each other except sorry.

"We should have eloped," I said.

"We should have known," said Abbie.

"We should hire doubles and go to Hawaii for the week," I suggested. "No one would notice."

"No one would care!"

"As long as the senior Casgall and the senior Leverett get precisely what they want, or wanted but neglected to mention yet expected to get anyway."

"Or didn't know they wanted but became utterly convinced they did want and in far greater profusion the moment they found the other wanted it on a more modest scale."

Neither of us would have denied our fathers' rights to unalloyed bliss in their dream wedding—had any of it remotely
concerned *us*. As things were, though, we both resented the way
these two overbearing patriarchs were intent on creating events
that entirely served their own interests and concerns, and just
happened to be taking place side by side at the same time in the
same place.

I found it miraculous that my father had accepted the event
should be held on the Casgall estate, but this was solely a result
of his reading of matrimonial tradition, which accorded some
kind of site tenacity to the bride's father. This privilege in no
way prevented the groom's father from acting as if the bride's
father's property were his own, however, to arrange or
rearrange, build upon or tear down as he saw fit—or as he eventually saw fit after much trial and error.

It was drawing close to being a nightmare from which we
might never be able to awaken. Of this we both agreed heartily,
lobbing our still-full paper tumblers of white-hot coffee-like
stuff into the steaming McGarbage can, as we returned to our
individual toil back along our equidistant roads.

This was also the day I received an invitation to lunch with
Caspar Weinberger, the secretary of defense.

Lunch was served in one of the Pentagon's private dining
rooms and I was the only guest, which was disconcerting since
I'd assumed there would be many people. A slim, handsome
man with something of a thirties matinee idol about his slicked-
back hair and foxy smile, Weinberger seemed careworn and too
busy to eat. We'd met briefly before, so there was no need for
preliminaries, and he got straight down to business, pulling a
copy of our guest list from his breast pocket.

"You have Franklin Barker on this list," he said, looking at
me with flat black eyes. "You might want to reconsider it."

"Why?" I was taken by surprise.

"He's got himself in a lot of trouble."

"He told me," I said. "But he's not the only one."

"He may be." Weinberger drummed his fingers on the table. "He may *have* to be."

"I understand." I realized he was saying that someone had to deflect the blame from, among others, himself. "Is that fair?" I said.

"Fair?" He made the word sound arcane, foreign. "It won't be fair to the American people to have their president made out to seem a liar, will it?"

"They're probably getting used to it," I said, smiling. "Barker got involved only so he could serve in this administration. He doesn't deserve to be keelhauled for it. He stood in the front lines and he pulled off something everyone wanted. He deserves a medal not a trial."

"I was in the infantry during the war," Weinberger told me. "My unit saw a lot of action. Every week someone was killed, friends. We all served, we did our duty, and we expected nothing in return. Why should he be different?"

"He's a good man."

"No one is going to see it that way, and you know it. They'll hang him out to dry."

"Your neck's on the line too, isn't it?"

"Secondary," he said, quietly. "The deal was in place by the time I arranged the financing. I'm not about to take the rap. *That* wouldn't be *fair*."

"When's this going to happen?" I asked, realizing it was too late to change anyone's mind about Barker.

"Soon."

"Does he know?"

"Listen, we've got the media digging through a lot of dirt in that area. It's only a matter of time. We had to ask the SAS to break into the London offices of the bank we were using, which they had to do with one of our finance people since there was no time to teach them what to look for. They just managed to get out before someone caught them, and I doubt if they would have done it had Thatcher not been implicated.

"We've been flying by the seat of our pants with this business—worthwhile though it is—and in my opinion we're not going to get away with it much longer. What would you do?"

"I'm afraid I believe in accountability," I told him. "I'd level with the public after carefully explaining why the deal was done."

"Ha," he laughed cynically. "And how would you explain why we sold arms to a country that invaded our embassy and took our people hostage? And why we used the profits to fund and arm a bunch of guerrillas in Central America trying to overthrow their government? We did it so they'd delay the hostage release and thus prevent the Democrats from winning the election? You think that would sound good?"

"So it's true?"

"Can you think of another reason we'd sell the Iranians arms?"

"To prevent Iraq winning the war?"

"Well, that is why we continue to do it, true."

I conceded that Iran-Contra was not something the public would understand—that I didn't understand it myself.

"I don't either," Weinberger sighed. "It is not something I would have ever sanctioned. I don't know what that idiot Bush was thinking."

"No one was thinking when this was hatched," I said. "Why doesn't Bush take the blame?"

"He might have to, but the agency won't be happy about that."

"So Barker is the fall guy?"

"Looks that way." He picked up his knife and fork. "Let's eat before it gets cold."

He was giving me a friendly warning, I realized, telling me to scrub Barker's name from the list. I wondered how close to breaking the scandal really was, forced to admit to myself that I didn't want a guest who would make everyone else uncomfortable, but I also didn't want to snub someone who had been good to me. I couldn't discuss any of this with Abbie or anyone else, either. She'd be shocked just to learn how corrupt we'd become. It was a National Security issue, so I would have to decide myself what to do. I decided to level with Barker and let him wrestle with the issue. It was a mistake, because he hadn't been told he was going to take the rap.

We met at Tony's Black Forest Inn, sitting out on the windy patio with dust flung in our eyes and deep embattled clouds overhead creating an ominous flickering light that appeared related to the rattling sound of leaves being tormented by rushing air. The world seemed to be speeding up the way it does in silent movies, humanity dancing crazily toward some random doom. There was a new maitre d', who didn't know Barker, and pronounced *oeufs* as oafs. We also learned that Tony, the owner, had been killed in a car crash, so the place would be changing hands soon. It had a forlorn abandoned feel to it, Campari umbrellas flapping, birds hopping across the tables after crumbs, the wind in the eaves sighing in exasperation.

"Fucking soup's cold," said Barker. "They don't give a shit any more."

He suddenly struck me as the kind of person who always felt waiters didn't give a shit about him, and was right in feeling it because they actually didn't give a shit about him. He seemed to have shrunk too. His clothes were baggy on him, which made them look cheap or like they were picked from the dingy bins of a thrift store. His beard was no longer bushy, it was merely unkempt. His fingernails were chewed and grimy. His eyes were small, and ill at ease. He was no longer ebullient; he was edgy and rude. At one point I honestly wondered if this was the same Franklin Barker I had so respected, and from whom I had learned so much. This shriveled effigy with bad nerves did not have anything I'd ever want to learn, surely? Even his words were all wrong. He was like someone with a bad memory and worse timing trying to tell jokes—minus the jokes. It hurt to see him like this, and it frightened me.

"They just don't give a fuckin' shit any more, do they?" Barker repeated.

I suddenly wondered if he meant the restaurant or the government. He sucked at the cold soup noisily.

"I want you to tell me that if you're dragged into this... *mess*, you won't come to the wedding," I said. "I can't do that to my father's guests."

"I'd have thought you'd be more loyal to old friends," Barker told me, smiling an empty smile. "But I guess not."

"Can you tell me what I asked?" I said firmly.

"That I'll just slink off and not embarrass your important guests?"

"If you want to put it that way..."

He shook his head. "No," he said. "I'm not going to do it. You'll have to cope with the price of friendship. You want me to stay away, *you don't invite me*—simple as that."

"I thought you'd be more understanding." I felt embarrassed now, and perhaps a little ashamed.

"You think my little girls are going to understand when they see their dad branded a villain on TV? You think their classmates will be understanding? Is my wife going to understand when I sell the house and cottage to pay lawyers? Is my son going to understand that I can't afford to keep him at Yale? Will I fuckin' understand when I have to get laid in some cheap motel because I've got nowhere else to take the little lady? And you thought I'd be *more* understanding...well, *you* thought *wrong*, didn't you?"

"It hasn't happened yet, Frank. Maybe it won't happen."

"And maybe we'll have a fuckin' democracy one day!" He hit the table so hard his glass of water spilled, running down onto his pants. He didn't even move his legs, making it seem that getting his pants soaked had become too negligible a problem now to be considered one at all any more.

"Fuck it," he blurted out, his voice almost a squeal as it rose dramatically in volume until everyone within thirty yards must have been able to hear. "You tell that cocksucker Weinberger that I'll make sure they know *his* fuckin' name. And that dip-shit fairy Bush better pack his bags and get out of town because I am going to *out* him if it's the fuckin' *first* thing I do—yeah, tell Poppy the jig is up. A Bush in the hand is worth quite a bit if you're a fuckin' *Contra*."

"Don't even joke about it, Frank," I told him, aware people were staring.

"You think I'm fuckin' jokin' about it, do you? The only person who's going to be okay when I've finished is the court jester himself. Ronnie's safe, don't fret. The American people might not like to hear his fuckin' brain has rotted in his skull and he gets lost trying to find the Oval Office washroom, though—but them's the breaks."

"I believe you're serious," I said. "But I am going to forget we had this conversation."

"So it's a good job that agency hack over there by the trees is recording it for posterity, isn't it?"

I looked over to the edge of the woods leading down to the Potomac just in time to see someone dodge out of sight into the mottled shadows.

"It's just someone walking their dog," I told him.

"Walking their parabolic microphone, you mean." He nodded back at the woods without turning, and I held up my knife to use as a mirror, seeing in it a man holding some kind of circular object. As I turned to get a clearer view, he dodged out of sight again. Ice replaced anything warm in my veins.

"You're playing with fire," I told Barker.

"So buy me some asbestos gloves," he said. "You can *afford* it."

"The way I heard it, you're the only person who can safely take the rap. They'll look after you, you *know* that. Just be a *mensch.*"

"That's right, break out the Yiddish at a time like this. Here's another word for your vocabulary: *Schmuck*, that's what I'll be— a fuckin' *schmuck*. And the way I see it is there's a lot of other little pricks who can take the rap with me."

"Why didn't you tell me earlier the spook was there?" I said, trying not to sound angry.

"Didn't see him."

He was lying. I knew damn well he was lying, just as I knew what I had to do now.

"I can't talk with you any more," I told him. "Be sensible, Frank, *please*...but you're on your own."

He looked it, looked so lonely. He'd been on his own all his life, though, since trudging out of Budapest. I told myself he'd survive, he'd be fine, he had spunk, moxie, *cahones*. But these are no match for the might of the State, with its laws and guns and power. I told myself whatever lies I needed to get me out of there.

Those legendary souls who stand alone against the armies of tyranny are just that: *legendary*. They make good stories, perhaps, but in reality they wouldn't even make first base before being obliterated. Sacco and Vanzetti, Joan of Arc, the Diggers, whoever they were, and all the others, past and yet to come, they all failed, or will fail, or else they're fictional. One man against the State is as foolish as King Canute against the North Sea. Twenty thousand men isn't much better. The man of true principle is a dead man. All we can do is accord martyrs an unverifiable achievement, based upon an invisible form of justice, in a place that may not even be there, courtesy of an entity whose existence cannot be proved. Martyrs always remind me of thwarted children who resort to wishing themselves dead, viewing death as an interval during which they will hide up on a cloud for long enough to see everyone wracked with grief and remorse before descending back into a life where their presence is sheer magic and all their wishes are once more paramount.

Only the Buddhist monks who ushered in nirvana prematurely with a can of gasoline and a match have ever remained with me as an example of where one man could truly be said to have defeated, if not the tyranny itself then certainly one of its armies. It is still the greatest image of protest I can imagine, and it said everything there was to say about the iniquity and depravity of Vietnam.

For decades I wondered why the suicide bombers who came after, even in their abject despair, could not see how infinitely more effective sacrifice would be if they followed the monks' example and imposed the burning agonies and twisted blackened death upon themselves alone. Two or three Muslim holy men may have even been able to shame peace from the hardest hearts and save countless millions of lives, if only they'd removed hateful revenge and its pride from their hearts for long enough to realize that a martyr can die alone only if his death is to truly be an offering, which is, after all, the nature of any real sacrifice. And Gandhi *won* his revolution.

As I walked away from Barker, biting my lip to hold back tears, all I could see was that image in memory of the burning man, arms raised, rocking from side to side still in his meditative posture amid the flames and smoke that had now turned him black and spared us the horror of a human being whose principles and spiritual convictions made him burn to death in torment rather than live comfortably watching others tortured to death by those who had no principles or convictions to die for, though plenty of reasons to kill.

* * *

It was the overwhelming need to be somewhere safe and familiar and comforting that impelled me to head straight over to my parents' house after leaving the Black Forest Inn. The house was none of those things any more, though, as I found upon arriving there. But I couldn't think of anywhere else to go.

Alone with my father, I wanted to talk about Barker, to ask him just how wrong my actions really were, and if there was anything I could do to help this man who had shown me nothing but generosity and friendship. But I could not find the words. Or did not want to squander them, nor the difficult feelings behind them, on a man who as often as not these days would happily talk all night to an emptying bottle. So instead, I asked him if he really believed in democracy. We were sitting with supper at the huge dining table's mahogany lake, which stretched out mournfully in the half-darkened room, inviting us to drown. He put down his knife and fork and said no one had ever believed in it:

"Even Rousseau didn't believe in it. He says it's a perfect form of government and that if there were a nation of gods, they would undoubtedly rule that way. But, he says, we're men, we're not so perfect, we can't handle it. This is the philosopher whose ideas fueled our revolution and that of the French—he doesn't believe democracy can work."

"He doesn't believe vested interests should be allowed near government, either," I found myself pointing out.

"It isn't realistic to think they can be kept out," my father said. "Which is why a prudent man makes sure his own interests are also represented."

"A prudent man?" I said. "Or do you mean a crook?" I put down my knife and fork, adding, "I find this all very, very distasteful, you know?"

"Pity," he said blithely. "*Mine's* rather good—you should have had the veal..."

If I had been trying to get him to admit on tape that the US was controlled by a handful of oligarchs who ran it for their own benefit, I would not have succeeded. He spoke in convoluted sentences that always referred back to something unsaid, or relied for their meaning on an inaudible word. A recording would have proved nothing. Yet, knowing him well, I knew he was really both confirming it and denying it. I was surprised that he'd never expressed these misgivings about democracy to me before, but, as I came to see that evening, they were not so much misgivings about democracy as they were pessimism about humanity. As such, they suited my mournful mood that night, and also gave me reasons to shake the guilt monkey off my back. The moat of alcohol my father plied me with during the course of intrepidly plying himself with even more of it did not exactly hinder this exercise in self-delusion either.

"Let's face it," my father said, "the *people* are generally stupid. Most don't even want to understand, the rest can't, or *basically* can't."

"That their fault or ours?" I asked him. "Because I haven't seen education as a priority in this bloody country since I returned from England."

I'm no drinker, not even half of a drinker. Some get witty, lively. I get dull, deadly.

He shrugged. Alcohol affected him in much the same way as being punched in the head constantly for two hours by Sonny Liston probably would have. "Look at Britain," he said. "A society of 'tirely equal opportunities. What happens, hmm? What? Most can't make use of 'em; some don't want 'em; a vast number just abuse social insurance, and the rich don't use the national elf because it's tied into government fortunes and canna be replied on. The educated man...men...they want nothing more than to drag everyone into the modern whirl, but they run up against the real problem: the oiks want stay back there in the fifteenth sentry. Who comes out to see the ol'

Queen? Whose trashy papers are filled with royal gossip? Who are the patriots, eh? Tell me that!"

"Who are the war dead?"

"Precisely."

I knew this speech well. I'd heard it many times. My father was a consummate diplomat, always responding to hard questions with something that appeared to be an answer yet was really completely and utterly irrelevant. These days it might not even make sense either. And having said it, now, he suddenly had no more to say. Yet for some obscure reason I needed him to say something. What I really wanted, I suspect, was for him to be again the big, strong, wise man he'd been throughout my childhood. Or was that just another childish misperception? You have to be sure you want to see what the Wizard of Oz is really like before you look behind the curtain, because once you've seen the reality there's no going back to the illusion.

"Am I going to end up as bitter and...and cynical as you are?" I asked him.

He laughed ruefully. "G'lord," he said, "I 'spect you'll be far worse than me. I see the crew you serve now and I ask myself where on earth we're *going*. Where, eh? Can new tell me *that*? Life's basically not worth livin'," he told me, as if revealing one of the greater mysteries. "Never wanted to tell you that, but someone tol' me years ago and I came to realize they were right. Life is *not* worth living—you'll remember I said it, mark my words."

"I wish I didn't have to remember, Dad."

I knew I would, though.

My mother had left him, and I could see why. Yet neither one of them would openly admit their marriage had failed and they were living apart—although my father occasionally told the same clanging joke about the solution to marriage problems not being separate beds but separate continents. Like those parents who try to hide the primordial evil of their continued cigarette smoking from their scornfully disapproving children, my parents imagined they were doing an astonishingly brilliant and seamless job of continuing to act like the parents who had been there, with me and for me, for ever. What kept causing a great bursting pool of sorrow to rise up in my heart was the thought that they simply could not see how bleak, depressing and lonely their house and its lives had become. Did they honestly believe I couldn't possibly guess what was going on, and walked in blithely oblivious to the massed ranks of misery stacked in their legions from cellar to attic. Even the staff were miserable, and changed so often that my father had simply given up attempting to locate names for his housekeepers, maids, gardeners, handymen and all the others of whom he knew nothing whatsoever beyond the fact he paid them—and that was no certainty any more these days.

"Not worth livin'," he repeated. "But, for God's sake, it doesn't have to be this damn *squalid*." He poured himself yet another huge cognac and sipped it noisily as if it were hot tea. "Thank God for this sweet poison," he said, now treating enunciation like a holy mission. "Don't know how I'd put up with't if it wasn't for Uncle Remy."

"Uncle Jack would help, no doubt," I told him.

"The ver' odd thing," he said, "John Fowles has a new novel out called a *Daniel Martin*."

"Eh?"

"That's like Drack an' Remy together, see what I mean? Jacan Rummy's what I mean."

Lordy-lordy, I thought, in the small part of the mind, or of *my mind* at least, that never gets drunk, that casts a cold eye on life, on death, and on sour mash. Was this the sort of drivel that went through his mind? *Daniel Martin* = code for Jack Daniels and Remy Martin? I wondered what he made of *The Magus*. An anagram for mute shag perhaps. Or smug hate. Oh God, oh God, was he becoming senile, this big strong man I thought was invincible and immortal? You can't tell gin from senility when someone's drunk all day though—it's just the same as senility. They get just as cunning at concealing it too. My father's finale of verbal mutilation, followed by blackout somewhere on the wooden hill to Bedfordshire, probably capped off a solid day's toil over many forms of alcoholic beverage, a large number of the earlier ones fairly deniable. I suspect ouzo was not high on his list of *favorite* tipples, but it offered the distinct advantage of having its odor on the breath easily explained away by the jar of anise-flavored candies on his desk. This was before he ran into the ex-president-Jimmy's wife, Rosalynn Carter, in rehab, where she told him the best eradicator of booze-breath bar none was peanut butter. Presumably, this wisdom derived from having a peanut farmer for a husband? I wondered if indeed it had been the sole perk from that pious frugal man. And I found it all so deeply tawdry and depressing, like all addictions and the deceptions that invariably accompany them like flies around fecal matter.

Far from comforted by the evening when I needed nothing but comforting, I felt terribly disturbed when I finally pronounced myself sober enough to drive home. Everything seemed wrong, the mottled road, the hunched trees, other vehicles, the lot. Even the stars looked unfamiliar, and I had to stop the car to get out just for the purpose of reassuring myself the same constellations were still up there. It is something that has always consoled me, though, gazing up at the heavens. Not for the grandeur of the universe, although that is humbling and awesome enough, but because it is all I know I have in common with my most distant ancestors back when history hadn't even begun, that ape-man or man-ape we generally feel no kinship with at all in our sophistication and technological finery. Yet I know he loped from his cave at night and looked up at all those twinkling lights studding the void, trying to grasp what they were, what they meant, where they came from each night, and where they went off to each day. I know too that I understand this night magic no better than he did, yet I wonder if I am a better creature than he was where it really counts. I suspect we are more similar than either of us would admit. Someone in the *New Yorker* proved this point by cleaning up Neanderthal, giving him a suit and hat, a shave and haircut. He looked like anyone you'd see sitting in a diner or on a bus.

We have come to believe in our veneers, our wrappings, which are now just another means by which the rich can oppress the poor, and the middle class can go deeper into debt. But the thing itself can't hide from itself. The poor, bare forked animal can't pretend it's sophisticated to the terrified thing in the mirror. Whether I retreat from the edge of impossible grandeur, beauty and mystery to my car or my cave, I thought, I am scarcely different as a being in all but the quantity of information I carry, none of which explains either my life or my death, none of which is *transforming*.

Standing there in this communion with the origin of the species, I had the odd yet distinct sense of being reprimanded by my avatars for letting us all down. *We can imagine utopia, but we cannot bring ourselves to create it*: the words came to mind unbidden, and would not leave when asked. The mantra had a strangely soothing quality about it, and finally I felt the comfort I had been seeking all night. I felt still, at peace, and strangely timeless, or as if I were no longer associated with time at all, time that washed over me like fine rain, millennia gone in a heartbeat, entire ages blowing in a mist that imperceptibly licked my cheek before vanishing. The shadows of dinosaurs fell quietly across the woods of Virginia if I held my breath, great dumb beasts whose time was over, crushing anything in their path as they lurched toward a squalid doom in the marshes and bogs of climate change, thinking always of the brave and bright new future awaiting their mere arrival. *We can imagine utopia, but we cannot bring ourselves to create it.*

CHAPTER TEN

★ ★ ★

Materiam superabat opus[*] (Ovid)

WITH EVENTS THAT OUGHT TO BE minnows but are pumped up into whales without any thought for where they'll be able to continue living, let alone where they might live happily, everything that has any real value or importance tends to be dismissed as minnow-think in a world that now lives for whale-talk. And so it was that only on the day itself did I notice Les Melton had not RSVP'd to his wedding invitation. No one at hand had heard from him in more than a week either. Les was not someone for whom life's formalities carried no meaning. He always wrote thank-you notes after parties. He always RSVP'd to invitations. We all did. Dean had. Even Mel had, despite the fact that a best man was hardly going to hold the ring and decline the party.

Our courteous card writing or responding was one of the things that prompted mothers to remark how well brought up we all were. We also all came from homes where parties were frequent and the importance of knowing precise guest numbers was always being harped upon, if not for the caterers then for the table arrangements, if not for them then for the transportation involved, and if not for this then, to be sure, for something vital to the success and splendor of the event, upon which hung

---

[*]The workmanship was better than the subject matter.

the social standing of...someone who would not be able to stand a loss in status, or a lowering of local opinion.

In the spare minute I did not have, between losing a button on the waistcoat of my morning suit and breaking the shaft of my cravat pin, I telephoned every number I had for Les. Those numbers answered by other Meltons could offer no better explanation for Les's whereabouts than the numbers answered by machines—even the machines that imitated Les's own voice.

Upsetting as this was, I simply could not allow myself to dwell on it any longer. I hoped dearly that he would just show up at the church, or the party at least. But he did not.

In an era when other couples were having wedding ceremonies conducted by space aliens, or channeled from pharaohs three thousand years dead via gifted actresses, and held on the summit of Mount Everest, or on the roof of a bullet-train traveling from Tokyo to Kyoto, I suppose ours was almost dull. We suffered the Anglican rite uncut, for richer, for better, in sickness, and all the way to death do us part. I accepted Abbie as my lawful wedded wife, not my first mate or vice president, and she took me as her lawful wedded husband, not partner or accomplice, promising to love, honor and obey me. It was all overwhelmingly conventional, I'm afraid. All I remember now is the sight of Theo Casgall pacing down the aisle beside Abbie looking for all the world as if he intended to be part of the happy union himself: *Do you take this woman and her half-mad father*...

But it all went off without a hitch. Melvin Cassel was even able to produce the ring without so much as a fumble, stumble or fall.

My mother, I was told, left immediately after the ceremony, driving off in the opposite direction to the reception. I wish she had taken my father with her, by force if necessary. He was tiresome at 10 AM, boring by noon, tedious at 2 PM, and downright intolerable in seven different varieties throughout the following

fifteen hours it took his body to sign off for the day on consciousness and fuel intake. Model of grace, dignity and
decorum, Burlington Bertie from Grosvenor Square he may
once have been, but in those far-distant days he did not, as far
as I know, insist that octogenarian American presidents barely
able to walk with any competence join him in a limbo-dancing
fiasco that would set them alight, not to mention covering
them with mud, some of which was not mud but dog shit, and
rattle their overtaxed brains severely enough to warrant medical
attention, which he then attempted to drive off by spraying
mouthfuls of Hennessy cognac at the doctor's face.

I heard someone aptly remark, "And we sent *him* to the
Court of St. James."

"Where all he found was the cork of some Jameson's, I'll
wager," added the local wag.

"At least yours is more fun," Abbie said, consolingly, in the
one shared moment we managed to wrest from the ordeal.

"I'll take yours any day," I said, wondering if I wanted either.

It took quite a bit of adjustment to accommodate my father,
and the embarrassment. The process was nowhere near comple-
tion by the end of that year, let alone that interminable day. At
one point I did try a firm, "Father, I think you've had quite
enough to drink, don't you?"

"Here's my *boy!*" was the response. "He's so hum-hum-
humorless and prim, so clueless an' so dim, that even Mayfair
tarts sing hymns...*instead o' fuckin' himmm!*"

"Dad, *please!*" I said, attempting to haul him off into the
house. "You are making a complete fool of yourself, can't you
see that?"

"Y'know, *Dave,*" he said, trying to focus on me, his nauseat-
ingly fermented breath hot on my face, "we have long
wondered where you come from, Buddy, I mean who your Ma
spread 'em for...because I don't see any my genes in ya, no sir!
Self-righteous fuckin' l'il tosser..."

I let go of his arm, watching him sway like a tree in the wind and peer around looking to see where I'd gone as I walked off into the shadows, saying, "Great party, Pappy, just the tops!"

I thought I heard him say, "Only a Leverett can sever it," but I wasn't sure, and had no idea what it meant anyway.

The reception was held on the Casgall estate in Maryland, and it was lavish in the extreme—the New York Philharmonic Orchestra, Ravi Shankar, and James Taylor were among those listed as entertainment—and no one seemed inclined to leave early. There were tents spread over the grounds, barbecue pits, two major chefs competing with each other, some of the finest wines in existence poured as if they were ginger ale, boxes of Davidoff cigars left lying around like cocktail sausages. The rich are so often a disappointment at events like these, but Theo Casgall had outdone himself, and, according to the press reports, anyone else. Ever. After all the months of bickering rivalry, my father couldn't even be bothered to assert his fifty percent in the extravaganza, didn't even notice Casgall taking all the credit—though behaving in the most scrupulously fair manner when it came to sending his daughter's new father-in-law half the bills.

My new father-in-law gave a rather embarrassing speech on the subject of our wedding, which he referred to as "a merger between American Titans," and then made rather heavy-handed allusions to "a politician in the family" who would "take the wheel and set a course allowing those whose hard labor had created this nation out of barbarism and wasteland to navigate more fruitfully into the unknown waters of the future. . . ." It sounded more acquisition than merger, and Theo sounded as if he had acquired an adult version of Thomas the Tank Engine—perhaps David the GOP Nominee? There were many here-heres and bravos. I had the vertiginous sensation of watching the tracks of my life fork and run straight into the golden sunset forever, a gleaming ladder leading on and on but really going round and round, spinning out the track on which my engine would run true, stopping here for babies, there for senatorial ambition, and on toward the presidential halt, the lion in winter and the final graveyard shift. And that would be all if I so much as relaxed my guard around Theo Casgall, for whom I represented a mildly threatening asset, but an asset nonetheless.

In spite of our careful seating arrangements, people sat where they wanted, in cliques and covens of mutual interest. My father-in-law shunted me around like a hotdog stand, offering me to guests as if I were an after-dinner mint or liqueur. I had to spend a deadly span of minutes with the Reagans, listening to Nancy prattle away about fund-raising to cover up the fact that Ronnie had no idea where he was much of the time. I felt sorry for her, realizing shame was not something she could handle, and that shame had decided it was going to be the one thing she would have to handle.

"I remember when Nancy and I were married," Ronnie said at one point, then stopped and repeated "Nancy" to himself a couple of times to be sure he'd got the right wife, and was about to continue when his wife cut him off with an anecdote about Princess Margaret that was rather cruel. Ron seemed baffled, his head bobbing affably, his smile broad and fixed like a rubber mask, waiting for an opening to say whatever it was he'd forgotten.

Vice President Bush sat at a side table flanked by two somewhat fearsome-looking older women, one of whom was his wife Barbara, who had someone fetch me over in a rather regal manner. For a moment, I pictured Bush wearing a dress and ugly hat, realizing how old-ladylike his presence was. He constantly looked around the room as he spoke, occasionally nodding to someone or flashing his unconvincing smile. I disliked him the moment I'd first set eyes on him some time earlier, and I noticed that few of his peers had much respect for him. He seemed weak, somewhat effeminate, and lacking in authority.

Where most guests were eager to start talking seriously about whatever their main interests were, Bush appeared content to make small talk and gossip. He seemed to lack some kind of essential component. I couldn't put my finger on what it was at the time. I came to see during the years ahead that it was a conscience. He lacked any philosophy too. He was a clever enough man, but he wouldn't have passed Philosophy 101 if he'd been obliged to take the course. He was easy to manipulate as well because of this, easy to persuade with facts and figures that white was black and up was down.

I was appalled to find he was the next president. Melvin Cassel was not.

Mel had performed remarkably well at the wedding's reception too, giving a bitingly funny yet tender and insightful speech, and generally charming everyone he met. I'd noticed that he seemed to have settled at Bush's table, leaving poor Ennis to cope with some ancient and dotty Casgall relative who wore a rather extraordinary hat with plastic fruit and a real stuffed finch on top of it.

Whenever I caught sight of Nancy Reagan, her mouth was gaping open and she was trying to take in the magnificence or sheer cost entailed in a particular excess of conspicuous consumption. She was overheard, or so I was told, complaining bitterly to Ronnie that she would never be able to throw a party like this on his salary. She needn't have worried, because the public soon associated the wedding with the general munificence of the Reagan era, and there were more pictures of her and Ron in the papers and magazines than there were of the bride and groom. There also seemed to be more pictures of Melvin Cassel everywhere than there were of the president.

And there were so many photographs of Dean Torrance dancing with Nancy Reagan that a week later Dean received by courier a handsomely framed photograph of President Reagan wearing a Stetson and pointing a Colt .45 straight at you. It was signed: *Dean, this town ain't big enough for the two of us. So scram! Fondly, Ronald Reagan.* The following day Nancy invited him to a White House dinner honoring Oscar de la Renta, where he sat next to the president's son, Ron Reagan, who—or so Dean claimed—tried to pick him up under the impression he choreographed for the Moscow State Ballet.

During the one moment I had alone with Mel at the reception, I managed to ask why he was hanging around Bush.

"He turns my crank," Mel said.

"Seriously."

"He's stinking rich and he's going to be the next president," he said. "What's not to like?"

"So what's in it for him?" I asked.

"Solid endorsement in my influential column."

I laughed at this, but he was serious, adding, "Although you think it's just a Jew crying in the wilderness, there are people who take it very seriously. It's not just the *Ruskies* who're coming in from the cold, you know," he said enigmatically. "We Hebes are coming in too."

"What's that supposed to mean?"

"*You'll* see," he said. "You'll remember you heard it first *here* too."

As I was walking away, wondering if Mel was very drunk or merely just drunk, I heard the plangent alien notes of Ravi Shankar's sitar wafting out of the twilight. Candles had been lit all over the grounds, and the smell of roasting meat mingled with the hyacinth blossoms and was carried back and forth in the wake of maids and waiters. The bright cloudless day had been swallowed up by the muted and mottled greens of the lawns and forests, from which seeped a rich dank musky odor, the fecundity and abundance of nature's hidden womb. A few bars of Shakespearian minstrel-song even wafted over through the thick, overladen air from a music source of some sort: *Spring come to you at the farthest, in the very end of Harvest, scarcity and want shall shun you, for Ceres' blessing so is on you.* I enjoyed that single moment more than all the rest of the day—and the week following it.

I walked down to the end of the formal gardens, where the lawn met the woods, and stood looking back to the bedlam of merriment that roared from the dome of light surrounding Theo's house, which resembled a giant head, the colossus of Casgall, marooned in its lone and level lawns that stretched away into a misty eternity. The scattered fires and burning tapers, along with the contorted silhouettes they made and the braying honking sound that these emitted reminded me of something else too, but I could not figure out what it was. Seeing, a little later on, Mel roar with laughter, his hand on Bush's shoulder, a fat cigar burning in its fingers, reminded me: Hieronymus Bush, Hieronymus *Bosch*, that was it.

What I kept thinking was the burning blood canyon of an unprecedented dawn about to break proved to be bonfires lit along the lakeshore as a prelude to a firework display the like and magnitude of which would not be seen again until the shock and awe bombardment of Baghdad that preceded the 2003 invasion. Theo bragged about his Pentagon pyrotechnic consultants, but our *Wedding Apocalypse Vow*, as the blitzkrieg was cutely titled in the Entertainments & Music program, did have an air marshal, a five-star general, and two propulsion experts from NASA heading up the list of nearly seventy-five technical staff that it took to terrify half of Maryland for over ninety minutes, during which more explosives were detonated than had been used throughout the entire War of Independence, 1812 War and the Civil War combined. It was over a week before the first birds began to return to the area, and they looked distinctly edgy to me, freezing in fear at the slightest thud and stepping along their twigs like over-caffeinated tightrope-walkers.

You could hear Casgall screaming with crazed delight somewhere down by the fires and launch site every time some object

whined up into the night to explode into thirty exploding
meteors, each of them sufficient to blind and deafen all life for
five miles around. It was a terrifying spectacle, and it seemed to
quite unhinge many of the WW II vets present, a lot of whom
fled indoors for cover. Predictably, the forty-minute finale
entailed the full New York Philharmonic, amplified beyond all
reason and crashing out from huge stadium speakers spread in
a half-mile arc throughout the woods, playing Attila the Hun's
version of Tchaikovsky's 1812 overture, with the cannons
scored for violin, and the aerial bombs scored for *Firebombing of
Dresden Meets Armageddon*. As the heavens literally fell, along
with Napoleon's army, guests went squealing and howling
under tables, into bushes, beneath automobiles, down to the
swimming pool floor, skidding across gravel to plunge into
garages, outbuildings, and of course scampering down to the
cellars of the main house.

It was only when the final planet-shuddering chord had died
away within rustling leaves and wreaths of sputtering cordite
smoke that we could hear the sirens closing in on all sides as several kinds of Maryland law enforcement officials raced to take up
arms in the war of the worlds. They found themselves, however,
looking down the laser-sighted barrels of large-caliber rifles
aimed by an entire SWAT team, backed up by two hundred Secret
Service officers brandishing chrome-plated Uzis, along with
numerous heavily armed private security guards. Virtually
everyone from the current administration as well as the three
previous administrations was now somewhere in the same square
mile, so it was only natural they'd have protection.

"Uh-uh," said an ancient little man crouching near me, his
silver toupee hanging from one ear like some tribal fetish. "Too
many spooks broil themselves like moths."

"Eh?" I said.

"I ran Special Ops for Warren Harding," the ancient gnome
explained, in a voice that crackled like the ghost of a Roman

candle. "We had shoot-outs with the agency all over the goddamn place. Once you got five different orgs all armed to the teeth and all on the same mission, you can kiss your ass goodbye, I can tell you that for nothin', kid."

"Thank you, sir," I said, heading toward the bristling security confrontation.

"Here, take a look at this," someone hollered, and a rolled copy of the morning's *Washington Post* hurtled out of the sky and into my chest.

I caught it before it fell into the now dewy grass, opening up the front page.

This was certainly going to be a day no one would ever forget. Not because of my nuptials, though, nor on account of Theo Casgall's rehearsal for the end of time. The *Post*'s headline said it all: "IRAN WEAPONS SALES FINANCED CONTRAS: Rogue Agent's Suicide Reveals Mastermind Behind Illegal Funding Scheme. But how close to the president does this really go?"

And there, right in the center of the page was a photograph of Franklin Barker, looking evil, guilty, unshaven, a scoundrel and the kind of man who ought to die no matter what he'd done or planned to do. They had found him in the shag pad with his brains spread across two walls, a .45 Magnum in his hand, and a pathetic suicide note begging for his family's forgiveness, for his nation's compassion. It wasn't even Barker's handwriting. The man didn't own a gun, and he certainly didn't feel he needed to be forgiven.

CHAPTER ELEVEN

★ ★ ★

*Summmum ius, summa iniuria** (Cicero)

SPREADING DEMOCRACY, THEY CALLED IT, but I could see that the proper term was coup d'état. It began in earnest with Panama in 1989. We simply went down there and took the president away with us, threw him in jail. We didn't like him. He had pockmarks and looked like a Latino narco-crook—in fact he looked exactly like the villain in *Scarface,* Al Pacino's Cuban cartoon, where dealing cocaine is glamorous until you die glamorously dealing it. Manuel Noriega's regime change was not so glamorous, however. We killed 3000 civilians while arranging it, but that part didn't get much press in the home of the brave.

George Herbert Walker Bush was president by then. Poppy to his friends. His secretary of defense was Dick Cheney, with whom I'd clashed on several occasions when he was chairman of the Republican Policy Committee. He was close friends with Donald Rumsfeld, Luposki's ally in the Team B enterprise, and the two of them had pulled off what was widely deemed to be a palace coup during Gerald Ford's lackluster presidency, which had completed Nixon's last term. Rumsfeld and Cheney contrived to box in Ford, forcing him to fire both his defense secretary, James Schlesinger, and his national security advisor,

---

* The extreme law is the greatest injustice.

Henry Kissinger, as well as urge his vice president, Nelson Rockefeller, to resign. This left Rumsfeld as the youngest ever secretary of defense, and Cheney, who was then only 34, as White House chief of staff, the second most powerful position there was in the White House at the time. Cheney had Bush the First wrapped around his little finger just as tightly as he was to have Bush the Second entwined, and before any of us knew it— and we were, it is to be remembered, those responsible for forming foreign policy—America was heading down an uncharted and dangerous path that had nothing to do with my Policy Planning Council or anyone else's advice.

At least Reagan had a disease to blame for the shambles of his mind. George H.W. Bush had no excuse for the mental incapacity that caused him to spend his days impersonating a fairly sophisticated plank of wood, with, however, the spiritual and emotional depth of a turnip. Although he had hunting dogs more engaging than Bush, Dick Cheney knew how to handle almost anything that had four limbs and wasn't human, so he kept Bush on a tight leash, setting him loose only to chase clearly defined prey, and even then usually accompanied by one of his brighter retrievers, just in case Bush fumbled, fudged or forgot what he was doing in the excitement of the chase.

I have been polite and diplomatic, my father's son, while discussing those in whose hands the rudder of our republic was placed until now, I think it is fair to say. Even in those for whom I had barely anything good to note, I suggest, I found some morsel or molecule worthy of respect, and thus treated them accordingly. But I have never understood why men in whom no goodness or decency exists, whose lives contain no benefit for the world, whose time has been one long conception and commission of wickedness designed purely to enrich themselves or increase their power, indeed whose very dreams bring a blight of discord and unease to swell the ranks of misery's serried minions and aide them in their labors which cling like mildew over the once-bright surface of pure joys and unalloyed love-supreme.... I have never understood why such men warrant the same respect we give to those worthy of respect. I believe all men deserve an honest response approximating the actual degree to which they merit any man's respect and gratitude for their deeds and the time they have sacrificed for others here. And that is what I mean to demonstrate by example in my treatment of our leaders from here on until the end of my account.

Euphemism will get us nowhere in the darkness ahead. We need precision in our thoughts and deeds, and in our words, if we are to put Humpty-Dumpty back together again, or rearrange the Linnaean classifications and retabulate the elements in readiness for the new world order hurtling our way like lightning, like ice from the sun.

I need to express my scorn for a creature like George H.W. Bush the way I need to sweat out toxins or excrete feces, the way I need to pull down from the violet air a fragile beauty unknown before now, whose lifespan is a thought from start to end, yet whose existence will be remembered until the stars fall. I need to hate, and I hate those who have made me hate, who have made me become like them, haters, sacks of bile and spleen, whose dawn chorus is a grating rant of blame, their sole excuse for the waste that has seeped into whiteness and purity, their only explanation for not creating the earthly paradise that was their entire mission.

Just the thought of these men unhinges me, sends the climbing sorrow pullulating up into my tiny brain. They say we are all to blame. They say it is fifty-fifty. They say wisdom begins when you accept that you alone are at fault. But they can spread the culpability across this entire universe for all I care, because I know the ones who really *are* to blame, the ones who saw something perfect, flawless and white, and had to smear shit all over it and smash holes in its clean geometry the very moment they looked upon that awe-inspiring purity with their filthy disease-ridden eyes.

I will admit that I did not survive all this unscathed. I would not have wanted to. To remain unaffected by the destruction of everything you loved and held dear, everything you valued, everything in which you had placed your hope and dreams, would be the same as not being capable of love, of not valuing anything, of being entirely bereft of hope and devoid of dreams.

The destruction occurred within my soul as well as out there, because when the target is what a man loves, *he* is the target. To have endured ten decades in this inferno of imbeciles is enough. To have been calm and polite almost every moment of every day is also enough. To have emerged from a hell that makes Dante look like *Bambi*, to have survived the unspeakable and unthinkable and claim one is still as sane as a country grocer would make a mockery of suffering itself. No, my mind is like a tattered life-raft in a pitiless black storm, thrown from here to there and on to places of which I tremble merely to imagine.

I won't mislead you any more. The mind with which I wrote these pages is now cracking beneath their burden of knowledge. I have eaten of the fruit of the tree of the knowledge, of good and evil. I have eaten of the fruit that is supposed to make men become as gods, knowing good and evil. Yet, unless gods are broken and oppressed by the weight of horror, unless gods are crazy from their knowledge, unless the fissures in their hearts have turned them around deep inside until all they see is fire and pain, unless gods have thus truly made us in their own image, I did not become as a god. Instead the fruit has made me looped and windowed, forked, bare, an animal more depraved than any beast, because I have tasted freedom and been poisoned by its awful truth forever, condemned to this emptiness. How beautiful and serene the history seems from this reach of time. Yes, the history calms me.

The golden age of Ronald Reagan was looking fairly rusty as it waned, I'm sorry to say. Iran-Contra hung over it like a fart at a perfume counter. Like Nancy, the stalwart core for whom Reagan was more a religion than a mere political brand, pretended the foul stench simply wasn't there. But the fact remained that it *was* there. What wasn't there was the president. There were quite lengthy periods in which he had no idea who he was, let alone a keen awareness of his responsibilities as leader of the most powerful nation in history and commander-in-chief of its armed forces, themselves then currently engaged in waging several wars around the globe. Admittedly, they were *small* wars.

There were of course a few responsible figures in the administration who wondered if it wasn't time to invoke the Constitutional Amendment that allowed a smooth transition of power from president to vice president in the event a president's mind suddenly turned to Swiss cheese. But there were also a good many thoroughly irresponsible crooks for whom a president without a functioning brain was like a fish without a bicycle and made the whole process of running criminal enterprises in the name of the US government so much simpler and smoother than it was when they first had to receive presidential approval thus had to not look like criminal enterprises, putting stress and strain on their perpetrators, who would be obliged to lie far more often than was good for their health, not to mention draw up entirely fictional proposals to conceal from the lily-livered, who were too weak to handle real issues like real men, a raw but genuine truth also deemed unpalatable. For example, the thriving business in cocaine trafficking that had been set up by the CIA and others, using US government airplanes and US military facilities, as a means of funding the right-wing Contra rebels in Nicaragua in their noble quest to overthrow the country's democratically elected socialist government, but without having to go through the irritating red tape and time-wasting rigmarole of asking Congress for money that it might easily refuse to grant anyway. If the quantity of unaccounted-for cash was anything to go by, this corporate-style narcotics importing enterprise funded a good deal more than the Contras. The agents in charge of the mission, for example, had had personal expenditures many times larger than their salaries for every year since the operation began. Ostensibly a wholesale business, it was not in fact that clear whether the agents were also retailing the cocaine, especially the hundreds of kilos they sold themselves at bargain prices.

The hovering stench of Iran-Contra, instead of going away, got larger and fouler, until the attention it drew made useful and enterprising business schemes like the cocaine importing impossible, whether the president's mind functioned or not. Various commissions probed the recesses of the astoundingly illegal dealings between Reagan's administration, the Iranians, the Contras, the Israelis and various other dubious concerns encountered along the circuitous route from Persia to Central America.

The US Congress itself concluded after its own investigation that Reagan's crew had exhibited "secrecy, deception and disdain for the law." All investigating bodies agreed that Reagan bore the ultimate responsibility for the actions of his aides, while admitting that his grip on the activities going on around him was probably not firm enough to accuse him of complicity. Numerous senior members in the administration were indicted on various charges connected to the arms deals, though, including the national security advisor, John Poindexter, who went on to be convicted on several felony counts of lying to Congress, obstruction of justice, conspiracy, and altering and destroying documents pertinent to the investigation. The convictions were all overturned on appeal, of course. Defense Secretary Caspar Weinberger ended up getting indicted for perjury, accused of lying to the Independent Counsel investigating Iran-Contra. He was pardoned by George H.W. Bush, whom the principle Tower

Commission went out of its way to reveal as innocent of any connection to the wickedness, a kindness for which the commission's key members were generously rewarded later on with high appointments in the Bush administration.

Also similarly rewarded were those up to their necks in Iran-Contra shenanigans who had kept their mouths shut no matter what the pressure or the enticements to talk. Bush even had to make Dan Quayle his vice president, in recognition of the fact that Quayle's law offices were a virtual sorting house for Iran-Contra business and its spawn of subsidiary enterprises and spin-off deals. Considering Quayle was so feeble minded it was a wonder he could feed himself—he once admitted he thought folks in Latin America spoke Latin—this was no mean sacrifice. Although some said the arrangement was Bush's insurance policy against assassination, an idea I for one did not buy, since Quayle, quacking fool that he was, still struck me as an improvement on the moral vacuum and pliable intellectual vacuity of Poppy Bush.

Iran-Contra should have buried all concerned or even vaguely connected with it, and certainly the entire Reagan crew, but it was carefully dulled in the public consciousness by an accommodating media. It should at least have left some robust food for thought, though, since the issues it raised were slightly crucial to the nature of the presidency, which had now begun the metamorphosis into a tyranny the like of which this world had never known in all the seven millennia charting humanity's subjugation under the heels and boots of ten thousand dictators, each one worse than any predecessors, all of them lacking that component we used to call the soul.

For instance, did the president have unconditional authority to conduct foreign policy over the objection of Congress and the laws it passed? Or could the president approve selling arms to a foreign nation without congressional approval? What information did the president have to provide to Congress and when should that information be supplied? What information did the president have to provide the American people? Could the president present factually incorrect information to the American people about key foreign policy initiatives if he believed his motives were just? What authority did Congress have to oversee functions of the executive branch? Did funding for foreign policy initiatives have to be approved by Congress? Who defined the entire spending budget and who regulated it? Was the provision of the 1978 Ethics in Government Act that created the position of independent counsel answering to the attorney general constitutional? What role did the Supreme Court have in deciding conflicts between the legislative branch and executive branch? And how much support was America entitled to provide to armed opposition forces seeking to replace governments with ones more sympathetic to the US?

Most, if not all, of the constitutional and ethical questions remained unresolved, unfortunately. If the American sheep had taken a little more interest in the machinations and strategies of those leading them inexorably to slaughter, their efforts would have been rewarded amply when they discovered they had been saving their own lives all along. Instead, they bleated and complained, following the sheep ahead along the winding track toward the abyss. I must have pointed out a thousand times that it looked to me that there were no legal remedies to fix the impasse arising if the legislative and executive branches of government did not wish to work together. I might as well have been claiming I saw fairies dancing on the White House lawn.

But once people have begun to slither down that slippery slope they cease to hear the cries of warning coming from below, knowing instantly that they have no way to get off the steepening slide any more and thus no use for cautionary imprecations.

Once Poppy had the helm, those who worked him like a glove puppet could finally steer the course directly.

The next fifteen years saw the steady erosion of ideals and the undermining of principles that it took many generations to earn. To the impartial observer it may have seemed to be error compounding error, yet it was not remotely anything to do with that. The dismantling of our republic was deliberate and planned, even if the deliberations were sly and underhand. Indeed, it was ripped apart as slowly and as methodically as it had been constructed, so few would notice the difference until nothing was recognizable at all.

This war on *us* had many fronts too, many distractions to lure suspicions away from the core tasks, yet every move was some part of the whole and vital in its elaborate and carefully controlled demolition.

Thus it is entirely appropriate for my purposes here to submit the transcript of a lecture I gave at Georgetown in 2005 on a theme of *Unacceptable Interventionism*. I was finally able to tackle the subject freely, too, able to be unapologetically and utterly objective at last—because I had by then resigned my State Department post, and was thus was no longer tormented by the censorious bogey-man of National Security.

Lecture at Georgetown University, October 17, 2005

Foreign Policy Limits in the Spreading of Democracy
During the past few years we have seen an acceleration of the number of "revolutions" breaking out all over the world. In November 2003, the president of Georgia Edward Shevardnadze was overthrown following demonstrations, marches and allegations that the parliamentary elections had been rigged. In November 2004, the "Orange Revolution" of demonstrations started in Ukraine as the same allegations were made, that elections had been rigged. The result was that Ukraine found itself ripped away from its previous geopolitical role as a bridge between East and West, and was placed on the

path to becoming a fully fledged member of NATO and the EU. Considering that Kievan Rus is the first Russian state, and that Ukraine has now been turned against Russia, this is a historic achievement. But then, as President George W. Bush said, "You are either with us or against us." Although Ukraine had sent troops to Iraq, it was evidently considered too friendly to Moscow.

Shortly after the US and the UN declared that Syrian troops had to be removed from Lebanon, and following the assassination of Rafik Hariri, demonstrations in Beirut were presented as "the Cedar Revolution." An enormous counterdemonstration by Hezbollah, which is the largest political party in Syria, was effectively ignored while the TV replayed endlessly the image of the anti-Syrian crowd. In one particularly egregious case of double-think, the BBC explained to its viewers that "Hezbollah, the biggest political party in Lebanon, is so far the only dissenting voice that wants the Syrians to stay." How can the majority be "a dissenting voice"?

After the "revolutions" in Georgia and Ukraine, many predicted that the same wave of "revolutions" would extend to the former Soviet states of Central Asia. And so it was to be. Commentators seemed divided on what color to label the uprising in Bishkek—was it a "lemon" revolution or a "tulip" revolution? They could not make up their minds. But on one thing, everyone was in agreement: revolutions are cool, even when they are violent. The Kyrgyz president, Askar Akayev, was overthrown on March 24, 2005 and protesters stormed and ransacked the presidential palace.

When armed rebels seized government buildings, sprung prisoners from jail and took hostages on the night of May 12–13 in the Uzbek city of Andijan (located in the Ferghana Valley, where the unrest had also started in neighboring Kyrgyzstan) the police and army surrounded the rebels and a long standoff ensued. Negotiations were undertaken with the rebels, who kept increasing their demands. When government forces started to move on the rebels, the resulting fighting killed some 160 people including over 30 members of the police and army. Yet the Western media immediately misrepresented this violent confrontation, claiming that government forces had opened fire on unarmed protesters—"the people."

This constantly repeated myth of popular rebellion against a dictatorial government is popular on both the left and the right of the political spectrum. Previously, the myth of revolution was obviously the preserve of the left. But when the violent putsch occurred in Kyrgyzstan, *The Times* enthused about how the scenes in Bishkek reminded him of Eisenstein films about the Bolshevik revolution, *The Daily Telegraph* extolled the "power to the people," and the *Financial Times* used a well-known Maoist metaphor when it praised Kyrgyzstan's "long march to freedom."

One of the key elements behind this myth is obviously that "the people" are behind the events, and that they are spontaneous. In fact, of course, they are often very highly organized operations, often deliberately staged for the media, and usually funded and controlled by transnational networks of so-called non-governmental organizations that are in turn instruments of Western power.

The survival of the myth of spontaneous popular revolution is depressing in view of the ample literature on the coup d'état, and on the main factors and tactics by which to bring one about. It was, of course, Lenin who developed the organizational structure for overthrowing a regime that we now know as a political party. He differed from Marx in that he did not think that historical change was the result of ineluctable anonymous forces, but that it had to be worked for.

But it was probably Curzio Malaparte's *Technique of a Coup D'état* that first gave very famous expression to these ideas. Published in 1931, this book presents regime change as just that—a technique. Malaparte explicitly took issue with those who thought that regime change happened on its own. In fact, he starts the book by recounting a discussion between diplomats in Warsaw in the summer of 1920: Poland had been invaded by Trotsky's Red Army (Poland having itself invaded the Soviet Union, capturing Kiev in April 1920) and the Bolsheviks were at the gates of Warsaw. The debate was between the British minister in Warsaw, Sir Horace Rumbold, and the Papal nuncio, Monsignor Ambrogio Damiano Achille Ratti—the man who was elected Pope as Pius XI two years later.

The Englishman said that the internal political situation in Poland was so chaotic that a revolution was inevitable, and that the diplomatic corps therefore should flee the capital and go to Posen. The Papal Nuncio disagreed, insisting that a revolution was just as possible in a civilized country like England, Holland or Switzerland as in a country in a state of anarchy. Naturally the Englishman was outraged at the idea that a revolution could ever break out in England. "Oh never!" he exclaimed— and was proved wrong because no revolution did break out in Poland, according to Malaparte because the revolutionary forces were simply not well organized enough.

This anecdote allows Malaparte to discuss the differences between Lenin and Trotsky, two practitioners of the coup d'état/revolution. Malaparte shows that the future Pope was right and that it was wrong to say that pre-conditions were necessary for a revolution to occur. For Malaparte, as for Trotsky, regime change could be promoted in any country, including the stable democracies of Western Europe, providing that there was a sufficiently resolute body of men determined to achieve it.

This brings us onto a second body of literature, concerning the manipulation of the media. Malaparte himself does not discuss this aspect but it is (a) of huge importance and (b) clearly a subset of the technique of a coup d'état in the way regime change is practiced today. So important, indeed, is the control of the media during regime change that one of the main characteristics of these revolutions is the creation of a virtual reality. Control of this reality is itself an instrument of power, which is why in classic coups in a banana republic the first thing that the revolutionaries seize is the radio station.

People experience a strong psychological reluctance to accept that political events today are deliberately manipulated. This reluctance is itself a product of the ideology of the information age, which flatters people's vanity and encourages them to believe that they have access to huge amounts of information.

In fact, the apparent multifarious nature of modern media information hides an extreme paucity of original sources, rather as a street of restaurants on a Greek waterfront can hide the reality of a single kitchen at the back. News reports of major events very often come from a single source, usually a wire agency, and even authoritative news outlets like the BBC simply recycle information that they have received from these agencies, presenting it as their own. BBC correspondents are often sitting in their hotel rooms when they send dispatches, very often simply reading back to the studio in London information they have been given by their colleagues back home off the wire. A second factor that explains the reluctance to believe in media manipulation is connected with the feeling of omniscience that the mass media age likes to flatter: to rubbish news reports as manipulated is to tell people that they are gullible, and this is not a pleasant message to receive.

There are many elements to media manipulation. One of the most important is political iconography. This is a very important instrument for promoting the legitimacy of regimes that have seized power through revolution. One need think only of such iconic events as the storming of the Bastille on July 14, 1789, the storming of the Winter Palace during the October revolution in 1917, or Mussolini's March on Rome in 1922, to see that events can be elevated into almost eternal sources of legitimacy.

However, the importance of political imagery goes far beyond the invention of a simple emblem for each revolution. It involves a far deeper control of the media, and generally this control needs to be exercised over a long period of time, not just at the moment of regime change itself. It is essential indeed, for the official party line to be repeated ad nauseam. A feature of today's mass media culture that many dissidents lazily and wrongly denounce as "totalitarian" is precisely that dissenting views may be expressed and published, but this is precisely because, being mere drops in the ocean, they are never a threat to the tide of propaganda.

One of the modern masters of such media control was the German Communist from whom Joseph Goebbels learned his trade, Willi Münzenberg. Münzenberg was not only the inventor of spin, he was also the first person who perfected the art of creating a network of opinion-forming journalists who propagated views that were germane to the needs of the Communist Party in Germany and to the Soviet Union. He also made a huge fortune in the process, since he amassed a considerable media empire from which he creamed off the profits.

Münzenberg was intimately involved with the Communist project from the very beginning. He belonged to Lenin's circle in Zurich, and in 1917 accompanied the future leader of the Bolshevik revolution to the Zurich Hauptbahnhof, from whence Lenin was transported in a sealed train, and with the help of the German imperial authorities, to the Finland Station in St. Petersburg.

Lenin then called on Münzenberg to combat the appalling publicity generated in 1921 when 25 million peasants in the Volga region started to suffer from the famine that swept across the newly created Soviet state. Münzenberg, who had by then returned to Berlin, where he was later elected to the Reichstag as a Communist deputy, was charged with setting up a bogus workers' charity, the Foreign Committee for the Organization of Worker Relief for the Hungry in Soviet Russia, whose purpose was to pretend to the world that humanitarian relief was coming from sources other than Herbert Hoover's American Relief Administration. Lenin feared not only that Hoover would use his humanitarian aid project to send spies into the USSR (which he did) but also, perhaps even more importantly, that the world's first Communist state would be fatally damaged by the negative publicity of seeing capitalist America come to its aid within a few years of the revolution.

After having cut his teeth on "selling" the death of millions of people at the hands of the Bolsheviks, Münzenberg turned his attention to more general propaganda activities. He amassed a large media empire, known as "the Münzenberg trust," which owned two mass circulation dailies in Germany, a mass circulation weekly, and that had interests in scores of other publications around the world. His greatest coups were to mobilize world opinion against America over the Sacco-Vanzetti trial (that of two anarchist Italian immigrants who were sentenced to death for murder in Massachusetts in 1921) and to counteract the Nazis' claim in 1933 that the Reichstag fire was the result of a Communist conspiracy.

The Nazis, it will be remembered, used the fire to justify mass arrests and executions against Communists, even though it now appears that the fire genuinely was started only by the man arrested in the building at the time, the lone arsonist Martinus van der Lubbe. Münzenberg actually managed to convince large sections of public opinion of the equal but opposite untruth to that peddled by the Nazis, namely that the Nazis had started the fire themselves in order to have a pretext for removing their main enemies.

The key relevance of Münzenberg for our own day is this: he understood the quintessential importance of influencing opinion formers. He targeted especially intellectuals, taking the view that intellectuals were especially easy to influence because

they were so vain. His contacts included many of the great literary figures of the 1930s, a large number of whom were
encouraged by him to support the Republicans in the Spanish
civil war and to make that into a cause-célèbre of Communist
anti-fascism. Münzenberg's tactics are of primary importance to
the manipulation of opinion in today's New World Order. More
then ever before, so-called "experts" constantly pop up on our
TV screens to explain what is happening, and they are always
vehicles for the official party line. They are controlled in various
ways, usually by money, flattery or academic recognition.

There is a second body of literature, which makes a slightly
different point from the specific technique that Münzenberg
perfected. This concerns the way in which people can be made
to react in certain collective ways by psychological stimuli.
Perhaps the first major theoretician of this was Sigmund Freud's
nephew, Edward Bernays, whose book *Propaganda* in 1928 said
that it was entirely natural and right for governments to organize public opinion for political purposes. The opening chapter
of his book has the revealing title, "Organizing chaos," and
Bernays writes,

> The conscious and intelligent manipulation of the organ-
> ized opinions and habits of the masses is an important
> element in democratic society. Those who manipulate this
> unseen mechanism of society constitute an invisible gov-
> ernment which is the true ruling power of our country.

Bernays says that, very often, the members of this invisible
government do not even know who the other members are.
Propaganda, he says, is the only way to prevent public opinion
descending into dissonant chaos. Bernays continued to work on
this theme after the war, editing *Engineering Consent* in 1955, a
title to which Edward Herman and Noam Chomsky alluded
when they published their *Manufacturing Consent* in 1988. The

connection with Freud is important because, as we shall see later, psychology is an extremely important tool in influencing public opinion. Two of the contributors to *Engineering Consent* make the point that every leader must play on basic human emotions in order to manipulate public opinion. For instance, Doris E. Fleischmann and Howard Walden Cutler write,

> Self-preservation, ambition, pride, hunger, love of family and children, patriotism, imitativeness, the desire to be a leader, love of play—these and other drives are the psychological raw materials which every leader must take into account in his endeavour to win the public to his point of view... To maintain their self-assurance, most people need to feel certain that whatever they believe about anything is true.

This was what Willi Münzenberg understood—the basic human urge for people to believe what they want to believe. Thomas Mann alluded to it when he attributed the rise of Hitler to the collective desire of the German people for "a fairy tale" over the ugly truths of reality.

Other books worth mentioning in this regard concern not so much modern electronic propaganda but the more general psychology of crowds. The classics in this regard are Gustave Le Bon's work *The Psychology of Crowds* (1895), Elias Canetti's *Crowds and Power* (*Masse und Macht*) (1980); and Serge Tchakhotine's *Le viol des foules par la propagande politique* (1939). All these books draw heavily on psychology and anthropology. There is also the magnificent oeuvre of one of my favorite writers, the anthropologist René Girard, whose writings on the logic of imitation (mimesis), and on collective acts of violence, are excellent tools for understanding why it is that public opinion is so easily motivated to support war and other forms of political violence.

After the war, many of the techniques perfected by the Communist Münzenberg were adopted by us, as has been magnificently documented by Frances Stonor Saunders' excellent work, *Who Paid the Piper?*, published here under the title *The Cultural Cold War*.

In minute detail, Stonor Saunders explains how, as the Cold War started, the Americans and the British started up a massive covert operation to fund anti-Communist intellectuals. The key point is that much of their attention and activity was directed at left-wingers, in many cases Trotskyites who had abandoned their support for the Soviet Union only in 1939, when Stalin signed his non-aggression pact with Hitler, and in many cases people who had previously worked for Münzenberg. Many of the figures who were at this juncture between Communism and the CIA at the beginning of the Cold War were future neoconservative luminaries, especially Irving Kristol, James Burnham, Sidney Hook and Lionel Trilling.

The left-wing and even Trotskyite origins of neoconservatism are well known—even if I still continue to be astonished by new details I discover, such as that Lionel and Diana Trilling were married by a rabbi for whom Felix Dzherzhinsky—the founder of the Bolshevik secret police, the Cheka (forerunner of the KGB), and the Communist equivalent of Heinrich Himmler—represented a heroic paragon. These left-wing origins are particularly relevant to the covert operations discussed by Stonor Saunders, because the CIA's goal was precisely to influence left-wing opponents of Communism, i.e., Trotskyites. The CIA's view was simply that right-wing anti-Communists did not need to be influenced, much less paid. Stonor Saunders quotes Michael Warner when she writes,

For the CIA, the strategy of promoting the Non-Communist Left was to become "the theoretical foundation of the agency's political operations against Communism over the next two decades."

This strategy was outlined in Arthur Schlesinger's *The Vital Center* (1949), a book that represents one of the cornerstones of what was later to become the neoconservative movement. Stonor Saunders writes,

> The purpose of supporting leftist groups was not to destroy or even dominate, but rather to maintain a discreet proximity to and monitor the thinking of such groups; to provide them with a mouthpiece so that they could blow off steam; and, in extremis, to exercise a final veto over their actions, if they ever got too "radical".

Many and varied were the ways in which this left-wing influence was felt. The US was determined to fashion for itself a progressive image, in contrast to the "reactionary" Soviet Union. In other words, it wanted to do precisely what the Soviets were doing. In music, for instance, Nicholas Nabokov (the cousin of the author of *Lolita*) was one of the Congress's main agents. In 1954, the CIA funded a music festival in Rome in which Stalin's "authoritarian" love of composers like Rimsky-Korsakov and Tchaikovsky was "countered" by unorthodox modern music inspired by Schoenberg's twelve-tone system.

> For Nabokov, there was a clear political message to be imparted by promoting music which announced itself as doing away with natural hierarchies...

Support for other progressives came when Jackson Pollock, himself a former Communist, was also promoted by the CIA. His daubs were supposed to represent the American ideology of "freedom" over the authoritarianism of socialist realist painting. (This alliance with Communists predates the Cold War: the Mexican Communist muralist, Diego Rivera, was supported by Abby Aldrich Rockefeller, but their collaboration ended abruptly when Rivera refused to remove a portrait of Lenin from a crowd scene painted on the walls of the Rockefeller Center in 1933.)

This crossover between culture and politics was explicitly promoted by a CIA body that went under an Orwellian name, the Psychological Strategy Board. In 1956, it covertly promoted a European tour by the Metropolitan Opera, the political purpose of which was to encourage multiculturalism. Junkie Fleischmann, the organizer, said,

> We, in the United States, are a melting-pot and, by being so, we have demonstrated that peoples can get along together irrespective of race, color or creed. Using the "melting-pot" or some such catch phrase for a theme we might be able to use the Met as an example of how Europeans can get along together in the United States and that, therefore, some sort of European Federation is entirely practicable.

This is exactly the same argument employed by, among other people, Ben Wattenberg, whose book *The First Universal Nation* argues that America has a special right to world hegemony because she embodies all the nations and races of the planet. The same view has also been expressed by Newt Gingrich and other neocons.

Other themes promoted include some that are at the forefront of neoconservative thinking today. First among these is the eminently liberal belief in moral and political universalism. Today, this is at the very heart of George W. Bush's own foreign policy philosophy: he has stated on numerous occasions that political values are the same all over the world, and he has used this assumption to justify US military intervention in favor of "democracy."

Back in the early 1950s, the director of the PSB (the Psychological Strategy Board was quickly referred to only by its initials, no doubt in order to hide its real name), Raymond Allen, had already arrived at this conclusion.

> The principles and ideals embodied in the Declaration of Independence and the Constitution are for export and... are the heritage of men everywhere. We should appeal to the fundamental urges of all men which I believe are the same for the farmer in Kansas as for the farmer in Punjab.

To be sure, it would be wrong to attribute the spread of ideas only to covert manipulation. They have their force in large-scale cultural currents, whose causes are multiple. But there is no doubt that the dominance of such ideas can be substantially facilitated by covert operations, especially since people in mass-information societies are curiously suggestible. Not only do they believe what they have read in the papers, they also think they have arrived at these conclusions themselves. The trick of manipulating public opinion, therefore, lies precisely in that which Bernays theorized, Münzenberg initiated, and that the CIA raised to a high art. According to CIA agent Donald Jameson,

> As far as the attitudes that the agency wanted to inspire through these activities are concerned, clearly what they would like to have been able to produce were people who, of their own reasoning and conviction, were persuaded that everything the United States government did was right.

To put it another way, what the CIA and other US agencies were doing during this period was to adopt the strategy that we associate with the Italian Marxist, Antonio Gramsci, who argued that "cultural hegemony" was essential for socialist revolution.

Finally, there is a huge body of literature on the technique of disinformation. I have already referred to the important fact,

originally formulated by Tchakhotine, that the role of journalists and the media is key in ensuring that propaganda is
constant: "Propaganda cannot take time off," he writes,
thereby formulating one of the key rules of modern disinformation, which is that the required message must be repeated very
frequently indeed if it is to pass.

> See in my line of work you got to keep repeating things
> over and over and over again for the truth to sink in, to kind
> of catapult the propaganda.
>
> *George W. Bush*

Above all, Tchakhotine says that propaganda campaigns
must be centrally directed and highly organized, something
that has become the norm in the age of modern political
"spin": British Labour Members of Parliament, for instance,
are not allowed to speak to the media without first asking
permission from the Director of Communications at 10
Downing Street.

Sefton Delmer was both a practician and theoretician of
such "black propaganda." Delmer created a bogus radio station that broadcast from Britain to Germany during WW II,
and that created the myth that there were "good" patriotic
Germans who opposed Hitler. The fiction was sustained that
the station was actually an underground German one, and
was put on frequencies close to those of official stations.
Such black propaganda has now become part of the US government's armory of "spin": *The New York Times* revealed
that the US government makes news reports favorable to its
policies that are then carried on normal channels and
presented as if they were the broadcast company's own
reports.[*]

[*] March 13, 2005, "Under Bush, a New Age of Pre-packaged Television
News," by David Barstow and Robin Stein

There are many other such authors. But perhaps the most relevant to today's discussion is Roger Mucchielli's book, *Subversion*, published in French in 1971, which shows how disinformation had moved from being an auxiliary tactic in war to a principal one. The strategy had developed so far, he said, that the goal was now to conquer a state without even attacking physically, especially through the use of agents of influence inside it. This is essentially what Robert Kaplan proposed and discussed in his essay for *The Atlantic Monthly* in July/August 2003, "Supremacy by Stealth." One of the most sinister theoreticians of the New World Order and the American empire, Robert Kaplan, explicitly advocates the use of immoral and illegal power to promote US control of the whole world. His essay deals with the use of covert operations, military power, dirty tricks, black propaganda, hidden influence and control, opinion forming and other things like political assassination, all subject to his overall call for "a pagan ethic," as the means to ensuring American domination.

The other key point about Mucchielli is that he was one of the first theoreticians of the use of bogus non-governmental organizations—or "front organizations" as they used to be known—for effecting internal political change in another state. Like Malaparte and Trotsky, Mucchielli also understood that it was not "objective" circumstances that determined the success or failure of a revolution, but instead the perception created of those circumstances by disinformation. He also understood that historical revolutions, which invariably presented themselves as the product of mass movements, were in fact the work of a tiny number of highly organized conspirators. In fact, again like Trotsky, Mucchielli emphasized that the silent majority must be rigorously excluded from the mechanics of political change, precisely because coups d'état are the work of the few and not the many.

Public opinion was the "forum" in which subversion was practiced, and Mucchielli showed the different ways in which the mass media could be used to create a collective psychosis. Psychological factors were extremely important in this regard, he said, especially in the pursuit of important strategies such as the demoralization of a society. The enemy must be made to lose confidence in the rightness of his own cause, while all effort must be made to convince him that his adversary is invincible.

One final historical point before we move onto a discussion of the present is that of the role of the military in conducting covert operations and influencing political change. This is something that some contemporary analysts are happy to admit is deployed today: Robert Kaplan writes approvingly of how the American military is and should be used to "promote democracy." Kaplan says deliciously that a phone call from a US general is often a better way of promoting political change in a third country than a phone call from the local US ambassador. And he approvingly quotes an Army Special Operations officer saying, "Whoever the president of Kenya is, the same group of guys run their special forces and the president's bodyguards. We've trained them. That translates into diplomatic leverage."

The historical background to this has recently been discussed by a Swiss academic, Daniele Ganser, in his book, NATO's Secret Armies. His account begins with the admission made on August 3, 1990 by Giulio Andreotti, the then Italian prime minister, that a secret army had existed in his country since the end of WW II, known as "Gladio"; that it had been created by the CIA and MI6; and that it was coordinated by the unorthodox warfare section of NATO.

He thereby confirmed one of the most long-running rumors in postwar Italy. Many people, including investigating magistrates, had long suspected that Gladio was not only part of a network of secret armies created by the Americans across Western Europe to fight in the resistance to a putative Soviet occupation, but also that these networks had become involved in influencing the outcome of elections, even to the extent of forming sinister alliances with terrorist organizations. Italy was a particular target because the Communist Party was so strong there.

Originally, this secret army was constructed with the aim of providing for the eventuality of an invasion. But it seems that they soon moved to covert operations aimed at influencing the political process itself, in the absence of an invasion. There is ample evidence that the Americans did indeed interfere massively, especially in Italian elections, in order to prevent the PCI from ever winning power. Tens of billions of dollars were funded to the Italian Christian Democrats by the US for this very reason.

Ganser even argues that there is evidence that Gladio cells carried out terrorist attacks in order to blame Communists, and to frighten the population into demanding extra state powers to "protect" them from terrorism. Ganser quotes the man convicted of planting one of these bombs, Vincenzo Vinciguerra, who duly explained the nature of the network of which he was a foot soldier. He said that it was part of a strategy "to destabilize in order to stabilize."

> You had to attack civilians, the people, women, children, innocent people, unknown people far removed from any political game. The reason was quite simple. They were supposed to force these people, the Italian public, to turn to the state to ask for greater security. This is the political logic which remains behind all the massacres and the bombings which remain unpunished, because the state cannot convict itself or declare itself responsible for what happened.

There is an obvious relevance to the conspiracy theories swirling around 9/11. Ganser presents a host of good evidence that this is indeed what Gladio did, and his arguments shed light on the intriguing possibility that there might also have been an alliance with extreme left-wing groups like the Red

Brigades. After all, when Aldo Moro was kidnapped, shortly after which he was assassinated, he was physically on the way to the Italian parliament to present a program for a coalition government between the Socialists and the Communists— precisely the thing the Americans were determined to prevent.

During my political career I have personally witnessed the same techniques for engineering coups d'états that are mentioned here deployed for similar goals.

From Chile to Lebanon via Kyrgyzstan, the iconography of revolution is always the same. The main tactics were perfected in Latin America during the 1970s and 1980s. Indeed, many of the operatives of regime change under Ronald Reagan and George Bush Sr. have happily plied their trade in the former Soviet bloc under Bill Clinton and George Bush Jr. For instance, General Manuel Noriega reports in his memoirs that the two CIA–State Department operatives who were sent to negotiate and then engineer his downfall from power in Panama in 1989 were named William Walker and Michael Kozak: William Walker resurfaced in Kosovo in January 1999 when, as head of the Kosovo Verification Mission, he oversaw the artificial creation of a bogus atrocity that proved to be the casus belli for the Kosovo war, while Michael Kozak became US ambassador to Belarus, where in 2001 he mounted "Operation White Stork" designed to overthrow the incumbent president, Alexander Lukashenko. During an exchange of letters to *The Guardian* in 2001, Kozak brazenly admitted that he was doing in Belarus exactly what he had been doing in Nicaragua and Panama, namely "promoting democracy."

There are essentially three branches to the modern technique of a coup d'état. They are

- non-governmental organizations,
- control of the media, and
- covert operatives.

Their activities are effectively interchangeable so I will not deal with them separately.

The overthrow of Slobodan Milŏsević was obviously not the first time the West used covert influence to effect regime change. The overthrow of Sali Berisha in Albania in 1997 and of Vladimir Mečiar in Slovakia in 1998 were heavily influenced by the West and, in the case of Berisha, an extremely violent uprising was presented as a spontaneous and welcome example of people power.

I personally observed how the international community, and especially the Organization for Security and Cooperation in Europe (OSCE), fiddled its election observation results in order to ensure political change. However, the overthrow of Slobodan Milŏsević in Belgrade on October 5, 2000 is important because he is such a well-known figure, and because the "revolution" that unseated him involved a very ostentatious use of "people power."

The background to the putsch against Milŏsević has been brilliantly described by Tim Marshall, a reporter for Sky TV. His account is valuable because he writes approvingly of the events he describes; it is also interesting because this journalist boasts of his extensive contacts with the secret services, especially those of Britain and America.

At every turn, Marshall seems to know who the main intelligence players are. His account is thick with references to "an MI6 officer in Priština," "sources in Yugoslav military intelligence," "a CIA man who was helping to put together the coup," an "officer in US naval intelligence," and so on. He quotes secret surveillance reports from the Serbian secret police; he knows who the ministry of defense desk officer is in London who draws up the strategy for getting rid of Milŏsević; he knows that the British foreign secretary's telephone conversations are being listened to; he knows who are the Russian intelligence officers who accompany Yevgeni Primakov, the

Russian prime minister, to Belgrade during the NATO bombing; he knows which rooms are bugged in the British embassy, and where the Yugoslav spies are who listen in to the diplomats' conversations; he knows that a staffer on the US House of Representatives International Relations Committee is, in fact, an officer in US naval intelligence; he seems to know that secret service decisions are often taken with the very minimal ministerial approval; he describes how the CIA physically escorted the KLA delegation from Kosovo to Paris for the pre-war talks at Rambouillet, where NATO issued Yugoslavia with an ultimatum it knew it could only reject; and he refers to "a British journalist" acting as a go-between between London and Belgrade for hugely important high-level secret negotiations, while people sought to betray one another as Milŏsević's power collapsed. (My suspicion is that he may be talking about himself at this point.)

One of the themes that inadvertently runs through his book is that there is a thin dividing line between journalists and spooks. Early on in the book, Marshall refers casually to "the inevitable connections between officers, journalists and politicians," saying that people in all three categories "work in the same area." He then goes on jokingly to say that "a combination of 'spooks,' 'journo's' and 'politicos,' added to 'the people'" were what had caused the overthrow of Slobodan Milŏsević. Marshall clings to the myth that "the people" were involved, but the rest of his book shows that in fact the overthrow of the Yugoslav president occurred only because of political strategies deliberately conceived in London and Washington to get rid of him.

Above all, Marshall makes it clear that, in 1998, the US State Department and intelligence agencies decided to use the Kosovo Liberation Army to get rid of Slobodan Milŏsević. He quotes one source saying, "The US agenda was clear. When the time was right they were going to use the KLA to provide the solution to the political problem"—the "problem" being, as Marshall explains earlier, Milŏsevic's continued political survival. This meant supporting the KLA's terrorist secessionism, and later fighting a war against Yugoslavia on its side.

Marshall quotes Mark Kirk, a US naval intelligence officer, saying that, "Eventually we opened up a huge operation against Milŏsevic, both secret and open." The secret part of the operation involved not only things like stuffing the various observer missions that were sent into Kosovo with officers from the British and American intelligence services, but also—crucially—giving military, technical, financial, logistical and political support to the KLA, which, as Marshall himself admits, "smuggled drugs, ran prostitution rackets and murdered civilians."

The strategy began in late 1998 when "a huge CIA mission (got) underway in Kosovo." President Milŏsevic had allowed the Kosovo Diplomatic Observer Mission to enter Kosovo to monitor the situation in the province. This ad hoc group was immediately stuffed with British and American intelligence agents and special forces—men from the CIA, US naval intelligence, the British SAS and something called "14th intelligence," a body within the British army that operates side by side with the SAS "to provide what is known as 'deep surveillance.'" The immediate purpose of this operation was "Intelligence Preparation of Battlefield"—a modern version of what the Duke of Wellington used to do, riding up and down the battlefield to get the lie of the land before engaging the enemy.

So as Marshall puts it, "Officially, the KDOM was run by the Organization for Security and Cooperation in Europe...unofficially, the CIA ran (it)...The organization was just packed with them...It was a CIA front." Many of the officers in fact worked for another CIA front, DynCorp, the Virginia-based company that employs mainly "members of US military elite units, or the CIA," as Marshall says. They used the KDOM, which later became the Kosovo Verification Mission, for espionage. Instead of doing the monitoring tasks assigned to them, officers would go off and use their global positioning devices to locate and identify targets that would be later bombed by NATO. Quite how the Yugoslavs could allow 2,000 highly trained secret service agents to roam around their territory is difficult to understand, especially since, as Marshall shows, they knew perfectly well what was going on.

The head of the Kosovo Verification Mission was William Walker, the man deputed to oust Manuel Noriega from power in Panama, and a former ambassador to El Salvador whose US–supported government ran death squads. Walker "discovered" the "massacre" at Račak in January 1999, the event that was used as a pretext for starting the process that led to the bombing which began on March 24.

There is much evidence to suggest that Račak was staged, and that the bodies found were in fact those of KLA fighters, not civilians as was alleged. What is certain is that Walker's role was so important that the country road in Kosovo that leads to Račak has now been renamed after him. Marshall writes that the date for the war—spring 1999—was not only decided in late December 1998, but also communicated to the KLA at the time. This means that when the "massacre" occurred and when Madeleine Albright declared, "Spring has come early," she was behaving rather like Joseph Goebbels who, on hearing the news of the Reichstag fire in 1933, is supposed to have remarked, "What, already?"

At any rate, when the KVM was withdrawn on the eve of the NATO bombing, Marshall says that the CIA officers in it gave all their satellite phones and GPS equipment to the KLA. "The KLA were being trained by the Americans, partially equipped by them, and virtually given territory," Marshall writes—even though he, like all other reporters, helped propagate the myth of systematic Serb atrocities committed against a totally passive Albanian civilian population.

The war went ahead, of course, and Yugoslavia was fero-
ciously bombed. But Milŏsević stayed in power. So London
and Washington started what Marshall happily calls "political
warfare" to remove him. This involved giving very large sums
of money, as well as technical, logistical and strategic
support, and including arms, to various "democratic opposition" groups and "non-governmental organizations" in
Serbia. The Americans were by then operating principally
through the International Republican Institute, which had
opened offices in neighboring Hungary for the purpose of getting rid of Slobodan Milŏsević. "It was agreed" at one of their
meetings, Marshall explains, "that the ideological arguments
of pro-democracy, civil rights and a humanitarian approach
would be far more forceful if accompanied, if necessary, by
large bags full of money." These, and much else besides,
were duly shipped into Serbia through the diplomatic bags—
in many cases of apparently neutral countries like Sweden
who, by not participating formally in the NATO war, were able
to maintain full embassies in Belgrade. As Marshall helpfully
adds, "Bags of money had been brought in for years."
Indeed they had. As he earlier explains, "independent"
media outlets like the Radio Station B92 (which is Marshall's
own publisher) were, in fact, very largely funded by the US.
Organizations controlled by George Soros also played a crucial role, as they were later to do, in 2003–4, in Georgia. The
so-called "democrats" were, in reality, nothing but foreign
agents—just as the Yugoslav government stolidly maintained
at the time.

Marshall also explains something that is now a matter of
public record: that it was also the Americans who conceived
the strategy of pushing forward one candidate, Vojislav
Koštunica, to unite the opposition. Koštunica had the main
advantage of being largely unknown by the general public.
Marshall then describes how the strategy also involved a

carefully planned coup d'état, which duly took place after the first round of the presidential elections. He shows in minute detail how the principal actors in what was presented on Western TV screens as a spontaneous uprising of "the people" were, in fact, a bunch of extremely violent and very heavily armed thugs under the command of the mayor of the town of Čačak, Velimir Ilić. It was Ilić's ten-mile-long convoy carrying "weapons, paratroopers and a team of kick boxers" to the federal parliament building in Belgrade. As Marshall admits, the events of October 5, 2000 "looked more like a coup d'état" than the people's revolution of which the world's media so naively gushed at the time.

Many of the tactics perfected in Belgrade were used in Georgia in November 2003 to overthrow President Edward Shevardnadze. The same allegations were made, and repeated ad nauseam, that the elections had been rigged. (In the Georgian case, they were parliamentary elections, in the Yugoslav case presidential.)

Western media uncritically took up these allegations, which were made long before the actual voting took place. A propaganda war was unleashed against both presidents, in Shevardnadze's case after a long period in which he had been lionized as a great reformer and democrat. Both "revolutions" occurred after a similar "storming of the parliament," broadcast live on TV. Both transfers of power were brokered by the Russian minister, Igor Ivanov, who flew to Belgrade and Tbilisi to engineer the exit from power of the incumbent president. Last but not least, the US ambassador was the same man in both cases: Richard Miles.

The most visible similarity, however, came in the use of a student movement known as Otpor (Resistance) in Serbia and Kmara (It's enough!) in Georgia. Both movements had the same symbol, a black-on-white stencil of a clenched fist. Otpor trained people from Kmara, and both were supported by the

US. And both organizations were ostensibly structured along Communist lines—combining the appearance of a diffuse structure of autonomous cells with the reality of highly centralized Leninist discipline.

As in Georgia, the role played by US money and covert operations has been revealed—but only after the event. During the events, the television was full of wall-to-wall propaganda about how "the people" rose up against Shevardnadze. All images that counteracted the optimistic view were suppressed, or glossed over, such as the fact that the "march on Tbilisi" led by Mihkail Saakashvili started off in Gori, Stalin's birthplace, beneath a statue of the former Soviet tyrant who remains a hero to many Georgians. The media were equally unconcerned when the new president, Saakashvili, was confirmed in office by elections that awarded him the Stalinist majority of 96 percent.

In the case of Ukraine, we observe the same combination of work by Western-backed non-governmental organizations, the media and the secret services. The non-governmental organizations played a huge role in delegitimizing the elections before they occurred. Allegations of widespread fraud were constantly repeated. In other words, the street protests that broke out after the second round, which Yanukovich won, were based on allegations that had been flying around before the beginning of the first round. The main NGO behind these allegations, the Committee of Ukrainian Voters, receives not one penny from Ukrainian voters, being instead fully funded by Western governments. Its office was decorated with pictures of Madeleine Albright and indeed the National Democratic Institute was one of its main affiliates. It pumped out constant propaganda against Yanukovich.

During the events themselves, I was able to document some of the propaganda abuses. They involved mainly the endless repetition of electoral fraud practiced by the government; the constant cover-up of fraud practiced by the opposition; the frenetic selling of Viktor Yushchenko, one of the most impressively boring men on earth, as a charismatic politician; and the ridiculously unlikely story that he had been deliberately poisoned by his enemies. (No prosecutions have been brought on this matter so far.)

The fullest account of the propaganda and fraud is given by the British Helsinki Human Rights Group's report, "Ukraine's Clockwork Orange Revolution." An interesting explanation of the role played by the secret services was also given in *The New York Times* by C. J. Chivers who explained that the Ukrainian KGB had been working for Yushchenko all along—in collaboration with the Americans of course. Other important articles on the same subject include Jonathan Mowat's "The New Gladio in Action: Washington's New World Order 'Democratization' Template," which details how military doctrine has been adapted to effect political change, and how various instruments, from psychology to bogus opinion polls, are used in it. Mowat is particularly interesting on the theories of Dr. Peter Ackermann, the author of *Strategic Non-Violent Conflict* and of a speech entitled "Between Hard and Soft Power: The Rise of Civilian-Based Struggle and Democratic Change," delivered at the State Department in June 2004. Mowat is also excellent on the psychology of crowds and its use in these putsches: he draws attention to the role of "swarming adolescents" and "rebellious hysteria" and traces the origins of the use of this for political purposes to the Tavistock Institute in the 1960s: that institute was created by the British Army as its psychological warfare arm after WW I and its illustrious alumni include Dr. David Owen, the former British foreign secretary and Dr. Radovan Karadžić, the former president of the Bosnian Serb Republic. Mowat recounts how the ideas formulated there by Fred Emery were taken up by one Dr. Howard Perlmutter, a professor of "Social Architecture" at the Wharton School, and a follower of Dr. Emery, who stressed that "rock video in Katmandu," was an appropriate image of how states with traditional cultures could be destabilized, thereby creating the possibility of a "global civilization." There are two requirements for such a transformation, he added, "building internationally committed networks of international and locally committed organizations," and "creating global events" through "the transformation of a local event into one having virtually instantaneous international implications through mass-media."

These are the victims of US foreign policy operations to date:

Panama	*1989*
Serbia	*2000*
Belarus	*2001*
Venezuela	*2003*
Georgia	*2003*
Ukraine	*2004*
Kyrgyzstan	*2005*
Lebanon	*2005*

You know me well enough by now to trust I can distinguish truth from fiction. None of this is conspiracy theory—it is conspiracy fact. The United States considers as a matter of official policy that the promotion of democracy is an important element of its overall national security strategy. Large sections of the State Department, the CIA, para-governmental agencies like the National Endowment for Democracy, and government-funded NGOs like the Carnegie Endowment for International Peace, which publishes several works on "democracy promotion," are devoted to it. All these operations have one thing in common: they involve the interference, sometimes violent, of Western powers, especially the US, in the political processes of other states, and that interference is very often used to promote the quintessential revolutionary goal, regime change.

You young men and women sitting here today will—many of you—comprise the governments of tomorrow. I leave it to your judgment to decide whether or not this is an acceptable policy for the United States of America to pursue, whether or not it exceeds the bounds of legality, and whether or not it is constitutional. It has been a privilege to take up so much of your valuable time, and I thank you for it.

★　★　★

There was a pattern too of infinitely more violent versions of regime change, which were later pointedly called by some "Wars of Mass Destruction." Iraq was the most shameful and egregious example. Poppy Bush's initial limp-wristed attempt to oust Saddam Hussein—terminated at the request of the Saudis—was followed by twelve years of bombing and sanctions that reduced the most prosperous, Westernized and secular of all Arab states to a wasteland of horrendous violence and Islamist fervor. One of the few political promises Poppy ever kept was the one saying he would return Iraq to "a pre-industrial condition."

The pretext used by us to attack Baghdad had been Saddam's invasion of Kuwait. He had reasonably legitimate grievances with the Kuwaitis over money owed, oil stolen and territory disputed, and he had consulted with our ambassador, April Glaspie, over the issue. She was quite clearly instructed to give Saddam a green light, claiming we would remain neutral—"have no opinion"—during any Arab–Arab dispute. We had our own problems with the Kuwaitis too. They were destabilizing the money markets by shifting from one currency to another with their bottomless well of petrodollars, and although we had asked them to cut it out several times, they were having too much fun making so much money, and they kept on doing it. The Kuwaiti royals always did whatever they wanted to do regardless of how it affected others. Unsurprisingly, this sort of behavior had not endeared them to other Arabs, many of whom had received at one time or other the dubious privilege of working for the royal al-Sabah enterprises—an experience usually likened to the punishments of hell. Nothing bad that happened to Kuwait or its haughty princelings would elicit an atom of sympathy anywhere between the Persian Gulf and the shores of the Atlantic Ocean. It was not so much that the al-Sabahs were regarded as un-Arab in their arrogance and greed, but rather that the Arab consensus questioned even their claim of being human.

Besides, no one thought Saddam would take *all* of Kuwait. We might even have let him keep the disputed territories, but he got both irrational and greedy.

CHAPTER TWELVE

★ ★ ★

*Legum servi sumus ut liberi esse possimus** (Cicero)

I WAS AS CLOSE TO THE CENTER OF power in Washington DC as I would have thought it was possible to get without actually holding that power oneself. Every day I met with the most senior officials in the administration. I reported directly to the secretary of state. I was intimately involved with creating the nation's foreign policy, yet I knew nothing of an entire gallery of squalid imperial schemes, ranging from murder to grand larceny, that had also become our stock in trade as leader of the free world. It was as if there were two governments, the one the public had elected, and the one that elected itself and didn't consult with or listen to the advisers for whom the taxpayers paid for their brilliance and skill in the arts of diplomacy. There was a whole other world that was utterly impenetrable for those of us not invited into it.

It was not until Gulf War One had ended, in the spring of '91, that the mystery of Les Melton's disappearance was finally solved. Les resurrected himself and called from New York saying he needed to see me urgently. But not at work, nor anywhere populous or trendy.

Although the four of us had not seen a lot of one another since we'd stopped sharing a house, it is incorrect to assume

---

* We are slaves of the law so that we may be able to be free.

friendship's embers had cooled down or died. I was especially fond of Les and had generally made a point of calling him at least once a month. He was a cheerful light-hearted soul, normally, and his company was a pleasure, so to hear his frail voice now creaking with emotion disturbed me to the core. The last time we had spoken at any length he had been working for Bowman, Tretherne & Pitt, a small firm of merchant bankers with some very large overseas contracts, so I naturally assumed his career had invaded his life, as mine had done, and was now a trigger-happy army of occupation, suspicious of intruders. I didn't push him for information on the phone, as much for my own protection as his, but I did meet him at Dulles Airport later that night.

He came hurrying through the gate holding just a briefcase, looking around with the pained eyes of a hunted animal. Something reddish had stained his tie, which also had egg on it. He was pale, and perspiring like a man in the tropics. We walked swiftly over to where I'd parked, and Les kept looking behind even when he was sitting in the passenger seat and we were driving toward the freeway. This kind of behavior is catching if one is an empathetic person.

Before long, I couldn't bear the tension, which hotwired steel filaments from Paranoia Central into my own nervous system. I felt as if I'd chewed a pound of dark roast coffee beans. The tendons in my neck were taut as reinforcing rods, and my mouth was so dry I could have stored rare stamps in it. I took a deep breath, feeling my lungs inflate with papery snaps and dusty crackles like an old Chinese lantern opened in the dark. I had no other option than to ask him what was wrong.

"You do realize," I told him, "you're behaving like a parody of someone on the run?"

"They said they'd kill me," he said, in a blank whisper that everyone within fifty yards would hear. "Just like that. They'd take away my life and leave me nothing, not even an explanation."

"Who would? Who did?"

"I wish to God I'd never met that monster, Parks," he said. "It's him. He's behind this."

"Parks?"

"You'll never be able to connect him, though. They've become so fucking clever with this global corporation stuff."

"Which stuff?" I asked.

"The Right Stuff, of course—the wrong stuff gets terminated with obscene prejudice before anyone can say it was ever there."

"Les, for Christ's sake ease up, old man. You're not making sense."

I got him to breathe slowly and deeply. As we drove in circles around DC, he started to tell me the whole story, starting at the beginning and heading for the end, in a language we both spoke.

When he'd begun working as a partner in the law firm that Parks had found for him, he was handed a file of clients apparently belonging to a partner who had just retired. Each of these clients ran companies registered offshore that were all subsidiaries of Azel Mahoon, the multinational electronics combine. There was a considerable backlog of paperwork, which took up the first three months Les was there. He tried to see each client to introduce himself and discuss aspects of their legal work that were not clear. Now he had only one client left to see, a man named Stelle, whose assistant acknowledged he was hard to reach a lot of the time. Les spoke to her on several occasions, and during the course of one of their conversations she let it slip that Stelle had not in fact dealt with any lawyer at the firm before Les Melton. So Les started snooping around the office, looking through old files, poking his nose into encrypted folders, following hunches, whims and links. He very soon concluded there had been no retired partner. But he was merely puzzled by this. He certainly didn't think it worth pursuing with the other partners. Perhaps it was just a silly joke?

A few weeks later, he managed to set up a meeting with Stelle, a lunch in Palm Beach, but when he arrived at the location, it didn't exist. There was no such address. He tried telephoning Stelle's assistant but he couldn't get hold of her, and the Florida number he had was out of service. He tried a different combination of digits for the address, but still had no luck. He tried the directory: no Stelle listed. Then, just as he was about to get a cab back to the airport, a chauffeured Lincoln pulled up in front of him, and who should be sitting in the back but V.S. Parks. Les found it a bit too much of a coincidence, and he said so forcefully. Then Parks showed him a Marine Corps photo ID that tagged him as "Lt. Col. Vernon Stelle Parks": *he's* Stelle. Why the deception?

Parks didn't answer but instead told him that Azel Mahoon was eager to get the contract to develop a satellite launching facility for the tiny Central American state of Auroco. He wanted Les to persuade Auroco's current dictator, General Puandaro, that Azel Mahoon was the only choice possible for such a vast and complex project. Parks conceded that Les would need special training to do this, and a familiarity with the company's various divisions, and so he'd already arranged for him to join an intensive course starting the following day right there in Palm Beach.

Les showed up at the appointed time to find the place was a government facility evidently doing bogus ecological research but in reality doing something else involving spooks and weapons. He was ordered to sign in, and discovered he'd just signed a National Security Act document promising he would not reveal anything he saw, heard, or did while at the facility.

"I was still feeling flattered," said Les. "You know, selected for special services, secret training, that sort of thing.... *Singled out for glory* ... It doesn't happen often...."

He was then given basic field operative training, how to detect a tail, lose a tail, be a tail, that sort of thing. Then he was handed over to a higher-level fellow, who told him the official name for the work he was being trained to do was Economic Hit Man, always abbreviated to EHM. Once you were in this kind of work, he was told with grim finality, you never got out of it. This was when Les began to feel scared. He described what the job entailed in simple terms so I wouldn't be bogged down in details, assuring me every few minutes that he was not exaggerating:

He would go to a country like Auroco to create a long-term economic plan for them. While there he would identify and cultivate a ruling elite, arranging for members of it lavish sinecures for adding their names to various boards, committees, commissions, or councils, and promising them Uncle Sam would make sure they remained in power. The key part of his long-term plan would be a vast project, a dam, a port, a satellite launching facility, something that would generally benefit these elites far more than it would the ordinary people. Les would then arrange for the state to get a loan from the World Bank or IMF, on condition the mega-project's tender was awarded to one of five or six major American companies without taking any bids. There was no real competition anyway because the nature of the job determined who got it. If it was big infrastructural construction, dams and so on, it went to Bechtel; oil industry upgrading and sinking new wells was Halliburton; airports were more cooperative ventures; sea ports, the Carlyle Group.

"You get the picture," stated Les. "The World Bank or IMF money mostly went straight into the pockets of a small band of super-wealthy US citizens—the same highly connected industrialist oligarchy you always see first in line at the Defense Budget tax trough or wherever the anticipated pour-off exceeds a few hundred million."

"But who is actually employing you at this point?" I asked him. "The US Government?"

"Of course not," he said. "I work for Bowman, Tretherne & Pitt, who've been hired as consultants by the State of Auroco."

"So it's pure fraud?" I said, unable to take it all in. "Is that your function?"

"Oh, no," Les told me. "Once I had redistributed global wealth more equitably for a US billionaire elite, my function was essentially to bankrupt the country. Construction costs would keep getting higher, so the World Bank or IMF, at my behest, would loan the little nation more and more cash, until it had amassed a debt larger than it could ever conceivably repay. Soon, all that stands between it and financial ruin is Uncle Sam's *largesse*."

"Why would we want to create a situation like this?" I said. It didn't make any sense to me.

"The place is, of course, an ally for life by this stage," Les explained. "Its reps will vote whichever way America votes at the UN, and it will always send a dozen soldiers, plucked from an army largely ceremonial in nature, to join the latest Coalition of the Willing—if not always exactly able—to fight beside us in our wars."

"We don't need a dozen soldiers, Les."

"No," he agreed. "What we need is their UN vote. But the real point is that this little fledgling state's seat of government will always from now on be here. It's a fucking *empire*..."

"Where does World Bank and IMF money come from?" I asked.

"It's a fund contributed to by the G7-8-9—the earth's fat-cat nations."

"They *have* to be aware what's going on, surely?" I said.

"When the Warlord of the Ostrogoths went to visit the emperor in Rome," said Les, "what did he have to remember not to leave home without?"

Tribute. All Rome required of the conquered was their annual cash payments, on time, in full.

"Jesus," I said, "it's just the Mafia writ large and global."

"Don't be tempted to say 'sophisticated' or 'grown up,'" Les told me. "Because it isn't. It's business as usual."

Les was informed that if he failed, the real hit men would be sent in, the covert ops guys. If *they* failed, the army would go in— and the army never failed. This is what had happened in Panama. The public was told that Noriega, the dictator, was a conduit for the Columbian drug cartels, a bad man. Because he *looked* like a bad man with his brutal pock-marked face, we didn't give it a second thought. He was tried in Florida and then thrown in jail. By his own account, however, Noriega had refused to channel money and weapons to the Nicaraguan Contras when asked to do so by marine Lieutenant Colonel Oliver North.

"—and *that's* why he was removed from power," said Les. "North is CIA."

"You never know who to believe," I said. "Everyone involved is some kind of crook, spook, carpetbagger, or they have a crate full of axes and an electric whetstone."

"The trouble is," Les said, "not precisely *everyone* is a crook. That's *our* cynicism, because the world still has a few decent honest men."

I looked Les straight in the eye, saying, "You knew the CIA wasn't doing social work."

"Of course," Les said. "But they've had the Cold War to keep them busy until recently. You can't untrain a team of assassins. We cut back funding, of course, but then they start getting entrepreneurial. They're self-funding through narcotics trafficking, David. They're fucking blowing back on us."

I sighed, pinching the bridge of my nose. My sinuses had been bothering me for months, and my eyes were strained.

"The agency was ostensibly created to counter the Soviet spy networks." I said. "A lot of people have been saying it ought to have been dismantled when the Berlin Wall came down. This is ridiculous."

"I haven't finished," Les said.

He had been flown to Auroco to begin his first project. But he soon discovered General Puandaro knew exactly what he was up to, and wanted no part of it. Les at first had wondered if his life was in danger. Was it like being caught spying? But Puandaro did not evidently take it personally at all, and continued using Les as an economic advisor. Gradually, the two men had become friends.

"He genuinely cared about his country," Les said. "He wasn't about to plunge it into debt, and he also had a financial plan of his own to finance the satellite launching facility—which was something they did actually *want* to build. It's a perfect business for Auroco. They even had advance orders for telecommunications satellites already from several small countries. Auroco is situated ideally for such launches, and the General's plan would have had the construction paid off within five years."

"He'd obviously never worked with Bechtel," I said.

"No, no," Les told me. "Puandaro wanted to award the contract to a Brazilian company, do you see?"

Les had felt obliged to tell Puandaro what would happen when Washington was informed of this. The general had taken it philosophically. He'd survived dangerous times before and could do it again.

At this point, Les had discovered his room had been broken into and his mission journal was missing. He suspected Puandaro's people at first, but then realized it must be the work of CIA assets who had infiltrated the Auroco military. This was as deep into intrigue and danger as Les Melton had ever wanted to get. Now he wanted out. But he felt almost certain he would not be allowed out. He was a liability to them. He became increasingly sure his every move and conversation was now being observed, and he did his best to make it seem everything was normal. He returned to New York on routine B.T. & P business, and even had a flight back booked for the following day. He wasn't tailed though, because he'd walked straight out the

BTP building's back door onto Wall Street and hailed a cab. He saw the tail parked across from the building half an hour later on his way to LaGuardia.

He gave me a nervous little smile, acknowledging this little triumph in a war he was otherwise certain to lose. But he couldn't even sustain the crease in his cheeks for more than five seconds before the smile became a twitch.

"They don't let you out, do they?" he asked me. "You have to stay in, working for them..."

He knew he wouldn't be able to handle much more of it. When they found out, they would probably kill him.

"Won't they, David?"

I felt certain he was right about this, but I did not know enough about covert ops and how the CIA functioned to come up with any useful advice to give him.

"My life is over," said Les. "I don't want to die. What should I do?"

All I could immediately suggest was that he stay with Abbie and me, while I tried to track down Parks and work out a deal of some sort myself. Les was literally trembling in the seat. He kept thanking me, and apologizing for being such a nuisance. I had to pull the car over and tell him to stop it.

"You're the brother I never had, Les," I said, giving his shoulder a pat. "You don't *ever* have to thank me. Not ever. I know you'd do the same if I were in trouble."

It was one of those awkward flashes of truth: because I knew the moment the words left my mouth that Les would not have done the same for me had the tables been turned.

It began to rain, and the water droplets sliding down the windows made the city's reflections look like glass offices and glass monuments that were on fire and slowly melting, cracking apart from larger structures, cascading into a crunchy luminous doom while burning crystal ropes were thrown to aid survivors and the wipers kept a tyrannically dull rhythm, *thump-thump, thump-thump*. I put my arms around his shuddering shoulders, the way an older brother would.

"It's the least I can do," I said. "Sometimes the least is all you can do, you know what I mean?"

I didn't know myself what I meant, so I am sure Les had no clue. But if there were any lingering doubts about the veracity of his story, they were soon put to rest.

Three days later, General Puandaro's Sikorsky helicopter blew up shortly after takeoff, crashing into the rip tide of a rocky cove. There were no survivors.

I met with Parks that very day, but before news of the crash came in. He was waiting for me in the lobby of the Sherry Netherlands Hotel, as agreed, but I wasn't staying at the hotel, and neither, I suspect, was he. We walked over to Central Park, talking. The haunted bare trees and the filthy crusts of snow still lingering on from a winter that seemed endless made for a desolate landscape, but one that suited our exchange perfectly.

Parks was bristling with hostility, unable to look me in the eye, the shoulders of his immaculately tailored camel overcoat raised almost level with the brim of a slate gray fedora he wore turned down on all sides. I had to invoke A-3 and remind him we were supposed to be good friends before he remotely calmed down. I told him Les was terrified for his life, and that I disapproved of this tremendously. I also told him I did not like the back channels through which he, Luposki and others operated.

"Imagine our fucking consternation," said Parks, the sarcasm flying off his words like slime from a wet dog.

"This isn't a moral or ethical judgment, Parks," I said, making sure he noticed that I was as angry as he had ever seen me.

"So what is it then, stylistic critique?" he said, sneering. "Or peer review, perhaps?"

"It's the fact that you don't know what it is," I said. "*That's* what it is."

"Funny," said Parks, "but I was just going to say that myself. Because you're the one whose ivory tower's under siege, if I'm not mistaken. You're the one who has to be dragged kicking and screaming into the twentieth century, when—*guess what?*—we're virtually in the twenty-first century, Leverett! And here they do things *differently*. They do them *my* way."

"And this will be how you explain it to the American people, will it?" I said. "The world's a bad place, but it's okay, because I'm badder. You should hear yourself, Parks. You sound like Al Capone running for office."

"From each his power to each his need, eh?" said Parks, coldly. "You take care of your needs and leave the power to those able to use it." He spat out something distasteful, pausing for a few seconds to clear his throat before adding, "I never realized what a self-righteous fool you were."

"My God," I said, "you're trampling over the ideals on which this country was founded, and *for which* it was founded...*and you don't even care, do you?*"

Parks stepped in front of me, stopping me dead in my tracks. He was standing so close to me I could smell the tobacco on his breath and see the yellowish stains on his pupils.

"If you ever question my loyalty to this country again," he said, in little more than a low whisper, "I will hack off your limbs one by one with a butcher's cleaver and feed them to alligators while you watch. Is that clear?"

He was serious, I realized, or serious enough to warrant caution. But I was not going to show him fear because something told me that would be more dangerous than antagonizing him further.

"Oh, your patriotism made you do it, I *see*," I told him, side-stepping his block to walk on ahead along the footpath, forcing him to run a few steps and fall in beside me again. "All that is clear to me, Parks," I said, "is that you are a *very* misguided man if you can justify this to yourself. You're completely at liberty, of course, to fool yourself in any way you like—and I'd fight for your right to do it—because the conscience will always be a free country no matter what people like you do with the rest of the world. Just don't ever try justifying it to me, because I am never going to see things your way. Is *that* clear?"

"You are consigning yourself to irrelevance," Parks said, a little less certainly than before, "as is your right. Yet I cannot help wondering why an intelligent man would do this to himself."

We had by now reached the area of parkland opposite that grim gothic edifice, the Dakota Building, where the widow of John Lennon had created a memorial garden to promote the hope for world peace and other nice things. An enormous black man was shoveling up last year's rotted leaves with this one's ice and trash, his shovel making a frighteningly human sound as it bit into concrete. Parks paused to retie a shoelace that had been trying to make him trip over and fall on his face for some minutes now. I was sorry it hadn't succeeded.

"We have rockets that can go to Mars," he growled, fumbling over the shoe, "yet we're still stuck with these fucking things on our feet."

The black man's shovel let out a howl of pain, and we both instinctively turned to see, framed in the rectangle of ground it had cleared, the word IMAGINE. It was set in a kaleidoscope of marble mosaic.

Noticing our attention to his labors, the man gave us a smile of inordinate sweetness and light, saying in a voice like a tiger's purr, "Yeah, yeah, that's all it take, don't it? The ol' world don't *have* to be this way. That's what Johnny tellin' us, man...*That's* what he sayin'. You have yo'selves a real nice day now."

Parks nodded at him, rolling his eyes to me.

"It's New York," he muttered, pulling the bow tight on his shoe.

"You and me, Parks," I said, shaking my head, "we're not the same species, are we? I've only just realized that there isn't room for both of us on this planet. This isn't a difference of opinion, a debate, not even an argument, is it? This is *genocide*."

We walked on again, passing a bench where a boy and girl kissed like drowning swimmers, clinging to each other for dear life.

"Spare me the metaphors and melodrama," said Parks. "I wasn't at Oxford, but I was at Harvard, so a little sophistry doesn't impress me."

"We may not have a perfect society here," I said, "but it's as good, if not better, than any other on the planet."

"Yawn," said Parks, veering over onto the 65th Street Transverse Road and disdainfully looking at his wristwatch. "What time does this end?"

We began heading back toward Columbus Circle. I ignored his rudeness and carried on with what I'd been saying:

"And although the Constitution doesn't protect it *perfectly*, it protects it at least sufficiently to keep it alive still." I pushed him gently with one hand, and said, "And I'm going to make sure it stays that way, because your America and my America cannot exist in the same space together. We don't have room for you."

I could tell the push, gentle as it was, had rattled him.

"With all due respect, old chap," Parks said, looking over at me and smirking, "you're not really in a position to be making any demands of me. You seem to forget there's a president down in DC for whom you work, to whom you are *answerable*. No matter how much old money and class you have, Leverett, *you* take orders *here*. Here *you're* not the boss. And *you* have not been doing the job that was asked of you, have you? Why is a policy planner sticking his snout into covert operations that are designed to protect this great nation from the jealousy and envy of her enemies? This little business with your friend

Melton makes you a traitor…technically speaking, I mean. Were you aware of this?"

"Let's see what cards you're holding, Parks," I said, laughing at him. "Yes, that's right, I'm calling your bluff."

He was silently furious, but trying not to show it.

"*Traitor*," I said again, trying to goad him. "It's absolute nonsense, and you *know* it." I raised both arms in surrender. "If I'm a traitor, have me arrested. *Now*, right now. Go on, I dare you because I will have one hell of a statement for them to take down and use in evidence against.…against whom, eh? Who's going to be charged in this little debacle? Who's going down if *this* shit hits, eh? It isn't *me*, Parks. It isn't going to be me."

"It's not a fucking game, David," he said, matter-of-factly. "You have no idea what I could do to you right now and get away with. No idea at all."

"Do it," I urged him. "Because we both know you can't. If any of this went public everyone on Capitol Hill would be in chains, but *you* and your neocon playmates would be in cages nailed to the city gates."

"We don't do this sort of thing in public, David," he said, looking up and down Central Park West for a taxi. Then he wiped his lips with a linen handkerchief.

The fear that suddenly went coursing like heat lightning through my nerves made me panic visibly. That affected wipe of the mouth with a crisp new handkerchief—he was giving someone a sign, wasn't he?

Parks had seen my spasm of panic, and seemed deeply gratified by it, just as he was by finding me scanning the rooftops and doorways across the road.

"One wipe is ready," Parks told me. "Two wipes is take aim. But it's only when I drop the handkerchief they fire thirty hollow-point shells into your head, and swear they did it because you pulled a weapon on me."

"I'm not armed," I said. "I've never even owned a gun."

"No one will care. The media won't be interested. They can't report every crime, can they? You'll have a gun in your hands by the time the police arrive, of course," he said. "That's all they'll care about. Man like me, important enough to have Special Ops snipers on his security team, they'll get the picture even before a special request from the President himself comes in to fast-track me out of here."

The smile on Parks' lips suddenly died. "Who did you think you were fucking with, *Dave*," he said, "a couple of local hoodlums? Some punks from *West Side Story*? Well it's not like that. We're a little bigger and more deadly than that...Here, catch!"

I was watching the hand with the handkerchief in it, and, without any warning, he suddenly threw the square of starched cloth at me. I caught it, but momentarily hunched over out of sheer instinct, expecting the dull pop of silencers to come from the skies.

"You're a riot," Parks said, laughing in a rather unconvincing manner and touching my arm. "I'm just joking with you. There's no security detail—look around. Why would I bring security to meet you?"

I was not convinced. Maybe he'd simply had a change of heart, or realized he couldn't get away with it? But also maybe I was tired and my nerves were on edge?

"I don't know why you do a lot of things, Parks," I said. "In fact, I don't really even know what you do at all."

"Well, I'll tell you one thing I'm going to do," he said, "—and not for old times' sake, but because we're on the same team—I'm going to make a phone call and smooth things over. Melton really screwed things up, you know? Big time. But this is the United States government, my friend, not the Black Hand Gang. When people screw up, we demote them or fire them. We don't kill them. But this time, just for Les, we're just going to forget it, pretend it never happened. Okay? He'll just come back to work at BTP and no one will say boo to him. Will that be all right for little Lester?"

He was lying, but why? Why was he so anxious to keep me happy when half an hour earlier he'd been threatening to cut my limbs off? It struck me that he'd have preferred me to fear him, yet since I did not, he didn't want to risk alienating me entirely, and so he was suddenly willing to do what I'd come to ask of him, although he had avoided even discussing the subject until now. Did he just want to make sure Les Melton came back to Manhattan where he was easier for Parks to find than he would be in Washington? The whole business was like a Chinese puzzle, boxes within boxes. Just when you thought you were going to open the final box and win its contents, the conjurer flipped them all over and you were opening the first box again, finding merely more boxes that contained only other boxes.

Abbie and I had moved into the Leverett Trust's Maryland estate after our brief honeymoon on Western Samoa, so this was where Les had been staying since I picked him up at the airport. His frayed nerves had begun to chafe against Abbie's normally robust state of mind, and she was happy to see me return from New York the same day, since I'd warned her it might take longer.

The three of us sat in the sunroom with drinks, as I recounted the highlights of my meeting with Parks, accompanied by the rattling of ice cubes in the glass of scotch held by Les's trembling hands.

He was so relieved when I got to the part where Parks promised to smooth it all over that he actually cried.

"I'm not going back there, though," he said, wiping his eyes. "I'd be happy if I never saw Parks again. There's something dark about that man...I don't know...And that little guy."

"What *little* guy?" I asked.

"Donner," said Les. "He's—"

"I know *Donner*. I met him at Harvard. He works for Parks... assistant or something."

"No, wrong," Les said. "*Parks* works for *him*. That whole office, BTP, they all work for him. You should have seen how they jumped when he was due in for a meeting. His own office is somewhere else, though. With Parks, I assume?"

"Odd," I said, remembering the meeting with Donner at the Fogg Museum. *"Call me Chris..."*

"What? Why?" said Les.

"Not *me*," I said. "Donner asked me to call him Chris— C.P. Donner was how he signed himself on the A-3 invitation."

"Donner sent you the A-3 invite?"

"Yes, the night Parks inducted me was at his invitation. Who sent yours?"

"Parks and Donner had nothing to do with A-3," Les said, looking so pale and overwrought I feared he might collapse. "All invites were sent out by the committee. Mine came from Reynolds, but Parks and Donner weren't on that committee. Parks had nothing to do with A-3."

"He told me he was treasurer," I said.

"Barclay was treasurer," Les pointed out. "Then Besdack after him."

"Maybe I'm confusing things." I didn't want to cause Les any more worry than he already had, so I was only too happy to claim faulty memory, when in reality I remembered everything all too clearly. "But," I told myself, aloud, "Donner was definitely an employee, a valet, or something of the sort."

"You're sure you've got the right guy?" Les said. "Not to be unkind, but he's a midget, right?"

"Or dwarf," I added.

"Hardly likely to be two of them, is there?" Les shook himself another scotch, tapping out an entire bar in ragtime with the decanter's stopper before managing to replace it in the neck with his quivering hands.

"Do something with those hands, Melton. Jesus, it's like St. Vitus' Dance or Smithsonian's Disease."

"Enough," Les complained. "It's not my fault. My nervous system feels like it's been on the road eighteen months as Jimmy Page's guitar strings."

"You know, I must admit I thought Donner was the big cheese," I said, "until Parks arrived in his big chauffeur-driven chariot. Then we just left the little guy on the sidewalk, so I assumed a different relationship. Nothing was ever *said*, though."

"We were told to call him Dr. Donner or *sir*—nothing else. It was evidently very important not to get his name wrong."

"Or very important for you to remember it."

"Possibly," Les agreed, knitting his brows. "And everyone was instructed to sit before speaking to him—and you were *never* to speak unless he spoke to you."

"They tell you who he was?" I asked, puzzled. "I mean, why you had to be so deferential?"

"Not specifically, come to think of it, no," said Les. "I guess it was just to make sure we were all suitably scared of him? When I saw him, of course, I assumed it was all dwarf-complex—you know, chip-on-the-shoulder inferiority thing. Of course, no one had bothered to tell me he was...you know..."

"A dwarf?" I said, growing exasperated with the ice rattling and the political correctness that had invaded my house. "You know, Les, we can say *dwarf*. We can say *cripple*, too, and *Mongoloid* or *retard* because this is my home and we're in America, where freedom of speech is non-negotiable. We don't have to whisper, either. What has gotten *into* you?"

I began to concede over the next few days that Les's experience was a life-changer for him. He told me several times that he just wanted to stay away from politics now. He wanted a quiet simple life. I felt obliged to point out that if he really wanted it he'd be ill advised to tell anyone else about the EHMS, let alone write about Auroco.

"I promise I won't write a word," he said, earnestly. "I won't say one either. I will erase the whole thing. Honestly!"

"I *believe* you, Les. For God's sake, I'm not the one you need to convince about this."

I don't think he ever had any intentions of writing about Auroco anyway. Within a few months, he had raided the Melton Trust's stock portfolio and purchased a dairy farm. I never heard from him again. Not directly. I did attend his funeral, though, with Dean and Mel.

I realized Franklin Barker had tried to allude to the EHMS when he explained our policies with regard to Saudi Arabia, and also when he recounted the real history of our involvement in Iran since the fifties. Possibly he knew no more, or was not permitted to tell me any more. But he had tried assiduously to open my eyes to political realities, especially when they skirted the boundaries of acceptable policy.

Now he was dead, of course. And two qualities—of soothsaying and death—might just be coincidentally related, death being related to everything while not necessarily being connected to anything.

Caleb Luposki returned to Washington in 1989 as undersecretary of defense for Policy, working with Dick Cheney. He invited me to lunch the day before he took up the position. For a long time, we discussed Indonesia, where Luposki had been stationed as US Ambassador, and, by all accounts, developed an admiration for the dictator Suharto. But our hearts were not in the subject, it was clear, or it was clear to me at least. For the subject we were studiously avoiding gathered mass and presence the longer it remained absent, and had begun to feel like a bloated thundercloud by the time Luposki suddenly said:

"So you and Parks no longer see eye to eye, I hear?"

"Is that what you hear?" I said, then I told him about Les Melton, told him that I disapproved of the underhanded techniques and back-channel maneuverings that were being employed. Told him the truth, and nothing but the truth.

He tut-tutted, shaking his head.

"I deeply admire your moral sensibility," he said at length, "but the world on the whole scoffs at such an approach. If we had taken that position with the Soviets, we would not be where we are today."

"You surely aren't claiming responsibility for the Soviet collapse," I said, scarcely believing my ears. "We both know that was internal. It was also being predicted twenty years ago."

In retrospect, I realize neither of us was much interested in discussing Les Melton's life-altering experience in the world of covert ops, mainly because neither of us was qualified to decide the facts of what had occurred. Luposki's disinterest was more related to his keen interest in discussing something else, however. As we had discovered when I worked under him at PPC, our respective talents in the area of long-term policy planning perfectly complemented one another. So much so that I quickly noticed he would always want to hear my views on anything important before committing his own to paper. Where he was headstrong and inclined to bluster, I was more cautious and diplomatic. His faults invigorated mine, and we openly recognized how we both benefited from the working relationship, what we both had learned from it.

I think he found emotion debilitating, though. He didn't view it as a weakness so much as see how weakened by it he could often be, and thus was better off without. He demanded much of himself—much more than he demanded of others. Too much, in fact. Because it blinded him to a whole part of his true nature, and in the end had him chasing his own shadow across the sun.

"Either way," he said, cutting me off with barely concealed irritation, "we're the only superpower left and we have a real chance to change the world, to spread freedom, to end these barbaric regimes in Syria, Iraq, Iran and elsewhere."

"Save the rhetoric for press releases, Caleb," I told him. "Installing pro-American regimes isn't spreading freedom—it's building an empire."

Luposki waved this thought away like a cloud of fruit flies, saying, in an almost weary tone, "Our first objective is to prevent the re-emergence of a new rival, for God's sake, not rape the planet."

"When does the rape come in?" I asked him, quite clearly as a joke. "Second or third?"

"Please," he said, sighing patiently yet not exhibiting much actual patience at all. "I'm telling you, this is a dominant consideration underlying the new regional defense strategy and it requires that we endeavor to prevent any hostile power from dominating a region—any region—whose resources would, under consolidated control, be sufficient to generate global power. As you well know, David, these regions include Western Europe, East Asia, the territory of the former Soviet Union, and Southwest Asia."

"What about Israel?" I asked him, but he ignored the question, continuing with what sounded to me like a policy statement.

"There are three additional aspects to this objective, and I want you to remember that I mentioned them before any journalist pointed them out to me, okay? First the US must show the leadership necessary to establish and protect a new order that holds the promise of convincing potential competitors that they need not aspire to a greater role or pursue a more aggressive posture to protect their legitimate interests."

"I want you to remember that I said this too, Caleb: if you think you are hiding the reality of that by fashioning it from lawspeak, you are sorely mistaken. It would be better received if you just said outright that our *might* will make us *right*."

"Not what I mean at all," Luposki said, brushing me off. "Second, in the non-defense areas, we must account sufficiently for the interests of the advanced industrial nations to discourage them from challenging our leadership or seeking to overturn the established political and economic order."

"Throw Europe some crumbs and it will remain a faithful lapdog and a useful proxy?" I suggested. "This is mesmerizing, Caleb, it truly is."

Of course, only he would have actually continued under such circumstances, now peering over his glasses quizzically at me as he said, "Finally...finally, we must maintain the mechanisms for deterring potential competitors from even aspiring to a larger regional or global role."

"You ban your bombs, we build even bigger ones—but only to make sure the status quo remains as it is. Is that a fair assessment?"

"No," he protested. "That is not what I am saying at all."

"But it is what you mean, isn't it?" I said.

"You're putting words in my mouth."

"If that's going to be a policy statement, which is what it sounds like," I said, "then one of us is severely out of touch with reality, because what you've just said is monstrous, besides being arrogant and ignorant. Our European allies will laugh at it—and they're the only allies we don't have to threaten or pay, so we shouldn't completely ignore their opinions. Jesus, Caleb! You make us sound like a bunch of inbred crackers sitting on the stoop with our shotguns, Wild Turkey and home-spun stupidity."

"So you think we should just leave regimes like Saddam Hussein's in place, turn a blind eye to the torture, the oppression, the—"

"Hypocrisy?" I cut him off. "Our first duty is to the American people, and they aren't particularly bothered by Saddam's regime—"

"*Some* are," he said, more forcefully than the words seemed to warrant.

"How many Iraqis are living in America, Caleb?"

"I didn't mean Iraqis," he said.

"Then who?"

He smiled a thin weak smile. "Go on," he said, "it's not important."

"The American people are not bothered by Saddam Hussein for the same reasons you don't seem to have been bothered by Suharto, or the Saudis," I said, "or Israel, for that matter."

"Israel?" he said, trying to make it sound like Finland. "Why would I be bothered by Israel? It's the only democracy in the entire region."

"Democracy?" I let the word resonate between for a beat or two. "I don't think so, Caleb. Over half the population don't have any rights at all."

"Palestinians..."

"Yes, Palestinians. They too are supposed to be citizens of Israel, aren't they?—because there isn't anywhere else they can *be* citizens of—yet they have virtually no human rights at all any more. But no one's supposed to mention that, are they?"

"I never would have pegged you for pro-Palestinian," he said, looking genuinely surprised.

"You think the rule of law doesn't apply to Israel? You think Helsinki doesn't accord Arabs rights? You think like that and you are damning your people to hell every bit as certainly as the Nuremberg Laws did, Caleb, because without the rule of law the existence of Israel, of America, of humanity itself, doesn't matter a jot."

"Israel was bought and paid for by the blood of six million," said Luposki.

I think the statement even surprised him, because in all the time I had known the man he never once expressed an emotional attachment to the Jewish state, or indeed anything.

"Maybe that wasn't what the Arabs had in mind for it?" I said, trying read what was written behind the pained expression in his eyes.

"You're suggesting they just pack up and leave?" He was openly scornful now. "They should just disperse, go home? The Palestinians are not the only ones without anywhere to go, you know. But the Jews should be the ones to leave? Is that what you're suggesting? Why don't you tell *that* to your friend Melvin Cassel?"

I knew he and Mel had an acquaintance by now, although I wasn't sure of its nature, so the comment took me by surprise.

"I'm suggesting they obey the law," I said. "That's all—the way everyone else has to."

"Didn't sound as if that's all you were suggesting."

"I'm sure it didn't," I said, "but that's all I *was* suggesting. Although I could easily suggest you can't use the law as a sword and still expect it to be a shield when you need one." It was my turn to sigh with frustration and weariness. "You know as well as I do that every other Israeli is beginning to worry about the way the Palestinians are being treated. Everyone knows what happens to those who live by the sword, don't they? But America isn't exactly the best teacher of ethics in statehood, I suppose, is it? What happened to Zionism? Ask yourself that, Caleb. Because you need *ideals* to win a war, and I don't see any. We're all bankrupt in that area, and I don't like the fact that we're now also both trying to row the same proverbial boat in opposite directions"

He laughed. Eventually. But he had not been at all sure what to do at first.

"I don't want to see anyone destroyed, Caleb. Writing policy that benefits shareholders of the military-industrial complex isn't going to do that. Going along with the suggestion of think tanks stacked with CEOs from weapons consortiums isn't going to do that. That's why I feel it's my responsibility to write policy that, in its even-handedness and objectivity, adequately reflects the egalitarian principles of America's Constitution."

"That's *precisely* my point," he said. "Those are the very same principles that oblige us to overthrow tyrannies and reward friends, particularly now that we have the ability to do so."

I knew he wanted me on his side, but I no longer trusted his motives or his honesty, and he realized it.

After the lunch with Luposki, I called Mel and suggested meeting for a drink.

The only time he had free was three weeks hence.

"It's just a drink, Mel," I said. "A drink with your old friend."

"I am double-booked 'til doomsday, pal," he told me. "I really am. I don't even have fucking time for God."

"Mel," I said, "just a quick question you'll almost certainly be able to shed some light on: Does it—I mean being Jewish—necessarily entail a blanket support for Israel no matter how misguided the country's political thinking becomes?"

"Correct," Mel replied, "although there are nuances, which we won't admit to the *goyim*. Israel can do no wrong."

"Be serious," I told him. "I really need to know."

"I am being serious."

"Okay," I said, "what about this: If a war broke out between the US and Israel, what would American Jews do?"

"Stop it," he said. "They'd stop it before someone got hurt. But that's *never* gonna fuckin' happen."

"Why are you so *sure* of that?"

"We *own* America," he said. "And we're not about to foul our nest here, are we?"

"Mel!" I was not really annoyed, of course, I merely seemed to be annoyed. "I need a *serious* answer...I'll be quoting you on this."

"Then mention that Cassel told you he was a Learned Elder of Zion."

"I will if you carry on like this."

"Please...don't jest about *that*," he said. "I'd have the anti-defamation league all over me like a cheap suit. Just say I told you Israel best serves US interests in the Middle East, and has proved over the years to be a loyal, effective and courageous ally."

"Great," I said. "That was *perfect*. Now, off the record, what's the *real* reason?"

"Israel's not much bigger than Dan Quayle's head," Mel said. "Think about it: One nuke, *booom*, and the war's over. Right?"

"Right. Good insight. Thanks, Melvin."

I could never really tell whether Mel was joking or not, and if he wasn't joking, whether he was lying or not. I realize he must have had a similar confusion about me, now I consider it. We assumed we were each comfortable with the framework of religions we no longer believed in still very much a mainstay in the infrastructure of our inner worlds. Never again would so flimsy a conceit as tribal superstition be permitted to excavate canyons between man and man—we truly and deeply believed this.

But in the long fading twilight of the Enlightenment it became increasingly difficult to tell where the lengthening shadows met the falling night. Like the abyss that, when you look deep and hard down into it, sometimes looks steeply up into you, the true distance between one soul and another was not hard but impossible to gauge. As Mel had once told me, when in a less facetious mood, the Kabbalists posited a terrible realm of shells and demons called the Klippot as an ultimate destination for all impure journeys in the soul. A man strove with tainted motives toward paradise and he would discover, all too late, that after a lifetime of psychic struggles, of hauling himself ever upward toward the eye of God by the skin of his teeth, he had in reality all this time been heading down into the mirror opposite of paradise, whose sweet respite and quenching waters of life were now a heartbreaking, mind-snapping lifetime away in the other direction.

This was our predicament, Mel and I. We imagined ourselves in the Elysian Fields of rational humanism, where every soul knew what it had done, and what it had left undone. We believed we were so free and clear of barbaric baggage that we could joke about the follies that had eaten through most of human history with callous indifference to the consequences. But we had fallen for a Faustian bargain, and when the *bonhomie* turned sour, we found those harmless little jibes and taunts, made to test the waters of our liberation, now flying at our faces like vicious harpies brandishing straight razors, screaming with blood-lust and rage.

The conversations, I remember them all too well. And it was the chicken that came before the egg, because Melvin Cassel had been an irredeemable goy-baiter as far back as Harvard Yard. A lot of them were, those gloriously well-read, whip-smart, darkly handsome, politically immaculate Ivy League Jews, who should have had a global conspiracy going because they *looked* as if they owned the world.

They knew we could tell they had an intellectual edge over us, and that it made us nervous, the speed and dazzle of their conversation, with its breadth and scope of allusive reference, and its sheer playfulness. Their nerves gave them the edge. No one needed to be jumpy in campus America as the Swinging Sixties waved Hello-Goodbye, some time around the mid-seventies. Yet *they* were jumpy. It was genetic, caffeinated, neurotic, *hopping*—and all we wanted was to know where *we* could buy some of *that* for ourselves. Civil Rights, Bob Dylan, Norman Mailer, Saul Bellow, Leonard Bernstein, the painters, the architects, the virtuoso musicians, Allen Ginsberg, Lenny Bruce, Hollywood, and all those accolades, scholarships, bursaries, gifted awards, the three titans of the twentieth century for Christ's sake—Marx, Freud, Einstein—the sheer intellectual weight in all the papers, seminal texts, breakthroughs, Nobel Prizes....It just isn't an achievement easily written off, is it? It is daunting, magnificent, threatening.

What the hell happened? This was what I kept asking myself, and what I would have asked Melvin Cassel if I thought I'd get a decent answer, and what I wanted to ask every Jew I encountered in the course of every day. But I knew I *couldn't* ask them, because something had changed. A circuit was rewired, and all the jokey attempts to ease off the tension of centuries now made the spring tighter.

No, this was not anti-Semitism. I can say it with a clear conscience: I didn't hate them. I *loved* them, loved everything they stood for. It seemed to me then they turned their backs and walked away, into the murky hall of mirrors that was to be neo-conservatism.

"Maybe we've had enough of bleeding hearts, lost causes, folk music," was as close as Melvin Cassel ever came to explaining it to me. "Maybe we want to make some money, move uptown, listen to Dire Straits and meet some blonde *shiksas* at Studio 54, kick back, relax, learn to fuckin' *enjoy* ourselves."

So here we were worrying about the intellectual trumping we got every time we went up against the Book People, while *they* were sweating over the quickest route to take into shallow, superficial, and Episcopalian. Was that the great mystery I'd been tracking down? I doubted it, but all the same I couldn't come up with a better explanation—better in the sense that it did not entail a vast conspiracy, bonfires, hoods and Jesuits.

It made me angry with myself for never having given the questions much thought until recently, too—and then it made me angry to find myself angry with anyone, particularly with myself.

CHAPTER THIRTEEN

★ ★ ★

*Pede poena claudo*** (Horace)

IT WAS OFTEN SAID OF BILL CLINTON that many people dealt with him as if he were two different people at the same time. Nearly everyone felt he did a helluva good job. His work had always impressed those around him throughout his life. But there were also those who, while they were as delighted as anyone, did not feel they could work closely with Clinton, because they did not trust him. They sensed he was a liar.

In Washington, statements like this amounted to a joke, because, between politicians and lawyers, we housed most of the nation's professional liars. In the old days, politicians simply lied about everything all of the time, and the voters could either tell, or they couldn't. Increasingly, now, though, politicians relied on the deceptive mutilations of language, the semantic landmines and ticking bombs, the ingenuity, cunning, unscrupulousness, and sheer criminal flair of America's finest legal minds. Ideally, of course, the politicians themselves were lawyers.

The ideals of justice for all, dispensed equally to president and pauper, and the impartiality, the implicit fairness of the rule of law were now merely quaint curiosities from a bygone era, no more relevant than the Declaration of Independence or the

---

* Punishment comes limping.

Constitution, with their flamboyant script and lofty utopian principles. The Museum of America was not supposed to represent an eternal goal, a shining example for people to emulate down through the ages, a pinnacle of socio-political achievement that would never be improved upon. It was simply a museum like any other displaying aspects of the way things were. I wondered what today's schoolchildren made of the pious pronouncements, austere resolutions, resolutely noble intentions, and unselfish daydreams. I wondered what they made of the fact that Thomas Jefferson was a slave-owner, and, at the time he drafted the Declaration and wrote about all men being born equal, owned 186 human beings. He even fathered children on some of them. He did not visit them for the purpose of fathering children—that was a *consequence* of visiting them—he visited them for sex. He had no *relationship* with them. They were mere vessels. He used them for his own pleasure. One can hear him say, "And why not, I *own them*, and I can do whatever I choose with my property."

For as long as I have paid attention to the matter, there have been books and essays discussing the question of whether Jefferson's slave-owning and slave-abusing antics, in the light of the ideals he professed in the Declaration, make him vulnerable to the charge of hypocrisy. The Founding Fathers, like all fathers, it seems, let us down.

Luposki's desire to topple Saddam Hussein may have been thwarted by the Saudi rulers' personal appeal to Bush, but throughout the eight years of the Clinton presidency his back-channel maneuverings saw to it that the UN embargo kicked in and that the country was kept under constant attack from British and US warplanes. I was right about him preparing a policy paper, though.

Dick Cheney, who was Bush's defense secretary and controller, was determined to wield long-term influence over post–Cold War policy, and had set up a "shop," as he laughably called it, to look into options. Within the Pentagon there were two schools of thought: hawks and realists. The former tended not to be military people and were headed by Luposki. The latter were represented by Colin Powell. Both of them were told to prepare an hour-long briefing for Cheney on May 21, 1990 from which he would select the material with which he would then brief the president on the new defense strategy.

Luposki and Powell arrived together for the meeting. Luposki was first to present, a situation Powell was happy with since he believed the last speaker carried the most influence on any audience. Luposki's presentation, however, went way over the hour, lasting nearly ninety-eight minutes. Since Cheney was the only one who could call time, and he did not, Luposki took up Powell's hour too. Cheney told him to come back to present three days later. It looked to me very much as if Cheney and Luposki had planned this to marginalize the dovish influence on policy.

But when the press heard rumors of what had supposedly been in Cheney's defense policy—such as the need to prevent the rise of any other great powers—they began to ask questions. By then it was clear that Poppy Bush had lost the re-election bid to Clinton, so the issue looked like a last gasp of molting hawks anyway. But Bush denounced the strategy and Cheney issued a version of his presidential briefing that had been thoroughly sanitized of all contentious points.

It appeared very much as if Luposki had been marginalized. He spent most of the decade teaching at Johns Hopkins, however, and that is far too close to Washington for anyone to assume he stayed out of politics. In fact, I was surprised at the number of lobby groups there were to hammer out Luposki policy suggestions. From the Committee to Free Iraq, through the Project for a New American Century and American Enterprise Institute, to the Iraqi National Congress, which posed as a government-in-waiting, Luposki was a very busy man indeed. But the repeated stubborn refusal of Bill Clinton to implement any of his recommendations infuriated him, often to a point where he ceased to be able to handle it well. His scorn for Kissinger was a petty trifling thing compared with the black hatred he harbored for Clinton, which occasionally revealed its hobgoblin presence when I was around and felt like a cold shaft of appalling cruelty that came hurtling out from somewhere far behind the black pupils of his hard eyes, from the space that was also the throne room of his austere and uncharitable intellect.

Clinton had been a Rhodes Scholar at Oxford when I was a freshman, so I knew him very slightly. Unlike most Americans among the dreaming spires, he was quiet and charming, and not inclined to found societies or clubs to promote loud and silly interests. We had little in common, however, and though I respected his intellect, I found his political and social views to be self-interested. He was radical only, I found, if the cause served him in some way. I certainly would not claim that I *knew* him in anything more than a superficial sense. The same way I way I knew Tony Blair, who was also there during my years. I don't think he and Clinton met. Why would they?

The thing with Oxford, on account of the decentralized nature of the colleges, is that one can expand or contract one's range of acquaintance as seems prudent. After all, at any given time over the last several hundred years a good third of world leaders were Oxonians, which meant that a good third of the world's future leaders were then studying there at the same time. My expanded though tenuous Clinton connection was enough, however, to provide me with several invitations to the White House, during which I developed a greater respect for his wife, Hillary, than I ever had for him.

It was Hillary who confided in me that she believed Luposki and his colleagues were responsible for tying up the last years of Clinton's presidency in legal problems that rendered him incapable of doing anything meaningful. She was very bitter about it. I do not think any man has ever been so publicly humiliated as Bill Clinton was over the issue of his sexual indiscretions. Foolish as they were, there was no harm done, and indeed no one had made any kind of complaint. To hear the braying media, though, the interminable stupid discussions about Monica Lewinsky's dress and fellatio skills, you would have thought someone had been murdered.

But all the trial by fire showed was that Clinton's skin was thicker than rhino hide. Similarly, investigations into alleged financial misdeeds by the Clintons—investigations that cost the taxpayer upward of $60 million and proved baseless—were turned over in the press and on television like manure on a coprophiliac's cornfield.

The frequency and obsessiveness of this news coverage began to give me misgivings about the role media were beginning to play in affairs of state. That they had the ability to decide who should be president, who was innocent, who was guilty, who should be promoted, who should be fired, and a thousand other democratic choices, was a dangerous enough thing in itself, but that they may be misusing this power was surely genuine cause for concern. Indeed, many were concerned about it, but not many in government—because in government everyone's job was on the line. It does not take Sherlock Holmes to discover that people who own major newspapers or national TV networks are going to be wealthy, nor that the wealthy tend toward conservatism, since they tend to be heavily invested in the status quo. As I have stated, none of this bothered me unduly at the time, and didn't bother me because I felt that media barons were smart enough not to interfere with the political process. It was taken for granted, of course, that they could have no possible interest in interfering with other news (unless it concerned themselves).

But, it may be argued, "capitalism is dead, consumerism is king." And consumerism requires the services of expert salesmen versed in all the arts (including the more insidious arts) of persuasion. Under a free enterprise system commercial propaganda by any and every means is absolutely indispensable. But the indispensable is not necessarily the desirable. What is demonstrably good in the sphere of economics may be far from good for men and women as voters or even as human beings.

The task of the commercial propagandist in a democracy is in some ways easier and in some ways more difficult than that of a political propagandist working for an established dictator or a dictator in the making. It is easier inasmuch as everyone starts out with a prejudice in favor of beer, cars and lipstick, whereas almost no one starts out with a prejudice in favor of tyrants.

It is more difficult inasmuch as the commercial propagandist is not permitted by the rules of his game to appeal to the more savage instincts of his public. The advertiser of dairy products would dearly love to tell his viewers and listeners that all their troubles, their fears and the high cost of living are caused by the evil machinations of a gang of godless international margarine manufacturers, and that it is their patriotic duty to march out and burn the oppressors' factories and offices. This, of course, is ruled out, and he must be content with a milder approach. But the mild approach is less exciting than the approach through verbal or physical violence. In the end, we know, anger and hatred are self-defeating emotions. But in the short term they pay high dividends in the form of psychological and even (since they release large quantities of adrenalin and noradrenalin) physiological satisfaction.

People may start out with an initial prejudice against tyrants; but when tyrants or wannabe tyrants treat them to adrenalin-releasing propaganda about the wickedness of their enemies—particularly of enemies weak enough to be persecuted—they are ready to follow those men with enthusiasm. In his speeches Hitler kept repeating words like "hatred," "force," "ruthless," "crush," "smash"; he accompanied these violent words with even more violent gestures. He would yell, he would scream, his veins swelled up, his face turned purple. As every actor and dramatist knows, strong emotion is highly contagious.

Almost all of us yearn for peace and freedom, but few have much enthusiasm for the ideas, thoughts, feelings and actions that make for peace and freedom. On the other hand, almost no one wants war or tyranny, but a great many people derive intense pleasure from the ideas, thoughts, feelings and actions that make for war and tyranny. Such emotions are too dangerous to be exploited for commercial purposes. The ad people accept this handicap and do the best they can with the less intoxicating emotions, the quieter forms of irrationality.

Effective rational propaganda becomes only possible when there is a clear understanding by all concerned of the nature of symbols and their relationship to the things and events symbolized. Irrational propaganda depends for its effectiveness on a general failure to understand the nature of symbols. The simple-minded tend to equate the symbol with what it stands for, to attribute to things and events some of the qualities that have been expressed by the words used by the propagandist—for his own purposes—to discuss them. For example: most cosmetics are made of lanolin, which is a mixture of purified wool fat and water mixed up into an emulsion, which has numerous wonderful qualities: it penetrates the skin, it does not become rancid, it's mildly antiseptic, and so on. But the commercial propagandist doesn't talk about the genuine virtues of the emulsion. He gives it a voluptuous exotic name, talks ecstatically and misleadingly about feminine beauty, and shows images of flawless blondes nourishing their tissues with skin food. A cosmetic manufacturer once wrote that he and his colleagues were "not selling lanolin, they are selling hope." For this hope, this fraudulent implication of a promise that they will be transfigured, women will pay hundreds of times the value of the emulsion, which has been skillfully related by the propagandists to a deep-seated and probably universal feminine wish—the wish to be more attractive to the opposite sex.

The principles underlying this kind of propaganda are laughably simple. You find some kind of common desire, a widespread unconscious fear or anxiety; then you dream up some sort of way to relate this fear or wish to the product you're selling; then build a bridge of verbal or pictorial symbols over which your customer can pass from fact to compensatory dream, and from the dream to the illusion that your product will make the dream come true. If the customer buys it. We don't buy oranges, we buy vitality. We don't buy merely a car, we buy prestige.

Everywhere, the motivation analyst finds some deep-seated wish or fear whose energy can be used to make the consumer part with money and so, indirectly, turn the wheels of industry. Stored in countless minds and bodies, this potential energy is released by and transmitted along a line of symbols carefully arranged to bypass rationality and obscure the real issue. Sometimes the symbols take effect by being disproportionately impressive, haunting and fascinating in their own right. Such are the rites and rituals of religion and now politics.

Hitler's annual Nuremberg rallies were masterpieces of high ritual and theatrical art. Sir Nevile Henderson, British Ambassador to Nazi Germany: "I had spent six years in St Petersburg before the war in the best days of the old Russian ballet, but for grandiose beauty I have never seen any ballet to compare with the Nuremberg rally." John Keats: "Beauty is truth, truth beauty, that is all ye know on earth and all ye need to know..." Perhaps the correlation exists on some ultimate, supramundane level, but on the levels of politics and theology, beauty is perfectly compatible with nonsense and tyranny. If it weren't there would be precious little art in the world.

The great masterpieces of painting, sculpture and architecture were produced as religious or political propaganda, for the greater glory of a god, government or priesthood. But most kings were despotic and all religions have been riddled with superstition. Genius has been the servant of tyranny and art has advertised the merits of the local cult. As it passes, time separates the good art from the bad metaphysics; but can we learn to make this separation while the event is actually taking place?

Listen to this:

"Under a scientific dictator education will really work—with the result that most men and women will grow up to love their servitude and will never dream of revolution. There seems to be no good reason why a thoroughly scientific dictatorship should ever be overthrown." That was written in the late 1950s by Aldous Huxley. By the beginning of the Third Millennium I knew we were living in that scientific dictatorship, yet it took me a long time to understand that I too was a victim of its brainwashing techniques and even my ability to think about it had been compromised significantly. Even my ability to fight against it was limited to the very methods and media I was fighting against. And even this thought of hopelessness in the face of omnipotent might was a product of its brilliantly cunning and flawlessly efficient propaganda machine, which you could not actually see as such because the state was its propaganda. There was no point where propaganda left off and reality began, because the only reality was propaganda. Therefore to contemplate truth and freedom was impossible because they could not coexist with reality, and you cannot persuade anyone to destroy everything they have ever known, to make all that is solid melt into air.

Sitting in the half-light with the sense of dread, I look at a page of my journal upon which, all those years ago, I have written:

UNEASE Propaganda—sapping of the will
Abbie + me = abbie/me
are we like a lot of wild
spiders crying together, but without tears?
The mirror held up by nature
The one swallow that makes a summer
Nothing is simpler than marking off the days and weeks
But the calendar's pages are glued together
With honey. . . .

Up and down I go, up and down,
Up and down—
My sole still point in all this turning
Is the nest of a startled bird
Swinging there,
The nest of the red and black bird
Up and down, up and down . . .

I am glad that many little moments occupy more room in my memory than the larger events of those years. It shows me how much more I valued the little truth there was.

* * *

Dean Torrance was now Senator Torrance from Vermont, a man with no cause to be angered by the media, which adored him the way everyone else did and unfailingly reported with the utmost sympathy the succession of tragedies that afflicted his family like a genetically carried disease. Even in the depths of personal grief Dean was irresistibly likeable. The deeply etched smile lines around his eyes and mouth seemed to belie sorrow.

Possibly he had tried to counter this by down-turning the mouth, which, however, merely created the impression that his grief had turned his head upside down. By now he had married Belinda Mahoon, the heiress, and they had five children, of whom one developed a rare cerebral affliction leaving her with the mind of a two-year-old,; another had been mauled to death by a safari park tiger that had dragged him through the window of a car; and a third had, at the time in question, vanished while shopping with his mother in Woodstock, Vermont, and was still missing three days later.

"They are doing everything possible," said Dean, pouring me a cup of tea.

I had flown out to be with him the moment I had heard, leasing two helicopters to add to the search efforts.

"I'm sure he'll show up," he added. "Probably just wandered off and lost track of the time. And now he thinks he'll be in trouble if he comes back. He's done it before."

"He has?"

"Well, not quite the same. But similar. He's a little rascal." Dean smiled wanly at the thought of his boy, and I saw him glance over at a framed photograph showing the two of them together.

He was so optimistic, and I wondered where he justified this optimism. His previous run of luck did not justify any optimism. It justified total despair.

We began talking about the role the media were playing in finding the boy, and the conversation wandered into the way Clinton was being treated, and then into the issue of media ownership. The election was coming up, and I had been somewhat dismayed to find George W. Bush, son of George H.W. Bush, going after the Republican nomination. I knew how it would look to Europeans to see dynastic tendencies in our presidency. Dean stated outright that the coverage of Clinton's misdemeanors amounted to interference, and that Al Gore, the vice president who was going for the Democratic nomination, was forced to distance himself from Clinton because of it, whereas he ought to have benefited from the connection to a strong and popular president.

"Without this fake scandal," Dean said, "Gore would be a shoo-in. Although I don't think he'll make a very good president."

"Can't be any worse than Spawn of Bush, can he?"

"That's who will win," Dean said, with a smile of resignation.

"What makes you think that?"

"I know it, I don't think it," he said, lowering his voice. "Belinda's dad told her...to make sure I don't back the wrong horse."

Edward Gurney Mahoon, besides the Azel Mahoon Electronics empire, owned or sat on the boards of several newspapers and a few TV stations. If he knew who would win the next election it was not because he was psychic.

"How?" I asked.

Dean leaned toward me, speaking so quietly I could barely hear him myself: "She didn't know specifically, but she said he had just returned from a meeting in New York that she couldn't discover the nature of because her father's assistants did not know it themselves. In her experience, that meant a closed-doors private meeting of other media fatcats. They're held regularly, you know?"

"Dean," I said, "this is really worrying."

"I'm glad you think so, David. I wasn't sure whether you would or not."

My head was aching from the burden of containing this information. I sat back in the deep chintz sofa, listening to Dean's grandfather clock tick away the moments of our lives. The air in the room seemed to ripple with waves of energy or something, and the walls and carpets and objects looked suddenly unreal—as if they were going to melt away to reveal some kind of absolute reality behind them. The wind sent a brace of thin branches tapping at the windows, startling both of us. The old black Labrador retriever that had been sleeping like a pile of laundry raised its big worried head with enormous effort and uttered a single woof at the noise. The dog looked over at me with stained old eyeballs in sockets so bloodshot and baggy it was surprising they hadn't fallen out. Then, still with the rest of its body crumpled in a heap, it wearily looked at Dean for an explanation regarding my presence.

"Great watchdog." I said.

"Whadda ya want, Leverett, she's fifteen years old."

I started laughing because his remark had suddenly seemed preposterous: that anything could be ancient at fifteen seemed to make nonsense of time itself. Some of us are very old at fifteen, though, or fifty, yet it has come to me only now, in my one hundredth year, when I am too old to care. For Dean's son, however, five would prove to be extreme old age. His body was found five days later mutilated under some tin siding in a wood seven miles away. An autopsy revealed he had been sodomized and forced to perform fellatio before death came as a mercy.

I had no idea what to say to Dean. How do you console anyone in a matter like this? Just thinking of the little boy's last moments myself was enough to make me retch. The media were just like a posse from some old cowboy movie. CATCH HIM, PUNISH HIM, THEN FRY HIM yelled the *Washington Libertarian*'s front page, alluding to its editorial suggestion that the killer ought to be beaten up and tortured before getting the electric chair. Next to it in the airport bookstore I noticed *The New York Times'* headline that announced Edward Gurney Mahoon was offering a $20 million reward for anyone supplying information leading to the apprehension of his grandson's murderer. I doubted the reward would make any difference in a case like this, where anyone who knew the killer would turn him in. I was wrong, as it turned out.

"My God, Dean," I said when I first saw him. He was pale as the ghost of an albino, and his eyes had lost their sparkle. He stammered slightly when he spoke too, and he had clearly not changed or washed in days.

"I don't know what to say to you. I don't know how you are still standing, still here."

"What would you have me do?" he said, in an old dry voice. "One death in the family a week is our quota."

It took me a while to realize he was making a joke. That was Dean, life always went on for him. This, however, was the worst of all his tragedies, and life did not go on for a very long time. He had a wife and other children who were dealing with their own grief to look after too. And he had a father-in-law who had embarked on a one-man crusade to put the penal code's clock back to about 1323. His $20 million had been claimed by a woman who turned out to be the mother of Dan Mankewitz, a thrice-convicted pedophile who would eventually confess to six other similar murders.

When Ed Mahoon learned he would be giving his money to the mother, he had his legal people add five pages to the existing contract specifying that the money could not be used for a legal defense or given in any way to her son. His newspapers and TV stations also revealed shamelessly the myth of their editorial independence, calling for revised legislation for child killers, and running two- or three-page spreads on every facet of Dan Mankewitz's miserable existence, including one that struck me as way out of line. It unearthed the medieval superstition that Jews sacrificed Christian babies during the Passover festivities—the abduction and murder had occurred during the week of Passover.

I had stayed with Dean for a few weeks, because he asked me to, and it was he who had first pointed out the sacrifice article.

I had also noticed that other newspapers gave the "Torrance Child Killer" very little attention, assuming this was another unintended consequence of the overkill coverage in Mahoon media. Apparently it was not. A month after the killer's arrest, Ed Mahoon had attended another of his media moguls' meetings, this time in Atlanta, where it is believed he was asked to stop running inflammatory articles because they were responsible for an alarming rise in anti-Semitic incidents across the country. I can well imagine what Ed's response had been to this request, and whatever it was, Mahoon media did not stop running inflammatory pieces. If anything, they increased the level of vitriol in them. Ten days after the meeting, on November 9, 2000, Ed's private Gulfstream jet blew up shortly after taking off from LaGuardia Airport, New York, killing everyone on board. It was never possible to determine the exact cause of the explosion.

CHAPTER FOURTEEN

★ ★ ★

*Difficile est longum subito deponere amorem** (Catullus)

THE MOOD IN WASHINGTON WAS at the lowest ebb I had ever seen. George W. Bush had been elected president only after a disturbingly long recount, mainly in Florida, a state governed by his brother John, who was known as Jeb. Initially, it looked as if Al Gore had won. I remember thinking that Belinda Torrance would be pleasantly surprised to find her father was wrong, but Dean would be miffed to find he had wasted his time campaigning for Bush. The nation was shocked to find the electoral process in such disarray, and it was widely believed that the Bush family had found ways to subvert it.

The day Bush was inaugurated, it rained relentlessly, emphatically, as if trying to make a heavenly point. Crowds turned up merely to yell abuse, and indeed the hostility was so palpable that Bush elected to drive instead of taking the traditional walk toward history.

After this, it struck me as if he had disappeared off the face of the earth. He spent most of his time back on his hobby farm in Texas. No one appeared to miss him, however.

Looking at the people who now occupied key positions, I thought I was back in the days of Bush Sr. The same people were

---

* It is difficult to give up a long-cherished love.

there, although in different spots. Dick Cheney was now vice president, with Luposki's student, Lewis "Scooter" Libby—who had worked with me in policy planning—as his chief of staff. Luposki was deputy defense secretary, under his old comrade Donald Rumsfeld, who, having been the youngest defense secretary under Ford, was now the oldest under Bush. He and Cheney were, of course, close friends, and it soon became apparent that the country was being governed through their alliance. Everything now had to be cleared through their offices. No wonder the president stayed in Texas: there was nothing for him to do.

My father was now in a nursing home near Falls Church and I used to visit him every week, although most of the time he had no idea who I was and we talked like total strangers about food and gardening. I drove straight from the office to the Seward Nursing Home, discussing the following week's schedule with one of my staff, Thomas Zegg, a freckle-faced farm boy from Missouri whose PhD thesis on *realpolitik* had been one of the most brilliant works of analysis I'd ever read. His presence always cheered me; he seemed to embody everything good about America.

I saw my father sitting on a bench near the pond. He had a tartan blanket over his knees and a bored-looking black nurse standing behind him. She noticed me get out of the car, and I could see her trying to direct Father's attention my way. Improbably, he started waving at me.

"Shall I just wait in the car?" asked Thomas.

"No," I said. "Come and meet my father... or what's left of him."

We walked over toward the bench, where my father was trying to stand up and the nurse was now trying to prevent him.

"He's been frisky today," said the nurse. "Say hello to your son," she told my father.

"Stop treating me like an idiot, woman!" said my father. Then as I reached his side he added, "David, thank God you came..."

He looked suspiciously at Thomas Zegg, whom I introduced.

Then he asked me piteously, "Can't we ever be alone?"

I nodded to Thomas and the nurse, who walked away together—and, I might add, struck up a friendship that ended in marriage fourteen months later.

"All my life I known all kinds of things," my father said when they'd gone. "All kinds. But I've always known what I could say and what I couldn't. You don't know that.... You *don't*. And they'll kill you, they will." He gazed at me with milky eyes. "Bang!" He'd made a pistol with his fingers. "Dead you'll be."

"Who's going to do this, Dad?"

He started laughing. Then he stopped and stared hard at me, narrowing his eyes until they vanished into wrinkles and hair.

"Tell Morgenthau to go fuck himself," he said, making a sucking noise with his lips.

"Dad?"

"You heard me, lickspittle!"

He turned away, looking at the calm surface of the leaden pond.

"Dad," I said. "It's me, David."

"Over there," he whispered, pointing out at the pond, "is a marsh-hen's secret nest. But I won't show you because she prefers it that way, you see?"

"I know you recognize me, Dad," I said.

"It's the sorrow," he said in a quavering voice. "It climbs up, you see? The sorrow climbs up and I don't recognize myself."

He turned back to look at me, and I saw the tears sliding from his eyes into the fissures of his old face.

"Who am I?" he said.

He died the next day.

I was not prepared for the outpouring of public grief. A state funeral was planned, but when I found out that my mother did not want to attend I tried to have it called off.

"Did you hate him that much?" I asked her.

"I didn't hate him at all," she said, adding after a long pause, "I just wish I'd never met him."

"I assume then that goes for me too?"

She made no reply. The static of the phone line seemed to hiss out laughter, so, to stop it more than anything, I asked her what I'd done to warrant her behavior.

"A parent hopes to see something of herself in the child," she said. "And I don't see it. Not at all. So..." I could hear her draw in breath and exhale slowly. "So just leave me alone, would you? Would you mind just doing that?"

"Of course," I said, and I hung up.

That night, I sat at my desk working until about 3 AM, then I walked out into the waiting room to stretch my legs, but instead sat down on the roomy sofa, put my feet up and gazed around at the photographs of previous policy planning directors that decorated the walls.

I was more distraught than I realized at the time about the holocaust in West Asia, about the end of the ideal of Israel; I was more of an ardent Zionist, I think, than I ever knew I was. Not a Luposki Zionist, but a ben Gurion Zionist. I began searching my papers and came across what I was looking for: President Dwight D. Eisenhower's final address to the nation on January 17, 1961. My father was then still our man at the Court of St. James. What I copied down was this:

Until the latest of our world conflicts, the United States had no armaments industry. American makers of plowshares could, with time and as required, make swords as well. But now we can no longer risk emergency improvisation of national defense; we have been compelled to create a permanent armaments industry of vast proportions. Added to this, three and a half million men and women are directly engaged in the defense establishment. We annually spend on military security more than the net income of all United States corporations.

This conjunction of an immense military establishment and a large arms industry is new in the American experience. The total influence—economic, political, even spiritual—is felt in every city, every Statehouse, every office of the federal government. We recognize the imperative need for this development. Yet we must not fail to comprehend its grave implications. Our toil, resources and livelihood are all involved; so is the very structure of our society.

In the councils of government, we must guard against the acquisition of unwarranted influence, whether sought or unsought, by the military-industrial complex. The potential for the disastrous rise of misplaced power exists and will persist.

We must never let the weight of this combination endanger our liberties or democratic processes. We should take nothing for granted. Only an alert and knowledgeable citizenry can compel the proper meshing of the huge industrial and military machinery of defense with our peaceful methods and goals, so that security and liberty may prosper together.

Akin to, and largely responsible for the sweeping changes in our industrial-military posture, has been the technological revolution during recent decades.

In this revolution, research has become central, it also becomes more formalized, complex, and costly. A steadily increasing share is conducted for, by, or at the direction of, the federal government.

Today, the solitary inventor, tinkering in his shop, has been overshadowed by task forces of scientists in laboratories and testing fields. In the same fashion, the free university, historically the fountainhead of free ideas and scientific discovery, has experienced a revolution in the conduct of research. Partly because of the huge costs involved, a government contract becomes virtually a substitute for intellectual curiosity. For every old blackboard there are now hundreds of new electronic computers.

The prospect of domination of the nation's scholars by federal employment, project allocations, and the power of money is ever present—and is gravely to be regarded.

Yet, in holding scientific research and discovery in respect, as we should, we must also be alert to the equal and opposite danger that public policy could itself become the captive of a scientific-technological elite.

It is the task of statesmanship to mold, to balance, and to integrate these and other forces, new and old, within the principles of our democratic system—ever aiming toward the supreme goals of our free society.

Another factor in maintaining balance involves the element of time. As we peer into society's future, we—you and I, and our government—must avoid the impulse to live only for today, plundering, for our own ease and convenience, the precious resources of tomorrow. We cannot mortgage the material assets of our grandchildren without asking the loss also of their political and spiritual heritage. We want democracy to survive for all generations to come, not to become the insolvent phantom of tomorrow.

Down the long lane of the history yet to be written America knows that this world of ours, ever growing smaller, must avoid becoming a community of dreadful fear and hate, and be, instead, a proud confederation of mutual trust and respect.

Such a confederation must be one of equals. The weakest must come to the conference table with the same confidence as do we, protected as we are by our moral, economic, and military strength. That table, though scarred by many past frustrations, cannot be abandoned for the certain agony of the battlefield.

Disarmament, with mutual honor and confidence, is a continuing imperative. Together we must learn how to compose differences, not with arms, but with intellect and decent purpose. Because this need is so sharp and apparent I confess that I lay down my official responsibilities in this field with a definite sense of disappointment. As one who has witnessed the horror and the lingering sadness of war—as one who knows that another war could utterly destroy this civilization which has been so slowly and painfully built over thousands of years— I wish I could say tonight that a lasting peace is in sight.

Happily, I can say that war has been avoided. Steady progress toward our ultimate goal has been made. But, so much remains to be done. As a private citizen, I shall never cease to do what little I can to help the world advance along that road.

So—in this my last good night to you as your President— I thank you for the many opportunities you have given me for public service in war and peace. I trust that in that service you find some things worthy; as for the rest of it, I know you will find ways to improve performance in the future.

You and I—my fellow citizens—need to be strong in our faith that all nations, under God, will reach the goal of peace with justice. May we be ever unswerving in devotion to principle, confident but humble with power, diligent in pursuit of the Nations' great goals.

To all the peoples of the world, I once more give expression to America's prayerful and continuing aspiration:

We pray that peoples of all faiths, all races, all nations, may have their great human needs satisfied; that those now denied opportunity shall come to enjoy it to the full; that all who yearn for freedom may experience its spiritual blessings; that those who have freedom will understand, also, its heavy responsibilities; that all who are insensitive to the needs of others will learn charity; that the scourges of poverty, disease and ignorance will be made to disappear from the earth, and that, in the goodness of time, all peoples will come to live together in a peace guaranteed by the binding force of mutual respect and love.

Now, on Friday noon, I am to become a private citizen. I am proud to do so. I look forward to it.

Thank you, and good night.

Dreams can be revived, but there has to be a dreamer. Now the dreamer was gone, and what we were left with was the nakedness of our own colonial greed.

I know I had a terrible dream that night, but the details of it were lost to me. Something came up from under the sea, a monstrous thing that stalked the land and killed everything in its path. I awoke to find a luminescence in the silent room, the sense that something had just left, a fading sparkle like the nanoseconds following a bubble bursting. The word "blessing" spoke itself in my head, and I did feel I had been blessed. But before I could ask by whom or by what, the feeling vanished.

Dawn was beginning to break beyond the windows, a milky peaceful dawn. I felt stronger, resolved, ready to deal with whatever might arise. Ready to die for the Republic, if that was what it required, ready to argue, state my case, take it to the people and get down on my knees to beg their forgiveness. For you do not give up on a dream like this, a noble perfect vision that was the beginning not the end of history, that had waited down the long blood-stained centuries, through the cruelty and barbarism, the self-seeking shabbiness, the vainglorious chronicle from cave to final catastrophe, the whole saga of halberds, kings and merchants, waited patiently biding its time to burst forth with the light of a thousand suns and say, *Behold! I am the god of reason and I bring you hellfire—have a nice day!* And it *was* going to be a good day, I felt sure, looking at my calendar so I would never forget the anniversary of my little illumination: Tuesday, September 11th, 2001.

★ ★ ★

"Let us stack it up," said Scooter Libby. "Somalia, 1993; 1993, the World Trade Center, first bombing; 1993, the attempt to assassinate President Bush, former President Bush, and the lack of response to that, the lack of a serious response to that; 1994, the discovery of the Al Qaeda–related plot in the Philippines; 1995, the Riyadh bombing; 1996, the Khobar bombing; 1998, the Kenyan embassy bombing and the Tanzanian embassy bombing; 1999, the plot to launch millennium attacks; 2000, the bombing of the *Cole*. Throughout this period, infractions on inspections by the Iraqis, and eventually the withdrawal of the entire inspection regime; and the failure to respond significantly to Iraqi incursions in the Kurdish areas. No one would say these challenges posed easy problems, but if you take that long list and you ask, 'Did we respond in a way that discouraged people from supporting terrorist activities, or activities clearly against our interests? Did we help to shape the environment in a way that discouraged further aggressions against US interests?,' many observers conclude no, and ask whether it was then easier for someone like Osama bin Laden to rise up and say credibly, 'The Americans don't have the stomach to defend themselves. They won't take casualties to defend their interests. They are morally weak.'"

"The use of force by a power like ours is a weakness," I said. "It shows we have lost faith in our own words, it shows our powers of persuasion have left us. It shows we don't believe in our own arguments, we don't take ourselves seriously. It shows our time is up, our star is waning. No, my friend, when you have the most powerful military machine in history, unequaled in the terrible might and sophistication of its weaponry, literally invincible, capable of waging war on all the nations of the earth simultaneously and unquestionably winning, capable for God's sake of destroying the entire planet ten thousand times over, of rendering it inhabitable for twenty millennia to come, and perhaps forever...when you have all this, you *never* use it. And you sure as hell don't use it to correct the ways of a two-bit dictator in a banana republic who's dying of cancer anyway. Hubris, Scooter, hubris is the word. You remember your classics—think of the Greeks, the attack on Sicily, which was going to be a cakewalk but turned into a funeral march. Hubris."

I was waiting to see Dick Cheney for the last time, and Scooter had invited me into his office in the Old Executive Building. It had been Teddy Roosevelt's office when he was assistant secretary of the Navy and had the aura of time and dignity about it. I liked Lewis Libby. He was bright, articulate and had a fine analytical mind, but we no longer viewed the world the same way. Something had reached inside of him and turned around the delicate mechanism of his inner self. If someone like him was sold on waging war in Iraq, I had realized, then there was no place for me in this administration.

"You're just plain wrong, David," said Scooter Libby. "The only thing these people understand is deadly force....Deadly force used with ingenuity and innovation."

"I haven't seen that," I said. "All I've seen is lumbering aggression, heavy-handed bullying. Let me ask you something—"

"Shoot."

"Can you honestly tell me that you can put aside the wishes of the state of Israel and view the Middle East with complete objectivity? Because I think you're rearranging it in Israel's favor."

"You're being unfair, David," Libby told me. "Look at what the president has done in Afghanistan, and look at his speech to the joint session of Congress," he meant the State of the Union message. "He made it clear that it's an important area. He made it clear that we believe in expanding the zone of democracy even in this difficult part of the world. He made it clear that we stand by our friends and defend our interests. And he had the courage to identify those states that present a problem, and to begin to build consensus for action that would need to be taken if there is not a change of behavior on their part.

"Take the Afghan case, for example. There are many other courses that the president could have taken. He could have waited for juridical proof before we responded. He could have engaged in long negotiations with the Taliban. He could have failed to seek a new relationship with Pakistan, based on its past nuclear tests, or been so afraid of weakening Pakistan that we didn't seek its help. This list could go on to twice or three times the length I've mentioned. But, instead, the president saw an opportunity to refashion relations while standing up for our interests. The problem is complex, and we don't know yet how it will end, but we have opened new prospects for relations not only with Afghanistan, as important as it was as a threat, but also with the states of Central Asia, Pakistan, Russia, and, as it may develop, with the states of Southwest Asia more generally."

"Iraq is what bothers me, Scooter. Why do we have to go charging in there? We've tolerated Saddam for thirty years, surely we can wait for him to die? What makes him suddenly so unacceptable? The fact that he's screwing around with the UN weapons inspectors? Come on!"

"The issue is not inspections," Libby said. "The issue is the Iraqis' promise not to have weapons of mass destruction, their promise to recognize the boundaries of Kuwait, their promise not to threaten other countries, and other promises that they made in '91, and a number of UN resolutions, including all the other problems I listed. Whether it was wise or not—and that is the subject of debate—Iraq was given a second chance to abide by international norms. It failed to take that chance then, and annually for the next ten years."

"I've seen the debriefing of Hussein Kamel," I said—Kamel was Saddam's son-in-law and also in charge of Iraq's nuclear program. He had briefly defected to the West, where he gave detailed information on the state of Saddam's military—"as have many people. You quote him extensively and authoritatively on the quantities of nerve gas and other toxic chemicals stockpiled, but you ignore the part where he also says that the nuclear program was abandoned in '91 and all the enriched uranium, along with the machinery, the reactors' cores, the warhead casings, and everything connected with destroyed or disposed of."

"We don't believe it," Libby said. "And we have hard intelligence data that says otherwise."

"Then show it to the American people, for crissakes—they're going to be paying for this little adventure."

"It's classified stuff."

"Show me then. Show me and I'll believe it."

"I can't do that."

"What if Saddam changes his behavior...in a way that you will be satisfied by?"

He ran a hand over his tired but handsome face and then gave me a frank stare, speaking slowly and deliberately.

"There is no basis in Iraq's past behavior to have confidence in good-faith efforts on their part to change their behavior. No basis at all."

"You're going in anyway, aren't you? The diplomacy is a sham, isn't it?"

There was nothing Saddam could do to avert this attack, which wasn't going to be a war at all. It was going to be a very violent coup d'état.

Libby said nothing, continuing to stare, the faintest trace of a smile on his lips.

"I'm here to hand in my resignation," I told him.

He nodded, moving his whole body back and forth in the leather executive's chair like a dipping bird toy, exhaling in a prolonged hiss of white noise.

"Give it to Dick then," Scooter said. "Because I won't take it."

All the power on earth in the hands of imbeciles will amount to little benefit, and I doubt if there has ever been a convocation of dunces quite as imbecilic as the administration of George W. Bush. I am inclined to forgive anyone born the son of George H.W. Bush most things, since born equal they were most certainly not, yet to be thus born and also afflicted with an identical name is a handicap few of us would have overcome. If history were still a subject of study, the confusion caused by two George Bush's both waging wars against a man named Saddam Hussein would occlude the era by itself, and if there ever was an era that deserved occlusion it is this one, and not the one following it, about which you know nothing. The son completes the work of the father indeed.

Bush, son of a Bush, began with the collapse of the World Trade Center in New York, and ended with the collapse of the entire country. By the halfway point of his scarcely believable two terms, there was no endeavor he had embarked upon that had not blown up in stupendous chaos or festered into ignominy. It had nothing to do with him, of course. He was a rat told he was king of the hyenas by the warthogs.

The predators and bottom-feeders had chosen him because they had so enjoyed the experience of working with Ronald Reagan, whose mind had simply walked off one day and not returned. The younger Bush looked promising because he seemed not to have possessed much of a mind from the very beginning. Power does, however, attract the basest of people, and by then the politcal stage was worse than the roughest holding cell in the most rotten urban ghetto in all the land. Thieves, con-men, liars, racketeers, pimps, hustlers, cheats, muggers, rapists, murderers, fools—it was a daunting prospect. The public knew, but they didn't care as long as everyone was well dressed, clean-shaven and personable. The perception was the reality, after all. They were conscious of voting for appearances, but they had come to think of it as what they were supposed to do.

Machiavelli was no doubt giving his Prince good advice back there in the Middle Ages, but those who imagine that this advice segues effortlessly into the Third Millennium are revealing their lack of common sense, not to mention the absence of any ability to observe or think. To be feared as ruler is not better than being loved any more. If it were we would have started electing terrorist leaders to the presidency long ago—and I'm not suggesting we would have been worse off by doing so. Fear brings a grudging obedience, a backstabbing conformity. But love elicits a total embrace, an open-armed tearful yearning to serve and do and adore. Love: it's the real thing. But, unfortunately, in being the real thing it also has a tendency to flip into its opposite: hate.

If there never was a love supreme like that for the commander-in-chief as he swore to protect and serve us all from the terror standing upon the sacred smoldering mound in New York City, there had not been a hatred for any president quite like the one that began to grip the country in the wake of the Middle East debacle. It would be facetious to add that the government did not take my advice, but they certainly did not take it. I do not pretend that this advice would have proved to be a magic wand, but it would at least have spared the nation and the president what must be the single most humiliating episode in imperial history.

This is what you are not supposed to know:

I was flying back to Washington from a fundraiser in California when the pilot announced there were unconfirmed reports that an atomic device had been detonated in Tel Aviv. After several minutes of trying, I got hold of General Arbuthnot at the Pentagon. He confirmed that their satellites had detected a massive explosion, and that sensors at various listening posts had picked up the electro-magnetic pulse of a large nuclear device, but so far they had been unable to speak directly to anyone in Israel. It was days before any concrete news came in, and even then it was sketchy. A spokesman for Al-Qaeda had initially claimed responsibility for the bomb, but as reports came in from Jordan of a massive death toll from radiation poisoning among Palestinians in the West Bank, three senior Al-Qaeda functionaries denied this claim as a Zionist plot.

A huge dust cloud had spread across much of the Middle East, so satellite images were impossible, and radiation fallout at dangerous levels was being detected as far away as Cairo and Athens. European aid agencies refused to authorize emergency assistance to Israel, citing lack of protective clothing for their people. Damascus and Amman radio stations both reported attempts to organize mass evacuations of their citizens before going off the air. The British claimed they had received a communiqué from Israeli central command that had stated their bunkers were leaking radiation and that rather than surrender all senior personnel had agreed to commit suicide after authorizing nuclear strikes on Teheran and Damascus. We were left to speculate why these had not occurred.

An emergency session of Congress was held to discuss the situation behind closed doors, but no clear actions resulted from the meeting. I heard later that the discussion had centered on whether or not to blame China for the Tel Aviv bomb.

Some weeks after the explosion in Israel, a BBC camera crew wearing protective clothing and carrying oxygen tanks broadcast live videophone images from Haifa, which had received substantial impact from the blast and was a partially flattened wasteland of smoldering rubble. Charred bodies lay all around, some looking as if they had melted in tar-like puddles. It was utterly silent. No birds sang, no flies buzzed—nothing was left alive. A UN force brought back images from Damascus that were still more terrifying: fires burned in various areas but otherwise the buildings were intact, yet streets were littered with bodies, some of them still alive. All were hairless and covered in bluish spots in parts, but in other parts the skin had disintegrated, leaving raw festering cavities. A few people, mainly children, were still able to stagger around, all of them bleeding from the eyes, mouth and nose, with huge open sores on their arms and cheeks. Some had been driven insane by what they had seen.

Jewish organizations appealed for help without knowing to whom they were appealing. But by the time governments— most notably that of India—recovered from the initial shock and began supplying radiation suits and emergency supplies, it was too late to help anyone in Israel. Even the few who had miraculously escaped the blast, shockwaves and direct ionizing radiation were killed by residual radiation within three months. The fields and orchards were dead; the grass had turned to ash; the soil itself, lacking micro-organisms, began turning into sand. The land lay dead beneath a chilled dark sky that produced sunsets like blood yet no noon or dawn. Stoic in their darkest hour, the World Jewish Congress issued a brief press release: WE HAVE NO HOMELAND. It stated the scientific reality that Israel would not be habitable for decades, possibly centuries to come. How had Israel's first president, Chaim Weizmann, put it? "The conflict between ourselves and the Palestinians is not a conflict of justice against injustice, but a conflict between two equal rights." All conflicts ended in equal wrongs, however, and every struggle for justice eventually reached only injustice.

The Palestinians in the West Bank fared no better than their oppressors. The handful of those who survived the year did not feel any victory had been won. None of them lived more than five years, a few having children born horribly deformed or even dead. Only the Bedu of south-eastern Jordan and those Syrians living in the extreme North escaped the fallout. By the rivers of Babylon I sat down and wept when I remembered Zionism in her dawn—pristine, generous, grateful. Everything dies. Everything.

The bomb went off in Seattle that same day. With two million dead, a widespread panic, and the army in command under a state of emergency, America deteriorated into military dictatorship, a republic of fear that tolerated no dissent whatsoever. The public had been so carefully conditioned by decades of fear politics and a media diet rich in nameless horror that, generally, they welcomed each new repression of personal liberty as a manifestation of patriarchal care and concern. No one discussed the hundreds of thousands detained, deported or executed on the spot. Anyone who gave credence to the rumors about a Special Ops commander who went insane and babbled about detonating the Seattle bomb either kept quiet about it or simply emigrated abroad. A man we'd never heard of before but who was very credibly shown to be Al Qaeda's number two official conveniently claimed responsibility for the bomb a week or so after it exploded, inciting the usual spree of attacks on mosques and individuals. Yet no matter how often we were reassured that the majority of Muslims were law-abiding citizens of America, few seemed convinced, and Muslims began to leave our shores, some returning whence they came, others heading or being taken to lands they had never seen before. It was planned this way. Those who remained either packed up their faith and put it out with the garbage, or else they practiced it in secrecy. One by one, the mosques were boarded up, sold off eventually to anyone unbothered by the old association. A few of the prettier ones remained, so we could deny the exodus, and the showpiece Rock Creek mosque in Washington was well-maintained for photo-ops but used only as an Islamic museum. Very few Muslim diplomats went out to pray, and those who did went to private houses. The old need to please the House of Saud had vanished with the Saudi princes, whose country became a dark side of which little was known, all of it terrifying. Over time, the almost total lack of Islamic associations in America made it impossible to continue presenting a faction in the religion as a threat, but long before then a new and greater evil had been discovered. Another faction, another fiction.

CHINA SUPPLIED ISRAEL BOMB read *The New York Times'* headline. Pentagon sources had leaked a CIA report that stated the only country capable of supplying the kind of bomb used in Tel Aviv was China. The Chinese recalled their ambassador that same day. Within a month, Americans found themselves back in another Cold War, as the administration began directing its foreign policy hostilities toward Beijing, which was suddenly held responsible for all manner of provocative actions, from the economic woes beginning to afflict our nation, through the unfriendly behavior of certain European states toward us, to the seething turmoil in the Middle East, where Islamist governments took our inability to defend Israel as a sign of our collapse as a military power.

Various Islamic leaders openly called for Jihad to drive out all remaining US troops in their countries. The Saudi monarchy was overthrown by Muslim fundamentalists, and it was only seven years later that anyone learned of the appalling bloodbath that had taken place there.

With their supply line from the Gulf cut off by Iranian troops blockading the Strait of Hormuz, the 150,000 troops in

Iraq mutinied, over half of them accepting offers to join various forces preparing for war on three fronts. Most were airlifted to Turkey, but the twenty thousand or so stranded in the desert were slaughtered by their own countrymen who had elected to remain as mercenaries for the main Shia faction of what passed for a government in Baghdad by the rivers of Babylon.

European countries initially opened their doors to our fleeing Muslims, but a public backlash in France made other countries think twice, and gradually all the avenues of escape closed off. While we were all wondering if there would be death camps and mass executions, the war with China came. It was obvious that soon Washington would celebrate Taiwan's independence and welcome it into the United Nations, something scrupulously avoided before now, since Washington's sinologists were well aware of how sensitive the issue was to Beijing.

US forces were not swift enough to prevent the Chinese army launching an intercontinental ballistic missile, which landed on the outskirts of Denver. It was a relatively small warhead by Chinese standards, yet it wiped out Denver and most of Boulder. Only a strong wind from the south prevented radiation from falling over the Midwest farmlands and poisoning food supplies for the coming year. Instead it fell on the Canadian Midwest, causing untold miseries in the oil patch and the cities of Calgary and Edmonton, where deformed children are one out of every three born to this day as a result. The oil was not affected, of course, and that was Washington's only concern.

Once the country had been locked down by the military, which imposed curfews and restrictions on all travel, it was slowly announced that security considerations had made it unsafe for a US president to reveal his identity in the media. Initially, this was made to sound as if the president would simply avoid public events, but it kept increasing in scope and was done so gradually that no one seemed to object at all and most found it an obvious and sensible move. Within four years, the entire administration was anonymous. Then the elections had to accommodate increased security needs, so we simply voted for a party, not a candidate, as we had once done long ago. The system of representation disappeared without the slightest fuss—indeed, its reputation for corruption and the system of lobbyists that caused it made many say we were better off without it. Perhaps we were too, and, besides, it had become a creaking anachronism in the age of mass media, which were the real tools of government, manufacturing all the consent a president needed, as long as he was allowed to have it. Thought control that could assure everyone it wasn't thought control allowed all other semblances of democracy to wither away and die. There was no need for anything to come between the rulers and the ruled when the rulers could ensure precisely what the ruled were thinking.

Thus the dismantling of bureaucracies and the institutions of democracy went off without a hitch, cheered on by a public instructed in what it felt, and instructed even in how it reacted to suggestions it was being instructed. It was an extraordinary spectacle to behold, if a dismal one, but security concerns dispensed with the possibility of dissent—it simply was not patriotic to object to actions taken for your own safety. And of course the next government had to be thoroughly secure too. With their control over the computer networks and Internet, all objections were smoothed away entirely.

I remember the air outside seemed smeared, as if there were stains on my cornea like paper-thin sheets of ice sliding down a window. The nerve in my left eyelid began to twitch. I attempted to assess what someone had found to be worth the cost of going to war with China, for that was where it all led. But I soon realized this was like wondering what a snake or spider is thinking. The distance between the mind of one man and that of another is sometimes unbridgeable. Some people want a world of peace and love, others just want to be rich. The positions are irreconcilable. One must exterminate the other for either to succeed.

With the encroaching gloom of a new dark age gathering around me, the sense of urgency I felt would often propel me to despair. I wanted to discuss these thoughts with someone, yet I knew I'd be signing a death warrant for whomever I told. Those who could see what was going on in the country, or could see part of it, or simply disapproved of what was going on no longer had a place in America. Their views were simply not heard or read in any medium, and it became rarer to hear anyone discuss dissent privately. There was no dissent.

For the masses, television continued pumping its opiates. Everything was fine. They went to work, they watched TV, they slept. But they could not fail to notice that life was steadily changing for the worse. They were used to a bit more than bread with their circuses, and the government knew this. With the rising price of oil, the price of everything crept steadily upward and before long signs of hardship were everywhere.

The Grand Egress was broken up by interludes that seized the collective imagination, however, little triumphs that renewed our sense of American greatness. The Friendship War, for example, resembled a crusade, although it was nothing of the sort in reality.

We had long interfered in Canadian politics, largely through the mergers and takeovers that were the merchant's version of war and invasion, but also more directly. Many Canadians hated us for it, too, but we managed nonetheless to create some loyal support among the conservative elements in the Western provinces, which had always resented rule by the East, where the so-called Liberal Party remained in power for such unhealthily long periods that it was more conservative than the Conservative Party, although just as corrupt.

The wild card in Canadian politics was always the French-speaking province of Quebec, which the Liberals catered to shamelessly, even making the country bilingual while the Quebecois had to speak only French. The Canadians flirted with socialism, but were kept in check by trade with us, which we used to punish them. If they refused to join our war coalitions—in which we did not need their actual help, merely their apparent support in the eyes of the world—we withheld tariffs or slapped huge taxes on Canadian products. But increasingly we became reliant on their natural resources, most of which we owned anyway but needed freer access to after a problem arose that we created ourselves. The border.

As our security needs called for ever-stricter border controls, the border became an impenetrable nuisance. As the oil price rose, too, the viability of Canadian oil from tar-sands increased. At $20 a barrel it wasn't worth drilling for or refining. At $80 a barrel it made Canada an oil superpower. So we treated them the way we treated any little country that had something we needed: we changed their regime for one subservient to our needs.

It was simply a matter of media control, and a few election gimmicks we used ourselves, so we knew they worked. Polls tell people who is going to win; media report the polls as if they are news, along with a little subtle boosting of their own. The result: our party gains power. We even provided a few incidents where the new leader could stand up to us, just to show the public he wasn't in our pocket, and of course we provided him numerous tiny triumphs, cozy summit meetings where he seemed important, much good advice, and we even repaid some of the money we'd confiscated as punishment for the previous government. We also told him to butter up Quebec if he wanted to win the next election without too much shameless interference on our part.

All went well until disaster struck. A Canadian we used as a conduit to the leader before he was in power, ferrying up campaign money and advice, got drunk and blabbed about his key role in the coup d'état to the wrong person. And some documents laying out the cunning strategy in Quebec—and written in a decidedly unsophisticated, inflammatory manner—fell into the hands of an Internet blogger, who published them. The result was what we viewed as a national security threat.

The friendly government we had installed was, by the vagaries of the political system there, in grave danger. So we went in to help them out. Not a shot was fired during the war itself, but the insurgency still continues, largely in Quebec. The event was portrayed to Canadians as a brush with death, a near escape from Communist tyranny, the evil influence of old Europe, the Islamic plague, and many other awful fates that we had saved them from. The result, after a lot of coaxing, was "the American–Canadian Union," a term we soon made vanish, like the Canadian government. We simply acquired another thirteen states, which became the United States of North America (USNA).

The Friendship War captivated Americans, who volunteered in droves to join the cause of liberating their northern cousins, and was extended far longer than necessary because media ratings were so high. The insurgency was hardly reported at all, and downgraded to "foreign terrorism" since most of it was in Quebec. Thanks to the media, the transition was so smooth that most Canadians probably didn't notice it at first, and many felt things were better than they had been. Even Americans who had never heard of Canada, or thought it was American to begin with, suddenly wanted to visit the place, and there was a Canadian craze lasting two or three years, in which beavertail franchises sprang up everywhere and teenagers wore plaid shirts with embroidered moccasins, both of which were usually made in the US. The Canadian use of *eh?* as a form of punctuation spread like wildfire after it was adopted as a signal of support for the Liberation by news anchors. With Canada's oil safely secured, free access to arctic oil, Great Lakes' water, and all the other resources we owned but had trouble getting to at times, the Greater American economy enjoyed another brief little boom. Oil prices fell, food supplies were once more abundant, and the good old days returned.

But even miracles of providence ran out in the end.

I shall not recount the long twilight during which it was debated whether one could term the period spent analyzing the failure of Western civilization a tail part of that civilization or a post-mortem feature, and I certainly won't waste the reader's time on the issue of whether or not the debate over this analysis itself could also be so considered. It would not surprise me to learn that this refusal to recount the whimpering finale has also become a subject of the same scholarly inability to face reality.

The decline and fall is never a happy time, but no civilization declined nor fell, nor declined its fall, with the staggering excesses of graceless and stubborn fury that we brought to bear on the task. Our response to the reprimands and critiques that flowed in from all corners of the globe was at first a baleful countercharge (*European Islamophilia* by T.F. Rozbic, at the high end, and *Taking Out the Eurotrash* by Pibby Ray Manto, at the low), which soon festered into spiteful threats of violence that were too muscular and impatient to remain as mere threats for long.

Only a sentimental cobweb of memory prevented the North American Aerospace Defense Command from launching the gigantic brace of intercontinental ballistic missiles, each carrying a two hundred–megaton hydrogen warhead, that were not just on their gantry but belching liquid oxygen at minus thirty and counting. They would have destroyed every living thing in a ragged arc between Paris and Warsaw.

I was unable to shake the overwhelming sense of shame and dismay that came at this moment and was not exactly sure how I'd expected to find myself feeling as the four dark horsemen's hooves clattered across the tiled rooftops into the sunrise of an American morning.

At that stage, it was still not widely known that the Pentagon had begun broadcasting on its own news network—PNN, in the same font as the CNN logo—because they wanted to smooth out the glitches before they promoted it. But the glitches were legion and the attempt to imitate CNN only *began* at the logo. Sets changed, lavish graphics were played with, spectacular technologies deployed, and a great deal of money spent—yet PNN was still unwatchably awful. Only when they stopped using soldiers who wanted to be on-air personalities and started using on-air personalities who wanted to be soldiers did the ratings improve enough for them to risk screening war movies in the afternoon, if there were no movies from wars in progress to show. But ultimately only when the other news networks found their local stations were having the annual applications to renew their broadcast licenses rejected by the FCC—pending amendments that no longer included the right to news broadcasts—did PNN start releasing its audience ratings. Since the filing dates for licenses varied from state to state and stretched across the entire year, it took nearly six months for the big five to grasp this predicament, then a further year for the venerable three to realize it barely made any difference since they had hardly broadcast any news since the mid-1990s anyway. Their viewers had been spoiled by the Gulf War and weren't interested in news programming that was less exciting—and if they did find something worth watching they watched it on CNN, with which the networks conceded they could not possibly compete unless they abandoned the major part of their business.

The art that should have been holding a mirror up to this mayhem was merely co-opted by it, which is not the same as satirizing it. Utter tripe was exhibited by serious museums.

Someone wrapped up buildings in plastic sheeting. Painters were people who couldn't paint. Sculptors no longer made sculpture. Music tried not being music, but it didn't work because you could hear the difference, and no asinine charlatan in a bow tie could persuade you that rubbish you could hear as rubbish was not rubbish. With everything else it was The Emperor's New Clothes staged as the Apocalypse of St John.

The backdrop to this seething bedlam, this eschatological Dunciad, was a sequence of political events that began by embarrassing me as a conservative and ended by making me ashamed to be human. The quest for empire turned into a desperate attempt to stay afloat, and the celebration of a freedom-loving folk turned into the most brutal repression of the human spirit ever seen on the weary face of the tired old earth.

No one went out much anymore. The malls were deserted, bare ruined boutiques where the pretty young things used to hang, shelves akimbo, dust and cobwebs engaged in their tasks of reclamation. The supermarkets still thrived, but every time anyone shopped it was obvious that supplies were in a slow but steady decline and imports were merely a fond memory. It was all winding down, and we knew that when the winding down ended the only thing left would be a horror vast and unspeakable, yet we could not bring ourselves to plan how we would organize against it—because we knew we couldn't overcome whatever force awaited after midnight. Luck, courage, strength, spirit—everything would run out when we were outrun by time, when the clocks struck none.

When those in control of time had so blatantly lost that control, we began to realize our vehicle was a rollercoaster which no one can steer and which has no brakes. I wasn't surprised the government wanted invisibility after this gross abrogation of responsibility. Luposki, Parks and the others simply vanished, thus accountability was no option. Melvin Cassel held me accountable for Israel's destruction, though, or so I assume, for he never returned my calls after that day. I kept up with him through his column, which deteriorated into bitterness and paranoia before vanishing into the Internet's black hole.

I was profoundly shocked to learn he had killed himself with sleeping pills, alone in a hotel room in the bath with a bag over his head, taped tight around the neck. There was a note, but it merely said, "The bastards ground me down."

"And then there were two," said Dean Torrence, as we walked through the drizzle from Mel's grave.

But there weren't. Dean and I never saw each other again, although we wanted to. We just couldn't look each other in the eye. Each suspected the other of doing more than he should have, or less than he could have. But I know Dean worked hard to atone. He chaired committees, he raised funds, he handed out ration cards, he opened his house to the poor at Christmas. And then he vanished.

We spoke occasionally, but he gave me no warnings. By this stage, we all knew what happened when high office beckoned: you vanished. Your old life ended and invisibility began. Some time later, it was rumored Dean was president, but it did not matter anymore to me. We had changed the world, and that mattered. That was why he hated me and I hated him.

I miss what we once were and what we could have been. I don't miss him, though. I sense he's dead because there is no one out there. No one to turn to.

I stayed at home in the country with Abbie, but we rarely spoke and hardly ever saw one another even if we shared a sofa. The potential for discord in any human transaction was so immense and forbidding that we came to fear even the most trivial exchange. Murders and suicides had assumed unheard-of levels, no longer reported anywhere, given over to the buzzing bleak domain of rumor which was ruled by fear. Husbands and wives became toxic combinations of recrimination, hatred, exasperation and sorrow. A suspect glance let alone words was enough to ignite arguments that could spiral into an unreal parallel universe of anti-marriage where language was a howling, a spitting, a clawing and a biting way to fight; where windows rattled and fine crystal wineglasses that had survived world wars were smashed into the tender gristle of a delicate ear whose coiled shell-like chambers, made for whispering and sweet music, now rang with screaming and the forms of ugliness.

Abbie and I were quiet, gentle people, but even we lived taut with mortal fear of what we might do to each other, of what we were capable of doing. Thus we who had watched perhaps ten hours of television a year, we who despised and loathed the busy bristling pushy window onto Planet News, now watched ten hours or more a day because its mild hypnosis and ceaseless affirmations of drivel, its merchants' mantras and the jingling simplexity with which it rendered all things great and small into the same kindergarten myths of the good defeating the bad were just plain soothing. Often I never knew if I had been asleep or awake, since the television's job was to make those transitions gentle, almost imperceptible, and to insert its strangers, its entertainers locked in a permanent role, into the heart as well as the home. Sitting there every day, I could feel the synapses in my brain shut down and the whole organ turning into a porridgy blob of numbed protoplasm. How much longer would it be before evolution decided we should lose it since we didn't use it?

I was wrong to resign, I finally realized. It was the consequence of weakness, the fear of battling impossible odds, fear of failure. I should have used the power of high office to make certain as many people as possible knew what had happened to our institutions of state. I should have blown the whistle where it would be heard. No matter how compromised, we would still have had a semblance of recognizable rule. Instead I had stupidly handed the invisible parliament on a plate exactly what its schemers wanted—absolute control and an appearance of being wronged more than most by the machinations of power. You can't fight this enemy, I told myself. Control of the media means control over reality. I would have lost before I even started fighting. Madmen fight reality.

Years of analyzing foreign affairs had taught me to avoid seeking patterns until all the pieces of a puzzle had been tipped out or all the dice had hit the board, so I had obstinately refused to examine further any anomalies or coincidences in the vast sequence of events that came cascading after 9/11, believing the sequence would naturally take longer to play out, when in fact it no longer corresponded to the old paradigm at all and had the appearance of an endless chain reaction. What it actually more closely resembled was a brilliantly audacious chess gambit.

I started to see this when I told myself idly one day that the desertion of US forces in Iraq had proved to be a stroke of luck for those nations that hired them as mercenaries and thus managed to hold an uneasy peace they wouldn't have been able to maintain for very long at all otherwise.

But then I noticed that the postponement of what was an inevitable war for that length of time provided the only series of factors that would have allowed the sequence of events leading to Israel's nuclear annihilation. What I was looking at, surely, was not a trail of random events but a carefully orchestrated plan. The destruction of Israel was part of that plan, but it was clear to me that it was not its final objective. I puzzled over it in my head, where I followed the chain of events back and forth across a huge map of the world. I became convinced I was seeing a pattern but the proof for it eluded me maddeningly.

I had, however, become accustomed to seeking patterns in an enclosed system where I always knew the center of power and where the events were self-contained. When the center of power was unknown, or moved around, it created the illusion that events were autonomous. Anyone wanting to create this impression would not operate from one center of power, which is why the socialist revolutions had been so worrying: it was hard to discern if they were indigenous events or ones created by Soviet agents working undercover in the countries concerned, and would have remained an open question if the Soviets had not been creating an empire.

I had been assuming that Washington was the power center in the pattern I was seeking, but it was only when I removed it that I saw a pattern. I was also used to seeking patterns from completed strategies and thus to throwing my timeline backward. What I looked at now yielded up its pattern only when I posited no center of power and an interlinked sequence of seemingly disparate events directed toward a clear goal in the future. It was only because I knew myself not to be a fantasist and had two dozen years' experience in geopolitical analysis that I was certain what I saw was not imaginary.

The reason so many events—in America particularly, but elsewhere too—were susceptible to conspiracy theories is that politics generally, and American politics notably, *are* a conspiracy. I am fortunate that my emotions have always remained uninvolved with the work of my mind, for there was no appropriate emotional response to the havoc being wreaked in the world. Yet I also know that it is because of men like me, whose hearts are cold and hard, who seek power because they cannot understand love, who deal in violence and pain because they cannot feel what others feel, that this planet has become our hell.

You may ask who the scientific dictator was, and the answer is terrifying: the state itself. We had long fantasized about computers running amok and taking over, but we failed to see that the state itself had also become an organism bent on a single-minded course of totalitarian power from which there was no turning back. When the computers go AWOL in a film I'm the one shouting, "Pull the plug out!" The state has no plug. It has no clearly vulnerable points at all. In order to modify its activities you have to join them. And if the masses are persuaded you are the right person to lead the state, you can lead it, but only because you have enough financial backing to persuade them, which is a marketing issue. You play to what you know are their underlying fears and desires—terrorism, chaos, lower taxes, security—and you have to keep it brief. Boredom = failure. Complex issues are reduced to all but meaningless simplicity because the medium of television cannot handle complicated realities—and even if it could, its audience couldn't. The marketing of politics guaranteed that no one would ever hear the truth about anything.

When madmen are in the asylum they rarely worry us, thus it is not madness that blows winds of primeval fear through our hearts. What we fear are men whose madness has driven them to become their own delusions, thereby proving irrefutably that they are sane. *All* madmen think they are sane, but the dangerous ones are those who *know* they are sane, for they make us think *we* might be the madmen.

The world offers no inducements to humility, kindness and compassion. None of us sees any evidence of a God rewarding those who keep his laws—not any, not anywhere. But everywhere we see the evidence that ruthlessness, avarice, cruelty, egoism, violence, selfishness and hypocrisy are rewarded by someone or something, and are indeed the sole tools for ambition in this world. The meek inherit nothing. It's all a lie.

The prophet Zoroaster identified the great duality as Truth and not–Truth or the Lie. Whatever wasn't Truth was the Lie. For the Hindus there was Reality and the Illusion. Whatever wasn't Real was an Illusion. The physicist sees only order and chaos, hopefully speculating that chaos might be a kind of order—the kind we identify as dis-order. The Lie is also a kind of truth, the kind that is not true. The Illusion is a kind of reality, too, the kind that is not real. Zoroaster did not say how much Truth there is compared to how much of what a human being faces is a lie. The Great War and the Great Work are struggles to die. There is Time and there is Eternity, and eternity is everything that is not time. Eternity is not history. Now, we are all people without a history.

The war has dragged on now for twenty years, during which the US has become US–Global, a super-government above all other governments. Whenever serious resistance emerges, it is crushed ruthlessly. The war in the East continues largely as an excuse to deploy barbaric measures whenever they are required. It is not a war so much as skirmishes with guerrilla forces and the Chinese Resistance. No end of it is in sight. No end is planned, since no end is desired.

The world I knew in my youth has vanished utterly into our tyranny. Generations exist now that have never known anything else but this, that have no idea of what I mean by the terms *thought, freedom, consent* or indeed any other terms.

I have been a guilty bystander for too long.

We have been lying to ourselves for too long.

Thus have I lost my center fighting the world. The dreams clash and are shattered. We wanted to create an earthly paradise, when none can exist. The only paradise is within, beyond the reach of tyrants and the vicissitudes of fortune. Seek it there.

DDL 1950–2050

ACKNOWLEDGMENTS

★ ★ ★

I WOULD LIKE TO THANK THE CANADA COUNCIL for the Arts for its assistance in the writing of this book, a task that Linda Pearce also made infinitely less onerous with her kindness, patience and hard work. David Murray and the Bank of Nova Scotia were as always instrumental in easing the financial burdens faced during the many months of no income.

For their ideas, both good and bad, and in some cases for their inspiration, I owe a debt of gratitude to: Aldous Huxley, Bernard-Henri Lévy, George Kennan, Noam Chomsky, David Sobelman, Barbara and Terri Jackman, Robert Locke, Leon Cherniac, Norman Snider, Daniel Lynch, Marc Gabel, Lorien Gabel, Yoko Ono, Jean-Luc Godard, Kara Williams, Martin Amis, Robert Lowell, Jessica Kronberger, David Lynch, Simon Harling, Lyndon LaRouche, Robert Duncan, Frederic Raphael, Frank Zingrone, John Perkins and John Laughland.

I would also like to thank the staff at Key Porter Books who have been supportive of this novel from its very inception: Marnie Ferguson, for her incredible enthusiasm, generous support and keen insight; my publicist Kendra Michael for all of her energy, time and effort; and Art Director Martin Gould for the beautiful cover design.

Most of my gratitude, however, is due to Janie Yoon, who not only suggested that I return to fiction and write this book, but had the courage, fortitude and sheer skill to work with me and help turn this novel into what you now hold in your hands. To say she is the kind of editor writers dream of finding barely scratches the surface of the thank-you I owe her.

PAUL WILLIAM ROBERTS is the bestselling author of seven books, including *A War Against Truth*, which was shortlisted for the Charles Taylor Prize for Literary Non-Fiction; *The Demonic Comedy*, which first appeared as a National Magazine Award-winning article in *Saturday Night* and *Harper's*; and *The Palace of Fears*, a novel. He is also an award-winning writer and producer for television, and has written for many magazines and newspapers, including *The Globe and Mail, Toronto Life, The Toronto Star, Harper's, Vanity Fair, The New Yorker, The New York Times, Atlantic Monthly, The Washington Post, The Times Literary Supplement* and *The Jordan Times*. He has been the recipient of several National Magazine Awards, and has also received the Canadian Author's Association Award for Fiction. He is considered one of Canada's top experts on Middle Eastern affairs, and is a scholar of Jewish and Arabic history and religions. In 2005, Paul William Roberts received the inaugural PEN Canada/Paul Kidd Courage Award for excellence and bravery in journalism.